Flight Surgeon

Michael R. Jennings

Flight Surgeon

Michael R. Jennings

ISBN—Paperback: 978-0-9855412-0-0 (13) 0985541202 (10)
ISBN—E-Book: 978-09855412-1-7 (13) 0985541210 (10)
Library of Congress Control Number: 2012911394

For bulk order and other information, please contact the author at: FlightSurgeon@aol.com.

Author Website: FlightSurgeonNovel.com

Printed in the United States of America

For William Morris Lowney
1923 ~ 2011

A father figure of forty-five years,
a true friend, a guiding light,
a rare man who truly knew the
meaning of love for all

Acknowledgments

The actual writing and publication of a novel, like many other things in life, takes a village. From the very first word laid down in this novel to its actual publication required the time, efforts and intelligence of a number of people—for without their contributions this novel would never have seen the light of day. First and foremost, I want to thank my dear friend and fellow author, Arion Golmakani (Solacers), for paving the way. His willingness to openly share the trials and tribulations of writing and publishing that he endured along the path toward the eventual publication of his memoir were immeasurable. Arion, I can't thank you enough for your unselfish contributions.

I would also like to thank my two sons, Brendan and Ryan, who allowed me the opportunity to write this novel in the quiet solitude of their home. The expansive view of the valley and river below your picture window is a writer's paradise. A father could not ask for better sons. And a very special thank you goes out to Diane Alexander who, with the help of a fresh supply of red pens, took the first crack at the editing of this novel—followed again by a second review prior to publication. Your critique of the two drafts and accompanying recommendations went a long way toward making this novel what it is today. Thank you for your painstaking efforts.

To my long-time friend, Matt Sylvester, what can I say but thank you many times over. As a commercial pilot, I relied on your expertise for all things related to the flying of an aircraft and more—though you are to be held totally blameless for those incidents where I took "literary license" with some of the factual information you provided. And thank you also, Matt, for patiently responding to my million and one questions.

A special thank you also goes out to Jeff Fielder, who not only designed the cover, but also provided many forms of technological assistance required to take the finished manuscript to its final, publishable stage. Also, to Kemberlee Shortland, romance writer extraordinaire, for your gifted advice . . . thank you.

While I have only thanked individuals, I would be remiss in not expressing my appreciation for all of the fellow writers, agents, editors and publishers out there on the Web, who openly and freely contributed vast amounts of information and advice via the multitude of online writer sites available to all. We've shared many a conversation on the art of writing from A to Z; I consider each of you a friend.

And last, but by no means least, to the countless others in my life who believed in me and offered encouragement along journey's way. As I mentioned in the beginning—it takes a village. And to my readers, I hope you enjoy reading this novel as much as I enjoyed its creation.

– Michael R. Jennings

Prologue

At this point in the flight, Michael stared out the pilot's window and drifted off into silence. A silence she let stand because she rightly assumed it was brought about when talking about his parents. She could only surmise that he still missed his parents immensely—as she would hers if something tragic were to happen to them.

And yes, Michael was thinking of his parents. He had graduated from medical school a week earlier when his parents left to attend a social gathering of fellow professors—something they had always done at the end of the school year. They were met with heavy rains and winds as they made their way home to their estate along the country road after midnight. They never made it. Around one-thirty in the morning, Frankie answered the phone. He knew instinctively that it was not going to be a welcoming call. They rarely are at that hour of the morning. On the other end of the line was Dr. Manning, a fellow professor who had attended the same social as his parents. He had been following behind his parents on his way to his own home a few miles farther on down the road. It was both dark and raining hard, and the winds were howling incessantly through the trees. Then, the apparently saturated roots of a tree broke loose and the tree fell on their car—killing his parents instantly.

Dr. Manning immediately hit the brakes of his own car—nearly crashing into the back of his parent's vehicle. Outside of dialing 911, he knew there was nothing he could do. The large tree, as if by design, had chosen to fall directly on top of the front seat. In a matter of minutes, Dr. Manning found himself standing amongst paramedics, police officers and fire rescue personnel; and later by the coroner himself. No rescue would even be attempted that night by those responding; one glance at the vehicle made it clear that no rescue was warranted. No amount of medical miracles could ever bring them back.

Frankie had the unfortunate task of going up to Michael's room after taking the call to explain what had happened. Between the two of them, they wept long after the sun had risen. Oddly enough, the storm had spent its fury and drifted away shortly after the accident—leaving behind that summer morning one of the most beautiful sunrises native Tennesseans had ever seen.

Three days later a funeral mass was held in the Cathedral of the Carnation, located in the very heart of Nashville. Every one of the thousand-plus seats was filled along with hundreds more lining the walls. Never before had the cathedral experienced this large a gathering for a single funeral mass—with the exception of a funeral some years back for a Cardinal.

The funeral mass itself lasted over two hours, with forty-five minutes of it devoted to eulogies by those who knew them well. Doctors, nurses and others came in from nearly all fifty states to pay their respects to their teachers, their mentors and peers. Michael's parents had both taught at Vanderbilt for thirty-three years; the same university where they had graduated, met and were married. Along the way, they accumulated thousands of friends and acquaintances; hence the large gathering at their funeral.

The four-and-a-half-mile trip from the Cathedral to Calvary Cemetery required the escort of sixteen motorcycle police officers and eight privately contracted tour buses. The burial ceremony at the gravesite took close to an hour and a half. A large block of that time was spent waiting for everyone to come into place around the gravesite before the Archbishop could even begin the graveside ceremony.

At the conclusion of the ceremony, all present were invited to Vanderbilt University to partake in catered foods and socializing. Michael remembered walking into the cathedral and walking out—but little in between. He fully remembered attending the graveside services—but nothing of what was said by the Archbishop. He also remembered going to the university afterward—but not who he met or what was said. If it were not for Frankie at his side at all times, he wasn't sure if . . .

Chapter One

Five Years Later

TWENTY-SEVEN YEAR OLD DR. MICHAEL THOMAS GUIDED HIS CESSNA Citation along its assigned path toward the outskirts of Nashville. Aboard his seven-seater aircraft were three fellow doctors and four nurses—all volunteers for Doctors Without Borders (DWB).

Twenty-minutes outside of Nashville, he switched on the intercom system.

"Okay everyone, we'll be landing soon. You know the routine."

It wasn't but a minute later when he sensed an uneasy commotion going on in the cabin behind him. He then heard the unmistakable voice of Dr. Tong yell out at the top of his voice.

"Grab the defib, stat! Easy Bill," he muttered as he tried to support his friend's upper body while clawing for the seatbelt's buckle.

Opened mouth and bulging eyes screamed silent panic as a great weight on Bill's chest stopped his breathing. His right fingers were like fat sausages, fumbling for the back of the seat ahead while falling sideways to hang over the armrest.

At the sound of the word defib, Michael instinctively knew that a member of the medical team had suffered a heart attack. And just as quickly, Heather poked her head into the cockpit.

"Michael, it's Bill," she spit out in a choking voice. "They have him on the floor."

"Thanks Heather, I'll get us down as quickly as possible. Keep me informed, please."

"Yes, Michael." And with that she quickly departed back to the main cabin just as his radio came to life.

"Flight Surgeon three-one-four, Nashville approach, expect vectors for the approach to Tune field."

"Nashville approach, Flight Surgeon three-one-four, we just encountered a medical situation on board, we are declaring an emergency, we'll need to divert to Nashville International."

"Flight Surgeon, three-one-four, roger, expect vectors for the visual approach, runway two-right, please state the nature of your emergency and assistance needed once on the ground."

"One of our passengers has, I believe, just experienced a heart attack; we're going to need medical support upon landing"

"Roger Flight Surgeon three-one-four, you can expect that."

Though only fifteen minutes away from the airport, Michael eased the thrust levers forward until he achieved maximum speed for the aircraft. This, he knew, would shave a few critical minutes from the flight time into the airport. He desperately wanted to be back in the main cabin assisting, but knew that his friend was in capable hands with the six other medical professionals on board. It was his job to get the plane down as quickly as possible.

Eight minutes later, Heather reentered the cockpit with less excitement in her voice. "Michael, they've got a pulse now. A weak one, but it's a pulse."

"Great news, Heather. Thank you. Let the others know that we will be touching down in a few minutes. Those of you that are not working on Bill, belt up. I'll try to touch down as gently as possible."

"Okay, I'll let them know," she replied as she quickly exited the cockpit.

With her exit, he immediately resumed his ongoing conversations with the Nashville controller.

"Flight Surgeon three-one-four, you are cleared to land, runway two-right, we understand your emergency, emergency vehicles are rolling out, upon exiting the runway, you are cleared to shut down and allow emergency services on board your aircraft."

"Cleared to land, two-right, will exit at taxiway Hotel-five and shut down there."

Following one of the smoothest landings he had ever made, he exited the runway as instructed to where emergency vehicles were waiting. Once the plane came to a full stop, he shut down both engines and quickly headed back to the main cabin to open the access door. Upon opening the door, the medical personnel immediately entered the aircraft. In just under seven minutes, the patient had been loaded into the medical vehicle and was being whisked away to the hospital with Dr. Patrick riding in the back. Michael was the first to speak up.

"Well gang, not the ideal way to finish off a productive two-week mission, was it?"

"Yeah," responded Harry. "It's hard to believe that it would happen to Bill of all people—only 55 and in great shape for his age."

"We'll know more later as to the cause, I suspect," chimed in Cammy. "I know from my own practice that heart attacks are not always a matter of chronological age."

"You're right about that," Michael responded in agreement. "Now, if you'll excuse me, I need to button up the aircraft and get us off the exit ramp. I'll take us over to the service terminal for those of you catching flights home. Jody, knowing that your car is at my place, you'll obviously be flying back with me."

"Okay, Michael," acknowledged Jody as she and the four others headed back to their seats.

After securing the aircraft and communicating with the ground controller, Michael proceeded over to the terminal to disembark his passengers. A half hour later, with only Jody onboard, Michael took to the skies once more for the ten minute flight to his home airport; barely climbing above 3,000 feet in the process.

After landing at John C. Tune Airport, he taxied the aircraft to its outer fringes. At the push of an overhead button, a gate opened wide and the plane continued taxiing onto a private taxiway, which led to a large hangar. With the push of a second overhead button, the two large doors on the leading face of the building began to open wide. As soon as they were fully opened, Michael carefully taxied the plane into the hangar. Waiting inside was an extended-length golf cart at the ready to take them to the main house—a mansion situated on five acres owned by Michael.

Following the short ride to the mansion's garage, Michael loaded Jody's personal belongings into the trunk of her car. After a brief hug, she made her way out of the garage for the three-hour drive back home to Memphis. Michael then made his way up the elevator to his third-floor bedroom. Following a routine of shaving and taking a quick shower, he climbed into bed and fell fast asleep.

The following morning, Michael received a call from Sandy at DWB headquarters concerning a pending fundraiser in Etenia—a small town located in the northeastern part of Tennessee.

"Michael, good news for a change," Sandy said. "No, change that—two pieces of great news. First off, Dr. Patrick called us both yesterday and this morning. Apparently Dr. Richardson is going to make a full recovery following his triple bypass. It pays to have doctors and nurses around when you need them. The other piece of good news being the vice president, along with his wife, Dottie, has agreed to make a brief appearance at the hospital benefit. We tried for both days, but his staff didn't go for that. Right now he has agreed to be there for the Saturday portion of the event, though the actual time of his appearance hasn't been finalized yet."

"We'll take whatever we can get, Sandy."

"And that isn't the only great news. From the list our staff was able to generate of potential country singers, we were able to get a tentative commitment from Briana Price who, by the way, also lives in Nashville. She's at the top of the charts right now, so that will make for a good drawing card. I'll e-mail her contact information to you shortly."

"Great. Can't say that I know much about this Miss Price, but I'll check her out on the Web."

"Michael, you may want to consider offering her a ride up to Etenia, given that you both live close to each other. Or not—that's up to you."

"I'll offer that up, thanks for mentioning it, Sandy."

"Well, that's about it from here, Michael."

"Thanks for all of your efforts, Sandy, and be sure to give the twins my love. Tell them that I'm still undecided which one to wait for. Better yet, let them know that I'm holding out to see which one gets the better high school grades. Maybe that will spur them on to study a little bit harder."

"As much as they admire your good looks, Michael, I'm not sure your suggestion will remotely work on those two. Right now, boys their own age are their number one priority, unfortunately."

"Are you implying, Sandy, that you've already forgotten what it was like to be their age?" Michael jokingly asked.

"Unfortunately, no. That's why I'm somewhat concerned. My parents, if they had known, would've killed me for some of the things I did when I was their age. Now I find myself worrying about what they're doing while away from the watchful eyes of hubby and me."

"Care to confess your youthful sins to Fr. Michael, Sandy?"

"I think I'll pass, thank you."

"In that case, I'll let you get back to work, and I'll go for a swim."

"Okay. Talk to you later, Michael."

"Bye, Sandy."

With that good news in his head, Michael made his way out to the pool for his daily swim. He had to admit to himself that he knew nothing about this Briana Price gal. Before calling her, however, he knew that some personal sleuthing was in order; he wanted to find out as much about her as possible. While swimming laps, he wondered if this Briana Price was another one of those reputed "spoiled performers" he had read about in the past. Following his swim, he decided to find out if he was right or wrong. He headed back up to his bedroom where he showered and changed before sitting down at his computer to Google Briana Price.

After an hour of searching and heavy reading, he was left with one word—"Impressive!" With what he had read online, he came to the conclusion that not only was she a talented pop-country singer but, unlike many other performers, she appeared to have kept her head on straight—at least he found nothing that would cause anyone to label her as a "wild child." Though at twenty-one, she was hardly a child. With the search completed, he made a mental point of calling her later in the evening. The call would have to wait, however, until he returned from visiting Bill in the hospital.

It would be seven-thirty p.m. before he would return home and make the call to Ms. Price. As Michael had guessed prior to actually making the call, he was greeted by a recorded message. After leaving his name and phone number, along with the purpose of the call, he retired to his study to catch up on a backlog of medical journals and mail that had been piling up while he was away.

At nine forty-five, the ringing of the house phone startled him awake. Coming back to his senses, he found it unusual for anyone to be calling this late in the evening. He arose from the reclining chair and made his way over to his desk. He first glanced at the phone screen which displayed the word "Private," before picking up the receiver and answering, "Hello."

"May I speak with Dr. Thomas, please?"

"Speaking," he responded, while not being able to identify the seemingly young female voice on the other end.

"Hi, Dr. Thomas, this is Briana Price. You left me a message earlier about the late November hospital benefit in Etenia. I hope I didn't catch you at a bad time?"

"No you didn't. And thank you for returning my call. I'm assuming you've heard about the Doctors Without Borders program?"

"Who hasn't? You folks do great work in faraway places for those in need of medical help."

"We do our best, but even that isn't good enough in most of those places. What few people know is that we also provide the same services closer to home—and that's the purpose of this call. As the DWB folks probably informed you already, we're trying to raise enough money to upgrade the only hospital in Etenia and surrounding towns. The conversation I had with a staff member with DWB earlier this morning suggested that you might be willing to help us in the fundraising event."

"Yes, the folks at DWB did inform me of the benefit. Fortunately, I have no engagements scheduled for that weekend, so I'd be more than happy to assist in any way I can. After all, I'm a Tennessean, am I not? I've never been to Etenia, but I do know that many cities and towns to the east are not exactly affluent by Nashville or Memphis standards."

"Exactly. I've been up there volunteering my services more times than I care to admit, and I keep coming back astounded at how run down and outdated both their hospital and equipment are. I think you'll understand better what I'm talking about once you see it for yourself."

"I'll take your word for it."

"If you can work it in your schedule, I'd like to meet with you beforehand to go over the proposed schedule of events that I've been putting together."

"I'm sure we can work something out. My mother is my manager, so why don't I have her give you a call to set up a time and place for us to get together?"

"Perfect. I'll be expecting her call. And Ms. Price, thank you again for volunteering."

"Ms. Price!" Briana exclaimed, in a mocking tone of shock. "That's a little too formal if we're going to be working together, Dr. Thomas. Everyone who knows me just calls me Briana."

"Then Briana it is. And, by the way, most people I work with call me Michael. I've never been one much for titles."

"Touché, Michael. I'll let my mother know in the morning of our conversation. And so you aren't caught off guard, her name is Debra, not Ms. Debra or Mrs. Price."

"Touché back! I can see you have a good sense of humor. For that reason alone, I look forward to meeting up with you. So on that note, I'll let you get some sleep and I'll await your mother's call."

"Goodnight, Michael."

"Goodnight, Briana."

Following his conversation with Briana, he returned to his reclining chair and reflected on the conversation that had taken place. It appeared to him that she was not a diva and he was actually looking forward to meeting with her. So, with pleasant thoughts running around in his mind, he jumped back out of the recliner and headed off to bed

Chapter Two

THE FOLLOWING MORNING, MICHAEL AROSE AT HIS USUAL TIME TO THE smell of bacon wafting its way up the stairway. This was a clear indication that Frankie had returned from his vacation to Cannon Beach, Oregon—a visit he made every year, spending time with his only sister and her extended family. Throwing on his bathrobe, Michael headed directly downstairs to partake of breakfast—the shower can wait, he figured.

"Welcome home, Frankie," Michael said as he entered the kitchen, aiming directly for the coffee pot where Frankie was standing.

"Welcome home yourself, Michael," he responded as he gave him a warm hug. "And how was your trip to Santo Domingo?"

"Exhausting, but fulfilling. And how are your sister and her family doing?"

"In spite of her age, she's doing fine, thank you. Being around her children and grandchildren has not only kept her quite active, but young in spirit, as well. I'm thinking she'll probably live to be 110 easily."

"Did you remind her that I requested the pleasure of her company here in Nashville?" Michael inquired. "It's been five long years since she paid us the pleasure of her company."

"That I did. And she appreciates your kind offer, but she's at that point in her life where she is comfortable being around her immediate family—which obviously, by omission, must not include me. Anyway, she's always afraid that if she travels she'll miss out on some important happening or activity in their lives, which is exactly why I have to travel to Oregon if I want to see her."

"Well, fortunately for you, you love Cannon Beach anyway, sister or no sister."

"That I do. There's something about the lazy summer days and the crashing waves of winter that have always appealed to me," Frankie stated, as he set Michael's breakfast plate before him.

"And still you won't retire and move there?"

"You know my feelings on retiring, Michael. I won't be leaving here anytime soon—at least until I have some observational assurances that you can boil water properly without burning it."

"I would tell you that your comment hurt, but there's a lot of truth to it. But you're the one responsible for it. You've never let my parents or me anywhere near the stove or oven. I'm thinking that it's always been part of your secretive plan for job security around here. You've spoiled us, and you know it."

"I've told you before, Michael, you are free to fire me anytime you feel like it."

"What! And allow me to starve to death, which I almost do when you're gone?" Michael responded, mockingly. "You've got to be kidding me. When you're ready to retire, Frankie, you have my full blessing. I'll most likely be forced to hire two or three staff members to handle your responsibilities, however. So don't let that added financial burden influence your decision in any way," Michael added, teasingly. "In all seriousness, you've been very loyal to our family, and you know that I appreciate everything you've done for us over the years. But enough of this conversation," he finally concluded.

"As you wish, Michael. Now finish your breakfast before it gets cold and I have to cook everything over again. I don't believe that reheating food is in my contract. So what else is new with your life?"

"I'm expecting a call today from a Debra Price, Briana Price's mother. No matter what I'm doing when the call comes in, please see that I talk with her."

"Briana Price, huh? As in the pop-country singer?"

"That would be one and the same. She's agreed to be part of our hospital benefit in Etenia at the end of November. Her mother, who I've learned acts as her manager, will be setting up a time for Briana and me to meet prior to the benefit. She will be the only entertainer for the benefit, so obviously we have a certain amount of planning to work out beforehand."

"Consider yourself lucky, Michael, as she is a class act."

"And how would you, of the swing band era, know anything of the likes of Briana Price, may I ask?"

"I may be old, Michael, but it doesn't mean that I live in a cave when it comes to hometown entertainers. I haven't seen one of her shows in person, but I've heard her sing a few times on TV specials. She's also taken her fair share of statues at the various award shows. I may be wrong, but I have a feeling that you've never heard of Miss Price until recently?"

"That's the problem with you, Frankie, you know me all too well. I've got to find a way to keep you from invading my mind."

"I probably know you better now than any future wife will ever know you."

"There you go again, assuming that I will ever marry," Michael threw back at him for probably the hundredth time.

"Trust me, you will eventually. You're intelligent, rich, and you have your father's distinguished good looks about you. You've kept yourself too damn busy to allow a woman the opportunity to get close to you, and when they do, you run the other way."

"I spend almost as much time away from home as I do at home. Not exactly the type of man most women would be interested in settling down with. I know that I wouldn't be particularly happy if my wife spent the majority of her time away from home. Right now, it's a matter of priorities for me; my involvement with DWB and the free clinic happens to be the strongest priority at this point in my life."

"Your parents would be very proud of you right now, but I'd also venture to guess that they would be less than enamored at your committed sense of bachelorhood. They were both very loving with each other, and they would have wanted the same thing for you."

"If it is meant to be, then it will happen," Michael stated, philosophically. "I find this conversation, which you love to bring up now and again, rather interesting, given that you have chosen a life of eternal bachelorhood. Seventy-six years of life, I might add."

"I've had my share of relationships in my younger days, but in none of them did I feel comfortable enough, or trustworthy enough, to spend a lifetime glued to their hips. It wasn't long after going to work for your parents that I realized what true love was all about, and no relationship of mine ever measured up to what your parents had."

"At least we both agree on one thing: that my parents were very special people. I've never doubted for a moment that I've had the best parents a son could ever ask for. Thankfully, I had the opportunity to tell the two of them that on many occasions before they were taken away from me—and from you."

"Your parents taught you well. Now go off and do them proud by getting married. Join one of those online 'singles only' clubs."

That suggestion brought a round of laughter from Michael as he slid out from the table and headed up to his study. Falling asleep in his recliner last night did not allow him the time needed to catch up on the mail—not to mention the latest medical journals. He would have been further behind, he thought to himself, had Frankie not taken over the household responsibilities following the death of his parents; the tedious task of paying the household bills, along with seeing to it that the contract staff was managed efficiently, fell willingly to Frankie. He wasn't sure what he would do if Frankie ever decided to retire— the hole left behind would be significant—and he knew it.

Chapter Three

BY MIDFTERNOON, MICHAEL HAD MANAGED TO GET THROUGH HIS MAIL and journals, and take in a run along the trails that ran throughout the property. Once back from the run he changed into his swim trunks with every intention of cooling off with a swim. Just as he was leaving his bedroom, Frankie came down the hallway and informed him that Debra Price was on the house phone; Michael quickly crossed the hallway to take the call in his study.

"Michael Thomas speaking."

"Good afternoon, Dr. Thomas. This is Debra Price, Briana's mother. Before my daughter ran off to the studio this morning, she mentioned something about setting up a time for the two of you to get together prior to the actual benefit. Which, if I recall, is the last weekend in November—at least according to the information we received from the folks at Doctors Without Borders."

"The last weekend in November is correct. I know that it doesn't allow for a lot of upfront planning on the part of you or Briana, so I apologize for that right from the get go."

"No need to apologize, doctor, we understand. As you can well imagine, we receive a lot of benefit requests each year, with a good 99.9 percent of them being turned down—there are only so many days in a year. Briana is well aware of the Doctors Without Borders organization, which she has a lot of respect for, I might add. And the fact that this benefit supports one of our own hospitals in Tennessee also appealed to her sense of giving back. So, even on short notice, we will do whatever it takes to support the cause."

"Thank you. I truly appreciate that. Can you tell me the first opening your daughter has that we might get together?"

"She's in the studio the rest of this week recording a new album, so the earliest opening she has would be this coming Monday. Are you, by any chance, available Monday as well?"

"Monday would be perfect. Is there any time of the day that she prefers?"

"My daughter is generally an early riser, so whatever is agreeable to you would work for her."

"Do you think she'd be open to meeting at my place at nine over breakfast? My cranky old cook is tired of preparing meals only for me, so I'm sure he'd appreciate the opportunity to show off his cooking skills for someone else."

"Over breakfast sounds great. I'll give you fair warning though. She may be tall and slender, but she can generally out-eat most men when it comes to breakfast foods. If she had her way—and she of-tentimes does—she would eat breakfast meals three times a day, and probably does now that she's living on her own."

"I'll be sure to pass that warning on to Frankie. You are more than welcome to join us if you like."

"Thank you for the offer, but my husband and I have an ear-ly-morning meeting with our son's guidance counselor at school."

"Another day, maybe. Would your daughter prefer that I send a car for her?" Michael asked, trying to be the gentleman.

"Heavens no!" came the quick response. "Thank you for the offer, but Briana is tired of being chauffeured around all the time when we're on the road. She's got her own sporty little Mustang that she loves to drive but seldom gets the opportunity to do so. All I need from you at this point is an address."

"I guess an address would come in handy," he jokingly replied. "It's 923 Airport Road. And for her point of reference, it's located at the southeast corner of John C. Tune Airport. When she pulls up to the gate, have her hit the intercom button. Frankie or I will let her in. Have her follow the road for about a thousand feet and park in front of the main entrance."

"That doesn't sound like a home, it sounds more like an estate," Debra replied, rather inquisitively.

"I guess you could consider it an estate. It was built for William Johansson and his family way back in the twenties. My parents picked it up from his estate. To me, it is simply a home—the only home I have ever known."

"I know the name Johansson well. His name is not only on buildings in the greater metropolitan area, but a major boulevard is named after him, as well. To be honest with you, I'm not even sure that Briana knows who he is.

"If I weren't living in his house, I probably wouldn't know who he was either. My parents made sure that I knew everything there was to know about him. Speaking of which, your family is more than welcome to visit the estate. If I'm not around personally to take you on a tour, then Frankie would love to guide you around. My parents not only purchased the estate but the furnishings, as well. Most of what is currently here pretty much resembles what was here back when the Johanssons furnished it."

"Wow!" Debra exclaimed. "The original furnishings! You may find my husband and me taking you up on that offer."

"A simple phone call is all it takes. And, on that note, I will let you go and, please, tell your daughter that I'll be looking forward to her visit on Monday. And tell her to bring her appetite."

"I will. It's been a pleasure talking with you, doctor."

"Debra, as I mentioned to your daughter last night, my friends call me Michael."

"Okay then, Michael it is. Hopefully, I'll get the chance to meet you personally someday, along with taking you up on that offer to tour your estate."

"Likewise, Debra. And just so you know, the best part of the tour is that it's free. I normally charge a thousand dollars an hour." He hears light laughter on the other end of the phone following his comment.

"Good—I like free," she responded, with lightness in her voice. "Bye, Michael."

"It's been a pleasure. Bye, Debra."

After hanging up the phone, he sat back down in the recliner to run their conversation through his head once again. He liked Briana's mother—she had warmth about her. Hopefully he would find the daughter as pleasant and easygoing as the mother; something told him that he would find the daughter to be a reflection of her mother. With that thought in mind, he grabbed a towel and went downstairs and headed outside for a swim.

He wasn't one for working out in a gym—not that he needed to, as the half-hour of aggressive swimming, mixed in with some running, kept his body well-toned. The only part about going on missions for DWB was the total lack of available swimming facilities. But then again, most of the people he dealt with in his role as a doctor had never even seen a pool, let alone a doctor; nor, he knew, would he even have the time for a swim anyway.

Chapter Four

MICHAEL SPENT THE NEXT FEW DAYS AND SATURDAY VOLUNTEERING HIS services at one of the local free clinics around town. If for no other reason, it helped to keep his mind off the upcoming visit with Briana. Even though he had yet to meet her, she was beginning to play mind games with him and, for that reason alone, sleep did not come easily most nights—though he wasn't quite sure of the underlying reason.

He surmised that his apprehensions came from never having had the opportunity to work with, or personally interact with, an entertainer before. He'd participated in previous DWB sponsored benefits before this one, but they were always handled entirely by the staff back in New York. This would be his first foray, at least partially, at pulling together a crucial component of a benefit. The hospital in Etenia took on the responsibilities for the onsite logistical support, while the New York office was handling the vice president's itinerary—Briana would be up to him.

When Monday morning finally arrived, Michael was fully awake at the all too early hour of four. He tried reading for awhile in his study, but found it much too difficult to concentrate, so decided on an early morning swim. At the completion of his swim, he returned to his room to shave and shower. He tried reading once again, but had no better luck at concentrating than he did on his first attempt.

An hour and a half later, however, he found himself awakening from a deep slumber. He immediately went into panic mode thinking that he had overslept and that Briana was already here—until he glanced at the clock and realized, with some relief, that it was only eight; meaning that he had one more hour before her arrival.

With that amount of time left, he decided to wander downstairs to see what Frankie was up to. Passing by the dining room he noticed that the table settings were already in place. Making his way into the kitchen he caught sight of Frankie in the process of cooking up a whole lot of bacon and sausage links. As for the actual breakfast meal, it made no difference if she wanted eggs, pancakes or French toast—regardless of her choice, Frankie was ready to go with any or all of the potential meal choices. As expected, it appeared at first glance that Frankie had everything under control.

"Good morning, Frankie."

"Good morning to you, Michael. Checking up on me, are you?" he responded, while at the same time turning around to glance at Michael. "From the pitiful looks of you, I would say that you forgot to go to bed last night."

"Well, thank you for the morning compliment, Frankie," Michael responded, without totally disagreeing with his observation. "I look that bad, huh?"

"Let me just say that you have looked better at this time of the morning."

Now feeling the need to justify his sleepless look, Michael said in response, "I've had a lot of things going on in my mind lately which have disrupted my normal sleep patterns. My swim and shower this morning obviously didn't mask my sleepy look any . . . at least according to you."

"I would tend to agree with that assumption," Frankie responded, in a matter-of-fact way.

"Maybe some of that strong, burnt coffee you always make will help," he added, with a sly smirk on his face.

"In your case, I'd have two or three cups before Miss Price arrives. And someday, Michael, I'll turn the coffee on before I go to bed—then you'll know what strong and burnt really taste like."

"Knowing you, Frankie, I wouldn't be surprised to find you doing exactly that. If, for no other reason than to teach me a lesson," he replied, while pouring the coffee into an oversized mug.

"I might do that, so be careful before taking that first sip each morning," he said, with a grin.

"Well . . . even though it's rather cool outside, I think I'll take a walk around the grounds. Unless, of course, you might be in need of some expert help in the kitchen? We are having a special guest, you know."

"Good idea on the walk. It might help to improve your looks. As far as needing help in the kitchen . . . that will only happen the day after I retire, expire, or get fired, whichever comes first. So get out of my kitchen."

Michael enjoyed Frankie's good-natured attitude, if for no other reason than it helped to wake him up in the mornings by means of their back-and-forth kidding. They'd always had a close relationship during his growing up years, but never as close as they'd been since the death of his parents. His continued presence in the house, and in his life, has remarkably eased the loss of his parents—in immeasurable terms.

Returning to the kitchen a half hour later, he found Frankie washing the pans used to cook up the bacon and sausage; enough to feed an army, he thought to himself.

"You should've considered taking a longer walk," Frankie remarked, after glancing at Michael entering through the doorway. "You almost look half-human right now."

"I don't know whether to take that as a dig or a compliment. But, for the sake of peace in the world, I'll take it as a compliment."

"It's a good thing Miss Price has never met you before. One look at you and she'll think sleep-deprivation is part of your normal look," Frankie said, with another of those slight grins showing at the corner of his mouth.

"I can only hope so," responded Michael, as he glanced over at the clock on the wall. "I think I'll run upstairs, freshen up a bit before she arrives. However, if she's anything like most women, she'll more than likely be fashionably late."

"Don't count on it. From what little I know about her, she's very professional in all matters. I'd bet my money on hearing the intercom buzzer go off right at nine."

"I'll take that bet. If I lose, I'll cook dinner tonight for the two of us."

"Maybe you didn't hear me very well earlier this morning, because you were still in a sleep-like stupor. What part of stay out of my kitchen didn't you hear and understand?"

"If you'd give me the chance, I might surprise you someday. Remember, I've survived while you've been on vacation before."

"Michael, have you ever wondered why I'm never sick? The very thought of you cooking a meal for me would kill me off for sure; like a prisoner having his final meal before being sent off to the gallows. As far as cooking for yourself while I'm gone, I intentionally stock the freezer with microwavable meals before I leave, and every year when I return, I've noticed that they are mysteriously missing."

"Okay, I can take a not-so-subtle hint. I'll go off and see if I can crawl my way upstairs with what's left of my pride."

"You better be quick about it; Miss Price will be here in less than ten minutes. Unless, of course, you have in mind being fashionably late yourself."

With that humorous notice of dismissal from Frankie, Michael headed quickly up the stairs to freshen up. No sooner had he made his way halfway back down the stairs, when he heard the intercom buzzer go off. Glancing at his watch, he noticed that it was exactly nine o'clock. Frankie being Frankie, he knew that he was going to be ribbed about her on-time arrival for days to come.

By the time he reached the kitchen, he overheard Frankie giving Briana the okay to come in through the gate. When Frankie noticed Michael entering the kitchen, he glanced up at the wall clock and then back at Michael—all without saying a word. Michael knew exactly what Frankie was telling him.

In order to save face with Frankie, Michael headed to the front door to await her arrival. Looking through the door's side window, he caught sight of a shiny red car rounding the corner a few hundred yards down the roadway. Because of the heavily tinted windows, it was impossible to see who was driving, even though he already knew it was Briana.

She brought her car to a stop directly below the covered driveway in front of the house, but made no attempt to immediately get out. Needless to say, the suspense was eating at Michael. After what seemed like an eternity, at least to him, her car door finally swung open. What stepped out of the car totally took his breath away. There, standing next to the car, stood a very tall, strikingly beautiful young lady. Having seen pictures of her on the Internet was one thing, but seeing her in person was quite something else. She wore a simple, light red blouse with dark blue slacks touching the tops of her low-heeled shoes, the colors highlighting her blond hair perfectly. Then there were the eye-catching, droplet earrings that flashed with the early morning sun; they too matched the color of her blouse. At 6'2" himself, he quickly realized that they would be almost standing eye-to-eye; they would be, he thought, if she were wearing high-heeled shoes as female entertainers most often do—at least on stage.

Watching her as she began her ascent up the thirty-two stairs leading to the front door, he decided to back up a few paces. The last thing he wanted was to have her catch him standing at the door, somewhat like an expectant child waiting for a freshly-baked cookie. God knows he didn't want to give her the impression that he was overly excited about meeting her; even though, in fact, that was actually the case.

Given her long legs, it took no time at all before she reached the front door and rang the doorbell. Michael hesitated a few moments before opening the door. Upon seeing each other, there was a moment of hesitation on both their parts as they stood taking one another in. Briana was the first to speak up.

"Unless you're the cook, butler or groundskeeper, I am going to assume that you are Dr. Thomas . . . I mean Michael," she remarked.

"Unless you're delivering flowers, running for office or trying to sell me some Girl Scout cookies, in which case I'll buy all you have—I am going to assume that you are Miss Price . . . I mean Briana," Michael humorously responded in turn.

At that, they both broke out in laughter. From that moment on they both knew they were going to get along well together. Michael then went through the motions of inviting her inside before escorting her directly into the kitchen to meet Frankie.

"Frankie, I would like to introduce you to Briana Price, our guest of honor for breakfast this morning."

"The pleasure is all mine, Miss Price."

"Thank you, Frankie. Apparently you don't have a last name, at least according to Michael's introduction, so if you don't mind, I will address you as Frankie . . . but only if you address me as Briana," she added.

"I've been called Frankie for so many years I'm not sure I even remember what my last name is anymore. If Michael only addresses me as Frankie, which he does, then you most certainly can. Besides, you're a lot prettier than Michael. So you can call me by any name you choose."

"Frankie, would you quit trying to butter up Briana and think about breakfast—unless you would permit me to do the cooking?"

"If you don't pretend to be a chef then I won't pretend to be a doctor," Frankie quickly shot back.

"Fair enough," Michael responded. "Are you at least going to inform our guest as to what the morning offerings are?"

"Certainly! I already have bacon and sausages warming in the oven, so whichever you prefer, let me know. You have your choice of hot cakes, French toast, eggs of any style, various breakfast cereals, a variety of oatmeal flavors, and waffles. As for beverages, we have coffee, tea, milk, orange juice, apple juice and, of course, water."

"Oh my God! I feel as though I'm in a high-class restaurant ordering straight off the breakfast menu," responded Briana. "How about four of everything?" After a moment's hesitation, she added, "Only teasing. I could probably go with two strips of bacon, two sausages, two eggs scrambled, one French toast, a cup of coffee, and a small glass of orange juice. Is that doable?"

"It most certainly is. And you, Michael?"

"I would like the same, please, except apple juice in place of orange juice."

"Okay then! If you two would please vacate my kitchen, I'll have breakfast up shortly."

"We know when we're not wanted," Michael jokingly remarked to Frankie as he escorted Briana into the formal dining room.

"I like Frankie a whole lot," remarked Briana, once they entered the dining room. "He's quite the character. How long has he been with you?"

"Frankie has been a part of this household and family since long before I was even born. What he does for me today, he did for my parents for years before I came onto the scene . . . only more so now. We constantly rib each other, but trust me when I tell you that he's irreplaceable. And, as you'll see, though it's only breakfast, he's an amazing cook, among other things."

"I'll take your word for it."

"While Frankie is putting together breakfast, why don't I take you on a quick tour of at least part of the house?"

"I would love that. My mom relayed some of the history on the house to me last week, based on your conversation with her. She's excited to see it for herself someday."

"I let it be known more than once during our conversation that she is welcome out here anytime for a personally guided tour. Or, if I happen to be out of town or the country, then Frankie will guide your family on a tour. He loves to show off the house."

"I'm impressed already, and I've only seen three rooms so far. I love the antique furniture."

"They're all original pieces from when the house was built, which adds a lot more history and ambience to the house. The formal dining room, as you probably noticed, can seat up to 16 people in one sitting. The original owners, as you can well imagine, loved to entertain or, as some historians have claimed, loved to show off their wealth and power. The living room, as you can also see, was built for entertaining large groups of people as well. Next to the living room is where the men would go off to smoke their cigars and pipes. Women, of course, were never allowed in there. I have my suspicions that a lot of deals were made in that room. Through this doorway, when the weather was agreeable, the men would sit out on the deck and talk about money and world affairs."

"Oh my God!" Briana exclaimed as they walked out onto the large deck area. "Look at the large pool and the beautiful, manicured lawn; not to mention the forest-like grounds behind it all."

"Back in the day, it was all part of impressing their guests. Their children may have used the pool, but I seriously doubt that the adults did."

"And look at the huge pond over there. Any fish in it?" she asked.

"Koi—somewhere in the neighborhood of forty or so—and a bunch of frogs and turtles thrown into the mix. During the summer months, I like to come down here and read. In case you didn't know it, koi are actually beggars. As soon as they see me, or anyone for that matter, they come over and expect to be fed."

"That is so cool," Briana remarked, in awe of it all. "I need to build one of those ponds in my new condo."

"Say what?" Michael replied, as if she had lost her marbles.

"A koi pond in my condo. Why not? It's something different. It will make it a one-of-a-kind condo."

"Now this I've got to see."

"You've been kind enough to take me on a tour of your place, so I'll reciprocate in kind."

"I may just take you up on that offer. After you build your pond, that is."

"You're on."

"Shall we go back in?"

"Sure."

Michael then led the way back through the sitting room, living room and dining room. "Back down this hallway," he continued as they walked along, "are three bedrooms, one of which is Frankie's, two bathrooms, and what appears to have been a sewing room in its earlier days."

"Well, at least the women of the house could claim one room for themselves," remarked Briana.

"Those were different times, Briana. Things like that were accepted as given. At the very end of —"

At this point in their tour, they were interrupted by Frankie's voice announcing that breakfast was ready. They both quickly turned around and headed back to the dining room. There before them on the table was everything—as ordered.

Frankie motioned to Briana where her chair was, and immediately pulled it out for her to sit down.

"Thank you, Frankie, that was very gentlemanly of you. Not something I've experienced too often in my short life, and the table and meal look as though they were prepared by a professional. Won't you be joining us for breakfast?"

"Thank you for the compliment, and no to the offer of eating with you two. I've already had my breakfast a good two hours ago. That's what happens to those of us early-riser types. But thank you for the offer anyway. Now, if you two will excuse me, I have some cleaning up to do in the kitchen. If you need anything else, you only have to give a shout and a holler. Enjoy your meals."

Both Michael and Briana thanked Frankie for breakfast as he began making his way out of the dining room and back into the kitchen.

"So," Michael said, as they started eating, "do you mind discussing the benefit while we eat?"

"Of course not—happens all the time in my line of work and, I believe, that's why you invited me over in the first place. Or was it to buy all of my Girl Scout cookies?"

Michael had little choice but to burst out laughing. When he finished laughing, he asked, "Have you always been quick on your feet with comebacks?"

"Yep. Ever since I was a little tyke. The only way I knew how to defend myself against the neighborhood bullies."

"Just so you know, I would have bought all of your cookies had you come to my door."

"I'll remember that . . . should I ever become a Girl Scout, that is. How did we ever get on this subject, anyway?"

"I believe you started it."

"Oh. I guess I did. Sorry."

"Now let's see, where was I? Now I remember. I was about to ask if you're free the Friday of the benefit?"

"Outside of some studio work, I have no concerts planned except for a Thanksgiving Day special the week before. I was informed by DWB, however, that the activities were going to take place on Saturday and Sunday. Have the plans changed?"

"Not at all. I was planning on flying up on Friday to work with the hospital staff on the finalized schedule of events. I'm a little nervous about everything going smoothly, so for peace of mind, I'm planning on a Friday arrival. Because you're a major component of the benefit, I thought you might wish to come up a day early . . . you know . . . to check out where you'll be singing and to see the hospital for yourself before the actual benefit."

"I'm sure I can leave Friday as well as Saturday . . . if, for no other reason, it will give me the opportunity to relax before the actual shows. I've been asked to do three performances. Are they during the day or evening?"

"Saturday is at three and seven, Sunday is a one o'clock performance."

"Sounds good. Is DWB handling the flights and room reservations? Or do I need to ask my staff to do that?"

"The rooms have already been booked. But remember, this is a small town, so the accommodations won't be up you your usual standards."

"I've spent the better part of my career living and sleeping on a bus. So anything they have to offer will be fine."

"Fair enough. As far as the flights go, I have a relatively new Cessna jet located on the back property. You're more than welcome to fly up with me. And, to give you some assurances, I've been flying since I was sixteen; jet certified at twenty-one. I use the jet primarily for our DWB missions. If you'd rather fly commercial or drive, I understand."

"I love flying," Briana responded. "Something I'd like to learn how to do myself someday. So, if you're offering, I'll gladly accept the free ride."

"Okay, that's settled. It's a relatively short flight up to Etenia, but I'd still like to leave around the noon timeframe. That will give us plenty of time to tour the hospital and work out the final details of the benefit, both for your performances and the small part that I will play in all of this. Are you comfortable performing solo or would you like to bring a part of your band with you? The jet is certified for eight passengers, with one of those eight being the co-pilot's seat."

"I've performed solo many times, but I would prefer, for this benefit anyway, to include my piano player; he lives in Charlotte, North Carolina. Would the DWB or hospital be willing to cover his expenses? I work benefits for free, but see to it that musicians I bring along are paid. He'll also need a piano."

"If you'll contact him about the benefit dates, I'll contact the hospital to expect a call from either him or your staff to make the necessary flight and hotel arrangements. Whoever makes the call, have them ask for Harold Brotherton—he's the money man for the hospital. I'll give him a call later today alerting him to expect a call from someone. In terms of a piano, can't say that I know for sure, but I'll see to it that one is made available. In case you have any further questions, here's my card with my cell and home phone numbers on it. Feel free to call me anytime."

After placing his card in her purse, she pulled her own card out and handed it to him.

"Any changes come up, contact me directly on my cell phone," Briana stated. "I'm not always immediately available, so please leave a message and I'll call back as soon as possible. I'll try to remember to program your number into my phone. If I don't do that, then there is a strong possibility that I won't even answer it. Very few people have access to my cell phone number . . . for obvious reasons."

"Thank you. In your line of work I can understand how you have to be careful with your phone number. How was your breakfast, by the way?"

"Everything was done perfectly. My compliments to the chef."

"Frankie must have cooked everything to perfection as I don't even see a need to wash your plate," he remarked, in an attempt at humor.

Briana let out an embarrassed laugh following that comment. "I'm sure my mother must have told you that breakfast is my favorite meal of the day . . . and that's why you intentionally invited me over for a morning meeting . . . right?"

"I believe she did mention something about breakfast being your favorite meal of the day. Would you like a refill on that breakfast?"

"Oh heavens no, thank you anyway. If I ate like this every day I'd be out buying larger-sized clothes before you knew it."

"Well then, now that we've gorged ourselves, would you like to continue the tour of the premises, or do you need to run?"

"No, I have nothing on my calendar today outside of this meeting. I'd love to see the rest of the house and grounds—or should I say, mansion?"

"Most people would refer to it as either a mansion or an estate; for me, it's a home—the only one I've ever known. We can head upstairs first, then I'll take you on a tour of the grounds. The grounds are rather expansive, so we'll use one of the golf carts for that part of the tour."

"That sounds like fun," she replied.

"Would you prefer the elevator or the stairs?"

"After that breakfast," she replied, "I think I need the exercise over the elevator. Did you have the elevator installed?" she inquired.

"Heavens no! Came with the house . . . it's an original Otis elevator. Johansson believed in only the best when he had this place built. The only time any of us use the elevator is to go down to the garage. We'll take it down when we tour the grounds."

After climbing the stairs, Michael took her on a tour of the bedrooms; one of which included his massively oversized bedroom with double bathrooms—apparently one for the man of the house and the other for his wife—or so the assumption was made. From there, he led her into his equally oversized study which immediately reminded her more of a library than a study. Two walls, floor to ceiling, were lined with nothing but bookshelves. The shelves themselves were filled with neatly positioned books and just enough artifacts to add a little touch of class to it all.

"Oh my God! That's a lot of books," she remarked, as she stood in awe of it all. "Have you read them all?"

"Heavens no!" Michael replied. "What you see here is a combination of books that came with the house, my parent's books, as well as my own. I love reading, but it would take me three lifetimes of straight reading to consume all of those books."

"Outside of this room," Briana commented, "with its modern recliner, it looks as though you and your parents have chosen to retain all of the original furnishings, including the period paintings on the walls."

"My parents could have totally refurnished the house, but chose to keep it in its original state. What you currently see here is pretty much what you would have seen back in the early twenties when the house was built and furnished. My parents did upgrade the plumbing, wiring and the kitchen appliances, but that's about it. I don't spend a lot of time at the house, so I'm content to leave things as they are . . . not to mention the fact that I have absolutely no skills in the area of refurbishing the rooms. I'll leave that up to the next owner. I do have enough sense to leave well enough alone."

"Are you thinking of selling anytime soon?" Briana inquired, sounding interested in purchasing it for herself.

"Absolutely not," he responded. "Unless there are major changes in my life, and I don't foresee any, I'll probably take my last breath in this house. It may seem large to you, given that only Frankie and I live here, but Frankie manages, through outside contract services, to keep all of it maintained—yard and house both."

"I don't blame you for wanting to stay here. It has such charm and so much history, aside from being the house you grew up in."

"All of that and more," Michael replied, as they entered the elevator. Once in the elevator, Michael pulled the gate shut, pushed the G button, pulled the lever down, and they immediately began their slow descent to the garage below.

"Oh my God!" she exclaimed. "Brass surfaces . . . latticed doors with glass . . . accordion gates. I can't believe that something this old still works," she finally said in wonderment while looking over at Michael.

"They knew how to make things last in the old days. Frankie has it serviced periodically to make sure that it continues working. The thought of ever having to replace the elevator with something modern doesn't appeal to me, so I spend what I have to in order to keep it running smoothly."

Once they reached the garage level, Michael pulled open the gate and guided Briana over to one of the two golf carts sitting outside of the elevator. After climbing in, they proceeded out the garage door and along a compacted dirt path that wove in, out and around the finely manicured lawns and garden areas. A short ride later the path eventually led them to the hangar.

With the push of a button on the golf cart dashboard, a side door opened wide enough for their entry into the hangar. Ten feet inside the doorway he brought the cart to a stop and climbed out. Glancing over at Briana, he noticed that she was making no attempt to leave the cart— her eyes being focused directly on the jet as though she were in a trance.

"Are you eventually going to get out or are you going to spend the rest of the day in the cart?" he asked, in a joking manner.

"Oh my God! I can't believe that someone would actually have a jet parked right on their property. Is there anything I can do to convince you to sell your place, jet included? I'll even throw in free Girl Scout cookies to sweeten the deal," Briana remarked, all with a sly, teasing grin on her face. "I could fly to my concerts right from my own home. How cool would that be?"

"Sorry. Not for sale, even with cookies thrown in. This hangar is the only new structure ever built on the entire property—architecturally built to match the house, of course. My father owned a jet as well, so he found it more convenient to park it right on the property for loading and unloading medical equipment, but out of sight of the main house for aesthetic reasons. In some ways, it made sense given that the property borders that of the airport—aside from the fact that he never had to pay hangar fees or parking space to store his aircraft. I currently contract with an aircraft servicing company to keep the plane refueled at all times, along with fulfilling the general maintenance requirements that go with owning any aircraft. Aside from using the plane for DWB missions," he continued, "I also use it for what I guess you would call mercy missions—patients who require more extensive care at specialized hospitals outside of the Nashville area. If I'm not available at the time, then I allow a few other carefully chosen pilots to use the jet for the mercy flights."

"Oh my God! I am so impressed," she responded, still in awe of it all. "Do you have any time left over for yourself?"

"Sure I do. The DWB missions, which usually last anywhere from two to three weeks at most, only take place about once every two or three months. Mercy missions that I volunteer for only average about one a month. I'll fly the patient and families to wherever they need to go and, if necessary, I'll go back and pick them up for the trip back home. In between those trips, to answer your specific question, yes, I have ample time to attend to my own needs. It may not sound like it to you, but I do."

"I guess, in many ways, we both seem to have the same kind of schedules. I go on tour for a month or two, return home, chill, hit the studio, chill some more, attend award ceremonies, chill some more, before doing my own thing—which usually means writing music. Looking at my own life, I know that I'm doing what I want to be doing. I guess the same can be said about your life. We're both busy, but busy doing the things we want to be doing."

"That pretty much sums up the two of our lives in a nutshell," Michael said, in concurrence. "Why don't we jump back into the cart and head back to the main house?"

"Okay," she responded. "You're the driver, so lead on."

The ride back to the main house was mostly in silence as they both took in the beautiful scenery, even spotting two deer along the way, a mere ten yards off to the side of the path.

"Oh my God! You even have deer on the property," she said, with childlike delight.

"Do you always use the phrase, 'Oh my God' a lot in your conversations?" he kiddingly asked.

"Only when I see or experience things that are so unbelievable. I can't help it. The whole place—the mansion, the grounds, the jet, the deer—all are so overwhelmingly impressive, not to mention Frankie's cooking," she added.

"What you're experiencing for the first time here, Briana, are the very things that I guess I take for granted—one of the downsides of living here all my life."

"Until I moved out on my own, I know exactly what you're referring to. Looking back, I probably took my parent's home for granted, as well. That's the fun part of experiencing new things . . . it forces your eyes and mind to see things in a new light, from a different perspective than what we're normally accustomed to."

About that time in their conversation, they found themselves re-entering the garage and eventually making their way up the elevator. This time, however, Briana was operating the buttons and lever of the elevator—much like a child in awe at having experienced something new. She found herself thinking that this would be a cool house to live in. Being a tad bit on the shy side, however, this was not something she was willing to say out loud to Michael.

She was thankful that the elevator door opened when it did for fear that she would reveal her true feelings about the mansion; let alone about her thoughts of Michael that had also started playing with her mind. She was impressed with everything about him. He was tall, handsome, obviously educated, and wealthy. He appeared to be compassionate toward others and, though somewhat reserved, had a playful sense of humor when the occasion arose. What wasn't there to like about him?

"Are you comfortable with the plans we made for your participation in the benefit?" Michael asked, returning to the subject of the benefit.

"Pardon me," she responded. It was obvious that she was still lost in her own thoughts, as she barely heard a word of what he had just said.

"Your mind must have taken a brief vacation on you," he responded with a grin. "I asked if you felt comfortable with the plans we've made for your participation in the benefit."

"Oh yes, for sure. All I need to do is whip out a potential playlist for both days along with contacting Bill, my piano player, to see if the dates work for him. If the dates don't work then I have a backup piano player I can call on. I'll take care of the entertainment part of the benefit—it sounds as if you've got enough on your plate as it is."

"Okay then, I appreciate that. If anything else comes up in the meantime, give me a call, and I'll do the same."

"Agreed." She was secretly hoping that they had more details to work out as she wasn't quite wanting to part ways just yet. So, as a stalling technique, she asked, "Is Frankie still around?"

"Not sure . . . but most likely," Michael answered. "Let's check his favorite hangout, the kitchen. Right about now he might be preparing lunch for himself and the hired hands."

As they entered the kitchen, she quickly caught sight of Frankie standing over the stove while stirring something in a large pot.

"Frankie," Briana called out, in a quiet voice so as not to startle him.

"Yes, my dear," he responded, as he cranked his head around to acknowledge her presence.

"Before leaving, I wanted to thank you for that wonderfully prepared breakfast. You may find me sneaking over here, when Michael is gone of course, to partake in some more of your delightful cooking."

"You don't have to wait for Michael to be gone, Briana. You can join us anytime, as my guest. I'm entitled to cook for whomever I please—and nothing would please me more then to see you back again."

Michael, of course, was highly amused by this conversation, but chose to stay out of it. Like Frankie, he would like nothing more than to have Briana return for another visit—or two. But he wasn't about to say so openly for fear of scaring her off by coming across as too forward. So, he stood silently, leaning against the door frame while the interchange between the two of them continued.

"Don't be surprised if I take you up on that offer, Frankie. Living by myself now equates to lousy meal planning; not that my meals are actually planned out in advanced, mind you. I'd be lying if I said they were."

"If I don't hear from you anytime soon, Briana, then I will have to assume that you either don't like me, or you didn't like my cooking this morning."

"I'll give you a call soon to prove that I like both you and your cooking. But don't ask me to choose between you or your meals, okay?" she said, with a big smile on her face.

Poor Frankie was starting to get a little embarrassed with all of this attention—and it showed on his face. "Either way, you are welcome here anytime, right Michael?"

"Anytime . . . anytime at all," he responded. And he meant it more than either one of them were aware. Well, maybe not Frankie.

"See you soon, Frankie, and thanks again for everything."

"Soon will be too late. Make it sooner than soon," he responded, with a twinkle in his eyes that even caught Michael by surprise.

Both Briana and Michael turned, exited the kitchen and headed for the front door. There was an awkward silence as they made the walk side by side. They were both sorry that it was over, but neither one of them knew how to prolong the stay any longer. Briana was the first to speak up.

"I'm going to give you some fair warning, Michael. My mother, guaranteed, will beat the gory details out of me about this morning. So don't be surprised if you receive a call from her asking for a tour of the house; you know, the one you offered to her last week."

"She's welcome anytime," he replied. "In fact, the whole family is invited, and you can lead the tour this time. Give us a call and we'll either make a breakfast, lunch or dinner tour out of it."

"That sounds like fun," she replied. "Then I'll get to see Frankie again. He is definitely a gem . . . a one of a kind." She said this knowing full well that it wasn't Frankie she wanted to come back and see. But what's a little white lie every now and again? Something she has been known to do before, and on more occasions than even she cared to admit.

"Okay then! I shall go sit by my phone awaiting your mother's call," Michael responded, with a smile on his face.

He then reached out, rather reluctantly, for the door knob. Once the door was opened wide enough, Briana passed through to the outside.

She immediately turned around, saying, "Thank you again for everything, Michael. I had a great meal and tour, and of course, great company. At this point, I can only say that I will see you when I see you."

"So long, Briana . . . and thank you again for being part of the benefit. Your presence will make for a huge difference in our fundraising efforts."

His statement was followed by a long period of silence between the two of them before Michael finally spoke again. "So . . . until we meet again."

With those words spoken, Briana turned around and headed down the stairs to her car. She opened her car door and slipped into the driver's seat without chancing a glance back up at Michael. She was afraid that he would notice the sad look in her eyes. How could this happen so quickly, she wondered, as she slipped the key into the ignition and started the car. With darkly tinted windows, she didn't even bother a wave as she circled around the driveway and headed back down the road for home. Moments later, she chided herself for at least not glancing up to see if Michael waved as she drove away. Now she would never know.

Chapter Five

A FEW DAYS FOLLOWING THE VISIT BY BRIANA, MICHAEL CLIMBED ABOARD his plane and headed up to Etenia. He flew there on the pretense, at least with Frankie, of making more preparations for the upcoming benefit. Only he knew that he could not get Briana out of his mind—so he decided to get away from the very place where he first met her—his own home.

Upon arriving at the hospital, he spent the first part of his day going over the details of the benefit with three members of the hospital staff—two from the administrative side and one from maintenance. He then made his way over to the Emergency Room to assist the always limited staff with an overcrowded waiting room.

Following six hours of work in the emergency room, he went home with Dr. Murphy, who graciously puts him up whenever he was in Etenia.

The following day, during a brief lunch break, he received an unexpected call from Sandy at DWB. "Did I catch you at a bad time, Michael?" Sandy asked.

"Not at all, Sandy, I was getting ready to sit down for a bite to eat. What's up with you?"

"We received word from the vice president's staff that he and his wife will be flying up there on Friday—same day as you—probably around two. He apparently wants to spend more time with his relatives and friends who still call Etenia home."

"Well good—maybe Briana and I will get an earlier opportunity to meet him and his wife."

"No schedule of events for Friday were given, other than spending time with friends and relatives. So I'm guessing that you may or may not see him until Saturday . . . but who knows."

"That's too bad. Oh well, it is what it is," Michael stated. "Thanks, Sandy. Any more updates, be sure to give me a call."

"Will do, Michael. See ya."

"Bye, Sandy."

Michael was now glad that he and Briana had agreed to arrive a day earlier than originally planned. Their arrival time should put them into Etenia almost an hour earlier than that of the vice president and his wife. With any luck, he thought, Briana might be able to meet the two of them—if not Friday then Saturday for sure. This was something he thought would deeply impress her.

Following a late dinner, Michael decided he had best place a call to Briana to inform her of the vice president's earlier arrival. While the vice president's schedule change probably didn't make much of a difference to her personally, or professionally, it gave him a viable excuse—and that is exactly what it was—to talk with her, to hear her voice once again. To call her, for no apparent reason, would give the appearance of being a little too forward, but this was business after all, or so he justified it as such.

He was quite surprised when following the third ring she actually answered the phone. Her voice almost left him speechless at the very sound of her "hello."

"Hi there," he finally replied, following a brief moment of silence. "I hope I didn't catch you at a bad time?"

"Not at all," she responded, with a sense of cheerfulness in her voice. "I had just finished a late dinner, if you'd call what I ate dinner. I was about to sit down and scribble some notes in my diary."

"Do you record everything that happens in your diary?" he inquired, with a heavy emphasis on the word everything.

"Not everything," she replied, "only the major events of the day. A lot of the music I write is taken from my diary notes . . . the good along with the bad."

"Well, then," he replied, teasingly, "I hope, if I ever make it into your diary someday, that it will be more good than bad."

"Actually, both you and Frankie did make it into my diary. And, so as to set your mind at ease, it was all good. How could it not be given the excellent breakfast and the grand tour of your estate?"

"Well, knowing about your diary now, I'm guessing I'd better be certain that I am always on my best behavior, at least when I'm around you. I'm not exactly sure that I want to be the main character for one of your songs."

"You have nothing to worry about in that department—I never name names. Plus, most of what I write about has to do with dating experiences, not working relationships."

"On that note, I guess I can rest easier then, huh?"

"Yep! Rest assured . . . you'll be able to sleep at night."

"Thank you for that assurance. The reason I'm calling right now is to let you know that the vice president has decided to fly into Etenia a day early, which means Friday. It won't alter when you and I leave, but it may somewhat change our afternoon tour plans. DWB is working with his staff to see if he is expecting a meet and greet with the hospital staff on Friday, or if he will stick to Saturday, as previously planned. He apparently wants to spend time with his relatives before the events of Saturday."

"I'm flexible either way. Give me a call back when you find out, please."

"Will do. I'm up in Etenia right now as we speak. I'm going to be here one more day before flying back tomorrow evening."

"You actually flew up to Etenia?" she asked, in a surprised tone. "Can't you work out most of the benefit details over the phone?"

"I could, but I came up here for more than that. I've actually been helping out in the emergency room the past few days. They are so short-staffed that they can use all the help they can get. It makes for a long day for some of the doctors, especially those doctors who refuse to go home until everyone has been seen. Those are the men and women who deserve the title doctor, if anyone does."

"And you are one of them," she remarked, in all seriousness.

"I wouldn't go that far, but thank you for the compliment."

"I seriously mean it. You could open up a practice anywhere . . . have dinner at home every night, weekends off, play golf. Instead, you spend the majority of your time away from home helping others at little or no cost to them. In fact, it is actually costing you to provide medical services to those who can't afford it. Now that is my definition of a dedicated doctor."

"Enough, please, you're starting to embarrass me. Thank God you aren't here to see the redness in my cheeks."

"So I make you blush, do I?"

"Can we change the subject, please?" Michael pleaded.

"Sure we can," she replied. "I may just let you off the hook—this time."

"You are so kind, especially given the fact that you're the one responsible for putting me on the hook in the first place."

"Sorry," she said, not meaning it, of course. She liked the idea that she could get to him—even if only in a small way.

"Okay, Briana. I'll let you get back to your diary while I make preparations for bed. I've got a busy day ahead of me starting first thing in the morning . . . probably while you're still in dream mode."

"Okay, Michael. We'll talk again another time," she responded, reluctantly ending her side of the conversation. "Bye!"

"Goodnight, Briana."

His third day of volunteering at the hospital pretty much resembled the two previous days—only different patients. Each patient offered new challenges—which is what he enjoyed as there was no monotony in what he did. At the end of the day, one of the nurses gave him a ride to the airport—an airport conveniently located a few minutes outside of the city. After a three-day stint at the hospital, he decided it was time to get back to Nashville and prepare for his recruiting efforts for DWB. As with previous mission preparations, he would spend time assisting DWB in their recruiting efforts of doctors and nurses for upcoming missions—relying largely on contacts made while in medical school and through his parents. The upcoming Haiti mission, fortunately, would come well before the benefit itself.

A few days following his return from Etenia, Frankie informed Michael that Debra Price had called, leaving a message for him to return her call. He wondered whether this was a professional call or a personal call—as in a tour of the mansion, or something to do with the benefit. After heading upstairs to his study, he dialed up the number that Frankie had written down. After four rings a man answered the phone.

"Hello," came a businesslike voice on the other end.

"This is Michael Thomas. I'm returning a call from Debra Price earlier today."

"Oh sure, doctor, one moment please."

Michael wasn't quite sure who he was talking with, but apparently he knew of him. He could only assume that it was Briana's father. After what seemed like a full minute had passed, Debra finally came to the phone.

"Hello, Michael, thank you for returning my call. You're probably a little curious as to why I'm calling, right?"

"Oh, that thought did cross my mind when Frankie relayed the message that you had called."

"Briana stopped by the day after meeting with you and, of course, I interrogated her for every morsel of detail about her visit—as only a good, protective mother would, mind you."

"Briana warned me that you might do exactly that. She obviously knows you well."

"She knows her mother much too well, I'm afraid. Anyway, after listening to my daughter talk about her visit, we were wondering if we could take you up on your previous offer for a tour of our own. Is that offer still open?" she inquired.

"Of course it is," Michael responded, rather excitedly. "I mentioned to Briana before she left that her family was welcome to take a tour of the place anytime that's convenient for them. I don't even have to be here to lead the tour. Frankie can take you around or, if Briana comes with you, then she can lead the tour. Frankie, as your daughter can probably attest to, would be upset if you didn't join us for breakfast, lunch or dinner as part of the tour. He loves to cook for guests, which we seldom have, so you might consider making his day by allowing him to prepare a meal."

"We don't want to impose to that extent," Debra responded unconvincingly.

"That wouldn't be an imposition at all. Frankie would look forward to the challenge of cooking for guests, as he gets a little tired of cooking just for the two of us. At least that's what I hear from him all the time. So you'd actually be doing me a favor by sharing a meal here. Consider it all part of the free tour I offered last week. After all, I would think that any good mother would want to know everything she possibly could about the man her daughter is going to be spending three days with, don't you agree?"

"You do have a good point there. It's hard to keep an eye on her now that she's moved out on her own. All of us here are pretty busy during the days . . . so how does a dinner tour sound?"

"Great! Dinner it is then. Throw out a date while I have my calendar in front of me."

"Looking at our own calendar I would say that we're free either Tuesday or Thursday of next week. If that doesn't fit your schedule, then maybe the week after."

"Thursday is booked solid for me, so how about Tuesday?" he said, knowing full well that Thursday was as wide open as Tuesday. The very idea of having to wait until next Thursday to see Briana again was too much—even waiting until Tuesday was going to be too long. Since returning back home, she was all he had thought about.

"I'll put us down for Tuesday then," she responded.

"And how many shall I tell Frankie to expect?" He asked this, hoping that Briana would be joining them.

"Three for sure . . . four if Briana decides to join us. That would be my husband, our son and, of course, myself. I'll talk to Briana before then to see if she'll be joining us. Either way, I'll call and let either you or Frankie know. I haven't met Frankie yet, but Briana went on and on about his cooking abilities—and something about the way he handles you."

"It appears that your daughter summed up Frankie quite well, I'm afraid to admit. In terms of dinner, is five an acceptable time, or would you prefer something later?" Without waiting for an answer from Debra, Michael continued on. "It gets dark early at this time of year, so if you can be here around four that would work best. The outside part of the tour would be best viewed before darkness sets in."

"Perfect!" Debra exclaimed, in agreement with Michael's suggested arrival time. "We'll see you at or around four then."

"Looking forward to seeing you. Give my best to Briana."

"Will do. Goodnight, Michael."

"Goodnight, Debra."

After hanging up the phone, Michael remained in his recliner and reflected on the conversation with Debra. He thought Debra seemed to be a personable lady, much like Briana herself, and was, therefore, looking forward to meeting her along with the rest of the family. Deep down, of course, he knew that he would be disappointed if Briana chose not to join them for the dinner tour—even though she had already shared both a meal and tour with him. Not to mention the fact that Frankie would also be disappointed if she didn't show up.

Shortly after his private musings, he headed downstairs to find Frankie, who was sitting in the living room reading another one of his many books. "Frankie!" Michael began as he entered the living room. "I had a conversation with Briana's mother, Debra, and we negotiated a dinner tour for next Tuesday. I suggested an arrival time of around four with dinner at five." Teasingly, he added, "Can you handle dinner for the four of them or would you like me to cook it?"

Looking up over his short-rimmed reading glasses at Michael, Frankie replied, "That was a pretty brazen offer, or threat, from a man who can't even boil water without burning it . . . or were you thinking of ordering in pizza? Or should I purchase more TV dinners?"

"I know, stay out of your kitchen. Briana's parents, along with her younger brother, will be joining us for sure. Her mother will call in a day or two to let us know if Briana will also be joining us for dinner. As always, I'll leave the menu planning up to you."

"That would be a smart idea on your part," Frankie remarked, without glancing up from his book that he had resumed reading.

"Okay, I know when my culinary skills are not appreciated, so I'll head back upstairs and do a little pouting. But, should you need my assistance, you know where I live," Michael added, before leaving Frankie to his reading.

"Don't call me, I'll call you if I need any help. Goodnight, Michael," he added, before making another attempt at reading.

"See you in the morning, Frankie," Michael yelled back, as he rounded the corner and began his climb back upstairs to change into his swimming trunks. Even though it would be a bit on the chilly side, he felt the need for a swim.

Chapter Six

TRY AS HE MIGHT, MICHAEL WAS FINDING IT DIFFICULT TO KEEP THE UP-coming dinner out of his mind. To do so, however, he headed out for one of the free clinics—arriving back home around six every evening. Following late dinners and a swim, he invariably found himself retiring early to bed. On the good side, however, was a call he had received from Debra, informing him that Briana would be joining her family for dinner—for this he was extremely pleased.

When Tuesday morning finally rolled around, he found his nerves to be more on edge than before. He slept in, knowing that he would not be heading off to one of the clinics today. Following a vigorous morning swim, he showered and dressed before coming downstairs for an unusually late breakfast. No sooner had he sat down to eat than a call came in from one of the local hospitals.

"Michael," Frankie said, as he handed the phone over to Michael. "It's for you."

"Michael speaking."

"Dr. Thomas . . . this is Mary, I'm a surgical nurse from Nashville General. We currently have a young boy here who was involved in an overturned school bus accident. We have him stabilized at the moment, but given his extensive bone damage, the doctors feel that the boy can best be treated at Shriners Orthopaedic Care Hospital in Lexington. Dr. Ashwood, whom you apparently know, had asked that I give you a call. Is there any possibility that you could provide air transportation for the patient to Shriners?"

This was not the kind of request Michael was expecting—especially on the very day of his dinner tour with Briana's family. As much as he personally regretted the call, he knew himself only too well to refuse the request, regardless of his own personal plans.

"Dr. Thomas, are you still there?" she asked, breaking his thought process.

"I'm here," Michael quickly responded. "I was glancing at my calendar for today. And sure enough, after making a few quick calls to readjust my schedule, I'd be more than happy to fly him up to Lexington. What time should I expect them to be arriving at the airport?"

"The doctor gave a tentative time of noon. They apparently want to do a little more work on him beforehand. Is noon agreeable with your schedule?"

"Noon works for me, Mary."

"One other question, Dr. Thomas," Mary stated, "would it be okay if his parents went up with you, along with Dr. Ashwood and one of the flight nurses?"

"Parents are always welcome to fly along, Mary. Will they be following behind the ambulance?" Michael inquired.

"I believe they'll be riding in the ambulance. I've been told that they don't have a car."

"Okay, I'll see everyone at noon, then."

"Thank you, doctor. I'll be sure to let Dr. Ashwood know. Bye."

"Bye, Mary."

While eating a leisurely breakfast, he started doing some mental time calculations in his head. If the ambulance arrived on schedule at noon, it would take a solid half-hour to load the stretcher into his plane and secure it into place. Once that was accomplished, he would then have the parents come aboard and see to it that they were buckled up, as well. He figured, at best, that it would be close to twelve forty-five before he was taxiing down the runway.

The Blue Grass Airport in Lexington was approximately 200 miles northeast of Nashville. Michael knew that he could arrive at the airport easily in well under an hour's time—this would put him into Lexington around one-thirty. According to his continuing mental calculations, he would then be able to begin the flight back home in the vicinity of two o'clock. This calculation took into consideration the unloading of both the patient and his family. Allowing for the time needed to deliver the doctor and nurse back at the terminal, and taxiing back to his hangar, he should arrive home prior to four o'clock—or so he hoped.

Once the calculations were all worked out in his head, he started feeling better about taking on this flight. If, for no other reason, it would take his mind away from thoughts of Briana—at least he hoped it would. Following breakfast he shared all of this with Frankie, assuring him that if all went as planned, he should return about the same time that Briana and her family would be arriving.

"Well, Michael," Frankie said, with a devilish grin on his face, "I guess this means you won't be able to help me prepare dinner after all. And to think that I was actually looking forward to the application of your culinary skills."

Even Michael had to chuckle at this. "No, Frankie, it looks as though you'll have to go it alone on this one. Follow the directions in the cookbook or on the back of the box and you should be okay," he remarked, with an even bigger grin than Frankie's.

"Haven't you got a flight to get ready for, Michael?"

"I'll take that comment as an early dismissal from cooking school,

Frankie. But you're correct . . . I'd better get out of here and prepare both myself and the plane for duty. I'll see you later this afternoon, hopefully before or around four."

Finishing up with Frankie, he ran back upstairs to change into more appropriate clothing for the flight. On the way out, he grabbed his medical bag, as he always did—just in case the need arose. Because he had extra time before the actual flight, he decided to walk from the garage out to the hangar. Next up, with checklist in hand, he walked around and under the aircraft to conduct his preflight inspection. Even though the aircraft was checked over by certified mechanics following 80 hours of flight time, he never took these preflight inspections for granted—something his father had drilled in him for many years.

Once on board the plane, he performed the same functions on the multitude of dials, buttons, switches and screens that make up the flight instrument panel. When the preflight checklist was completed, he opened both the back and front hangar doors before firing up engine number one; ninety seconds later he fired up engine number two. After a few minutes of engine warm-up, he slowly taxied out the forward doors of the hangar. Thanks to his father, both sets of hangar doors were programmed to close fifteen minutes after each departure and arrival to allow for the dissipation of fumes from the two engines.

After pulling up to the gate leading directly onto the airport grounds, he pressed the push-to-talk switch to activate the VHF radio for communicating with any planes in the vicinity of the airport.

"Tune area traffic, Flight Surgeon November three-one-four is at the private gate, any traffic in the area, please advise." Receiving no feedback, he reached up and depressed a button which opened the gate for access to the airport perimeter. With the assurance that no aircraft were landing or taking off, he made his way directly across the runway to the small terminal office. After disembarking the aircraft, he went inside the terminal office to await the arrival of the ambulance.

"Hi Shirley," he said, as he entered the office. "You sure are looking rather lovely this morning. Got a hot date later tonight?" He wasn't exactly clear on this rumor, but he believed that she was seventy-five going on eighty—and she looked every year of it. But a more spirited and fun loving person one could not find anywhere.

"Well doctor," she responded, while looking up from her desk. "I was actually hoping that you stopped by to whisk me away to an opera in San Francisco. You know, just like that guy did with Julia Roberts in Pretty Woman. I always want to make sure, as you've probably observed many times, that I look my best; you know, so we can leave right from here when my shift ends. Oh, I know what you're thinking—but don't you worry—my husband wouldn't even know that I hadn't come home. Unless the fridge is out of beer, that is. That's why I make sure it's always full."

"Well, Shirley, I was actually thinking that very same thing this morning when all of a sudden I received a call for a mercy flight. But if you seriously want me to cancel the flight and take you to San Francisco, you just say the word. I'll be at your beck and call."

"A mercy mission, huh? I guess I'll have to take a rain check on the opera. Even an old coot like me has her morals and knows the priorities in life. Where you headed off to this time?"

"Up to Blue Grass. LIFEGUARD status. The patient will be arriving by ambulance at noon which, if your wall clock is correct, is in about fifteen minutes."

"Oh, so that's the call we received earlier from the hospital. We were asked to have the service gate opened up around that time for access to the flightline. They didn't mention your name—only that a plane would be waiting."

The two of them chatted back and forth with Michael teasing her repeatedly—and she loved it. Twenty minutes had passed between them and still there was no sign of the ambulance. Fifteen minutes later, Shirley received a call that the ambulance was making its way through the service gate and would arrive shortly. Michael then said his goodbyes and headed out to the plane to await their arrival.

A half-minute later, the ambulance pulled up alongside the aircraft. Dr. Ashwood and the accompanying flight nurse immediately opened the back door and set about removing the young boy from the ambulance. Once planeside, the stretcher was maneuvered into the plane. Using tie-downs, they then secured the stretcher in place, directly across from the door and behind the cockpit where an eighth seat had been permanently removed.

During all of this transfer activity, the parents of the young son were standing alongside the ambulance with obvious looks of apprehension on their faces. Michael motioned for them to come on board. Without hesitation, they quickly came over, climbed the stairs and entered the plane. Michael quickly introduced himself to the parents before guiding them to their respective seats. After sharing words of encouragement, he then returned to the cabin door, raising the stairs before securing the door into place. Following quick introductions with the flight nurse, he immediately stepped into the cockpit to ready the plane for flight.

When the engines were sufficiently warmed up again, he continued to taxi out and radioed Nashville departure control to receive his route clearance and IFR release. With his mission being classified as LIFEGUARD status, the controller advised Michael that all incoming and outgoing aircraft had been properly sequenced for his departure. Upon reaching the runway itself, he wasted no time in revving up the engines before releasing the brakes and racing down the runway towards eventual lift off.

Once airborne, he was informed by air traffic control that the skies would be clear and the winds minimal all the way from Nashville to Lexington. After reaching an assigned cruising altitude of 19,000 feet, he glanced back at the passenger cabin where both parents, not surprisingly, had their eyes focused on the activities of the doctor and nurse. While their son was kept sedated, Michael could only imagine what mental anguish they were experiencing during this entire ordeal; though he has witnessed this same situation many times over, it never got any easier for him.

Michael seldom liked to prejudge people but, in this particular case, he sensed that the parents were not people of means. One quick glance at their clothing led him to that conclusion, along with the fact that they were without a vehicle. So, while still in flight, he contacted the staff at the receiving hospital and requested that nearby hotel accommodations be made available for the couple—at his expense—along with taxi vouchers.

Shortly after making those arrangements, he noticed that the lights in the cabin behind him were intermittently flickering off and on. His flight control panel was, thankfully, not affected. He then reached over and flipped a switch that would automatically initiate a diagnostic assessment of the aircraft's systems—hopefully it would detect this unexplained lighting problem. Within three minutes of running the diagnostics, the results came back indicating a faulty fuse; a relatively minor issue which brought an immediate sense of relief to Michael. He would have the mechanics at Blue Grass install a new fuse prior to his heading back to Nashville. At twenty minutes out from the Lexington Airport, Michael's radio came to life with what was to be a series of instructions from various controllers just prior to landing.

"Flight Surgeon three-one-four, descend and maintain one-one eleven thousand, proceed direct Lexington."

"Descend, maintain eleven thousand, direct Lexington, Flight Surgeon three-one-four, roger," Michael replied. Fifteen miles out came further instructions handing over radio control of his flight to the Lexington controllers.

"Flight surgeon three-one-four, contact Lexington Approach One-two-zero point one-five."

"Contact Lexington approach on one-two-zero point one-five, Flight Surgeon three-one-four, take care," Michael repeated back in acknowledgment of the instructions given prior to making contact with the Lexington ATC.

"Good afternoon Lexington, Flight Surgeon three-one-four level at eleven thousand with Papa."

"Flight Surgeon three-one-four, Lexington Approach welcome! Descend and maintain four-thousand, expect vectors to ILS runway 22."

"Descend and maintain four thousand, vectors to ILS 22, Flight Surgeon three-one-four," he repeated back in the ongoing conversation as he approached within ten minutes of the airport. Michael looked forward to these conversations as it broke up the solitude of flying an aircraft for extended periods; ongoing conversations between pilots and controllers that the general public seldom were aware was taking place in the cockpit. With the landing only a few minutes away, Michael flipped on the internal PA system and advised both the doctor and nurse to take a seat and buckle up.

"Flight Surgeon three-one-four, turn left heading three-one-zero, descend and maintain three-thousand two hundred."

"Left heading three-one-zero, three-thousand two-hundred, Flight Surgeon three-one-four," Michael repeated. Shortly thereafter, he received the last of two directional turns.

"Flight Surgeon three-one-four, turn left heading two-five-zero, you're three miles from SADDL, you're cleared for the ILS runway 22 approach, Contact Lexington tower one-one-niner-point-one."

"Left turn two-five-zero, cleared ILS 22, contact Lexington tower, Flight Surgeon three-one-four," Michael responded as he began banking to the left for his final approach. After achieving a straight-on view of the runway, Michael received the last of two commands from the tower controller.

"Flight Surgeon three-one-four, Lexington tower, cleared to ILS land runway 22."

"Cleared to ILS land runway 22, Flight Surgeon three-one-four." Moments later, he brought the plane down as gently as he could onto the designated runway.

"Flight Surgeon three-one-four, exit runway as able, contact ground one-two-one-point-nine."

"Will exit left, ground point nine, Flight Surgeon three-one-four," Michael replied. Once clear of the runway and as directed, he made contact with the ground controller.

"Lexington Ground, Flight Surgeon three-one-four is clear of runway 22, request taxi to Aero-Tech via Alpha."

"Flight Surgeon three-one-four, Lexington ground, taxi via alpha, good day."

"Taxi via Alpha, Flight Surgeon three-one-four, good day."

With the communications now completed, he continued along the taxiway until stopping twenty feet short of a waiting ambulance where three individuals were standing alongside. The flight nurse and Dr. Ashwood unstrapped all of the stretcher restraints and were ready to go by the time Michael had the door opened and the stairs secured in place. The moment the stretcher was on the ground, Michael motioned for the parents to disembark the aircraft. There to meet the young boy were both a doctor and nurse from Shriners Hospital.

Between the two sets of medical staff and the driver, they quickly proceeded to wheel the stretcher directly into the back of the waiting ambulance. Once the stretcher was secured inside, along with the Shriner staff, the driver closed the back doors before motioning to the parents to climb into the front of the ambulance.

Michael explained to both Dr. Ashwood and the nurse that a mechanic should be arriving shortly to swap out the faulty fuse. Because he knew he was running potentially late for this evening's dinner and tour commitment, he had phoned his concerns ahead to the aircraft servicing company. Thanks to the wonders of the plane's self-diagnostic system, it not only told him the fuse number, but where the fuse box was located on the aircraft. The change out, he figured, should only take a matter of minutes, at best.

Fifteen minutes later the mechanic had yet to show up. The waiting for his arrival was slowly starting to eat at Michael. When speaking with the company, he had informed them of his need to get back to Nashville shortly after landing. When ten more minutes had passed, he reached for his cell phone to see what the holdup was. Just as he was about to hit the call button on his phone, he caught sight of the service vehicle approaching the plane.

The mechanic climbed out of his vehicle as Michael approached him and immediately offered his apologies for being late. With fuse and clipboard in hand, he followed Michael up into the airplane and went straight to work—completing the change out in less than ten minutes. He then proceeded into the cockpit, flipping the light switch on to confirm that they worked correctly—which they did. Michael then signed off the work order and the mechanic exited back down the stairs.

With that out of the way, his next urgent assignment was to go in search of both of Dr. Ashwood and the nurse, who had disappeared into the terminal in search of something to eat. They had offered to find something for him, but he assured them that he wasn't hungry. The truth be known, he was actually hungry, but he was saving his appetite for dinner with Briana's family. He couldn't personally blame the doctor and nurse for being hungry, but their timing could not have been worse—at least for him. As he was about to open the door to the terminal, the two of them came out with prepackaged sandwiches and drinks in hand.

As soon as the stairs were repositioned back into the aircraft and the door secured and latched, he proceeded to the cockpit to make ready for the flight home. After warming up both engines and checking all systems, he radioed ground control of his intent to fly out. Following a two-minute wait, ground control then gave him clearance to taxi back to the same runway from which he had landed. Arriving short of the runway, he found himself lined up behind four other aircraft. This, of course, did little to calm his already jangled nerves. If only I were still on LIFEGUARD status, he thought to himself.

In between watching planes both land and take off on this particular runway, he made the mistake of glancing at the control panel clock. With all the activity going on, he was surprised to find that it was already three-thirty. This, he knew, meant that he would be lucky to reach John C. Tune Airport any earlier then four-fifteen—and would not make it back to his own hangar for another fifteen minutes after that. After landing, he knew that he still had to drop his two passengers off at the main terminal for their ride back to the hospital. Thoughts of being part of the Briana family tour were quickly dashed.

Once airborne and cruising at his assigned altitude, he quickly placed a call to Frankie.

"Frankie, Michael here. We had a few delays along the way, so it looks as though I won't be home until sometime before five."

"Not a problem, Michael. I'll ask my good friend Briana to take her family on the tour while I continue with dinner preparations. And with you out of the kitchen, I'm positive that dinner will be a hit with everyone."

Michael was not in the mood for Frankie's humor, but quietly bit his lip before the possibility of unleashing his selfish frustrations took hold of him.

"That's a good idea, Frankie. Briana knows the house and the grounds well enough from her own tour. Let her know that she's free to take them into any room in the house . . . with the exception of yours, that is."

"She can show my room anytime she wants. I have no dark, deep secrets hiding in there—as you well know."

"Whatever!" Michael responded, still somewhat frustrated by the turn of events. "Please apologize to them for my absence and let them know that I'll see them at dinner."

"As you wish! We will see you at five or thereabouts."

Michael hung up the phone and proceeded to make up as much lost time as he could—but not so much as to put added strain on the engines. As his father advised him many times over, "Never be in too much of a hurry when operating an airplane—that is an invitation to an accident." He'd done his best in the past to heed his father's advice, and so far, it had never failed him.

As with the flight over to Lexington, the return flight was uneventful. Prior to landing, he made another quick call to Frankie. After the fourth ring, Frankie picked up the phone.

"Yes, Michael."

"I'm twenty miles out . . . will be landing shortly."

"Take your time. Briana is upstairs taking the family on the first part of the tour. As expected, she has everything under control. Dinner is slow-cooking, so no concerns on that part either."

"Okay. I'll see you soon."

Shortly after hanging up with Frankie, his wheels hit the runway at exactly four thirty-five. Michael immediately taxied the plane over to the terminal where a hospital van was waiting to take both Dr. Ashwood and the nurse back to the hospital. After saying their goodbyes, Michael raised the stairs and secured and latched the door before proceeding around the outer fringes of the airport to his private gate. After the gate opened, he slowly taxied the plane to the hangar doors, which began to open. At this point in time, it was four-fifty. He was a little less stressed now knowing that dinner would not be served without his being there.

When the doors were fully opened, he noticed Briana and her family sitting on the six-seater golf cart just inside the side entrance. He surmised that they were on the last leg of their tour; though they couldn't see him, he smiled at the sight of her, exhaling with a deep sense of relief.

Chapter Seven

With the engines shut down and all systems shut off, he proceeded to unlatch the side door and, with the push of a button, the stairs unfolded downward. Before descending, he glanced over at the four of them now standing alongside the golf cart with a look of wonderment on their faces. He could only surmise that they weren't used to seeing an airplane in a private hangar—and at someone's residence, no less.

Michael acknowledged their presence with a wave of his hand before descending the stairway. With medical bag in hand, he quickly made his way over to his guests. Briana was the first to speak up.

"Welcome home, Michael," she said with a warm smile on her face.

"Thanks, it's always good to be back home," he responded with a smile of his own. "I wasn't sure if I was going to make it home in time for dinner."

"Michael, this is my mother, Debra, my father, Alan, and my younger brother, Ryan. Of course, my family already knows who you are, professionally known as Dr. Michael Thomas, but to your friends and associates, known simply as Michael."

"Very accurate introduction," said Michael, as they all shook hands. "I'm assuming that the four of you have already taken a tour of the house and grounds before coming out to the hangar."

"Yep, this was our last stop. Because you weren't here, Frankie said that it would be okay if I acted as the grand tour master," Briana responded, with that same smile lighting up her face. "Frankie told us of your last minute call this morning for some kind of mercy flight."

"Not the kind of call I was exactly expecting this morning, but then again, mercy flights are seldom preplanned. As much as I was looking forward to taking the four of you on the tour, this particular child was in obvious need of more advanced treatment at Shriners."

"You did the right thing, Michael," Debra remarked. "Though not to purposely change the subject, but you should think about installing seat belts on the golf cart for when Briana is at the wheel again. You might also consider installing speed signs, or speed bumps, along the path . . . she damn near took out a poor deer."

This onslaught of Briana's driving ability by her own mother brought about a lot of laughter from her parents and Ryan—Briana included.

"Speaking of the cart," Michael interjected. "We should all climb in and head back to the main house, or Frankie will be a little more than unhappy with all of us."

"Before we left for the tour of the grounds, Frankie mentioned that he had already slowed down the cooking and that dinner would be served at five-fifteen or thereabouts," Briana remarked.

"That would be Frankie."

The five of them climbed into the golf cart with Briana behind the wheel and Michael riding shotgun. After proceeding into the garage, they rode the elevator up to the main floor with Briana, once again, acting as the official elevator operator. Michael took notice of how comfortable she appeared in her new surroundings—along with taking control of matters—like the tour—when and where appropriate; he was liking that she appeared to be at ease around here.

After exiting the elevator, Michael suggested that they retire to the living room while he headed off to the kitchen to chat with Frankie.

"How's dinner coming, Frankie?" Michael asked, while spotting him removing a container from the oven.

"Very well, Michael, even without your assistance, I might add."

"That's okay, Frankie, at least there's a good doctor in the house in case anyone gets sick after eating. Come to think of it, I should invest in one of those stomach pump machines for the house. You know, in case someone eats some undercooked food."

"A good host does not abandon his guests," Frankie fired back. "Why don't you go out and tell them that dinner will be served in twenty minutes. And possibly they would like a glass of wine or something from the liquor cabinet. Make yourself useful Michael—anywhere but in my kitchen."

"As usual, I can take a hint. See you in twenty minutes then," he remarked in parting as he walked out of the kitchen.

Rejoining the group in the living room, Michael asked, "Would any of you like a glass of wine or something from the liquor cabinet?"

"If it isn't any trouble," Debra responded, "I could go for a glass of red wine."

"Make that two," added Alan.

"Briana, what would you like?" Debra asked, glancing across at her daughter.

This comment caught Briana a little off guard—her mother knew that she wasn't much of a drinker. Quickly thinking about what her mother had just said, she decided to act more grown up in front of Michael.

"I would like a red as well, please," she responded, feeling proud of herself.

"Any particular type for any of you?" Michael inquired of the three of them.

"Whatever you select will be fine with us," Debra answered.

It was at this point that Michael looked over at Ryan and realized that he had nothing to drink. "I apologize for being a bad host, Ryan, what can I get you to drink?"

"Nothing, sir," he replied. "I'll have a glass of milk with my dinner, if you don't mind."

"This must be your lucky day then . . . we milked the cow this morning, just so it would be fresh for you."

"You actually have cows living here?" Ryan asked, in total amazement.

"Not really, Ryan, I was only teasing you. We do have the room, obviously, to raise a few livestock, but not the time or inclination. Now, if you'll excuse me for a brief moment, I'll go down to the wine cellar and see what I can find in the way of a red."

Briana immediately spoke up, asking, "You actually have a wine cellar, too?"

"It's downstairs. I guess I forgot all about that room during our tour. Would any of you like to see it?"

Briana spoke up immediately. "I would love to see it, if you don't mind my tagging along."

"You are more than welcome to tag along," Michael replied, glad that she had asked to come along.

"If you don't mind, Michael," Debra stated, "the rest of us will stay put."

Briana quickly rose from her chair and followed Michael to the elevator.

"I don't suppose you'd like to play elevator operator?" Michael teasingly asked.

"I would be most honored to take you down to the dungeons below," she replied, jokingly. "Who knows what creatures await us," she added, in a haunted-like voice.

Michael rolled his eyes while looking up at the ceiling of the elevator before saying, "Lord, please forgive me for making a monster out of this formerly nice lady—for the devil has taken hold of her."

Briana could not contain her laughter as they ever so slowly descended to the garage level. With smiles still on their faces, they exited the elevator into the garage. Off to the right of the elevator was another door that led down to a lower level containing the wine cellar. After opening the door and flipping on the dimmed lights, they descended below to where the wine was stored.

"Oh my God!" she exclaimed in total amazement after viewing what appeared to be two hundred or more bottles lying on racks. "This is sooooo impressive."

"My parents, unlike myself, did a lot of entertaining with their fellow professors from the university. I know a little about wines, though nothing like my parents, so let's look for a nice red and hope for the best."

"What little you know is still a hundred percent more than I know," she remarked, still in awe at the variety and quantity of wines lying on the racks. "The only thing I know for sure about red and white wines is that they are red and white," Briana remarked, with a bit of clearly intended humor.

"Ah, here's one of my parent's favorite wines," Michael said, while lifting a dusty bottle off the rack. "I'm pretty sure that the three of you will enjoy it—at least I hope so."

"What is it?" Briana inquired, while secretly wishing that the two of them would become trapped in the cellar.

"It's Dom. Romane Conti of 1997 vintage," he answered. "Speaking of age, we had both better hurry upstairs; dinner should be ready about now. And trust me, Frankie does not like serving cold dinners. If that happens, stick around after dinner and watch as my hide gets tanned alive by Frankie."

Briana let out a laugh with the picture in her mind of Michael being tanned by Frankie.

The two of them took the elevator back upstairs where Michael wiped down the bottle before expertly uncorking it and filling the four glasses. The entire time he was doing this, Briana's eyes were fixated on him. Aside from his other attributes, she thought to herself, he is also a man of culture—apparently his knowledge appears to go beyond that of medicine. I wonder what other attributes he has that have yet to be revealed, she silently fantasized.

Michael brought her out of her thoughts when he handed two glasses of wine before her. Quickly coming to her senses, she took the wine glasses from Michael's outstretched hands and carried them into the living room. Briana presented one to her mother while Michael presented the other to Alan. After Briana sat down, Michael remained standing and presented a toast to the four of them.

"To health, wealth and happiness," he toasted. "But always health and happiness before wealth," he added. He didn't feel the need to disclose that the toast was actually his father's favorite.

As he finished up with the toast, Frankie walked into the living room and announced that dinner was ready to be served. The four of them rose and followed Michael into the formal dining room. Ryan, by Michael's design, was placed at the head of the table while Debra and Alan were seated to his left and Briana and Michael to his right.

As Briana approached her chair, Michael pulled it out and, after she had seated herself, helped to ease her chair closer to the table. After pushing her chair in, his right hand lightly brushed her shoulder and neck as he moved over to his own chair. This touch sent immediate shivers of pleasure running down Briana's spine. It was probably an accidental touch, she thought to herself, but it felt so, so good—if only his hand could have stayed on my shoulder a little longer.

"Thank you, Michael," she said, after regaining her composure from the thoughts that had entered her mind from that simple touch—thoughts that even made her blush a little.

Alan, apparently taking his cue from Michael, did the same thing for his wife.

"Thank you, dear," she remarked to her husband.

The two men then took their respective seats just as Frankie was coming in with a large serving cart containing five small plates of salad with four varieties of dressing. The ensuing conversation amongst them was light and friendly, not formal and stuffy as many gatherings are. Briana, Alan and Debra all took turns toasting their host on the excellent selection of wine.

After the salads were finished, Frankie, in his unobtrusive manner learned from years of service to the Thomas family, cleared the table of the empty salad plates. He then returned immediately with a large roast on a platter—the meat already sliced for easy serving. After placing it on the table, he quickly returned to the kitchen for the rest of the dinner. Aside from the roast, he had prepared mashed potatoes with roast gravy, corn, broccoli, fresh-baked cornbread muffins and a tall glass of milk for Ryan.

"Thank you," Briana said, after Frankie placed the last of the dinner items on the table. "It all looks so delicious."

"Thank you for the compliment, Briana," he responded. "Now everyone enjoy. If you need anything at all, I'll be in the kitchen. Before leaving you, however, would anyone like a little more wine to help wash the dinner down?"

Both Debra and Alan said yes, with Michael and Briana declining as both had only taken a few sips of their wine up to this point. It was apparent to Michael that Briana's parents enjoyed his selection of wine—for this he was pleased. Frankie then refilled their glasses and quietly disappeared back into the kitchen.

The dinner conversation touched on a variety of topics—everything from Michael's work with DWB, free clinics and mercy flights, to bits and pieces about Briana's pop-country music career. While his parents may have unintentionally ignored him, Michael made sure that young Ryan was included in the conversation by asking questions about his school and extracurricular activities. This inclusion did not go unnoticed by Briana, as she put another mental check mark alongside his positive attributes.

Debra was curious as to how Michael came to be a doctor at such a young age.

"I graduated from high school after turning sixteen. From there I went directly onto college and graduated three years later. I managed to carry extra classes each semester along with taking classes during the summer. By this time, I was nineteen and entered medical school. After graduating three years later, I took up my residency right here in Nashville. Then, to make a long story short, I went straight to work for DWB."

"A child prodigy of sorts?" Debra inquired.

"I wouldn't go that far," Michael responded. "Let's just say that it was a combination of good genes, exceptional parenting and having established personal and professional goals early on in my life."

"And don't forget my contributions," Frankie interjected, as he entered the room to clear the plates and serving dishes from the table.

At this, Michael let out a hearty laugh.

"Yes," Michael responded, "you fed the stomach that nourished the mind. Plus your nagging to stay out of your kitchen kept me up in my room studying longer. Not to mention help with my homework—though I believe I got D's in those subjects."

At this, everyone laughed before moving to the living room at Michael's suggestion. Ryan, Debra and Alan chose the large white couch, while Michael and Briana chose the love seat. He wasn't quite sure if it was considered proper etiquette to sit next to Briana or not, but he did so, nonetheless. He only hoped that it did not place Briana in an awkward situation—though a part of him wanted to get as close to her as possible—etiquette be damned.

As it turned out, he wasn't the only one happy with the seating arrangement—Briana felt honored that he chose to sit next to her instead of at one of the other available couches and chairs in the expansive living room. She wasn't quite sure what to make of all this, but she had to admit to herself that she liked having him beside her.

Before anyone was aware of the time, the grandfather clock began to announce that it was eight o'clock. Realizing what time it was, Debra commented that they needed to leave.

"So early, mother," Briana remarked, obviously not wanting to leave just yet.

"Ryan still has some homework to finish up before bed," Debra responded. "And you know how he needs his sleep, Briana. Much as you did when you were his age."

"All of you are welcome to come back anytime," Michael interjected, "even weekends, when you can stay longer. It's not exactly summertime but the pool is well heated, so feel free to bring along some swimsuits—and I'm sure if we beg long and hard we can get Frankie to provide some eats."

"That sounds like a lot of fun, Dr. Thomas," piped in Ryan.

"Do you know how to swim, Ryan?"

"Sure do," he replied, excitedly. "But we don't have a pool at our house." He said this as if his parents were poor people for not having a pool.

"But I do. If your parents or Briana can't make it, then you are more than welcome to spend some time over here, with your parent's permission, of course. I'll even come get you if needed. We men need to stick together on these things, you know. If you have a couple of friends you want to bring along, that's okay too."

"Can I really?" he responded, in an excited voice.

"You can count on it, Ryan. I'm a man of my word."

"Okay, enough talk of pool dates, young man, we've got to get your homework done and you off to bed," Debra said to her son as they rose from their chairs and began heading toward the front door.

"Michael, it's been a pleasure meeting you and we thank you for your hospitality," Alan remarked. "And be sure to extend our heartfelt appreciation to Frankie for the excellent dinner. Any chance that we can send Briana over here to learn how to cook from Frankie?" he quipped.

The four adults all chuckled at that comment. Michael surmised that cooking was not one of her many attained skills.

"To answer your question, Alan, Frankie pretty much kicks me out of the kitchen every time I even think of cooking something for myself. Should Briana enter the kitchen, however, he would most likely lock the doors and never let her go home."

Once again, everyone chuckled, though Briana's cheeks appeared to be turning slightly pink as the given attention switched from Ryan to her. Upon reaching the front door, Alan opened it and stepped outside, followed quickly by both Debra and Ryan. After one more polite thank you and the requisite goodbyes, they began descending the stairs to their car; Briana, meanwhile, held back for a moment.

"Thank you, Michael, for the wonderful evening on behalf of my family and me—that was very generous of you."

"You are most welcome, Briana. You and your family have an open invitation to visit anytime you like."

"If you seriously mean that," Briana responded, looking directly into Michael eyes, "then maybe you will see one of us very soon."

"As Frankie once said to you, soon would not be soon enough," he responded, realizing after having said it that it may have come out as a sign of neediness.

Briana then put out her right hand and said, "Goodbye, Michael."

He sensed sadness in both her words and in her eyes—as if they would never see each other again.

Michael took her hand into both of his and said, "Goodbye, Briana, until the next time."

After releasing her hand, which he held onto longer than he knew he probably should have, she turned around and hastily made her way down the stairs. Upon reaching the car and opening the door, she turned around and gave Michael one last glance, followed by a gentle wave of her hand. A few seconds later she was in the car and her father began slowly driving around the circle before making his way down the long driveway toward home.

Michael could not deny the emptiness that enveloped his whole body when she disappeared out of sight. It was not like he hadn't felt emptiness before—as in the case of his parent's death—but this was something totally different. He found that he enjoyed her company, her quick sense of humor and playfulness—as in the elevator heading down to the wine cellar. She had a mischievous look in her catlike eyes that he found captivating—not to mention a face and figure that were more than easy on the eyes. It had been longer than he cared to admit to himself since he'd felt this good about being around a woman. When she walked out the door and into her parent's car, a part of Briana remained in his thoughts—and would for many days to follow. After holding the door open longer than he had a need to, Michael closed it, turned and headed directly for the kitchen.

"Thank you for the wonderful dinner, Frankie."

"It was my pleasure, Michael. They appear to be a very nice family." He hesitated before saying, "especially that Briana girl. She's very special—and it's obvious, at least to me, that her parents did a great job of raising her. She will make some lucky man proud someday," he added for Michael's benefit, before eventually turning around and pushing the button to start the dishwasher.

Those comments by Frankie only made his feelings of emptiness more profound. Given that, he knew of only one way to take those feelings out of his mind. He turned around and raced up the stairs to his room. Changing into his swimsuit, he came back down and out to the pool. A half-hour of doing laps faster than normal totally wore him out. He climbed out of the pool and into the chilly evening air, dried off before going back upstairs, took a quick shower and fell into bed exhausted. As a doctor, he was well aware of the fact that strenuous exercise does wonders for both the mind and the body; even so, thoughts of Briana kept him awake for another half hour.

Chapter Eight

IT WOULD TAKE A COUPLE OF DAYS BEFORE MICHAEL COULD FULLY CON-
centrate on matters at hand without thoughts of Briana entering his
mind. He was grateful for that, as he was readying himself for his two
week DWB mission to Haiti.

On the day before his trip to Haiti was to take place, he decided to
call Briana on her cell phone. The purpose of the call, of course, was
business. His intentions were simply to inform her that he would be
gone for two weeks and that if she had any questions about the benefit, she should contact DWB directly—or wait until his return. The
real reason for calling her, however, had nothing to do with the benefit
at all—he basically just wanted to hear her voice again.

After dialing Briana's private number, it rang four times before
going to voice mail. At first, he thought of hanging up rather than
leaving a message, as it was Briana that he wanted to talk to, not some
lifeless recorder. He changed his mind, however, when he realized that
his phone number would most likely be seen by her as a missed message. He left a brief message about his trip, the upcoming benefit, and
his hopes that she had a productive day in the studio. Michael could
have said more before hanging up, but women and phone messages
were not exactly in his repertoire of skill sets.

Later that evening, he received a call back from Briana on his cell phone but, as luck would have it, he had gone downstairs for a swim before bed. It wasn't until after his return from swimming and his shower that he realized he had a missed call and message. He was upset with himself at having missed the call. Michael then depressed the voice mail button and waited, with much anticipation, to hear what she had to say:

> *"Hello, Michael. Sorry I missed your call earlier, but I've been in the recording studio most of the day. If I have any questions concerning the benefit, I'm sure they can await your return from Haiti. Please have a safe trip and I'll see you after your return. Talk to you later. Bye."*

After listening to her message, more than once, he went to hit the delete button before deciding against it; if he couldn't have her in person than at least he could have her voice.

The following day, the doctors and nurses who would accompany him to Haiti began to arrive early in the morning. Frankie managed to keep himself busy feeding them breakfast prior to their expected three-and-a-half-hour flight to Port au Prince. Always one to think ahead, he also prepared a variety of sandwiches and fruit for their in-flight lunch—along with two large containers of nonperishable food items. Shortly after ten, all food and equipment needed for their mission was securely stored in the two cargo areas of the plane. As soon as the main cabin door was secured and latched, and everyone was buckled up in their seats, Michael entered the cockpit to begin preparations for the flight. Five minutes later, with both engines fully warmed up, he proceeded out of the hangar. Fifteen minutes later the wheels of the aircraft lifted up from the runway. In twenty minutes time, Michael was flying at his assigned altitude of 41,000 feet.

In just under two hour's time, Michael brought the plane down in Miami for refueling before quickly returning to the skies. After landing in Haiti, they were bused by the Red Cross to what would become their makeshift medical site. They quickly went about setting up the medical tent before erecting the two sleeping tents. As is always the case in these situations, residents of the city began forming a line to be treated before the tents were even erected. With an unemployment rate reaching sixty percent or more, the majority of the country's people could ill afford even the basics of medical care for themselves or their families; disease and premature deaths were an accepted given in countries such as Haiti. A sad state of affairs, Michael thought, given the wealth of many countries around the world.

On the fourteenth day, with both a sense of sadness and reluctance, the staff gathered up their equipment and headed back to the airport for the flight back home. This flight home was, as were the others before it, a quiet one for Michael and the staff—all worn out from their experience. With the exception of Michael, who had a plane to fly, the rest of them basically slept the entire time. No one even bothered to come forward and sit with him in the cockpit this time around. While he enjoyed having company while he flew, he fully understood their exhaustion; even though they had all slept reasonably well the last night there, they were still feeling the effects of the past thirteen days, and most likely would for a few days to follow.

Briana had entered his conscious thoughts from time to time, but he congratulated himself on staying focused on the mission at hand. But now, alone in the cockpit, he found his thoughts returning to her—saddened by the notion that there wasn't much time between now and the benefit for the two of them to spend some time together.

By late afternoon, Michael taxied the plane into his hangar—unlike the latenight arrival from their Dominican Republic trip. As it was still relatively early in the day, the doctors and nurses who made up this trip decided to head straight for their homes or to Nashville International Airport for their respective flights back home. He was actually thankful for this as all he wanted to do was take a shower and head straight for bed—even though it was still early. It was either hit the sack or stay up and think of Briana. So, after saying an early goodnight to Frankie, he headed off to bed.

Chapter Nine

THE PREVIOUS TWO WEEKS HAD BEEN THE LONGEST OF MICHAEL'S LIFE. He hadn't seen Briana since the dinner with her family, though they did converse on the phone a few times, but it was mainly to discuss matters related to their upcoming trip to Etenia. Though the conversations were trip-related, he was encouraged by the notion that she had generated the calls to him. God knows he'd wanted to call her, to hear her voice once again, but he couldn't think of a reason to do so without appearing too forward. She obviously didn't think twice about calling him, but he attributed that to her apparent sense of self-confidence. There was little doubt in Michael's mind that she was an accomplished, take-charge type of person—which he assumed went a long way toward explaining her successful singing career.

While lost in thoughts of Briana, his cell phone rang. Picking the phone up from the side stand in his study, he could see that it was from Briana.

"Hi there," he quickly answered.

"Hi Michael. I hope I'm not catching you too late at night?"

"No you aren't. As a matter of fact, I was sitting here in my study reading a book. Between a good read and a swim, it's how I like to relax before going to bed."

"The reason I'm calling is to confirm that we're still scheduled to leave at noon tomorrow for Etenia?"

"High noon it is."

"Good. My piano player will arrive tomorrow afternoon, as well. He's volunteered to set up the sound equipment for my guitar and microphone, so that's one less thing I have to concern myself with. And the even better news is the hospital brought in a baby grand for him. Not sure where it came from, but thanks for coordinating that for him."

"I requested a piano but had no idea it would end up being a baby grand. I'll have to remember to thank whoever it was that donated it. On another note, with a little more free time on your hands tomorrow, maybe you'd like to join me as I work out last-minute details with the hospital staff? Or you can choose to stay in your hotel room or even wander around town, though there isn't much to see."

"I'd love to join you. Besides, I've seen my share of hotel rooms, thank you very much."

"Okay then, hospital rounds we'll make together. When you arrive tomorrow, why don't you drive directly into the garage. That way we can load your suitcases right onto the cart. Plus it will keep you dry as heavy rains are expected for tomorrow. You've obviously become an expert at operating the elevator, so come straight up when you arrive."

"I can handle that—the elevator, that is. I kind of like that old fashion elevator. It may be slow, but it definitely adds character to the house. If I arrive at say, eleven-thirty, will that give us enough time to load up and still leave at noon?"

"Eleven-thirty is fine. I'll most likely have my stuff already on the plane by then as I'll probably do my preflight checkup long before we leave anyway."

"I'll see you tomorrow then, Michael. And I want you to know," she added, "I'm actually looking forward to doing this benefit."

"And so am I. You don't know how much I appreciate your giving up a full weekend for the benefit. I know how busy you are with your music and all."

"Let's consider it payback for the meals and the tour of your house."

"Paybacks are not necessary. I did those things because I wanted to. Besides, even those things don't add up to what you're doing for the benefit."

"Let's call it a draw then," she responded. "We're both simply meeting each other's needs."

"I'll settle for that," Michael answered, while liking the part referring to "meeting each other's needs."

"Okay then. I'll let you get back to your reading while I get myself ready for bed. A girl needs all the beauty sleep she can get, you know."

"I would say that you apparently get plenty of sleep," he responded. As soon as the words left his lips, he worried about it sounding too forward.

"Thank you for the vote of confidence. If only I could get my mirror to agree with you," she quipped, in reply.

Her comment quickly set Michael to laughter; a laughter that was soon joined by her own. Once the laughter calmed down, they both said their goodbyes and hung up. Michael sat for a long time with the phone still in his hand—and a smile on his face that was in no hurry to leave. He had to admit to himself that her comment was pretty cute. After sitting there lost in thought for awhile, he finally headed off for a quick shower before retiring to bed. As tired as he thought he was, he still found difficultly in falling asleep. But fall asleep he eventually did, with thoughts of Briana still caressing his mind.

At the all-too-early hour of six-thirty, he awoke and found himself still thinking of Briana and their upcoming three days together. Following a quick shower and shave, he headed downstairs to the smell of freshly-brewed coffee emanating from the kitchen. This, of course, was no surprise to him as Frankie always had a sixth sense as to when he was up. He was never quite certain of it, but it was just possible that Frankie could hear the shower running each morning.

"Good morning, Michael," Frankie greeted him. "You're up awful early this morning. Didn't sleep well?"

"I slept very well, Frankie. I simply went to bed earlier than usual, given the busy day ahead of me."

"If you're hungry this early I'll have your breakfast ready for you shortly."

"That would be much appreciated. I see that the weatherman didn't disappoint us in his prognostications of heavy rains today."

"No, he most certainly didn't. The clouds opened up about an hour ago, along with some pretty stiff winds. It looks as though you and Briana may be in for a pretty rough ride to Etenia."

"That we might," Michael replied. "I'll have to request an altitude that takes us above the clouds and winds."

"Before you leave, I'll have some sandwiches made up for you and Briana for lunch."

"Thank you, Frankie. Again, much appreciated."

With that said, Michael poured himself a cup of coffee and retired to the living room to await breakfast. He grabbed a magazine off the table and made a concerted effort at reading, but his mind was only focused on Briana. He knew that the hours were going to tick by slowly before her arrival, but there wasn't much he could do about it. He had to find ways to keep himself busy until then. Fifteen minutes later he heard Frankie announcing that his breakfast was ready.

Following breakfast, he decided to kill time by going out to the hangar to perform his preflight checks. An hour later he returned, going directly up to his room to pack his one suitcase. He was disappointed that the activity of packing only consumed fifteen minutes of his time. So, from there he headed off to his study where he plopped down in his recliner to read. An hour later he was surprised to find that he had actually fallen asleep. Oh well, he figured, at least it killed another hour. Now he only had another hour and fifteen minutes to kill.

With that in mind, he let the recliner back down, closed his eyes and went back to thinking about Briana in ways that he knew he had no right to think about her. If she knew what he was thinking right now, he thought to himself, he might find himself being slapped in the face—and deservedly so. Michael couldn't help wondering if she too were thinking any of the same thoughts about him. He reasoned that this trip may be the tipping point in any potential future relationship with Briana. While she has never hinted, one way or the other, at having a male companion in her life, he wishfully hoped that she didn't. She was young enough, pretty enough, and obviously very talented, therefore, she would be a substantial catch for any man who had his senses about him. Or maybe, he thought, she was too busy with her career to have any time for a serious relationship—much like himself.

He was taken from his thoughts of Briana by Frankie's call up the stairway that she would be arriving momentarily. Taken from his moments of fantasy, he headed off to the bathroom to freshen up before her arrival. Even before finishing up, Michael thought that had he heard the sounds of a car approaching the driveway leading into the garage. She's early, he thought to himself, but that was timely as it broke up the waiting. Quickly finishing up, he headed down to meet her at the main-level elevator door. Once the elevator door opened, he had to hold himself back from wanting to greet her with a warm embrace.

"Hi there," she was first to speak at seeing him standing there. "Been waiting long?" she added with a smile.

"Hi there, yourself," he replied back. "As a matter of fact, I was walking down the hallway when I heard the elevator coming up. As I don't get many visitors, I could only guess that it was you—and, as usual, on time or ahead of schedule."

"I hope I wasn't messing with your routine by being a few minutes early," she responded.

"Not at all . . . I was trying to find ways to entertain myself until your arrival."

"Unlike many of my fellow performers, I've developed a habit of beginning my performances on time. If a performance ticket indicates that a show will go on at a certain time, that is when I begin. In years past, I've been to a number of live performances that started as much as forty-five minutes late. I don't feel that it's fair to keep my fans waiting. One can only surmise that other performers are either ill-prepared, or they let their egos get in the way of starting on time."

"That's very thoughtful of you. If I'm ever invited to one of your performances, I'll remember to be on time."

"Well then," she replied. "Tomorrow is going to be your lucky day. I happen to be performing at a place I know you'll be at, as well. If you aren't too busy schmoozing with the dignitaries and the good-looking, monied ladies, that is."

"I obviously have no choice but to spend time with the various dignitaries who'll be there. I will make every effort, however, to break away from the ladies long enough to hear you perform. If, for some reason, I can't break away, I hope you won't hold it against me?"

"No, I won't hold it against you," she responded back. "I may be young, but I've been around this business long enough to understand the inner workings of benefits. Worst case, I'll give you a private performance."

"To paraphrase you, 'Oh my God!' A private performance, huh? I may find myself skipping your performances this weekend just for a chance at a private one."

"I'm beginning to think that the devil has gotten ahold of you this morning, Michael, and it's still early," she replied, with both a devilish grin on her face and a twinkle in her eye.

"Let's blame it on too much sleep," he remarked, in an effort to save face. "Let's also say that we further discuss your performance—and the devil—on the plane," he added, in a second attempt at getting his foot out of his mouth.

"Fair enough."

"Instead of standing here at the elevator any longer, why don't we head to the kitchen and say our goodbyes to Frankie. He'd be deeply disappointed if you left here without at least saying hello . . . and goodbye."

The two of them headed down the hallway and into the kitchen where Frankie was sitting at the table polishing silverware.

"Hello Frankie," greeted Briana, with a warm smile.

"And back to you," responded Frankie, with an equally warm smile to match hers. "It's been a long time since I've seen anyone smile in this house," he added, in an apparent jab at Michael's melancholy mood of late.

"Why, I find that rather hard to believe, Frankie. Why just a few minutes ago, when the elevator door opened, I saw a rather nice smile on Michael's face."

"That, my dear, is simply because it was you getting off the elevator, not me."

"Enough about smiles and me, you two," Michael interjected, in an attempt to get the subject off of him. "We have a plane to catch, a mission to go on, money to raise."

Is it true that Michael perhaps has some feelings for me? Briana wondered silently. She sure hoped so; though she wasn't going to further embarrass Michael by saying anything that would make him uncomfortable. They were going to be spending the next three days together, and she didn't want to get it started off on the wrong foot.

Michael broke the momentary silence by asking, "Frankie, you've got some lunch and drinks stored away for us here somewhere?"

"It's all down in the garage, back of the cart."

"Thank you. And while we're away, Frankie, work on improving your smile, but don't break the mirror trying too hard."

With that slight crack Michael immediately turned around to leave. Briana, on the other hand, had other ideas. She walked over to Frankie, threw her arms around him, and gave him a big, long hug—something no woman had ever done since the passing of Michael's mother. He was deeply touched by her gesture. Even Michael, who had turned around to witness this display of kindness, was deeply touched. If only that embrace were meant for me, he thought.

Without words being spoken, she then turned away from Frankie and walked with Michael out of the kitchen and down the hallway to the elevator. No words were spoken here, either. As soon as they stepped into the elevator, Briana took control of the appropriate buttons and handles before slowly descending to the garage below.

When the door opened, Briana proceeded directly over to her car where she grabbed a small handbag off of the trunk. Reaching down, she took hold of a rather large suitcase in one hand and her guitar case in the other and carried them over to the cart where Michael was standing. Michael took the items from her and placed them alongside his own suitcase and the lunch basket that Frankie had prepared.

"I would have brought your things over from the car, Briana," Michael stated, a little embarrassed at her independence.

"There was no need to," she replied. "On our road trips I'm used to handling my own things. It's something that I've always done. If you find fault with that, blame my upbringing. My parents have taught both Ryan and me to be independent. I do rely on other people—but I also pay them for it."

"Point well taken," Michael replied. "It's just that I was raised to assist ladies . . . you know, like carrying their bags, opening doors, etc. Something I watched my father do a thousand times over for my mother and others."

"In that case, then you will permit this lady the privilege of driving the cart to the hangar."

"Fair enough, James, drive on, but for God's sake, watch out for the deer."

Briana could do nothing but laugh as she sped out of the garage for the hangar. She was still laughing when they reached the side door to the hangar, having called out, "Here Bambi, here Bambi," along the way. Michael couldn't help but laugh as well.

Once inside the hangar, Michael grabbed their bags and, one by one, set them inside the cargo hold area before strapping them down. The lunch basket, guitar case and her handbag were stowed in the aircraft's cabin. After securing the door, Michael then proceeded to the front of the aircraft and took his seat. Realizing that Briana had not followed him into the cabin, he went back to where she had already found a place to sit.

"You're more than welcome to join me up front if you like."

"I would love that. I've always thought that only flight crews were allowed up front."

"That doesn't hold true for private aircraft. As long as you don't try to take over the controls and fly the aircraft yourself, that is."

"I promise to behave myself, and will resist every urge to take over the controls. Unless I notice you falling asleep at the wheel of course."

"Too wide awake for that to happen."

After the two of them were strapped securely into their seats, Michael reached up and pushed a single button, opening up the front and rear hangar doors. Then, with the push of another button, one of the two engines came to life. Ninety seconds later, with a push of another button, the second engine roared to life.

"Aren't you going to . . . what do they call it . . . a preflight check, or something like that?" she inquired.

"Already took care of that earlier this morning. Most likely while you were still asleep."

"This may come as a surprise to you, Michael, but I'm actually an early riser. I've got one of those unfortunate minds that never seems to shut itself down. Besides, there's so much to do, and I can't accomplish anything in my sleep."

"Speaking strictly in a doctor/patient relationship, sleep is good for you. Eight hours of sleep is what you should aim for each night. As your body needs sleep to rejuvenate itself, so does your brain if it's to function at full capacity during the waking hours. So, if you start going a little batty on me, I'll know what to attribute it to."

"Thank you, doctor. I'll keep that advice in mind—especially the batty part. Though I don't think it will work in my case; I've been operating on six hours of sleep for as long as I can remember."

By now the engines had warmed up enough that Michael began easing the plane out of the hangar and onto the asphalt-paved roadway leading to the airport gate.

"Aren't you going to close the hangar doors?" Briana inquired, out of curiosity.

"No need to; they'll automatically close in fifteen minutes. That allows the engine-generated fumes sufficient time to dissipate before the doors close."

"I'm guessing that I need to keep my mouth shut," Briana responded, somewhat embarrassed at herself for even having asked the question.

"You don't learn new things by not asking, so ask away. I probably asked my father a thousand questions back during the times he flew." Michael broke away from the conversation as they came upon the electronic access gate to the airport.

"Tune Field, Flight Surgeon November three-one-four is at the private gate, will be taxiing out on taxiway Alpha to runway two-zero, any traffic in the area, please advise." Michael's call received an immediate response from another pilot.

"Cessna November one-five-two is also on taxiway alpha heading out to runway two-zero. It looks as though you're ahead me so I'll give way."

"Roger, thank you," Michael replied.

Briana could hear some kind of response through his headphones but couldn't make out the exact words. She watched as Michael guided the plane onto the perimeter road and proceeded directly to the end of the runway.

"Nashville Tower, Flight Surgeon November three-one-four is ready for takeoff."

Briana heard a few more garbled words through Michael's headphones, and the next thing she knew, the plane was racing down the runway and into the air. While all of this activity was taking place, Michael had said nothing to her, giving his full attention to the aircraft. And she, for her part, thought better of saying anything until he spoke first.

"So how do you like the bird's eye view of everything?" Michael asked, breaking the silence.

"Wow! I love it," exclaimed Briana, with obvious excitement. "This is so cool to be up front instead of looking out a side window. You can see everything from here."

"Flight Level One Niner Zero, Flight Surgeon three-one-four, thank you," Michael said into his mouthpiece.

"What?" responded Briana.

Michael, noticing a slightly perplexed look on Briana's face, figured out her puzzlement. "Sorry—I was given permission by the air traffic controller to climb to an altitude of 19,000 feet. That will put us well above the rain clouds and hopefully some unstable winds."

"Oh," she responded. "For a moment there I forgot that you have piloting duties. I was talking to you about the beautiful view when all of a sudden you started talking some kind of mumbo-jumbo. Now I understand why."

"I heard every word you said about loving the view and always having to look out the side windows when flying. In spite of these headphones, a pilot can still hear what's going on around him."

"Okay then. If I hear anything else coming out of your mouth that sounds rather strange, I will ignore it. But only if you're piloting a plane, that is," she added, with a hearty laugh. Michael found himself laughing, as well.

"And what's this bit about ground control and tower? Aren't they one and the same? Aren't these dudes and dudettes in the same tower?"

"Wow! A lot of questions, young lady. And no, not exactly. Ground controllers have responsibilities different from that of tower controllers. And yes, they oftentimes sit together in the same air traffic control tower . . . usually in smaller airports. In short, ground controllers coordinate and handle all of the aircraft movement on the ground. The tower controllers are responsible for the actual sequencing of inbound landing airplanes, clearing aircraft to land, and giving takeoff clearance for departing aircraft. They are all Air Traffic Controllers, or ATC for short, but their individual responsibilities often vary. Today, the dude or dudette who is the ground controller right now could be the tower controller after his or her lunch. Does this short explanation make any sense?"

"It does now, thank you. I thought it might be fun to learn how to fly someday, but it sounds like one needs to learn a whole lot more than just how to fly an airplane."

"Flying a plane is actually the easy part. I'm guessing that about eighty percent of what they teach in flight school has little to do with the actual flying of an aircraft."

"I think for now, I'll just stick to being a passenger. I can't afford to fry anymore brain cells by sitting in a classroom of any kind." Her comment about "frying brain cells" brought about a polite chuckle from Michael.

"I don't suppose I can talk you into retrieving Frankie's food basket from the cabin," Michael asked.

"Not a problem, Captain. Your wish is my command." With that being said, she unbuckled her seat belts and headed back to the cabin. When she returned, she buckled herself back up and placed the basket on her lap. "What would you like? We have sandwiches, chips, bananas, two apples, orange juice and water."

"A sandwich and orange juice will do. That should hold me over until dinner."

"A sandwich and orange juice it is. And just so you know," she added, "I like being up here a whole lot."

"I'm glad you're enjoying the flight . . . and hopefully the company as well."

"I'm enjoying all of it. You, the jet, the view—it's all a new experience for me, and God knows that we all need new experiences to give meaning to life, to make us want to get up each and every morning with the knowledge that something exciting is about to happen." Following a brief pause, she continued. "Sorry, didn't mean to get all philosophical on you."

"Nothing to be sorry about. I like knowing what's going on in that brain of yours. It probably goes a long way toward explaining why you write your own songs and where you get your inspiration from. Most people look at something new but don't really see anything. You, on the other hand, appear to see the beauty and wonderment in everything you see. And that's what makes you who you are."

"Wow! You sure have me all figured out in short order."

"Not really. Just an observation and commentary on my part."

Following an interval of silence between them as they ate, Briana finally broke the silence again. "So tell me everything a girl would want to know about you, Mr. Fly Boy. You only have to Google my name to learn everything I ever did, from the day I was born until now. In fact, I'll share a little secret with you first. The last time I Googled my own name, it revealed over 30 million mentions of me. I was blown away by that. I'm saying that not to impress you in any way; that's not my style. It means that every time I had the sniffles, or uttered even a single word on any topic, someone would write about it. And before you knew it, it would end up on the Web for the whole world to read."

"But I am impressed," Michael replied. "It's simply an indication of how popular you have become."

"Maybe," Briana countered. "It could also be the case that those 30 million hits on my name could be all negative comments."

"You and I both know that's not the case where you are concerned. Your performances wouldn't be sold out in a matter of hours without your having a huge fan base, which you obviously do."

"You must have spent hours Googling my name," she remarked, with a slight condescending look on her face.

"Guilty as charged," he admitted. "But I did it for professional reasons. I had heard of you, but didn't know much about you . . . so yes, I Googled your name to see if you would be a good match for the benefit . . . and here you are."

"With that vote of confidence from you, I'll let you off the hook for Googling me. And see, it goes back to what I said earlier, you know everything about me and I know very little about you."

"I would suggest," he responded, "that you simply Google my name as I did yours. Or have you already done so?"

"Nope. I thought about it, however, but decided against it. I figured that if I did I would only find doctor-related stuff anyway. Besides, I like a little mystery in the people I meet. Or would I have possibly found some dark, dark secrets about you on the Web, had I looked?"

"Sorry to disappoint you, but 'Boring' is my middle name. You'd be lucky to find even a page related to my name, if that much."

"Okay, I'll take your word for it. But everyone has a story . . . even people with the middle name of Boring have a life. So what's yours?"

"Not much to say, really. If you recall, I've already shared a lot about me over dinner. I'm an only child, born and raised right here in Nashville. As I've said before, the house I currently live in is the only house I've known, and even Frankie preceded me there. My parents were both doctors and spent most of their careers teaching at Vanderbilt. They both served with Doctors Without Borders for many, many years. My father, like myself, flew his own jet. It was he who taught me how to fly. He and my mother were both killed in a car accident shortly after I graduated from medical school."

"Oh my God!" Briana remarked in a voice of shock. "You didn't mention that at dinner. I'm so sorry to hear that, Michael."

"Thank you. I know that it comes across as mushy, but they were great parents. They valued education, obviously, but didn't force it on me."

A good ten minutes of silence would pass between them as Michael's thoughts went back to the death of his parents and the days that followed.

"Earth to Fly Boy! Earth to Fly Boy!" Briana loudly stated in an attempt to get Michael's attention.

"Huh!" he responded, as if in a daze. "Oh . . . I'm sorry . . . were you talking to me?

"And was I ever. I could have read the entire works of Shakespeare before you would've noticed. I must really be boring."

"Sorry, Briana. I'll be honest with you . . . I was thinking of my parents. Obviously thinking a little too hard. I appreciate your pulling me out of it or who knows what state or country we would have ended up in. It's a good thing that I had the autopilot on. And no, you're anything but boring."

"That's okay," Briana responded, with the deepest of sincerity and compassion. "It's one thing to lose one parent at a time, let alone both parents at the same time. That has to be tough on even the strongest of souls."

"Frankie's the reason I'm even here today. He handled everything concerning the funeral while I, a doctor, sat alone in my room and cried. It took him months of patience and perseverance but, like a true father, he brought me to the point of acceptance for what happened to my parents. I initially blamed God. And oh, how I blamed Him. And when I did, Frankie would say nothing. He knew that I had a need to get the venom out of my system. And it worked. I finally wore myself out trying to blame God and others."

"Wow!" Briana exclaimed, before unbuckling her seat belt and going up alongside of Michael and wrapping her arms around him. "I'm sorry that you had to go through that, Michael." She immediately went back to her seat and buckled herself back up.

Michael was taken aback by what Briana had just done—so much so that he was utterly speechless. He appreciated her action—he sincerely did—but it totally caught him off guard. Following a few moments of silence, he was finally able to speak.

"Thank you, Briana. I hate to admit it—it's a guy thing—but I needed that."

"You are most welcome," Briana responded, in a soft and caring voice. "It's one of the virtues we women inherit at birth from our mothers. And I want you to know there's plenty more where that came from, so don't be ashamed to ask if and when the need arises."

"I'll do my best to remember that."

The next ten minutes went by in silence once again before Briana broke the silence. "Anything else to add to your life story that might be of interest to me, Michael?"

"Not too much. In fact, I don't even recall where I left off."

"I believe you left off at graduating from medical school."

"Oh. Following my internship and residency, and because I have the financial wherewithal to do so, I have dedicated myself to DWB and donating my services at the various free clinics around Nashville. Aside from helping out up in Etenia, that is. That pretty much wraps up the life story of Dr. Boring," he concluded.

"Not boring at all. With the passing of your parents, that helps to explain the close relationship you appear to have with Frankie."

"Frankie and I have always been close, even before the death of my parents . . . but more so since. I guess you could say that I had the privilege of having a mother and two fathers. He's very smart—a self-educated man, a voracious reader on anything and everything.

Even I know better than to question most of the facts that he throws my way."

A moment of silence passed between them before he began again. "Life would not be the same right now without him. You might say that I've been spoiled by him. He's always been treated as a member of the family, never as a servant or hired hand. He may have cooked all of our meals, but he sat down and ate with us at every one of those meals. No family secrets were kept from Frankie—he was part of the family."

"You're a lucky man with Frankie in your life. But I'm still curious about one thing. I remember . . . " She suddenly stopped in the middle of her conversation at the sound of Michael's voice.

"Flight Surgeon three-one-four, roger."

"What was that about?" she inquired once again out of curiosity.

"Notification from the controller to begin my descent as we approach Etenia," he responded.

"Oh! Are we that that close already?"

"We are. We've been cruising along at 350 knots or, in layman's vernacular, approximately four hundred miles per hour, so it doesn't take long to reach our destination. Etenia is only three hundred miles away from Nashville. If we had driven, it would've taken us close to five hours to get there."

"Ah, the advantages of flying," she remarked.

"Three-zero, thank you. In case you were wondering, ATC was informing me which of the runways to expect for landing."

Briana decided to remain silent upon realizing that Michael was becoming more involved in communications with the air traffic controllers. She wanted to learn more about Michael, but decided that it would be best to dig it out of him later when he wasn't so preoccupied with flying. Maybe another hug later would loosen him up a bit more. Or maybe even two hugs.

Chapter Ten

FOLLOWING ANOTHER ONE OF HIS SMOOTH LANDINGS, MICHAEL TAXIED UP to the far end of the terminal; an area reserved for visiting aircraft like his. Having had the foresight to call ahead, a taxi was waiting to take them to their hotel. Soon after arriving at the hotel and taking care of the customary check-in routines, they and their belongings were taken up to their respective rooms by a porter.

At the prearranged time of two-thirty, Michael quietly knocked on the private door that separated their adjoining rooms. Not getting any response from Briana, he knocked once again, this time a little harder than before. A half minute later the door finally opened to a sleepy-eyed Briana.

"Sorry," she said, looking up at Michael standing there. "The bed looked so comfy . . . I must have fallen asleep."

"Nothing to be sorry about. How about meeting down in the lobby in say, fifteen minutes? The hospital is only three blocks away, so we can easily walk it. If you'd rather sleep some more, I can go it alone," he added.

"No, I want to go with you. Give me a few minutes to freshen up and I'll meet you in the lobby."

"I'll see you downstairs then." Michael closed the door and grabbed his notebook from the desk before heading out the door leading to the second-floor hallway.

Ten minutes later he caught sight of Briana as she entered the lounge area of the hotel from the elevator. She walked over to him as he arose from the lounge chair.

"You clean up well," he remarked, jokingly.

"Did I look that bad a few minutes ago?" she asked in response.

"Not at all. You look good half asleep, as you do awake."

"I will gladly take that as a compliment then. Thank you."

"You're welcome. I'm returning the favor for the earlier hug. Ready for a walk?"

"As ready as I'll ever be."

Michael then took her elbow and guided her to the main doors leading out of the hotel. After opening the door for her, they began their short walk to the hospital, engaging in light conversation as they walked.

"Are you still meeting up with your piano man today?"

"Yes. I gave him a call before coming down to the lobby. I figured that you'd be busy with the hospital staff for awhile, so we agreed to meet on stage at four."

"And for that I apologize," Michael interjected.

"Apologize for what?"

"The stage, as you referred to it, is nothing more than a makeshift stage in the cafeteria. Not exactly the type of venue you're used to performing in."

"Trust me when I tell you, Michael, that when I first started out performing, I played in far worse rooms than a cafeteria. I think they were considered dives. So a cafeteria would be heavenly. If nothing else, at least I can eat while I sing."

With this mental picture of her singing while holding a sandwich in one hand, Michael broke out in laughter.

"That's number six or seven," Briana commented.

"Number six or seven what?" Michael inquired.

"The number of times I've observed you laughing since I met you."

"Oh, so now you're keeping some kind of score on me, huh?"

"Kind of. I like it when you smile or laugh, because it adds a warm character to your face."

"Oh, so if I'm not smiling or laughing, then my character is cold appearing to you, huh?" he fired back, teasingly.

"Not cold," she quickly replied back in an effort to save face. "You're a very warm and caring person on the inside—it's just that it doesn't always show up on your face."

"Well, I guess your challenge on this trip, should you choose to accept it, is to keep me laughing and smiling then."

"I'll give it my best shot," she replied, with a smile on her face. "And, should I fail miserably in my attempts, don't totally lay the blame on me . . . it takes two, you know."

"Okay—I hear you. Once I finish up here this afternoon, I'll see about taking my serious face off. And here we are at the hospital. Before I track down some of the staff who'll be assisting with the benefit, I'll take you on a quick tour. By the time we finish touring, it will be just about time for you to meet up with Mr. Piano Man."

"He actually has a name by the way—it's Bill."

"So it's Bill the Piano Man, huh?" he replied, with another one of those grins that was becoming more commonplace since being around Briana.

"Okay, Bill the Piano Man it is," she responded, with a wide grin.

Being a relatively small hospital, the entire tour of the two levels took just under forty-five minutes. It would have taken less time, but they stopped and talked to a few doctors and a nurse along the way that Michael knew personally. The two of them concluded their tour at the cafeteria that was to function as the "performance arena" for

Briana's mini-gigs tomorrow and Sunday. Over in the far corner of the cafeteria, on a raised, makeshift stage, was apparently Bill the Piano Man practicing his trade. Before she left to work with Bill, they both agreed to meet up again in about an hour's time.

Michael then left to meet with some of the hospital support staff to iron out last-minute details for the weekend's activities. He had heard from one doctor that the vice president had, in fact, already arrived in town; he and his wife would not, however, be coming to the hospital until tomorrow. Michael was still hopeful that his presence would attract a number of potential donors to the hospital's remodeling and equipment upgrade efforts.

After finishing up with the benefit-support team, Michael headed back down to the cafeteria to meet up with Briana. As soon as he opened the doors to the cafeteria, he spotted her up on the stage rehearsing with Bill. Even though it was only a rehearsal, he was surprised to see a large crowd of folks, either standing or sitting at the tables, watching them perform. Michael hung back by the entrance and listened to her sing—he was quite impressed with what he was hearing.

Briana eventually caught sight of him and waved. At the conclusion of that particular song, she glanced back at Bill on the piano; that glance apparently told him that the rehearsal was finished as he immediately got up and stepped away from the piano. The crowd, finally realizing that Briana was through rehearsing, slowly started to make its way out of the cafeteria—except for those who wanted her autograph—and there were many. Michael continued to hold back until the autograph seekers were finished before making his way to where Briana was waiting.

"You sing very well for a girl," he remarked, teasingly.

"I haven't heard a compliment quite like that before, but thank you anyway. I wish I hadn't left my guitar in the hotel room. I felt naked up on the stage without it."

"You looked and sounded great—even naked without your guitar as a crutch," he remarked.

"You're right, it didn't start out as crutch, but over the years, I think it became one. That's why I felt naked without it."

"Speaking of feeling naked—care to bust out of here and grab something to eat?"

"What does feeling naked have to do with eating?" Briana asked, with thoughts of amusement at the number of times he had mentioned the word "naked."

"Absolutely nothing," he stated, with a slight grin on his face. "It was a nonsensical lead-in to wanting something to eat."

"That was a very good attempt at humor on your part. There's hope for you after all."

"That, if I recall, is the second time you've mentioned something about hope for me after all. I may have to check in with my psychiatrist friend for a second opinion; it sounds as though I may be developing a serious condition here."

"No need for a second opinion. That's what you have me for. And best of all, I'm free." As soon as she said those words, she wished that she could have taken them back. It may, she thought, have left him with the insinuation that she was "free and easy." Which, she mused, she could be—with the right guy.

"I'll be sure to give your services some serious consideration when I start to doubt myself. You do have a license to practice psychiatry, don't you?"

"You bet I do," she quickly answered. "I'm a woman. It's one of the things we do best in life—giving free advice and hugs."

Michael broke out in laughter because he knew how true her statement concerning "free advice" was—when it related to a woman, that is. Briana, meanwhile, stood there looking up at him with a big smile on her face—grateful for his laughter.

"Well then, Miss Psychiatrist, are you ready to find some food in this town? Even over a good meal I'm sure you could continue to analyze my deep-seated behavioral problems; maybe even better."

"Only if the patient will escort me and treat me to the finest dining experience that this metropolitan city has to offer," she answered, with another one of those beautiful smiles that Michael was hoping to see more of.

On that note, he hooked his arm through hers and escorted her out of the cafeteria, just as it was beginning to fill up with even more staff and patient families for dinner.

Chapter Eleven

With the sun already out of view below the mountain range, the evening chill quickly set into their bones as they strolled, arm in arm, away from the hospital. It wasn't four blocks into their journey in search of a meal when both of them caught sight of an approaching motorcade some two blocks ahead of them. The various vehicles, with emergency lights flashing, were being escorted by two motorcycle officers in the lead and two behind. Following the two lead motorcycles were a black, unmarked car, a black limo directly behind it, and one more unmarked car behind the limo.

"If I were a betting man, I'd put all my money on that being the vice-presidential motorcade," Michael said, breaking the comfortable silence of their walk. "I don't know if I happened to mention this to you before, but the vice president was actually born and raised right here in Etenia, and both his immediate and extended family still live here. Needless to say, his roots here had everything to do with his willingness to volunteer his presence for this benefit."

Briana said nothing as the two of them continued to walk, all the while observing the motorcade's slow approach. Others along the sidewalk were equally entranced by the motorcade—a sight most of the townspeople have never witnessed before—with the exception of funeral processions from one of the local churches out to the lone cemetery.

The motorcade eventually passed them, though the darkened windows prevented anyone from seeing who was inside the limo. As soon as the limo had passed, they picked up their pace and continued heading off in the opposite direction in search of some much-needed nourishment. They had barely made it thirty feet from where the motorcade had passed them when suddenly they were both startled by the sounds of screeching tires, breaking glass and what sounded like metal on metal.

Instantly turning their attention to the intersection behind them, they saw what had happened. Under the street lights of the intersection, they observed that a pickup truck, unconnected with the motorcade, had smashed directly into the side of the limo. In less time than it took them to observe what had happened, they noticed the movement of two suited men jumping out of the lead vehicle and two from the vehicle behind. They wasted no time in rushing toward the limo.

Michael, without even thinking, instinctively grabbed Briana's hand and ran toward the intersection. Just short of reaching the accident, they were both stopped dead in their tracks by one of the dark-suited men yelling at the two of them. Michael knew exactly why they were commanded to stop.

"I'm a doctor!" Michael quickly yelled out.

The agent had to think about this before finally motioning for him to proceed. Michael found the man's slow response rather interesting given the circumstance of what had just taken place. Letting go of Briana's hand, he made his way quickly around to the limo at the same time as a man was stepping out of the pickup truck, seemingly unharmed, but dazed. As Michael approached the passenger side of the limo, he noticed two of the dark-suited men assisting a woman out of the back seat. At first glance, she also appeared to be unharmed, though seeming to be in a state of mild shock. The first thing Michael did was look into her eyes—then the doctor in him came forth.

Glancing at the two agents, he immediately started barking orders. "She appears to be in psychological shock—lay her down in the back seat of one your vehicles. Elevate her feet and legs about twelve inches. If you have an available blanket, place it over her. Do not—I repeat—do not elevate her head. Keep her still until medical help arrives."

As soon as she was carefully escorted away from the limo, Michael slid inside to check on the condition of the vice president, finding him still strapped in his seatbelt and in an upright position. By virtue of the overhead light, Michael immediately looked into his eyes and could readily see that he was in trouble. Not only was he unconscious, but there was the appearance of significant amounts of blood oozing out from the left side of his head.

Michael knew that his first priority was to stop the bleeding. He quickly slipped his jacket off, ripped off his shirt and immediately tied it tightly around the vice president's head. Though having a sense that time was of the essence, he knew that removing the patient from the vehicle would serve no purpose at this point—and might even result in more damage to the patient. Hearing the sounds of sirens approaching, he decided to wait for the medics to arrive. When the time came, he knew that he would need assistance from one or both of them in easing the vice president out of the vehicle. He knew from experience that they were better trained at removing injured people from automobile accidents then he was. No sooner had those thoughts left his mind when the aid car pulled up alongside the limo.

"He's taken a severe blow to the head and left side of his body, hypotension, pupils of different size, unconscious but breathing, hemorrhagic shock," Michael spewed out loud enough for both paramedics to hear. "Obvious concussion coupled with a severe gash to the left side of his head. Suspect possible bone fractures to the left side also given where he was sitting at the time of the impact and the looks of the door. Right now he needs both a c-collar and a cad board, if you have one, to keep him immobilized. As soon as the patient is loaded into the ambulance start a normal saline drip using a 14–16 gauge IV."

When the two medics quickly returned with the c-collar and spinal brace, Michael slid out of the back seat to make room for them. The two medics immediately climbed in and began applying both the neck and spinal braces. After carefully cinching up the straps to hold the spinal brace in place, they began the arduous task of sliding the patient along the seat to the open door.

Once the patient was moved to the doorway, one of the two medics retrieved the back board and angled it up against the seat. The medics then carefully slid the vice president onto the back board and slid him partway down. Once he was in position, they released the cad board holding straps from around his legs and laid him down flat onto the back board. Using spider-straps, they quickly secured him to the board. They then applied two head blocks to keep his head from moving during transport. With the assistance of one of the Secret Service agents, the four of them lifted the patient onto a stretcher and quickly rolled him into the medic van.

It was at this point that Michael caught sight of Briana on the sidewalk in the midst of a large crowd—standing right where he had left her. He pointed in the general direction of the hospital and waved goodbye to her. He felt some remorse at having to leave her alone here, but he knew that she understood the crisis at hand. He was pleased when she raised her own hand and gave him a gentle wave back.

As soon as the stretcher was secured inside the ambulance, Michael, remembering both the vice president's wife and the truck driver, requested that one of the medics stay behind to care for the two of them until a second medic team arrived. Michael immediately climbed into the back with the vice president while one of the Secret Service agents climbed up front with the driver. Within seconds, they departed for the hospital with sirens wailing and lights flashing while being escorted by two motorcycle officers in the process. Thankfully, the hospital was only five or six blocks away from the accident site. By the time they reached the emergency entrance, Michael had the saline IV drip in place. In less than one minute from pulling up they had the stretcher lowered and moving quickly through the doors leading into the emergency room hallway—all of this taking place under the watchful eyes of the lone agent.

"How many doctors on staff right now?" Michael unapologetically barked at the receptionist sitting behind the counter.

"Two, doctor. Dr. Woods is seeing a patient experiencing acute stomach pains, and I believe Dr. Sibenhauler is currently in surgery setting a broken arm." The receptionist, whom Michael didn't know, instinctively surmised that he was a doctor by his commanding presence and the way he fired off questions.

"See what you can do to break one of them free, stat," he commanded. "Also, see if you can round up Dr. Murphy at home to assist in surgery. Check the weekend roster and see what neurologist is on call; ask whoever it is to get in here ASAP; if they live far out, request police assistance in getting them to the hospital. We'll also need two surgical nurses. If they're not currently on site, call them in. Let everyone know that we now have the vice president as a patient."

The receptionist immediately looked up at Michael in almost total disbelief, before quickly picking up the phone—first calling both staff doctors on the intercom of the existence of a "stat" situation. A few seconds later both a nurse and an orderly came wandering into the area—seemingly without a care in the world. Again, without hesitation, Michael commanded the two of them to transport and prepare the patient for immediate surgery. They both looked at Michael in disbelief and then at each other with a look that implied, "and just who do you think you are?" Before either one of them had the opportunity to inquire, however, they heard the receptionist behind the counter yell, "Stat!" Apparently, this was all they needed to hear before realizing that this blood-stained, t-shirted man was either a doctor or someone else of importance. The two of them immediately took hold of the stretcher and began rushing it down the hallway—followed quickly by the agent on their heels.

"Hold it!" Michael yelled at the agent. "Where do you think you're going?"

"With the vice president—it's my duty to remain with him at all times," he yelled back.

"Not on my watch!" yelled Michael in return. "You either scrub up and change into surgical clothes or you will remain outside of the operating room. Come into the operating room in your germ-laden street clothes and you put the vice president at risk of infection and possible death. If that happens, figure out how you're going to explain that to your superiors."

Immediately turning back around, he said to the receptionist, "I'll be scrubbing up for surgery. Let whoever shows up to assist know which surgical room we're in. And we'll need either an anesthesiologist doctor or nurse along with an x-ray technician available, stat as well. I'm sure there's a radiologist on staff—let them know what's happening and ask them to stand by." With those final words, he headed off to the surgical scrub room with the agent in hot pursuit. After scrubbing up he was met by Dr. Woods at the doorway as he was coming out.

"Hi Tom, thanks for joining me," greeted Michael.

"I understand we have the vice president as our guest."

"We do. Aside from a major head wound, we're looking at the possibility of internal injuries to the left side; possible fractures would be my guess. I've asked for x-rays and an MRI. Right now I'm more concerned about the head wound. He was bleeding pretty heavily when I reached him. As a staff doctor here at the hospital, he's all yours now. I'll be there to assist, as needed."

"Thanks, Michael," responded Dr. Woods. "As you well know, this is more in your line of specialties, so I would appreciate your taking the lead. You already know more about what happened and what to look for than I do."

"Okay, I'll see you in surgery," he responded as he hurried out the door. On the way to the operating room, with the agent alongside of him, Michael gave him a quick speech on the run.

"Let me make this clear. You are not, in any way, to impede the movement of hospital personnel in or out of the operating room. Do I make myself clear?"

"Yes, sir!" responded the agent, sounding none too happy at being told what he could and couldn't do.

Michael found it amusing that the agent opted out of scrubbing up and changing into a surgical gown—his pride apparently won over his sworn duty to remain with the vice president at all times.

Meanwhile, Briana, having lost her appetite and not wanting to go back to the hotel, quickly made her way to the hospital. If she were eventually to be reunited with Michael, she figured, the Emergency Room would be the best place. When she finally got back to the hospital, she entered the waiting room where there were two people apparently waiting to be seen by a doctor. One middle-aged man had a wet, bloodied hand towel wrapped around his right hand with a twenty-something year old woman sitting next to him; she was showing more signs of pain on her face then he was.

Briana couldn't see what was going on with another pair over in the corner of the room. All she knew was that a man was holding a plastic bag with ice in it on top of his head. She guessed that taking two aspirin and calling the doctor in the morning didn't work this time around—at least for that elderly gentleman. His wife eventually left him and stepped outside the Emergency Room entrance and lit up a cigarette. So much for hospitals and health, Briana mused.

No one was talking to anyone, so she decided to pick up a magazine to read. The first one on top of the stack featured none other than herself on the cover. Not bad looking, she thought—thanks to a lot of makeup and photo retouching, that is. She would never admit that to the paparazzi, of course. She found it amusing that the magazine was two years old; someone either donated the magazine, or the hospital actually was hurting for money, she guessed.

The man with the bleeding hand was called and escorted away by a nurse. Soon after, a young boy of seven or eight came in with his distraught parents. Briana overheard the mother telling the receptionist that her son may have broken his arm from a bike fall. Briana, glancing at the boy, first noticed the sobbing before noticing the swollen elbow; she immediately felt sorry for him. After a full hour of trying to read outdated magazines in the waiting room, the time was starting to wear on her—so up she rose and headed straight for the admitting desk.

"I don't suppose there is another waiting room close by?" Briana asked, of the unknown person behind the desk.

"Yes, ma'am. We have the Surgical Waiting Room around the corner and down the hallway. Are you waiting for someone in surgery?" she inquired, trying to be helpful.

"Yes and no," Briana replied. My fiancé, Michael—I mean, Dr. Thomas, came in with the vice president about an hour ago. I'm waiting for him." Fiancé has such a lovely ring to it, she thought.

"Oh! So that's who the doctor was that brought him in—nice looking, I might add."

"Yep! That would be the one," Briana proudly replied at hearing the "nice looking" comment.

"Not sure if he will be the one, but one of the doctors, usually the primary doctor, will visit with the family in the waiting room following surgery. If he's primary, then there's a good chance you'll meet up with him there first."

"Thanks . . . any news on the vice president's wife? Is she here? Is she okay?"

"Yes, she is here, and yes, she is okay. She apparently suffered a mild case of shock but quickly recovered. The chances are pretty high that she's in the Surgical Waiting Room right now. One other thing, if you don't mind my asking, but you look kind of familiar. Have we met before?"

"Don't think so," Briana replied. "I'm just a country hick from Nashville. Tagged along with my fiancé for lack of anything better to do this weekend," she lied. Briana wasn't sure why she said what she said, but had to admit that it sure was fun being someone other than herself for a change.

"Oh . . . never hurts to ask, you know."

"Sure doesn't. Why just last week I was mistaken for that country singer . . . let's see, what was her name? Oh, yeah . . . Briana Price. Ever hear of her?"

"Oh yes. Love her singing. Why, as a matter of fact, she's going to be here tomorrow doing two or three benefit shows. My nephews and nieces plan on attending her performances. If I didn't know better I believe my oldest nephew . . . let's see . . . he must be sixteen by now, is madly in love with her. As for me, I'm holding out for Alan Jackson to become single."

"Can't blame you for wanting Alan; he's a hunk alright. But that sure is a coincidence, with Briana Price and me in the same place at the same time. I'll have to wrangle me a close up look at this gal and see how much alike we really are." By now, Briana figured that this conversation had gone on long enough—any longer and the sun would soon be rising.

"Well, it was nice talking with you, ma'am, but I had better mosey on down to that other waiting room if I'm going to catch my man."

"You ever think of giving him up, you be sure and let me know. If I wasn't already married, I'd sure like to take him home with me—no offense, ma'am."

"None taken. I actually see that as a compliment. See you around," Briana said, as she turned and made her fast getaway around the corner.

Reaching a sign over the doorway that read Surgical Waiting Room, she recognized one of the Secret Service agents that she had seen at the accident. As she had somewhat expected upon seeing him, she was stopped from entering the waiting room.

"Sorry, ma'am," he said politely, but sternly, as she tried to reach for the door knob. "For security reasons, I can't let you in," he added.

She instantly thought to herself that letting him know who she was might gain her access. Then she just as quickly realized that the Secret Service could give a hoot about any performer, actor, or anyone else of note; they lived and died according to strict rules. So, she thought to herself, this agent isn't dealing with your everyday, run of the mill country girl.

"Pardon me, sir. If the vice president's wife is inside, would you please let her know that I am Briana Price, the fiancée of the doctor who is operating on her husband right now as we speak." If this little white lie doesn't work, she thought to herself, then nothing will.

The agent, probably thinking that she looked harmless enough said, "Excuse me for a moment," and entered the waiting room while she remained at the door. A moment later he returned, holding the door open for Briana to enter.

"Thank you, kind sir, much appreciated."

There was, however, no response from the agent.

Once inside, Briana noticed a strikingly beautiful woman sitting all alone in the far corner of the room. It was obvious at first glance that she had been crying. Glancing up at Briana, the woman motioned for her to have a seat directly across from her.

"Hi," Briana said softly. "My name is Briana, Briana Price. But then you already know that. My friends just call me Briana."

Still the woman said nothing.

"You probably don't know me," Briana continued, but I was out with Dr. Thomas, my fiancé, when the accident happened." She had already lied twice about being his fiancée, one more time wouldn't hurt, she figured. "Dr. Thomas rushed to your husband's aid as soon as he saw what had happened."

"I know," the woman finally said. "It was most fortunate for my husband that he was so close by at the time. And for myself, I might add."

Once again she fell into silence while glancing around the room— but having that look in her eyes as if seeing nothing. Briana chose to remain silent, as well. Now was not the time to force a conversation on the obviously grieving woman. When she was ready, Briana reasoned, she would speak on her own accord.

A full five minutes of silence passed between the two of them before the woman finally spoke again. To Briana, it seemed as though an eternity had passed as she had nothing better to do than play with her hair while waiting for some kind of response.

"Yes, dear," she finally spoke, "we have never met before, but I know very well who you are. We have two adorable teenage grand-daughters who absolutely worship the ground you walk on. As a matter of fact, we gave both of them your latest CD for their birthdays."

That comment about "worship the ground you walk on" brought a flush of embarrassment to Briana's cheeks. She appreciated a strong, supportive fan base, but the word "worship," she felt, should hardly be used in conjunction with her name—but still it was pleasant to hear.

"And," she continued, "my husband and I both knew that you were going to be a major part of the benefit. If the girls were not busy with school and sports right now, we would have brought them along with us to watch you perform. My name, by the way, is Dottie."

"I would be absolutely amazed," Briana responded, "if there were anyone in this country who didn't know of you, or at the very least, your name. You are both beautiful and obviously a stylish, trendsetting dresser—aside from being the wife of the vice president."

"Well, dear, I hope that I'm known for far more than only looking beautiful, though I thank you for the compliment. We women like to hear those words from time to time, don't we?"

"No doubt about it," Briana answered. "I believe, or so I've heard from reliable sources anyway, that giving compliments only exists in the female gene pool. I've also learned, believe it or not, that when conducting a DNA analysis of male genes, the gene for giving compliments was found to be very weak; in some men it was nonexistent altogether."

At that, Dottie broke out in a wide smile. Even in a moment of grief, Briana thought, there's still room for a touch of humor.

Dottie's smile was soon broken by the sound of the door opening. The agent approached Dottie and politely informed her that members of her husband's family had arrived. Dottie asked him to let them in.

"With your relatives here, I'll disappear out into the hallway," said Briana.

"No, please stay. I informed the agent that when they arrive, and I knew they most certainly would, that they were to stay no more than fifteen minutes. I'm not in the mood for entertaining relatives right now."

"Okay. But why don't I head over to the cafeteria to grab a bite to eat while they're here. I haven't eaten anything since lunch."

"That would be fine, dear."

"Can I bring you anything?" Briana inquired, before making any move to leave.

"No, but thank you for asking, though. My husband and I had just finished with dinner ten minutes before the accident."

Briana rose from her chair and made her way through the six or seven family members who were heading directly over to where Dottie sat. Apparently none of the relatives recognized her, as they never batted an eye when walking past her. As far as Briana was concerned, that was good. She was in no mood herself to engage in conversation with people she didn't know. Or maybe they were so focused on Dottie that they saw right past her.

As she walked down three different hallways on her way to the cafeteria, she wondered if the accident would change tomorrow's scheduled benefit activities. Will they cancel everything—or will the show go on, as they say in show business? She presumed that such decisions will probably not be made until tomorrow morning at the earliest. Given how emotionally exhausted she was feeling right now, she knew that she would not be disappointed if the benefit were even canceled;

she felt this way even knowing that Michael had gone to considerable lengths to make this benefit a success. If worse came to worst, she further reasoned, she could easily make a charitable contribution to the hospital from her Foundation. Besides, she concluded, if the benefit were canceled, that would give her more time alone with Michael.

After consuming a cold sandwich of dubious origins, Briana decided to swing by the Emergency Room on her way back—with the sole intention of eliciting information about the vice president; it never hurts to ask, she figured.

"Hi there," Briana said, to a new person sitting behind the Emergency Room counter.

"May I help you?" came a patented response.

"Yes, you possibly can. My name is Briana, I flew up here with Michael, I mean Dr. Thomas, for the benefit this weekend. We were heading off to eat dinner when we came upon the accident scene that the vice president was involved in. I'm going to assume that Dr. Thomas is still in surgery?"

"Yes he is," was her obviously patented, three-word response.

"Can you tell me," Briana continued, pressing on, "If I have a long wait ahead of me or a short one for Dr. Thomas?"

"Don't know for sure."

"I see," Briana replied, sounding purposely disappointed. "I guess I had better plan on settling in for a long wait then."

"Yep! I'm afraid you're right."

Well, Briana thought, at least I have her up to five-word responses now. This was definitely an encouraging sign of progress.

"Dr. Thomas is very skilled at what he does, but I hope there are other doctors assisting him."

"As a matter of fact," she willingly offered up this time, "two or three other doctors have joined him. Word has come down that a team of specialists will be flying in from Walter Reed Hospital, to either assist or take over. You know how those military doctors can be sometimes; always wanting to be in control so as to take full credit. If anything should go wrong, however, the Walter Reed docs will blame it on our staff doctors."

Wow! Briana exclaimed, to herself. This woman clearly doesn't have a lot of love for military doctors; either that or she's overly protective of the staff doctors.

"I would have to agree with you on that one," Briana replied, in a continuing attempt to establish the woman's trust. "At least those are the same sentiments I recall Dr. Thomas uttering in light conversation awhile back. I wonder how long it will take them to get here?"

"According to a call I received a bit ago, we were told to expect their arrival sometime around ten."

"They can get here that fast?" inquired Briana, in a further attempt to divulge more information from Miss Tightlips, or whatever her actual name was.

"Military jet. A hospital-equipped military jet, to be exact. Loaded to the gills with the most up-to-date medical equipment as could be found anywhere. None of which could be found in this hospital, however. They rely on their fancy equipment while we rely on the skill of our nurses and doctors to pull our patients through. Your Dr. Thomas is a perfect example of a highly-skilled doctor. The staff doctors here keep begging him to come to work here full time."

The only part of her rambling conversation Briana picked up on were the words, "your Dr. Thomas." She liked the sound of that.

"I apologize for taking up so much of your valuable time, but I must get back to Dottie, the vice president's wife. I left her saying that I was only going to be gone long enough to grab a quick bite to eat." It never hurts to name drop, Briana thought.

"No problem. I enjoyed the break in my routine. Except for the vice president, things are unusually quiet right now, at least since I came on duty. Stop by again if you're in the neighborhood," she added, with a half smile.

"I'll be sure to do that," Briana replied, as she turned to walk away. She knew that she didn't get any news about the medical condition of the vice president, but she at least got some tidbits to share with Dottie about military doctors being flown in.

As she approached the waiting room, the same agent was standing ever so rigidly at the door. By the time she reached the doorway, he turned sideways and opened the door for her to enter.

"Thank you," Briana said, as she passed by him.

"You're welcome, ma'am."

Apparently Briana was gone just long enough that the "unwanted" relatives had already left. Dottie was still sitting in the same chair by herself.

"Hi there," Briana said, as she sat down in the same chair as before.

"Hi," Dottie responded back, obviously pleased to see Briana. "Did you have a good dinner?"

"I think the cold sandwich that I partook of had been previously rejected by one of the patients," she half-jokingly replied.

"That bad, huh?"

"I quickly learned that when one is hungry, one will eat almost anything. And that sandwich was right up there with almost anything. Forget about raising money for new medical equipment and facilities—they need to spend it all on an updated cafeteria and new magazines—might save more lives that way."

"I like your sense of humor, Briana."

"Yeah, I have been accused of having an over-active sense of humor at times. In fact, I will let you in on a little secret. I've been working on Dr. Thomas' under-active sense of humor of late. Given enough time I believe that I can save him from himself. It's a well-known medical fact, you know, that people without much in the way of humor in their lives die younger than their counterparts who have strong humor characteristics. So it's become my sole purpose in life to save him from himself. Not to change the subject, but I see that you managed to extricate yourself from your relatives in short order."

"After twenty minutes of listening to them whine and cry, the agent came in and basically threw them out. Don't get me wrong, I love my relatives, but I'm not looking for any pity or shared tears right now."

"Oh, that reminds me," Briana interjected. "On the way back from 'Café Doomsday,' I made a stop at the Emergency Room desk. My intentions, I will unashamedly admit, were to pry some privileged information out of Miss Tightlips behind the desk. With the help of a small crowbar that I always carry in my purse for just these occa-sions, I was eventually able to draw out a few spicy tidbits. Unfortu-nately, nothing about what was actually taking place in the operating room, though she probably doesn't know anything. Anyway, there are currently three or four doctors in there working on your husband. I also found out that a team of specialists is flying in on a medical-ly-equipped plane, as we speak, from Walter Reed. Miss Tightlips also informed me that they would be arriving here around ten. This means that at any moment now, we should be seeing a swarm of insurgents attempting a takeover of the hospital. Sorry; that last part was cour-tesy of Miss Tightlips. I never found out why, but she has a distinct dislike for military doctors. I'm thinking that a number of them have ditched her at the altar—and one look at her and her disposition, and you'd understand why."

"Good job, Briana," Dottie replied, with obvious interest in what Briana had to say. "If ever my husband needs to extract information from a political opponent, I'll ask him to get in touch with you as a last resort," Dottie stated, in an attempt at humor herself.

"I'm available, but not while I'm trying to extract humor from Dr. Thomas," Briana stated, with a wink. "Speaking of which, I was about . . . "

Briana was cut off midstream by the opening of the door that separated the waiting room from the hallway leading to the three operating rooms. Dressed in light-blue hospital garb was none other than Michael, who was quite surprised to see Briana sitting alone with the vice president's wife. Briana's eyes lit up at the sight of him. He wasted no time in coming over and sitting down on a chair across from the two of them. Before starting any conversation with Dottie, however, he first glanced at Briana and gave her a quick wink of acknowledgment. Whatever concerns were contained within her from the evening's activities, they soon faded away. And to think that all it took was a simple wink.

"Mrs. Stevenson," he started, "my name is Michael Thomas. I'm one of multiple doctors who took care of your husband tonight. To set your mind at ease, your husband is going to be okay. He experienced a deep laceration to the left side of his head. That was our biggest concern from the get-go and where we spent most of our efforts. There is no need at this point to give you a blow by blow account of what procedures we performed; I'll sit down with you personally tomorrow morning and explain everything." At this point, Michael let a moment of silence pass before continuing.

"He also had a badly dislocated shoulder. We had to go in, reset it back into place, along with repairing some associated ligament damage while we were in there. Following that, our next challenge was his left elbow. I'm assuming that he had it sitting on top of the door's armrest because it took its share of the impact. We had to insert a number of pins in the elbow, which may or may not require more re-constructive surgery down the road; it's too early to tell yet. We'll leave that decision up to the Walter Reed folks who will be taking control of his care upon their arrival, and, by the way, I received a message a few minutes ago that they had arrived at the airport fifteen minutes ago. They should be here shortly. Your husband also has three cracked ribs on his left side. Those, in our opinion, will not require surgery. Given time, they should heal on their own. But again, we'll leave the final decision to the Walter Reed staff. We are gathering up copies of the x-rays and MRI's that were taken for them to look at and take back with them. They have better equipment than we do, so don't be sur-prised if they conduct further diagnostic tests on your husband. We do the best we can with what tools we have at our disposal. His legs are fine outside of some deep bruises. It appears that his head and upper body took the brunt of the impact. Because of the concussion he suf-fered, along with the deep head wound, we have temporarily placed your husband into a coma—reversible within a short amount of time, I assure you. Our intent for doing so is to allow his body time to heal without putting undue stress on the wounds, especially to his head. Right now we believe his body can recover faster by restricting his ability to move, and that includes trying to communicate with anyone. Again, the doctors from Walter Reed may choose to do otherwise. The only thing I can tell you for sure is that he will require a lot of physical therapy, rest and TLC. In time, he will be as good as new, if not better. We're going to keep him in the operating room in case the Walter Reed folks see something that we may have missed. They will be the ones to let you know when he has been transferred to intensive care or a recovery room for you to visit."

Michael waited a moment to let this entire update sink in before continuing. "Now it's your turn for questions," he finally concluded.

Briana couldn't speak for Dottie, but she for one was blown away at how professional and exacting he was—in a remarkably calm and caring manner. He said nothing that didn't give Dottie hope for an eventual and full recovery. Briana felt that she obviously didn't need to teach him anything about his bedside manner—only his humor needed working on. She also found herself proud of being associated with him—humor or no humor in his gene pool.

"No, doctor," Dottie finally responded. "You did a very good job of explaining everything, which went a long way toward easing my fears in the process. Not only did you ease my fears, but your fiancée here did as well, I might add. She's quite the catch if you ask me. I probably would have been a total wreck had she not been here."

Michael immediately switched his full attention from Dottie to Briana who, all of a sudden, started squirming in her chair as her cheeks began to turn red. "Ah, yes," he said in a matter of fact tone, "Briana and I had planned on discussing that very subject this weekend. You will wait for me at the Emergency entrance, won't you dear?"

"Of course, Michael," she responded, rather sheepishly. "Silly of you to even ask that question. You know that I always go where you go." Briana now knew that she was in big trouble and would have a lot of explaining to do in short order—not something she was looking forward to at the moment. She hadn't given her "little white lies" a second thought as she threw them out randomly during the course of the evening. Nor, however, did she quite anticipate Dottie throwing out the word "fiancée."

"Do see that we get an invitation to your wedding," Dottie interjected. "I would love nothing more than to be part of what I see as the perfect couple for each other."

"Oh, I assure you, Mrs. Stevenson," Michael said, rather empathically for added effect. "Briana will see to it that you are the first to receive an invitation, if and when the time arrives. Now, if the two of you will excuse me, I need to get back to a certain patient of interest. The doctors from Walter Reed are probably being updated by one of the other staff doctors right now. And Mrs. Stevenson, I'll let the incoming doctors know where you can be reached." Turning to Briana, he said, "And I'll see you in about a half-hour at the Emergency entrance, my dear." With that last, biting comment, he rose from his chair, turned, and went back through the same door he had previously entered from—giving Briana one last, steely-eyed glance.

Briana, meanwhile, found herself speechless. She knew that she had less than a half hour to come up with a logical reason, other than the real one, for leading Dottie on about being engaged. Maybe, she thought, the truth is the right way out of this mess that she had created for herself. After all, she reasoned, experience has taught her that one white lie results in more white lies to cover up the first white lie. One thing she realized for sure—she did not, in any way, want to upset Michael any more than he probably already was—the truth, she concluded, would be the best way out.

"Briana, are you on another planet by any chance?" she semi-heard Dottie remark.

"I'm sorry," Briana answered, "were you talking to me?"

"Well, let's say that I thought I was talking to you, but obviously your mind was somewhere else at the moment. I'm going to place my money on Dr. Thomas."

"You win the bet—I was thinking about Michael. It's obviously been a long day for him. He's probably sore, tired and hungry right about now as we were headed off to dinner when the accident happened."

"He looks to be able to handle it. Plus, with a little TLC this evening from you—if you know what I mean—he should be as good as new by tomorrow."

Oh my God! Briana thought to herself. By "TLC," was Dottie implying what I think she was implying? We haven't even gone beyond one episode of holding hands yet, let alone engaged in any "TLC" as she refers to it. Right in the middle of her thoughts, she sensed that someone was talking to her again.

"Did you say something?" Briana inquired of Dottie, for the second time in as many minutes.

"Yes," answered Dottie, "but when I received no response I figured you were off to another planet again. Take my advice, go for a short walk outside in the cool air and then wait for Dr. Thomas. It's better that you be waiting for him than the other way around. After a long day and night, I would like to believe that he would want to get back to the hotel as soon as possible; maybe for a good massage to relieve the tight muscles he's probably experiencing right about now."

"Okay," Briana replied, now fantasizing about giving Michael a massage on top of some of that Dottie ordered TLC. "In the absence of my mother, I will take your advice, Dottie. Are you going to be okay here by yourself?"

"I'll be fine, dear. The trauma of the evening is somewhat behind me now, and my husband is going to be okay thanks to your Michael and the other doctors. Now skedaddle on out of here. And Briana," she continued, "thank you for spending time with me. You'll never know how your presence helped until you've been in this situation, and hopefully you never will be. But, if ever you are, be strong, be by his side—always."

"You are most welcome. I think we helped each other. And yes, if ever Michael needs me, I will be there for him, I promise," she added, before rising to leave.

"And Briana, don't forget that wedding invitation."

That not so simple statement of hers brought back a rising sense of uneasiness in Briana, for now she knew that it was time to go off and face the music, as they say. She hopefully wondered if the adage, "And the truth shall win out," or something like that, would prove to be the case in her current predicament with Michael. She was only minutes away from finding out.

"I won't, Dottie," she finally replied. "Like Michael said, you will be the first to receive an announcement. I'm not sure about tomorrow's benefit schedule, if it will even come off now, but hopefully we will meet up again, either tomorrow or Sunday."

"Most likely I will be in one waiting room or the other come tomorrow, or with my husband. So be sure to stop by and at least say hello. Now, on your way—don't keep your Michael waiting."

Before Briana had the opportunity to turn around and leave, Dottie rose from her chair and gave Briana a warm embrace. Briana liked that, as it reminded her of her mother's hugs. But even while she was being hugged, she couldn't get the words "your Michael" out of her mind. Briana liked that thought, but knew that soon she would be lucky if "her Michael" would even be speaking to her. Still lost in her troubled thoughts, she turned around and headed out the door. The agent she first met a few hours ago was still standing at attention in front of the doorway.

"Goodnight," Briana said, as she walked past him.

"Goodnight, ma'am," he responded, a little more warmly than on her first two encounters.

Chapter Twelve

BRIANA FOUND HERSELF FEELING MORE THAN APPREHENSIVE AS SHE MADE her way to the Emergency Room waiting area to meet up with Michael. She knew full well that Michael was not about to ignore the conversation in the waiting room where he found out that they were engaged—nor would she expect him to forget something that shocking.

"Hi there," Briana said, as she approached Miss Tightlips. "Got the late nightshift duty I see."

"Yep," she responded, "my favorite shift to work."

"I'm assuming that Dr. Thomas is still in conferring with the military brats?"

"Yep," she responded again. "Came in like storm troopers and demanded to know where the vice president was. No manners at all, mind you. I don't know who their mommas are or were, but they obviously failed to raise them properly. Maybe I should go find them and have a . . . "

Their conversation was abruptly ended with the appearance of Michael and two of the doctors who apparently had operated on the vice president with Michael. Just short of where Briana was standing, they stopped briefly to finish whatever conversation they were engaged in. Briana knew that it was soon to be all over for her as she watched the three of them shake hands. One of the doctors headed back inside the doorway while another exited out the entrance door of the Emergency Room, apparently heading for home, she surmised. Michael then made his way to where Briana was standing—staring at her with an expressionless look in his eyes.

"Ready to go?" he asked, without any emotion in his voice.

"Ready as you are," she replied, trying to sound chipper in spite of the crisis that lay before her.

Once outside the door, Michael wasted no time in asking the fatal question that Briana knew was coming. "Care to explain our so-called engagement?" he asked.

"Would you like the truth?" she countered, "or would you like a reasonably good story that I've been working on the last half hour?"

"The truth works best for me; and it may work in your favor as well. You've got exactly three blocks to explain yourself," he added, still with no warmth in his voice.

"Okay," she started out, hoping that the truth would get her back in his good graces. "I think I can do it in one block." Then she proceeded to explain the whole scenario with the Emergency Room receptionist, the Secret Service agent guarding the entrance to the waiting room, and Dottie. When she had finished, Michael said nothing for what seemed like an eternity to her.

"That was the best you could come up with?" he finally stated, still with no emotion in his voice.

"Well," she answered, "it's not like I had an hour to think about it, you know. Sometimes you say things that pop into your head. And yes, given the split-second decision I had before me, that was the best I could come up with."

"I don't like the potential ramifications of our 'engagement,' but I accept your explanation. You may have a lot of explaining to do down the road if Mrs. Stevenson mentions anything to the press about your visit with her. The paparazzi would be all over this one in a heartbeat. You do realize that, don't you?"

"I hadn't thought about that," Briana responded. "I'm sorry, Michael. I didn't do it to with the intent of causing you any discomfort, but obviously I have."

"I'll survive it. Like I said, you're the one with the explaining to do. And if it comes to that," he added, "you might try starting with the truth."

With that subject seemingly behind them, Michael slipped his arm in the crook of her arm. With that gesture, Briana immediately felt as though she had been set free of a heavy burden—a burden of her own making, of course. She promptly reached over and placed her free hand on his arm while at the same time looking up at him with an expression that said, "thank you." He, in turn, gave her a wink. Even though it was chilly outside as they walked, she never seemed to notice—at least for the last block and a half before reaching the hotel entrance. The truth, she thought to herself, did end up setting her free.

Walking through the lobby, they proceeded directly to the elevator with nary a soul in sight, though they could hear music coming from the direction of the lounge. After reaching the second floor, they said goodnight to each other before entering their separate rooms. Surprisingly, neither one of them had even made mention of tomorrow's benefit. After the events of this evening, all Michael could think of was sleep—and the sooner it came the better.

After entering his own room, Michael quickly stripped off his bloody street clothes and headed off for a hot and relaxing shower. This time, however, he allowed himself the luxury of taking an extended shower—not his usual three-minute shower when at home. With the hot water caressing his stiff muscles, his thoughts went back to how uncomfortable Briana appeared at trying to explain their "engagement" on their walk back to the hotel. Under normal circumstances, he probably would have remained mad for a long time had some woman put him into that same situation, but Briana was different. She was young and worldly in many respects while at the same time a little naive, he thought. A result most likely of having to grow up fast given the performing environment she lived in. But he also saw in her youthfulness a freed bird long held captive. He liked that about her, as it ran counter to his knowingly serious nature—and that, he felt, was what he needed. The very nature of his profession was one of seriousness—at least for the most part. He appreciated her many attempts to nurture his lighter side, even though he would never give her the satisfaction of directly knowing that.

With his shower and thoughts of Briana behind him, he slipped on a pair of clean shorts and a t-shirt before brushing his teeth. The hot shower, he noted, clearly went a long way toward relaxing his sore muscles—brought on more by the intense surgery than anything else. It's not every day that one is required to operate on the vice president of the United States, he mused.

After turning off the bathroom light, he proceeded straight to the far side of the bed where he slipped quickly under the covers. A small amount of moonlight managed to sneak in through the curtains—but he was too tired to get up and readjust them. As he lay there, he could perceive no noises coming from the door that separated his room from Briana's. He imagined that she too was already in bed and likely fast asleep.

Fifteen minutes later, however, he was awakened by what he thought was a light knocking at their shared door. Not being sure what he heard, he stayed where he was. Ten seconds later he heard the same light tapping. This time, however, he knew where the tapping was coming from. He quickly slipped out of bed and headed for the door without giving any thought to slipping on his bathrobe. When he opened the door, he found Briana standing there in her bathrobe.

"I can't fall asleep," she said softly, while looking at him with an apologetic look in her eyes for possibly having awakened him.

Without uttering a single word, he took her by the hand and led her over to the side of the bed. He then slipped the bathrobe from her shoulders and let it fall to the floor by her feet. He quickly observed, without noticeably staring at her, that she was wearing a short night-gown that left little to the imagination. He then pulled the covers back and guided her down onto his bed and situated her on her left side, facing the opened door that no longer separated their two rooms.

As soon as he had placed the covers over her, he walked around to the other side of the bed and slipped under the covers. Without giving it any thought, he scooted over to where she lay quietly. Pressing his body as close to hers as possible, he then slipped his right arm over her side with his right hand enveloping her silk-covered left breast. Her breast was neither large nor small as it fit perfectly in the cusp of his right hand. He could sense a slight shivering of her body when he did so.

A few seconds later she moved her right hand directly on top of his. At this point he sensed that her body had eased into a mode of contentment. There was no shivering, no tenseness, only complete relaxation on her part. Her closeness, coupled with her firm yet sup-ple breast in his hand, felt right to him. It wasn't but a matter of a few minutes lying there together, however, before he heard the gen-tle sounds of sleep emanating from between Briana's lips. Content in both his thoughts and his physical closeness to her, he too slowly slipped off to sleep.

Chapter Thirteen

THE FOLLOWING MORNING FOUND BOTH MICHAEL AND BRIANA IN THE same position in which they had both fallen asleep. It apparently was a solid sleep for the two of them as his hand was still spread out over her left breast, with her hand still resting over his. As he lay there awake, his thoughts were torn between his need to learn how things were progressing with the vice president and his desire to remain lying next to Briana. Her body, he selfishly thought to himself, belonged right where it was—right next to his own. And he so wanted to massage her firm breasts, but he knew in doing so, she would inevitably awaken from her sleep. Should that happen, he knew that he could not resist the urge to take her, to make passionate love to her—and never stop making love to her. Without actually knowing it to be a fact, he believed that she was a virgin. Did she willingly want to give up her virginity for him? Is that why she came to him last night? Would she respect him for taken her to the greatest level of intimacy, he wondered; especially if that were not her actual intention for coming into his room? Questions—nothing but unanswered questions filled his mind.

At this point, he was more than willing to take their relationship to greater heights of mutually shared fulfillment. But first and foremost, there was the pressing matter of his patient still weighing on his mind. He quickly thought— as if searching for a valid reason to remain in bed with Briana—did not the doctors from Walter Reed assume full responsibility for the patient upon their arrival, thereby relieving him of any and all responsibilities? Yes, they in fact did, he thought, answering his own question.

No sooner had he answered his own question, however, than he realized that the answer was not the essence of who he was, or what he had learned from his parents. He had assisted in bringing the vice president back from near death—so now was not the time to walk away from all that he had invested in by his efforts. So, with that sense of duty—or was it simply guilt playing games with his mind?—he slowly began removing his hand and arm from her soft body, his fingers slipping tenderly across her nipple in the process. Now I know what sweet torture is, he cried out silently to himself. Why must there be a vice president? Why must there be a benefit today? Why must I be denied the pleasure of her beautiful, tender body?

In spite of all his pleadings with himself, he quietly slipped out from under the covers and made his way into the bathroom, quickly changing into the clothes he had laid out the night before. After brushing his teeth and running a comb through his hair, he made his way over to the small desk. Sitting down quietly, he wrote out a short note on the hotel stationary with what little light passed between the curtains. Placing the note on her bathrobe, he quietly crossed the room before turning and taking one last look at Briana, who was still peacefully asleep. Tearing himself away from looking at her any longer, he let himself out the door.

It was a few minutes past six-thirty by the time he arrived at the hospital. There was an eerie quietness in the Emergency Room section of the hospital; a place where he would normally be observing nurses and doctors scurrying around—but then he had to remind himself that it was still early. An unfamiliar nurse or receptionist, he wasn't sure which, sat behind the admitting desk.

"Hi there," he said in a rather jubilant tone, "I'm Dr. Thomas. Can you tell me if the vice president is still here?" That was a rather silly question, he said to himself as soon as he uttered the words. Of course she knows if he is still here.

"Yes, doctor," she replied. "He is in Intensive Care, room two. They moved him there sometime during the early morning."

"Thank you. Can you also tell me if his wife is here?"

"No, doctor, I can't say that I've seen her. At least she hasn't made her way past me in the last hour. Though she may have come in via the main entrance and gone directly to the waiting room. Would you like me to call the nursing station and check if they've seen her?"

"No, thanks, that won't be necessary. I'm heading over to see the patient anyway, so I'll keep my eye out for her. If she does come in behind me, would you please have me paged?"

"No problem, doctor. By the way," she continued, "there are glowing reports going around about how you saved the vice president's life last night."

Michael wasted no time in setting her straight. "Those so-called reports that you hear going around are misleading. There were multiple doctors who worked along with me, not to mention a gifted team of nurses and other support staff. So do everyone a favor, please, myself included, by spreading those words around the hospital and with the media. Speaking of the media, why haven't I noticed any of them swarming around? In a situation such as this, I would have expected a multitude of cameras facing me as I came in this morning."

"On the radio this morning, I heard that the media has been asked to stay away, that all press releases concerning the vice president's condition would be issued out of Walter Reed Medical Center. They also mentioned that no interviews or cameras would be allowed on hospital grounds. When I arrived for work, I saw official notices plastered all over the place, forbidding any of us from releasing any information to anyone outside of the hospital concerning the vice president. I've only been here an hour and already I've taken five calls from the media requesting information. I'm not sure what part of Walter Reed they don't understand."

"As you probably well know, the competing media outlets want to be the first with the latest scoop. They'll try every tactic in the book to beat out the competition. Anyway, thanks for the media information. I guess I was too tired last night to give them a thought. I'll check in with you on my way out for any sightings of Mrs. Stevenson," Michael concluded, as he turned and headed down the hallway leading to the Intensive Care section of the hospital.

Before passing by the nursing station, he stopped long enough to ask if anyone else was currently in with the vice president. The on-duty nurse informed him that two doctors from Walter Reed had been with him all night, with a third doctor joining them about twenty minutes ago. He thanked her for the information and proceeded down the hallway to room two.

Standing outside the doorway was a Secret Service agent. This particular agent, however, was not one that he remembered seeing last night at the accident scene—though, as he recalled, he was preoccupied with more weighty matters at the time.

When he had arrived within a few feet of the agent, he displayed his hospital badge as well as stating his name. The agent quickly drew out a small, electronic device from his shirt pocket and began, using one finger, typing something into the device. After closing the device and reinserting it into his shirt pocket, he motioned for Michael to go in.

Michael, in a showing of consideration, lightly tapped on the door.

He was immediately greeted by Dr. Howard, whom he had conferred with post-surgery. Stepping inside, Michael was quickly introduced to Drs. Nichols and Stevens.

"How did the night go for the patient?" Michael inquired of anyone who would answer.

"Quite well, actually," Dr. Nichols answered. "Putting him into a coma was the right decision. All things considered, his vitals have remained at reasonably expected levels throughout the night."

"Our first inclinations were to transport him to Walter Reed first thing this morning," interjected Dr. Stevens. "After consulting with each other, however, we've decided it best to keep him here one more day and night. In addition, so as not to add any undue stress on his body, we have also decided to keep him in a comatose state until after arriving back at Walter Reed. Again, that was a smart decision on your part to induce the coma."

"That decision, gentlemen," Michael quickly replied, "was not mine alone. A team of doctors made the collaborative decision."

"Well said, doctor," replied Dr. Stevens. "However," he continued, "you did take the lead on the surgery. Based on the original x-rays and MRI's, and the follow-up ones that we ordered, you apparently did an exemplary job. You're to be congratulated."

"Again, gentlemen," Michael retorted, "there were multiple sets of eyes guiding that scalpel. A mistake by one of us would have been a mistake by all of us." He said this in the hopes of getting his point across that this hospital works on the "team" theory. He was beginning to get the feeling that military doctors work strictly from a theory of "competition."

"Again, well put, Dr. Thomas," responded Dr. Stevens, who reluctantly acknowledged the reasoning behind Michael's unwillingness to accept individual praise for his accomplishments.

"Well, gentlemen," Michael stated, "I'll leave you alone with your patient. I now need to turn my attentions to a DWB benefit we're holding later today and tomorrow—the very reason the vice president was here in the first place."

"Again," responded Dr. Nichols, on behalf of the others, "our heartfelt praise to your whole team for an excellent job. Apparently a skilled team, I might add."

"Thank you, doctors all. I will relay your thanks and praise to the team before the weekend is out. Have a safe trip home if I don't see you before you leave."

"Good luck on your benefit, doctor," stated Dr. Nichols, as Michael was in the process of turning around to leave.

"Thank you," Michael replied as he opened the door and headed back to the Emergency Room admitting desk. As he walked down the hallway, he thought about the conversation that had taken place. He wondered again if the military actively promoted competition amongst themselves, as opposed to teamwork amongst their doctors. Based on the conversation he had just witnessed, he had to believe that they were, in fact, driven by competition.

Stopping off at the nurse's station on his way out, he inquired of the same individual if she had heard from, or seen, Mrs. Stevenson yet; her reply was a negative. She probably returned late last night or early this morning to wherever she was staying, he figured. He chastised himself for failing to inquire of the doctors as to whether or not Mrs. Stevenson was eventually able to see her husband before leaving the hospital. He hoped so, as she would have her own "recovery" period to go through.

He had entered the hospital this morning in near darkness and was greeted by the bright rays of the rising sun; he was grateful for the fact that no rains were predicted for the weekend's activities. Glancing down at his watch, he saw that he had over a half hour to kill before returning to the hotel. The message he had left for Briana mentioned that he would pick her up for breakfast at eight sharp. So, with time on his hands, he decided to stroll along the main avenue and do a little window shopping—an activity he had never taken the time out to do on his previous trips to Etenia.

Passing by a jewelry store, his eye caught sight of a beautiful necklace draped around the neck of a mannequin bust and with what appeared to be matching earrings. Noticing that the proprietor was in the process of unlocking the door, he quickly followed him inside to have a closer look.

"Good morning," greeted the elderly gentleman as he sensed Michael walking in behind him. "Looking for anything in particular?" he inquired.

"Just window shopping," came Michael's short response.

"Looking for something for that special lady, perhaps?" asked the inquisitive shopkeeper in the hopes of making his first sale of the day.

"Possibly," Michael repeated. I'll just look around if you don't mind."

"Feel free—lots of excellent, high quality merchandise to look at."

As the shopkeeper went about his business of opening up, Michael headed directly over to the mannequin in the window. Both beautiful and unique, he thought to himself upon closer inspection. Glancing down at the base of the bust was a card which described the jewelry on the mannequin. Picking up the card he read that the necklace was a "21 carat, rose gold cultured freshwater pearl and diamond accent pendant with matching earrings." He wasn't sure what all of that meant but was still in awe of how stunning they looked on the mannequin. He readily admitted to himself that he didn't know much about jewelry, so was somewhat taken aback by the price tag of $1800. Ten minutes later, in spite of the cost, he found himself walking out of the store with the jewelry box inside his coat pocket.

Meanwhile, a still half-asleep Briana raised her head from the pillow to read the time on the nightstand clock before resting her head back down on the pillow. A quarter after seven, she read—plenty of time for a little more shut eye. Two seconds later she was startled back up into an upright position. "Oh my God!" She exclaimed to herself out loud. "I'm not even in my own bed."

It took a few seconds longer before fully realizing how she had ended up in Michael's bed in the first place. I was wound up, couldn't sleep, she recalled. So what possessed me to seek out Michael's bed? Or was it Michael I was seeking out? I distinctly remember him guiding me to his bed from our shared doorway. The next thing I remember was his loosening my robe and letting it slip from my shoulders to the floor. And I'm sure that he saw everything through my sheer, silk nightgown. Next, he sat me down on the bed before laying me down on my side. The last thing I remembered was his arm being wrapped around me with his hand tightly cupping my breast.

"Oh my God!" She repeated aloud, over and over. He actually touched my breast. I remember how comforting his hand felt—though it scared me at first. I think I even remember placing my hand over his hand. No man has touched my breasts before and yet, here I was, lying next to a man I hardly know; though, if I recall, I didn't want his hand to leave my breast because it felt so soothing. Did I dream all of this, or did it all actually happen? she continued, in her questioning thoughts about the events of last night.

Did he try to take advantage of me? No, she quickly answered, I most certainly would have known that. Did he not find me attractive enough to even desire to make love to me? Did he leave this morning thinking that I had thrown myself at him? This is all so confusing, she thought to herself. It was at that moment she noticed a piece of stationery lying on her bathrobe.

She quickly reached down to pick up the note and began to read:

Briana,

> *A quick note to let you know that I am heading off for the hospital—need to check up on our special patient. Unless there are some unforeseen circumstances, I expect to return to the hotel no later than eight. Hopefully you will have arisen by then, and your "appetite" is raring to go. I know mine is.*
>
> *See you at eight. Hope you slept well. I know I did, thanks to your body being snuggled up next to mine.*

Michael

"Oh my God!" That's less than forty minutes away, she said, as she grabbed her bathrobe from the floor and raced from his room back into hers. As she was heading into the bathroom, she suddenly realized that she hadn't closed the door that separated their rooms. I wouldn't want Michael to come into his room and see me stark naked, she thought. Or would I? With that tantalizing thought racing through her mind, she quickly closed the door and headed directly for the shower.

Following his expensive window-shopping experience, Michael concluded that there was a compelling reason such activities would never become a mainstay in his life; window shopping was boring—except for the jewelry, that is. He couldn't even conceive of how most women could get overly excited at the offer of a window-shopping experience with their lady friends. During the morning stroll, he witnessed only one elderly gentleman involved in the sport of window shopping—and the poor fellow appeared to be unwillingly dragged along by his wife.

At the stroke of eight, Michael quietly slipped the key into his door and opened it ever so gently. The last thing he wanted to do was startle Briana if she were still sleeping—a quick glance told him that it was not the case. He obviously had no idea when she finally woke up, but he had little choice but to tap on her door to see if she was ready to go. Before he had finished his fourth knock, the door opened wide.

"Good morning, Michael," she said, with unusual exuberance in her voice. "I'm starving, how about you?"

Michael found it rather amusing that the first thing out of her mouth was about food—intentionally ignoring the fact that they had slept together last night.

"Given that I haven't eaten since we both consumed Frankie's sandwiches yesterday on the plane, I'm starving as well; probably more so than you," he added for extra measure. "You look lovely, by the way." He said this for the simple reason that she did, in fact, look lovely. Actually, she looked ravenously beautiful to him. She must have gotten up right after he left to look that made up, he thought. Her appearance brought back memories of his mother spending an eternity in the bathroom before she and his father would go out on a date or to a party. He assumed that such behavior was true of all women.

"Where are you taking me for breakfast?" she inquired, still ignoring the issue of last night.

"While I was out window shopping this morning to pass the time, I came across a charmingly quaint little place on Main Street. The place was almost packed, so I'm going to take that as a good sign. Grab your purse and let's hit the road."

"Don't need a purse," she replied. "You're paying, remember?"

"Shucks, and to think that I was planning all along to stick you with the bill," he said, with a wide grin on his face.

"Nice try; but won't work on this girl. My momma done taught me to look out for your type," she said, with a purely southern drawl.

"Let's see if we can both walk and talk at the same time. It's a learned behavior, you know. So consider this a test of your walking/talking skills."

As they headed out and down the hallway to the single elevator, Michael felt obligated to ask for clarification on her previous statement. "So, your mother reportedly taught you to look out for my type, huh? And what is my type, may I ask?"

"Oh, you know," she started out, while stalling for the right words. "The type that would take advantage of a young, defenseless woman like me—at her weakest of moments, I might add."

"Funny," he quickly responded, "I don't recall having taken advantage of you last night—even though you practically threw yourself into my bed against my will."

"I did not!" She exclaimed, loudly enough that people in the lobby looked over at the two of them as they exited the elevator. "I was tired. I couldn't fall asleep. As a matter of fact, I believe that I was sleep-walking. Being a doctor, you should have easily recognized that sleep-walking look in my eyes, so there!" she proclaimed, rather emphatically.

"I find that rather hard to believe, given that I graduated at the top of my class in sleep-walking identification." This was a little white lie, of course, and he knew it, but she didn't, and that was all that mattered at the moment.

"Well, you missed diagnosing my case because it obviously was dark at the time," she quickly remarked in defense of her honor—or at least this friendly tug-of-war with Michael. "Besides, was it not you who led me over to your bed and practically ripped the robe from my body?"

"Wow!" Michael exclaimed, "are you sure we were in the same room together last night, and into the early hours of the morning? I don't recall ripping anything off. I do recall gently removing the robe from your shoulders and letting it fall to the floor—that much I will openly admit to."

"Okay, maybe you did gently remove it as you say. I was sleep-walking, remember. And who was it," she continued in her attempt to get back on the offensive, "who cuddled up behind me and placed his hand on my breast? And how do I know that you didn't take advantage of me last night?"

"You raise a good number of questions and concerns," he stated, rather calmly as they continued their walk along Main Street. "Allow me to answer two of them right away. First off, if you went to bed a virgin, you woke up a virgin . . . though I did have thoughts of taking you, but you fell asleep on me before I had the chance. Secondly, I find it rather amusing at your uncanny ability to recall so many details of what happened last night. Why? Because research has shown, conclusively, that the vast majority of sleep-walkers have no recollection of what they were doing while sleep-walking."

"Once again," she replied rather calmly, to match his calmness, "I am the exception to the rule. My mother always said that I was an exceptional child. And another thing, why didn't you take me? Did you not find me attractive enough?"

"As a matter of honest fact, I find you extremely attractive. Last night, however, may have been the right place, but the wrong moment. You could hardly expect me to make love to a sleep-walker."

"Oh, that's right. Thank you for taking that into consideration," Briana responded. "And thank you for finding me attractive," she added.

"We're almost there," Michael informed her, more as a means to change the subject than for any other reason. With only a half-block remaining, Michael slipped his arm in hers. With that little gesture on his part, he received a warm smile in return from Briana.

Their conversation during breakfast was filled with lots of humor, which brought about an occasional burst of laughter from Michael. There was no further mention of what took place the previous night, which apparently suited the two of them just fine; especially Briana, who knew that she, more than Michael, applied the delicate art of exaggeration to defend herself. She knew exactly what she was doing last night—she didn't want to openly admit it to Michael, however. But apparently, he was willing to let it go, and she was grateful for that.

They walked arm in arm again back to the hotel to freshen up prior to heading over to the hospital. Michael had a final strategy meeting to attend at ten-thirty before the opening ceremonies began at noon. Briana was not set to begin her first performance until three, but agreed to go with Michael; she had no desire to be left alone in a hotel room—at least not without "her Michael" being there with her.

Chapter Fourteen

FIFTEEN MINUTES LATER, THEY FOUND THEMSELVES ONCE AGAIN, ARM IN arm, making their way toward the hospital. It was becoming apparent to the two them that they were "coupling" without any words being said to that effect. Aside from last night's episode of physical togetherness, their relationship was evolving along a smooth path—not that last night would be considered an "unsmooth" path.

Upon entering the main entrance to the hospital, it was clear that something was about to happen. Administrative staff members were seen scurrying around the hallways pushing loaded carts or carrying boxes; activities related to setting up for the benefit were apparently in full swing.

The two of them then entered the only conference room in the administrative wing of the hospital. Sitting at the large table were a half-dozen staff members already gathered for the benefit briefing. The meeting began right on schedule and concluded a half-hour later. While tours of the hospital were planned, it was announced at the meeting that the Emergency Room, Intensive Care and the Recovery Rooms were designated as "off limits" to visitors; their associated waiting rooms were off limits, as well. This designation came at the request, or insistence would better describe it, of the Secret Service. As expected, given the circumstances of last night, they had flown in a team of additional agents immediately following the accident. Their overwhelming presence could be seen and felt in every nook and cranny of the hospital.

While the accident itself was unfortunate, Michael was quick to observe that it resulted in putting the city of Etenia, Tennessee on the national map of awareness. This would, he conjectured, hopefully result in bringing out more of the curious to the benefit. Whether donations to the hospital would increase as a result of this notoriety was unknown, but it undoubtedly would do little to undermine it.

Following the meeting, and with plenty of time to spare, Michael escorted Briana down to the Intensive Care waiting room. To no surprise of either one of them, they were greeted by two agents in front of the door.

Speaking to both agents, Michael asked, "Can you tell me if Mrs. Stevenson is in the hospital, please?" The response he received was as he had expected.

"Do you have a need to know?" one of the two agents inquired, sounding more like a robot than a human.

"I'm Dr. Thomas, I was one of a team of doctors that operated on her husband last night. When meeting with her, following the surgery, I promised to meet with her again this morning."

"Do you have any hospital identification?" responded the same agent.

Michael immediately pulled out his identification badge from his shirt pocket and handed it to the agent. The agent examined the badge at some length, front and back, before handing it back to Michael. As expected, he pulled out the now all too familiar electronic device from inside his suit jacket. Opening up the device, he performed a few keystrokes—obviously authenticating Michael's need to be there. A few seconds later, he turned to the other agent and gave him a nod. The second agent then turned around and appeared to be talking into some device attached to the lapel of his jacket.

"And you, ma'am?" asked the same agent, looking directly at Briana.

"I'm Briana Price," she replied, finding all this pomp and circumstance kind of amusing. "I was with Dottie, I mean, Mrs. Stevenson, last night during the surgery—at her request, I might add."

"ID, ma'am."

"I didn't bring any with me," she responded. "It was his turn to buy breakfast, so I left it at the hotel on purpose as he's always trying to stick me with the bill." The agent, apparently passing on her humorous jab at Michael, once again typed away at his little device—but said nothing after inserting the device back into his pocket. The second agent then disappeared into the waiting room. It would be a full five minutes before he returned with Mrs. Stevenson following right behind him.

"Can you vouch for these two, Mrs. Stevenson?" said the second agent, standing with her at the door.

"Oh yes, please come in, you two," she stated, obviously happy to see them.

Following her in, they then headed off in the direction of three comfortable-looking chairs. To Briana, Dottie looked a whole lot better than she did last night. She could only assume that it was from a combination of sleep, fresh makeup and her husband's favorable prognosis.

"So, how are you two?" Dottie asked, with a renewed sense of liveliness in her voice over that of last night.

"All things considered, we're doing fine, thank you," Briana responded. "We found a cute little restaurant that served a great breakfast. Michael ordered one of everything on the menu—if you can believe that," she added, while looking at Michael. He shook his head in exasperation, but chose not to say anything in response to her teasing. Now was not an opportune time to get into another tug-of-war with Briana, he thought. Besides, he had quickly learned that Briana was somewhat of an expert at twisting stories around—all to make her look like the victim, of course. If he didn't know better, he'd swear that she must have taken some lessons straight from Frankie's playbook of jabs.

"It sounds to me as though you're going to be one busy woman in the kitchen," Dottie said, while looking directly at Briana. "Our men do love to eat."

"I'm sure I will," Briana answered, regretting the back-door reference to their "pending" engagement.

Michael, wishing to change the subject, quickly inquired, "And how are you doing, Mrs. Stevenson?"

"I'm actually holding up quite well, all things considered. Knowing that my husband is going to be okay, thanks to you and your team, goes a long way toward reducing my stress level from that of last night."

"Along those same lines, do you have any questions of me concerning your husband that may have gone unanswered last night during our brief visit?"

"Oh heavens no. Between what you relayed last night and what the doctors from Walter Reed have told me this morning, I think I know everything that I want to know. Speaking of which, I understand that you were in checking on my husband bright and early this morning."

"I was."

"Thank you for doing that. I know you're no longer responsible for his care, but I appreciate your checking in on him. Not many doctors would do that."

"Michael is not your run of the mill doctor," Briana piped in.

"So I've come to learn, dear."

"Well, I know you want to get back to spending time with your husband, Mrs. Stevenson, so if you have no questions, Briana and I will get back to matters related to the benefit."

"I'm sorry that we put a damper on the benefit," Mrs. Stevenson responded.

"It wasn't anyone's fault outside of the drunk who ran into your vehicle," Michael replied, in an attempt to relieve her of any feelings of guilt. "Outside of a few changes, it will go on as planned." With that being said, Michael rose from his chair and extended his hand to Briana to help her up—not that she needed any help in the first place. Briana was quite moved by his gesture. Another example of being brought up well by his parents, she thought, as she rose from her chair with Michael's assistance.

"If you need anything, anything at all, Mrs. Stevenson, please let either Briana or myself know. And, if we don't see you beforehand, have a safe trip home tomorrow."

"Thank you, doctor. Thank you, Briana. Between the doctors tending to my husband, and way too many Secret Service agents floating around with little to do but intimidate people, I think I'll be okay. Again, thanks for stopping by—and good luck with the benefit."

As Michael turned to head for the door, Mrs. Stevenson rose from her chair and gave Briana another hug—the same warm and affectionate hug she had given her last night.

"Briana," she whispered in her ear, "Stay with Michael to the end, no matter what life throws at you. Put your faith and trust in him. He's definitely a keeper. If only I were thirty years younger and unmarried, you would most definitely have some competition."

"I know he's a keeper; and I will be there for him, if needed, just as you have been here for your husband. That much I promise you." Briana was moved by this repeated gesture of kindness on the part of Dottie— along with her sage words of advice that she promised herself to keep.

Chapter Fifteen

FOLLOWING THEIR BRIEF VISIT WITH MRS. STEVENSON, MICHAEL AND BRI-ana headed back to the hotel to rest up before tackling the busy day they knew would soon face them head on. The walk back for Briana was one filled with optimism, as her "little white lies" between her and Michael were apparently a thing of the past—at least she hoped they were. No more of those little white lies and unexplained nightly forays into his room, she promised herself. Well, except for the forays into his room, that is.

Coming to a street corner that was unusually busy for this small town, they waited patiently for the traffic to clear. Spotting some clearance between approaching vehicles, Michael grabbed onto Briana's hand and yelled, "Let's go." The two of them, in a fast walk, made their way quickly to the other side of the street.

Briana found herself somewhat stunned by Michael's actions; not so much the taking of her hand, as the not letting go of her hand once they continued walking down the sidewalk. She liked that. In fact, she had to admit to herself, she really, really liked that. His hand felt comfortable holding onto hers and she had no intentions of letting go anytime soon. Was he aware of what he had done? she asked herself. Was he sending her an unspoken message that led her to believe that their relationship was rising to a new level? Will he take it, she wondered, to even another level before they return home tomorrow? A part of her was hoping to experience the "next" level—whatever that might entail. More questions than answers, she concluded.

As they headed down the hallway, Michael eventually stopped with Briana at her door. "Your performance is at three. What time do you feel you need to be there?" he asked, in a soft tone.

"Probably no later than two-thirty," she replied, looking dreamily into his eyes.

"Okay then; that gives us about two hours for a cat nap. I'll set my cell phone right now for two-fifteen," which he did as she watched. "See you then."

"Michael," she said softly, with eyes that could melt an iceberg. "I don't want to be alone. Any chance I can persuade you to rest with me?"

Michael was pleasurably surprised by her request. "Are you sure that you aren't sleep-walking again?" he asked, softly.

Looking up into his eyes, she responded, "Neither this time . . . nor last night."

Michael, without saying another word, unlocked her door, took her by the hand and led her inside. Closing the door behind them, he then led her over to the couch and repositioned the pillows before motioning for her to sit down. He then lowered himself next to her, put his arm around her shoulder and eased her down with him as he laid his head on the pillows. With his arm still around her, he pulled her head onto his chest while she, without hesitation, willingly wrapped her free arm across and around his chest.

Once she was snuggled in, Michael began to gently and rhythmically massage her left temple. Feeling both safe and comfortable, along with being lost in her fantasies, Briana quietly drifted off to sleep in short order. Michael continued to massage her temple until he too fell fast asleep. The events of the last night had, without question, taken their toll on the two of them.

At exactly two-fifteen, they were both startled awake by the cell phone's alarm—but neither one of them said a word or moved. They were both content to spend the rest of the afternoon right where they were—in each other's arms.

"Briana," Michael finally spoke up. "We need to grab your guitar and get moving."

She knew he was right, but the performance was the last thing on her mind. She had never before been in this position—never before felt this calm and relaxed. "Michael," she said softly, "I'd rather spend the rest of the day on the couch with you."

"So would I. But I just happen to know a special young lady who has some singing to do in forty-five minutes." To this statement, there was no response forthcoming from Briana. Michael, taking the initiative on his own, raised her up to a sitting position before sliding off the couch. Leaning over, he then took her hands in his, gently pulling her up to her feet.

"Give me fifteen minutes to freshen up and change clothes," she said, half groggily.

"Okay, fifteen it is." he replied, before heading through the shared door into his own room.

At half past the hour, with Michael carrying her guitar case, the two of them began making their way to the hospital once again—this time with a clear sky and the midafternoon sun warming their backs. Briana said nary a word along the way, and Michael was respectful of her apparent need for silence. Still feeling somewhat tired, he presumed that her silence was directly attributable to her also being tired.

They entered the cafeteria via the service door as the courtyard entrance was already teeming with visitors awaiting her performance.

Had she gone through the courtyard, she would have been mobbed by those who came specifically to see her—which was everyone. She was, without question, Tennessee's favorite sweetheart. They both stopped short of the doorway that led from the stockroom into the cafeteria.

"Good luck," Michael said, while handing over her guitar. Without saying a word, she leaned up, kissed him on the cheek, turned and quickly disappeared through the door.

Their first kiss was not exactly passion-filled—but Michael considered that a first step to whatever she was willing to offer. The operative word being "willing," Michael thought. Maybe that kiss, along with cupping her breast in his hand, was as far as she was willing to go for the time being—or ever. He never considered himself to be the overly aggressive type in relationships, so he was content to let her make the next move—or no move at all.

Michael left through the same door they had entered from and quickly walked around the building, reentering the hospital via the main entrance. The younger generation, he surmised, was obviously in the cafeteria or courtyard, as those milling around inside the foyer were primarily adults and little children. Michael carefully threaded his way past those who were there to take in all of the displays that had been set up earlier by the staff. If his eyes didn't deceive him, he also took note of what appeared to be a few Secret Service agents making their own "observations."

Using his electronic badge, he slipped into the employee's lounge and headed out a second door leading into another hallway. From there he wound his way around until finally reaching the employee entrance to the cafeteria kitchen. Badging himself in again, Michael found himself standing before a large number of white-coated employees and what he presumed to be volunteers. This was a 24-hour hospital, after all—patients still needed to be fed along with the various working employees, he mused. The volunteers, on the other hand, appeared to be solely responsible for the preparation of finger foods for the assembled crowds to munch on.

After speaking with a few of the employees who recognized him, he made his way across the kitchen area to his final destination—the backside of the food service display cases. From this vantage point, he could take in Briana's performance without being crushed by the gathering fans. He was convinced that it was a wise choice of viewing arrangements on his part, as it appeared there wasn't room left for even air to circulate in the main room. He had a gut feeling that the local fire officials were intentionally over-looking the room's maximum occupancy limits. Glancing out through the windows, he felt sorry for the hundred or more young people who weren't able to make it inside. At least the doors had been left wide open; an ample number of speakers were thoughtfully set up on the roof overlooking the courtyard. The planners, whoever they were, obviously had the foresight to anticipate the overflow crowd.

It was Michael's original intention to pass on the performance itself. He fully expected himself to be milling around the main entrance to the hospital—answering questions and providing directions. But things changed. Those original intentions were both pre-Briana and the vice president. None of these feelings would have manifested themselves had it not been for her "sleep-walking" herself into his bed—and directly into his life as well, he thought.

Turning his thoughts away from Briana and onto the stage, he noticed Bill the "Piano Man" testing the microphone which, from his vantage point, appeared to be working properly. Glancing down at his watch, he noticed there were only two minutes remaining before show time. That was, if she actually started on time as she claimed she always did.

Two minutes ticked by and Michael became an instant believer in her word—with the exception of those words last night at the hospital and again this morning on the way to breakfast, that is. The Piano Man began to tickle the ivories as she came onto the stage strumming her guitar. She was looking more attractive and livelier than when he'd left her twenty minutes before. He could easily understand why her fans had come to adore her—he certainly knew why he did.

The fans, of course, went crazy the moment she appeared on stage. Michael wasn't certain as to why, but she apparently chose not to sing, but simply to play her guitar—which was probably a wise decision given that the crowds cheering, screaming and clapping would have drowned out her words anyway. At the conclusion of that first number, Briana moved up closer to the microphone.

"Hi there," she said to the young crowd. Wrong words, Michael thought to himself, as the young and overly enthusiastic crowd went back to cheering and screaming. Once the noise level from the crowd somewhat quieted down, she continued.

"What's with you guys and gals . . . couldn't find anything better to do this afternoon in Etenia?" Of course, this set the crowd off once again. Michael had to give her credit for knowing how to work up her fans. She's learning how to work me up, as well, he said to himself as a smile lit upon his face. On cue from Briana, Mr. Piano Man started with the next number. Michael had to give him credit as well—he certainly knew how to play the piano.

Right in the middle of the second number, he and Briana's eyes locked in on each other. At that moment, he perceived that her voice had faltered a bit; if it did, the crowd never appeared to notice. She apparently could do no wrong this afternoon.

Before Michael was even aware of it, a full hour of music had quickly passed by. Given that a second performance would take place at seven, it was agreed beforehand that Briana would do a one hour set for each performance; thereby not allowing too much strain to be placed on her vocal cords. But still she played on for a full twenty minutes before finally bringing the miniconcert to its conclusion.

The fans, however, had other ideas. Three minutes after leaving the stage, they were still screaming for more. It must have worked, because once again she reappeared to thunderous applause and screaming.

"One last song," she told them, as her guitar came back to life. Her final number, from what Michael could hear over the crowd noise, appeared to be about a young couple's yearning to find the meaning of life through love—true happiness is achieved when two become as one, she sang. Give love a chance, open up your heart, she continued. Love can be found through a simple touch, a hand in yours, an unexpected wink, a warm embrace that feels so right, she sang as the crowd quietly took in her words.

Michael strained to hear her every word. While she was periodically glancing his way during the song, he wondered if she didn't sing it for his benefit or, was he only wishing she had? Pretty heavy lyrics for one so young, he thought, remembering that she wrote her own songs. She sang the lyrics as if she truly was one of the two lovers. The passion in her voice brought a lump to Michael's throat.

Following the last song, Michael managed to find a doorway off the kitchen that led to the back of the makeshift stage. When he eventually found her, she was kneeling on the floor, placing her guitar back into its case. Seeing movement out of the corner of her eye, she glanced up and noticed Michael standing to her left.

"Nice performance," Michael stated with sincerity. "And let Mr. Piano Man know that he plays a pretty mean piano; not sure if that's the correct term, however."

"Close enough," she replied, giving off the warmest of smiles while looking up at him. "But it is better than no compliment at all. I'll let him know that he has received his first adult approval of the day."

"Are you playing with me?" he asked.

"Not yet," came her quick response. As soon as the words left her mouth, her cheeks instantly turned beet-red from embarrassment—which resulted in her immediately throwing out an apology. "Sorry, that wasn't meant to come out the way it did."

"No offense taken—I knew exactly what you meant." He actually didn't know what her thinking was behind the statement, but decided to have fun with this one for reasons of payback. "On second thought, what did you mean by that 'not yet' statement?"

"Can we change the subject, please? Or is my apology not being accepted at face value for some reason?"

"The answer to your questions is, "we can" and "it is." And to change the subject even more, I'm hungry, how about you?"

"Starving. As if that should come as any surprise to you."

"Starving wins out then. It should win out, given that neither one of us has taken the time to eat. How did we let lunch get away from us, anyway?"

"Cuddling on the couch and napping won out," she replied, with a grin. "Two important happenings in a girl's life, I might add."

"At the risk of being considered girlish, I'm going to agree with you on that. Here, let me take your guitar," he offered. "We can either walk along Main Street in search of a place to eat or we can eat at the hotel—any preferences?"

"I'm content with eating at the same restaurant as this morning if you are."

"That works for me."

As soon as they were outside, Michael instinctively reached for her hand—a hand she was more than willing to give him. Aside from that matter of a slightly missing humor gene, she thought to herself, he is a keeper—at least if this weekend can be used as a barometer of his attributes, that is. And to add credence to her own feelings, Dottie believed that he's a keeper, as well.

Finishing up a relaxing dinner just before six allowed them no time for another nap—much to their mutual disappointment. It was becoming apparent, without having to openly say as much to each other, that naps and cuddling were their newly discovered priorities.

Given the lack of time for personal pursuits, Briana opted for a quick shower and a change of outfits. Being the professional that she was, she had brought along three outfits—one for each of her scheduled performances. Michael, while still feeling the exhaustion from last night's long surgery, decided to play it safe and read as opposed to attempting a short nap—a nap he was afraid he wouldn't want to wake up from anytime soon.

At six-thirty on the nose, he heard a light tapping on his door. "Come in," he said, with a raised voice as he rose from the couch.

"My, oh, my! Don't you look absolutely beautiful this evening," he commented, as soon as Briana entered his room.

"Thank you," she said, in response. She liked that he freely gave compliments.

"Ready to go?" he asked, while finding it difficult to take his eyes off her outfit—and her in general.

"Ready as I'll ever be," Briana answered, as they started heading out Michael's door.

"Good. Plan on singing without your crutch tonight?"

"Oh my God!" she exclaimed, as she hastily turned and headed back into her room.

"Have your mind on other things, do you?" he remarked, when she reappeared with guitar in hand.

"I think some of my brain cells got washed out in the shower," she quipped, while revealing a devilish grin.

"I'm thinking that you have plenty of brain cells to lose," he commented, taking the guitar from her hand.

"Thank you. I'll take that as one of your many compliments of late," she remarked, as the two of them headed out the door.

As was the case with the earlier performance, she started this one at the appointed hour. The gathered fans were as numerous as earlier in the day—and seemingly as enthusiastic. Those forced to watch and listen from the courtyard did not appear to take notice of the chilled night air—but who could blame them, thought Michael, as he took up the same spot behind the serving counters. She puts on a classy performance—even without benefit of an elaborate stage or flashing-colored lights and other professionally orchestrated props. The fans surely didn't care—they came to both see and hear their Tennessee idol. It would be safe to say, Michael continued in his thoughts, that the majority of those gathered tonight, in this out-of-the-way small town, had never experienced a major attraction the likes of Briana—and not one of them would soon forget her or her performance. When this weekend was concluded, neither would he. At the moment, he considered himself to be her biggest fan—for reasons that went far beyond her music.

Chapter Sixteen

WITH THE EVENING'S PERFORMANCE BEHIND HER, THE TWO OF THEM MADE their way back to the hotel. They both agreed that this had been an extremely long day, and the events of the past twenty-four hours had worn them down. And still ahead was tomorrow's one o'clock performance for Briana.

Michael was grateful for the fact that the hospital staff relieved him of any responsibilities related to the actual two-day event—including the speech he had previously prepared. They were deeply grateful for his proposing of the idea of the benefit in the first place and would work around his absence. The CEO of the hospital agreed to step in and deal both with the public and dignitaries that arrived for the daily tours in his place. He had fully planned on being there to assist in any way possible—but that all went out the window with the vice presidential surgery.

With the wind seemingly gone out of their sails, the walk back to the hotel was met with mutual silence. There appeared to be little room for conversation as they were both lost in their own private thoughts—he of her and she of him. When they finally reached her room, it became apparent to both of them that neither of them wanted to say goodnight—in spite of their exhaustion.

"Briana," Michael said softly, after setting her guitar case down on the hallway floor. "I have a favor to ask. You can say no to my request and I won't be offended."

"Yes, Michael, what is it?"

"Would it be too forward of me if I asked to kiss you goodnight?" he said warmly, while looking directly into her mesmerizing, cat-like eyes.

"Dr. Michael Thomas, do you realize that you just wasted fifteen seconds of valuable kissing time trying to get that out? And if you hadn't asked the question, then I would have taken the initiative on my own—without first having to ask any questions."

With that, he leaned down and placed his arms around her upper body, pulled her into him and kissed her. It turned out, however, to be more than your typical "goodnight kiss"—it was a kiss of unbridled passion; a passion that had been building up in him since she entered his room, and his bed, the night before. And she obviously felt the same as she fully engaged in kissing him back just as passionately, if not more so, as her arms fought to bring him closer into her body.

When he finally pulled his hungry mouth away from her equally hungry mouth, his arms refused to allow the air to flow back in between them. He raised his hand up to her head and gently pulled it onto his shoulder. If any hotel guests happened to walk past them, they didn't take notice—nor did they even care. This was their moment—and their moment alone.

After what seemed like forever, Michael slowly released his hold on her back. Placing his hands on both shoulders, he looked into her eyes and said, "Thank you. If I hadn't asked you for that kiss, I know I would have laid awake the entire night wondering what it would be like to taste the warmth and softness of your lips—and now I know."

"It is I who should be thanking you, Michael, for taking the initiative. Though if you hadn't, I would have. Sometimes we girls have to take control when dealing with our timid men."

"Being around you these past two days has been quite an experience for me."

"Tell me, Michael," Briana inquired softly, "has it been a good experience so far, or a really, really great experience?"

"It has obviously been a really, really great experience, thanks to you. You not only sing well, but you kiss even better."

The two of them knew that the evening had to end sometime, but neither one wanted to be the first to say goodnight—until Briana finally spoke up.

"What time would you like to meet for breakfast, Michael?"

"Around nine—or is that too early or too late for your appetite?"

"Nine is fine. By the time I change, shower and unwind, it will be well after ten before I hit the sack. A girl does need her sleep, you know."

"After last night and today's events, I'm all for sleeping in myself. Goodnight, Briana . . . sweet dreams."

Little did he know, however, that Briana wasn't about to settle for a simple goodnight. She reached up, placed her hands behind his head and pulled him down far enough that her lips met his. Michael, for his part, once again wrapped his arms around her back and pulled her into his chest. Given his unsatisfied desire for her, he had no intentions of releasing her until she made the first move to pull away. He has kissed his share of women before, and even made love to a few, but this was different—she was different. That, he knew without a shadow of a doubt, explained the rising passion that reverberated throughout his body. He wanted her—he needed all of her as he had never needed a woman before.

As much as he wanted to rip her clothes off right there in the hallway, he knew better. His mother's words came ringing back to him, "respect and self control." Respect the woman you're with and practice self-control, she told him right around the time he was halfway through college and seriously starting to date. But still, her kisses were driving him wilder as her tongue darted in, out and around the insides of his mouth. It didn't take him long to realize that she was passion-filled as well, as her body slowly started to gyrate against his. He knew that if she didn't pull away quickly, then he would have to, as he was mere seconds away from losing it all—so he reluctantly pulled away. His mother would be proud, he thought to himself, even though it left him feeling extremely frustrated.

When he looked into her eyes again, he saw a look he had never seen before. Her eyes were almost rolled back into her head as if she were trying to look back at herself. He seriously doubted that she had the capability to see anything at the moment. Her breathing was labored, and Michael was forced to tighten his grip on her as her knees started to buckle out from under her—not that his ability to remain upright was any better than hers right now.

He continued to hold her up until she was able to lock her knees back into place. Her eyes took a little longer, but they eventually returned to normal. Neither one of them had the energy left within them to speak. Moments later, however, Michael reached over and unlocked her door before picking up the guitar case and handing it to her.

This obviously meant "goodnight," she thought to herself. She knew that this couldn't go on forever—especially in a hotel hallway, but heavenly it was while it lasted, she admitted to herself. What if someone was to walk by who recognized her? Or worse yet, God forbid, take a picture of the two them engaged in an over-the-top kissing, hugging, lusting marathon? She could vividly envision tomorrow's headlines:

Briana Price Seduces Innocent Doctor

"What are you chuckling about, may I ask?" Michael inquired while looking at her.

"I was thinking of tomorrow's headlines if the paparazzi caught us in an impassioned kiss—on film, no less. It made me chuckle, that's all."

"May I ask how you envisioned the headlines reading?"

Doctor Seduces Innocent Briana Price

She replied, with a big grin on her face.

"Are you sure that it shouldn't read the other way around?"

"I beg your pardon," she responded, with a mischievous smile. "I'm a good girl, I am."

"You're obviously a fan of My Fair Lady."

"I am. I can relate to her."

"Well how about 'relating' to one hot shower and a warm bed to crawl into."

"Only if you're offering the warm bed," she said, with a look of innocence in her eyes. "In my bones I feel another one of those sleep-walking episodes coming on—quickly."

"Yes, I've studied that syndrome at great length. Short of taking drugs, the only known cure is to crawl into a prewarmed bed. Goodnight, Briana." With that, he gave her a peck on the lips, turned around, and headed for his own door.

Briana had yet to move a full minute later. What have I committed myself to? she wondered, flustered at the many images that ran through her mind. I don't need a hot shower—this girl is in serious need of an icy shower. She then turned around, walked in and closed the door quietly behind her.

While the hot shower felt refreshing, Michael was too tired to extend it beyond his usual three minutes. After throwing on a fresh pair of shorts, he laid out a fresh set of clothes for the morning. He finished up by brushing his teeth before eventually slipping under the covers. He was tired, and he knew it, but he had to force himself to stay awake on the off chance that Briana was serious about doing her sleep-walking routine once again. The thought of her lying next to him again sent his pulse racing. He was all for a repeat of the hallway passion scene—but this time in the privacy of his room.

A half-hour later, Briana gently tapped on the door. Not receiving an immediate response, she then quietly opened the door. Leaving the door wide open, she made her way over to "her" side of the bed. As she started to pull the covers back, she clearly heard the unmistakable sounds of breathing—not your normal breathing mind you, but the breathing of one who was fast asleep. But that was okay, she thought, remembering that it was she who fell asleep on him last night—now it was his turn—even though sleep wasn't exactly what she had in mind for the two of them tonight.

Asleep or not, she loosened her bathrobe and let it slip to the floor—revealing nothing but pure nakedness which the bathrobe once covered. In a stealthy manner, she eased her naked body down and under the covers. There was enough moonlight coming in from between the curtains that she could see Michael lying on his right side, facing away from her. She slowly inched her way over to where he lay, eventually pressing her bared breasts against his back. Her left arm then reached over his upright side before coming to rest on his chest. He was still asleep—victory, she thought.

Her claim to victory was fleeting, however, as Michael, having not reached the deepest part of sleep, slowly stirred awake. He lay there, motionless, until all of his senses had awakened. The first thing he noticed was her hand lying gently across his chest. He could also feel her exposed breasts pressed tightly against his back. Without removing her hand from his chest, he slowly rolled onto his back. He then slipped his left hand and arm under her shoulder and gently lifted her head onto his chest. With his remaining free hand, he cupped one of her breasts. This time, however, his hand upon her breast did not startle her as it did the night before. That was a clear signal, he thought, that she had come to bed with the full intentions of making love.

As with last night, neither one of them said a word—none were needed at a moment like this. Briana slipped her arm farther around his chest until it reached his back—before pulling herself closer to him. She wasn't about to let him get away from her tonight. This night was set aside for one thing—and one thing only.

Michael slowly and methodically began to massage her temple with his left hand and her right breast with his right hand—her nipple hardening almost immediately under his touch. We are heading to the next and final stage at last, he said to himself. It's not what he wants—it's not even what she wants—it's what the two of them desire as one. He liked the sounds of that—much like the song she sang earlier about finding true love. He firmly believed that his mother would approve. It would be but a few more moments, he told himself, before he would raise her lips to his and the passion of the hallway scene would start all over again. This time, however, it would not stop until they had both been intimately consumed by their natural passions.

When it came time, at least in his own mind, to raise her head to his, he recalled the same sound that he had heard from her last night—she was peacefully asleep. He couldn't, for the life of him, understand how this could happen two nights in a row. He could wake her, he thought, and bring her back to life with both his kisses and caresses. He could lower his head to her already hardened nipples and make them even harder by teasing them with his tongue and lips. She wanted it—he knew she wanted it. And God knew that he wanted it; one strategically placed touch from her would reveal that all too clearly.

The longer he thought about it, however, the more difficult it became for him carry out his longings. She was asleep. Would she really be awake enough to be a willing and active participant? Could he hold his head up high in the morning knowing that he possibly took advantage of an apparently sleep-deprived woman? No, he sadly answered—he could not. And with that answer, he reluctantly allowed himself to join her in sleep.

Chapter Seventeen

WHEN MICHAEL FINALLY AWOKE FROM HIS SLUMBERS AT EIGHT O'CLOCK, the first thing he noticed was that he was lying in bed alone. Glancing over at the door he noticed that it was closed, so he naturally assumed that somewhere during the night she had returned to her own room. Could she not sleep? Was she disappointed that he had not made love to her? The answers, unfortunately, would have to wait until they got together at the arranged hour of nine o'clock for breakfast.

At the appointed hour, Michael lightly tapped on their shared door. When she opened the door, the first thing he noticed was a well-rested looking young and beautiful lady.

"Hi there," she said. "I was wondering if you were going to wake up in time for our date."

"I guess I did sleep; obviously longer than you."

"That you did. I woke up a little before seven. Figured it was time to get ready for our last day here. My bags are packed and I'm ready to go."

"I vaguely remember those words—from an old song, if I recall."

"Your recall of songs and musicals is amazing. I can't seem to pull any lines on you, can I Michael?"

"And I'm hoping you never feel the need to."

"This conversation is one of those that could go on forever. Hungry?"

"Sleeping with the right woman makes me hungry," he said, with a grin and a wink of his eye.

"I'm referring to breakfast hungry, not me hungry."

"Sorry. I was hoping to try out a new pick-up line on you."

"Michael Thomas! You are already starting to be impossible to deal with this morning—let's go eat."

"Okay! Downstairs or that quaint little restaurant again?"

"Clear skies . . . sun's up . . . let's walk."

"I do know that you have sleep-walking down pat," he remarked. "Want to try your hand at walking/talking again?"

"Like I said, you're being impossible."

"Wait a minute . . . for some reason you look naked."

"I beg your pardon," she responded. "What is it with you and the word naked the past few days?"

"You've got clothes on, obviously, but you don't look completely dressed." Reaching into his pocket, he pulled out a small jewelry box and opened it.

"Oh my God! Those are so beautiful," she responded, in total awe and surprise. "Are those real diamonds and pearls?" she inquired.

"Real diamonds and pearls," he answered. "You deserve only the best for participating in the benefit. Now turn around please, and let me put the necklace on you." At that, she turned around as he slipped the pendant around her neck and clipped the two ends together.

"The pendant just adds to your beauty. Now why don't you slip into the bathroom and put the earrings on."

After taking the jewelry box from Michael's hand, she quickly headed off to her bathroom, reappearing moments later with earrings in place.

"Now you don't look so naked," Michael stated when she reappeared. "Besides looking even more beautiful," he added with all sincerity.

"Thank you. Right now I feel beautiful, thanks to you. But when did you find time to pick these up? Or did you bring them up with you from Nashville with the sole intent of winning me over with nice jewelry—and then taking advantage of me?"

"Actually, I bought them yesterday morning while you were busy taking up space in my bed."

"That was very considerate of you. Though if you had said that you bought them to take advantage of me, that would have been okay too," she remarked with a smile on her face. She then reached up, placing her hands around his neck before pulling his head down and proceeded to kiss him passionately.

"Wow!" Michael said when she eventually pulled away from him. "I may have to buy jewelry more often just to keep the rewards coming."

"Now look at who's being impossible again! Let's go eat. We can talk about taking advantage of each other on the way to the restaurant," she added.

"Okay, works for me—let's go."

After getting off the elevator, they passed through the lobby where a number of guests were in the process of checking out. Once on the sidewalk, Michael took her hand and turned her in the direction of the restaurant.

"So, I have to ask," Michael started out. "Were you at all disappointed that we didn't make love to each other last night, and into the wee hours of the morning?"

"Yes I was," came her reply. "But I don't blame you. I'm the one who apparently fell asleep on you—again. Damned if your massaging of my temple doesn't put me to sleep. Last night, plus an afternoon on the couch, I might add. And the massaging of my breast just speeded up the process."

"Sorry! I'll never massage you like that again."

"Don't you dare say never; I liked it. I liked it a whole lot, as a matter of fact. I just need to make sure that I'm more awake next time—not so sleepy."

"Does that imply that there will be a next time?" he asked, with a note of hopefulness in his voice.

"I hope so," she replied, "even if I have to take the initiative and attack you; asleep or awake."

"Now that would most definitely be a new experience for me," he said, with a chuckle.

"As making love would be a new experience for me. Yes, I'm a virgin . . . but I'm taking an educated guess here that you already figured that out."

"Absolutely nothing wrong with being a virgin; we all were at one time—and only one time," he said, with a laugh—which in turn caused her to laugh.

At that particular moment, Briana felt as though she were on cloud nine. She liked being around Michael. Not only was he both strikingly handsome and a skilled doctor with compassion, she thought to herself, but he treats me as a lady would wanted to be treated—with respect. He didn't put me down—even when I might have deserved a scolding—which admittedly I have on a few occasions already this weekend. I felt comfortable when telling him that I was a virgin. He lightly joked about it, but the joke was not aimed directly at me in a belittling way. He's a terrific kisser—a plus in any girl's book. Two nights in a row he had the opportunity to take advantage of me physically, sexually—but he chose not to. God knows that his hormones were probably at their highest peak during those two nights in bed together—I know mine were—and yet he put my needs above his own. I failed him in bed and yet he still apparently wants me. How could

I have been so lucky to have found him? she continued in her private thoughts. Oh wait, he found me first—I like that even better.

Following an excellent meal and delightful conversation between them, they made their way back to the hotel for checkout. Because of her one o'clock performance, Michael prearranged to have their bags stored at the hotel until their actual departure.

Reaching her room, Michael unlocked the door and followed her inside. "Briana," he said, "come here, please."

She wasn't sure why he asked her to come back to him, but she wasn't going to ask. He remained in place until she stopped about a foot away from him. When she stopped, he grabbed ahold of her, pulled her tight against him, and kissed her. Not any kiss, mind you, but one of those kisses that a girl would not soon forget. He was gentle while at the same time forceful—he had been fantasizing about this kiss while sitting across from her at the breakfast table. In the absence of taking her to bed, this kiss would have to last him until they returned home later this evening.

Briana felt his passion and desperately wished that she could satisfy his obvious hunger for her. She instinctively knew that she had a lot to learn when it came to making a man happy, but she was more than willing to do whatever it took to make "her Michael" happy. She had only to look as far as her own parents to understand what a happy relationship was all about—they were her role model for successful relationships—much as Michael's parents had been to him. And right now she was giving back to Michael what he asked for, her kisses. If he wanted anything else, she was willing to give him that too.

Following a series of deep-throated kisses that reached seemingly clear to their toes, coupled with four hands searching each other out, they reluctantly pulled away. Neither one of them wanted it to end— but end they knew it must. In the back of their minds, they both knew that last minute packing and changing into her performance outfit had to be dealt with, as checkout time was only a half-hour away.

Looking up into his eyes, Briana said, "Sorry."

"Sorry for what?"

"For not taking care of your needs," she answered, apologetically.

"Don't be—we both have unrealized needs. Our time will come and, in some respects, we will be grateful for the wait, and the passions will only be greater for it."

"There's a time, there's a moment," she stated.

Sounds like another lyrical line you picked up from somewhere."

"I did, as a matter of fact. It was written by Michael Lynch, I believe. A song I picked up on in church—one of my favorites to both listen to and sing, but not on stage."

"Maybe you should write a song titled, Stolen Kisses. You know . . . a song that would capture where we are at this moment in time."

"I might do that," Briana said. "Now we both need to get ready, and I'm thinking that you have more packing to do than I do. I pretty much finished mine up while you were still sawing logs, Mr. Lazy Bones."

"You got me on that one. So, on that note of dismissal, I'll disappear off to my lonely room, pack, and freshen up before taking our collective bags down to the lobby and check out. How about we meet down in the lobby at eleven?"

"I'll be there. I wish we had a little more time," she added wistfully.

"That makes two of us, but duty and obligation call. There will be more tomorrows."

"Now there's a song title if ever I heard one," she responded. "Mind if I steal it for a song someday?" she asked, jokingly.

"Be my guest. But be nice if you happen to allude to me in the song," he said playfully.

"Only happy songs where you're concerned, Michael, only happy songs. Now get out of here," she said, teasingly, given that neither one of them wanted to be alone.

Before leaving, Michael grabbed the oversized suitcase that she had already packed, and took it into his room.

Without fail, Briana came into the lobby at exactly eleven with her guitar case in one hand and her handbag in the other. The first person she noticed was Michael sitting in one of the lobby chairs reading the paper. When he noticed her, he rose and took the guitar case from her hand.

"You look absolutely stunning," Michael commented, as they both walked over to the counter and handed her handbag to the desk clerk. "Are you sure you wouldn't like to go back up to our rooms?" he said quietly, with a wink of his eye.

"Michael Thomas! You behave yourself right now!"

"Hey, can you blame a guy? You are absolutely beautiful in your performance get-up. You don't even have to sing a word on stage and I would still fall head over heels in love with you."

She was startled. He used the word "love" for the first time. It wasn't exactly an "I Love You," but it was a decent first start, she thought. But then again she realized, neither had she used those same words before—outside of in the pages of her diary, that is. Slow and easy, she reminded herself—slow and easy—but not too slow and risk losing him.

"Earth to Briana!" Michael said, taking her from her thoughts.

"Sorry!" She stated, "I was thinking of the performance; possible changes and all that," she fibbed.

"We've got an hour and a half to kill. We can either sit in the lobby and read or talk, or we can wander around town and do some dreaded window-shopping or, we can wander directly over to the hospital and see what's going on."

"So many choices, what's a girl to do?" she exclaimed, in jest. "I know—why don't we go over to the hospital and see if Dottie and the vice president are still there?"

"Excellent idea. I've been kind of curious myself."

Taking her hand in his, they walked together out of the lobby and headed in the direction of the hospital. The best information on the vice president, Michael assumed, would be had at the Intensive Care nurse's station.

"Hi Martha. And how are you this fine Sunday morning?" Michael greeted her with a big smile. Martha was, without question, one of the oldest employees of the hospital. She could have retired years ago but, with the loss of her husband some years back, the thought of retirement no longer appealed to her. She needed to stay busy and loved mingling with people, especially Michael.

"Well, Michael," she replied, with a smile to match his. "I heard that you were around these parts, but I'd about given up hope, thinking you no longer wanted to romance this beautiful body of mine anymore." Looking over at Briana, she continued. "Oh wait, I think I know why—have you been two-timing me, by any chance?"

"Martha, you know full well that you're my one true love. Why do you think I keep flying up here whenever I get the chance? I only have eyes for you until time immemorial."

"And who is this pretty competition you brought along? If a jealous woman may be allowed to ask."

"This is Briana, Briana Price, a singer. Briana, this is Martha, the longest serving employee of this hospital."

"Hi Martha," Briana said, with a smile. "Always glad to meet my competition . . . now I know the real reason Michael flies up here so often."

"We can share, dear. Be sure, however, to leave me some leftovers—

don't totally wear him out before sending him up here. I don't want my men falling asleep on me."

"Oh, I won't, trust me," Briana answered.

Both she and Michael looked at each other at Martha's comment about "falling asleep on me."

"Anyway, Martha," Michael continued, "Briana has been the sole entertainment for our benefit. You know, the benefit that hopes to raise enough money to keep you gainfully employed and off the streets, and away from eligible bachelors who are screaming for your hand."

"You tell a pretty good story, Michael, that's why I like you. But I'm still holding out for those three magic words every woman wants to hear. The hell with those old geezers out there."

"I'll grow old someday too, you know; then what becomes of me?"

"Oh, I'm sure that other young, studly doctors like yourself will pass through these doors just as you currently do."

"Martha, my dear, I am hurt knowing that I can be replaced so easily."

"Not to worry, Michael, I'm thinking you have at least thirty good years left in you."

Briana was amused by this back and forth bantering. She took an immediate liking to Martha—even though she was openly trying to steal her man away from her.

"So, Michael," Martha inquired. "What brings you here outside of playing with my heartstrings?"

"We came by to get the latest update on the vice president. And if anyone knows, it would be you."

"He's apparently doing fine. Those Walter Reed docs wheeled him out of here about an hour ago on a stretcher for the trip back. It looks as though you did a fine job of patching him up—even if he is a Democrat."

"A team patched him up, Martha, you know that."

"Michael, when are you ever going to accept credit for what you do?"

"When I work alone, Martha, then I will."

Looking directly at Briana, Martha remarked, "Have you ever found Michael to be impossible at times?"

"Most of the time," Briana responded in concurrence.

"Okay you two—why don't you find someone else to pick on. Someone without feelings," Michael countered, in an attempt to change the conversation away from him.

"We girls have to stick together, right Briana?"

"Right you are, Martha," Briana replied, still grinning.

"Oh my!" Martha exclaimed. "I almost forgot something. Here's an envelope addressed to the two of you from Mrs. Stevenson. She dropped it off on her way out," she added, while handing up an envelope to Michael.

After saying their goodbyes to Martha, they proceeded over to a couple of chairs located across from the nurse's station. Sitting down, Michael then handed the envelope over to Briana. "Go ahead, you read it."

"Are you sure?"

"It's addressed to the two of us, isn't it?"

"Okay," she answered, as she carefully opened the envelope and began reading the letter aloud:

Dear Dr. Thomas & Briana,

There aren't enough words in the English language to express my (our) heartfelt thanks for saving the life of my husband. And to you Briana, for being both a supportive listening post and a friend when I needed one.

Your sense of humor went a long way toward relieving the stresses I was feeling—don't ever stop laughing. I assure you, keep laughter in both of your hearts at all times, for it will smooth out the rough patches that we all encounter in our marriages. And Briana, don't ever stop telling those wonderful stories that seem to just pop out of your head.

Once my husband has fully recovered, we would be most honored to have you over for dinner some evening when you are in town—no other guests—only you two.

Much love & best wishes to the two of you,

Dottie

P.S.—And don't forget that invitation. And Briana, remember what I shared with you.

"Yikes!" Briana silently exclaimed to herself. "Did she have to include that P.S.?"

"Nice letter," Michael said. "Though I would feel guilty accepting the invitation; I may write and tell her that."

"Michael! Whatever for?" Briana inquired, with a puzzled look on her face.

"It was a team effort. If there is to be a dinner, the whole team needs to be invited."

"Michael, Michael, Michael. Accept praise when it is given out."

"Like I told Martha, Briana, when I become a team of one, I will. Until then, it doesn't feel right."

"Your Martha gal was absolutely right about something else, Michael. You. Are. Impossible."

"Briana, let me give you a brief background for my behavior. My parents were both highly educated, dedicated doctors; but you already know that. They seldom took individual credit for anything, especially where others were involved in their accomplishments. They gained more respect and admiration from their peers and others by accepting accolades as a team for their accomplishments than others did as individuals. I've seen it firsthand—back then and now. It's a part of who I am, so please, don't try to change that one part of me. Anything else you may want to change—go for it."

Briana was silent for a moment, before leaning over and planting a kiss on Michael's cheek. She was proud of him. Keeping one's ego in check is not the usual character trait displayed by those in her own entertainment field—at least for the majority of them.

"Michael, it's noon already. I think I'll wander over and help Bill set up and practice some tunes I've been working on."

"Okay! While you're doing that, I'll go over to the main foyer and check out all of the displays and mingle with the visitors."

Once up from their seats, Michael leaned down and gave Briana a quick kiss on the lips.

"Thank you for the kiss. Will I see you at the performance?"

"Wouldn't miss it for the world—and don't be jealous," he added, "but I understand the headliner is some beautiful, sexy chick with a great voice. I may have a problem keeping my eyes—and my thoughts—off of her, though she reportedly is well known for falling asleep on her men."

"Michael Thomas!" She exclaimed, while at the same time displaying a huge smile on her face. "You are absolutely impossible today." With that, she picked up her guitar case and headed down the hallway.

After milling around the various displays, Michael went over to the cafeteria just in time to catch her opening song. He didn't have to look at his watch to know that it was exactly one o'clock. Some aspects of her personality were predictable. Being on time was one of those that he appreciated—not to mention her uncontrollable episodes of sleep-walking.

At twenty past two, the overflow crowd began to disperse at the conclusion of her final encore number. Michael then made his way over to the stage, but waited below while she conversed with Bill the Piano Man. Having finished with whatever she had to say to Bill, she picked up her guitar case and came over to where Michael was waiting below the makeshift stage. To his utter amazement, she set the case back down before immediately jumping off the stage and into his arms.

"Hi there," she said, while being cradled in his arms.

"Aren't you aware, young lady, that a lot of people just witnessed that little display of affection on your part?"

"You know what, Michael," she replied, while still smiling, "right now I don't care. I'm happy where I am in my life . . . thanks to you. Besides, if anyone asks, I'll tell them that you're my personal body-guard, assigned to look lustfully after the welfare of my body. I will also inform them that you miraculously saved my sexually-deprived body from becoming physically hurt beyond repair."

"Would you explain one thing to me, please," Michael asked, as he set her down on her feet. "Tell me how and where all of these off-the-wall thoughts and comments come from? You know, the ones that are forever spewing forth from your extremely beautiful and kissable lips? The ones that even Dottie made reference to in her letter?"

"I don't know. You're the doctor, you tell me."

"I would, but medical science isn't that far advanced yet. As soon as we get back, I will financially back a research team to study your body and mind for the answer."

"Sorry, but that's your job, and your job alone—to study my body, that is—and so far you've been off to a good start. But your own personal research is not complete yet. Your proposed research does include the 'hands on' approach, does it not?" she asked, ever so suggestively.

"Oh, absolutely." he responded. "There are known pressure points on a person's body that, when correctly massaged, can send them out of this world. It takes years and years of practice, however, before perfection is achieved."

"This may come as a surprise to you, doctor, but I happened to have years of free time available to devote to this sensuous, enticing study you're proposing. If I didn't know better, oh dear doctor, I would venture a guess that you're just trying to take advantage of another helpless patient. In this case, that would be me."

"You know what, young and beautiful potential-patient, you keep this kind of talk up and I'm going to be forced to rebook our hotel room for one more night."

"I'd be more than happy to begin your research as soon as possible—in fact, the sooner the better. There is, however, one slight problem with that."

"I can't wait to hear your excuse this time."

"Don't blame the last two nights on me. If you hadn't intentionally massaged my temple and/or my breasts, I wouldn't have fallen asleep on you. Besides, I think you purposely put me to sleep so that I wouldn't make love to you—probably figured that you couldn't handle the likes of one such as me."

"You still haven't answered why you can't spend one more night here, Miss Storyteller."

"Oh—you've got me so wound up I don't know what I'm thinking or saying anymore. Tomorrow, at eight I believe, I'm gathering with my fellow musicians in the recording studio for the entire day. Locked up, as they say. Though," she added with a twinkle in her eye, "a night with you might result in some brand new love songs."

"Or songs about falling asleep on your potential lover."

"Really funny, Michael. I write all of my songs, as you're already aware from Googling me, but some things are better left unsung, at least for the time being. A girl can't share all of her secrets with her fans, you know. If she did, then there'd be no mysteries left to keep people curious."

"Well then, it looks like we're off to the hotel, grab our bags and a cab and head for the airport. The mysteries of our bodies will have to remain mysteries until another day."

Chapter Eighteen

THE CONVERSATION WAS LEFT RIGHT THERE AS THEY PROCEEDED BACK TO the hotel for their luggage before heading to the airport. Following his customary preflight responsibilities, they established liftoff at four forty-five with the sun hanging low in the sky behind them.

Once the plane had achieved its assigned cruising altitude of 38,000 feet, Michael spoke to Briana through their respective headsets. It came as no surprise to Michael that it was Briana who suggested that she wear a headset as well. "Pilot to copilot—do you read me? Over."

"Read you loud and clear, Fly Boy. Over and back to you, Rover," she replied, with laughter.

"Boy, have you ever got a lot to learn. Would you like me to call ahead to Frankie and see about having dinner ready for us when we arrive? Over."

"Copilot to Fly Boy. That's a negative. Got to unpack, gather up my music, call my mom, get a good night's sleep, alone I might add, and rise by six. I'll take a rain check on the free meal though. Over and in."

"It is not over and in. Try over and out."

"I kind of like over and in, mind you. Over and out makes it sound as though it is all over with. Back to you, Fly Boy."

"Briana! If you're thinking what I think you're thinking, then you should be ashamed of yourself. It's a good thing that I had the foresight to switch off the controllers from hearing any of this. I had the premonition, right when I handed you the headset, that something like this would happen, and you didn't disappoint. Dottie is absolutely right about you."

"Sorry, but you bring out the devil in me. You have awakened my senses, as someone once said."

"You're thinking of the John Denver song, You Fill Up My Senses, I believe."

"Okay. I'll try to behave myself . . . but no guarantees."

"Thanks. It's not easy on me either, but I need to focus on getting us home safely or there will no tomorrows for either one of us to share."

At ten after six, they found themselves inside Michael's hangar. While he was in the process of opening the exit door and lowering the stairs, Briana came up behind him and wrapped her arms around him.

"Michael," Briana purred, while continuing to hold him tightly against her. "I'm begging you for one last kiss—a kiss to remember you by until we see each other again."

Turning around, he grabbed onto both of her shoulders and said, "You never have to beg for a kiss; or anything else for that matter."

"I know . . . it just sounds sexier that way."

At that, he pulled her close, wrapped his arms around her back and kissed her as passionately as he had done in the hotel hallway. This time, however, he didn't hold back—he brought his hands from her back and slipped them under her loose fitting blouse until they came to rest on her two breasts; her nipples hardening instantly under his sensuous, massaging fingers. She in turn slid her hands down to his buttocks and pulled him into her so that nothing separated the two of them any longer. As his tongue continued to move around hers, she felt him, rock hard, pressing tightly against her. She was hungry for Michael. All of Michael.

After a few minutes of kissing and groping, she was rapidly losing control of her physical self—and she knew it. She was relishing this never-before-experienced feeling of excitement that was quickly rushing through her body. This seemingly unstoppable feeling of arousal caused her to gyrate around and against his hardness. She had no idea, being new in these matters, that being up against a man like this could drive a woman to unbelievably frenzied heights. She quickly found that she couldn't stop herself. Nor did she want to stop herself. She wanted to go for it—all of it. She wanted Michael to take her—all of her—right here in the plane—anywhere. Even should he attempt to slow down or stop her, she wasn't about to let him. Whatever the feeling was that was taking hold of her entire body, she desperately needed to bring it to its end.

Without much in the way of warning, she totally lost it. Michael knew the very moment it happened as her body started going into uncontrollable convulsions. He pulled his mouth away from hers and rested her head against his shoulder as she continued convulsing. It would be a full minute before her body eventually quieted down. He somehow sensed that she could no longer stand on her own two feet, so he picked her up and took over to the nearest seat. He sat down with her cradled in his arms as her arms tightly wound themselves around his neck.

She began to cry, at first softly, before unleashing a flood of tears which fell against his neck with each burst of sobbing. Michael fully understood what was happening—and he was happy for her. The fact that his own needs were not met was of little concern at the moment—he knew that they would be met eventually. She was a virgin—this was unfamiliar territory for her. As a matter of medical fact, he reflected, she was still a virgin.

Ten minutes later, she was at peace with herself—so at peace, in fact, that he could have sworn he heard, once again, the distinct sounds of sleep slipping from between her lips. He wasn't sure whether to let her sleep or to wake her—so he opted to let her sleep. Fifteen minutes later, she began slowly waking up from her well-deserved mini-nap, but he continued to gently hold her head in place.

"Oh my God!" she whispered softly against his neck. "Where am I?"

"Right now you're situated on my lap . . . still on the plane. Twenty-five minutes ago you were somewhere beyond the heavens."

"Oh my God!" she whispered once again. "I had no idea it could feel so good—good doesn't even begin to describe it. Now I know what they mean when someone refers to 'seventh heaven.' I am so relaxed I'm not even sure I can stand up, let alone walk."

"No need to rush anything. Take your time; enjoy the moment."

"Oh Michael . . . I don't know whether to feel happy or ashamed."

"Don't ever feel ashamed about your sexuality, Briana. God gave it to mankind as a gift, meant to enjoy and to be shared. All with the right man, of course . . . so please, don't ever see it as something shameful or demeaning."

"You seem to have a knack for putting me at ease—if not asleep."

"I do my best, especially where and when it involves you. Do you feel up to testing out your sea legs yet?"

"I think so, though I'd rather stay in your arms longer—say until tomorrow about this same time."

Michael couldn't help but chuckle at the thought of holding her until tomorrow. "Okay, I'm going to lift you over the armrest slowly. When I do, plant your feet on the floor and try to stand up on your own. I'll be holding on so don't worry about the possibility of falling."

With Michael's assistance, she managed to place her feet on the floor and stand up on her own. Michael then scooted out of the seat and stood behind her, holding firmly onto her waist.

"I'm okay now, thanks. I think I will mosey on back to the powder room to freshen up a bit. I certainly don't want Frankie seeing me like this."

"Hold on a second—I'll be right back." He then disappeared into the cockpit and came back with her oversized handbag in his hand.

"You think of everything, don't you, Michael?"

"I've already told you, my mother taught me more things than the average mother would have, especially where it concerned women. And you don't need to worry about Frankie . . . your car is in the garage, so you can leave from there."

"I never thought about that. Do you think he'll be upset by my not coming up to say goodnight?"

"I'll let him know that you were running late. He'll understand."

"Okay. I'll be back in a jiff."

Michael then set about doing what he'd tried to do awhile ago—opening the door and letting the stairs down. Once the stairs were fully deployed, he went back into the cockpit to collect his flight bag, returning to the cabin as Briana was exiting the powder room.

"No evidence of any serious crime having been committed on that face anymore; you clean up well. Though I do notice a slight redness in your cheeks. Either you have high blood pressure or you have been engaged in some serious exercise recently."

If she wasn't blushing before, she most certainly was now. "It's your entire fault, you know. I was trying to escape the plane, but you refused to open the door until after you had your way with me. You should be ashamed of yourself, Michael Thomas."

"That's funny, I don't quite recall it happening that way. Maybe my memory is failing me. It's been doing quite a bit of that over the course of the past three days, but it only seems to fail me when I'm around you."

"Didn't your mother ever teach you never to argue with a woman? Even when we're wrong, which we seldom are, we're right."

"Can't say that she ever did. Speaking of which, if we don't get you moving and home soon, you won't be talking to your mother at all this evening. Unless you plan to wake her up, that is."

After unloading their luggage from the cargo hold, Michael whisked them along to the garage. On the ride, his mind was filled with the notion of having to say goodbye. The vice president's accident aside, he felt as though he had experienced the best three days of his life; and, if he were any judge of women, he had to believe that it ranked pretty high on Briana's list of best weekends also—if not the first few days, then surely the conclusion. If only, he privately wished, they were both far away on some tropical island together; maybe someday, he thought—hopefully sooner than later.

Pulling up alongside her car, he quickly unloaded her suitcase, handbag and guitar into the trunk as she stood there watching. After closing the trunk, he walked over to where she was standing, took hold of her and kissed her—not fiercely as on the plane, but passionately, nevertheless. They hadn't talked about when they would get together next, so he made sure that this kiss would carry him through until they did. She hadn't even driven off yet, and he could feel the pains of missing her already. When he finally pulled his mouth away from hers, he noticed a single tear rolling slowly down her cheek. He leaned down and kissed the tear away.

"Cry not, my love, for the morrows shall bring hope and sunshine," he said softly.

"Well, aren't we poetic all of a sudden," Briana said, grinning. "Where did you steal that line from?"

"Not sure—it somehow came out without much thought on my part."

"Well then, keep it coming—we girls like poetry, jewelry and flowers from our men. But then I'm sure that your mother already mentioned those things to you," she added.

"I'm sure that she intentionally let those words slip from her mouth from time to time; but always in front of my father, of course. You know that we're stalling, don't you?"

"I know . . . I never realized how much a goodbye could hurt. Right now I want to climb into your bed and lie beside you again. But this time I want to make love to you . . . and you to me. I want to feel you inside of me . . . wanting me, needing me, having your way with me."

"I do need you and want you . . . badly. But those needs and wants will have to wait for another day, another time."

Resisting the urge to take her right there in the garage, he pulled her tightly against his body. Just as quickly, he released his hold on her, took her by the hand and walked her to her car door. He then leaned down, kissed her gently on the lips before opening the door. She quietly slipped into her seat and Michael closed the door. Nothing more was said. He watched as she fired up the car, backed up slowly, before eventually exiting the garage for home. He waited until she was out of sight before loading his suitcase and flight bag onto the elevator and disappearing straight up to his room. He was hungry, but he wasn't quite ready to face Frankie just yet. Frankie had been around long enough to recognize the look that most likely remained deeply embedded on his face.

Chapter Nineteen

THOUGH EXHAUSTED FROM THE WEEKEND'S ACTIVITIES, SLEEP DID NOT come easily for Michael. When it did eventually take him, it didn't let loose of him until eight the next morning; he couldn't remember the last time he'd slept in that late—except after each of his missions, maybe. He had gone to bed thinking of Briana and waking up was no different. When he awoke, he found himself clutching his extra pillow as if he were holding Briana in his arms again—or so he wished.

His senses quickly picked up the smell of freshly brewed coffee as he came down the stairs and into the kitchen. Frankie was standing over the stove in the process of preparing breakfast.

Without turning around, Frankie said, "Good morning, Michael; you apparently slept well."

"Long weekend," came his short reply, as he poured himself a cup of coffee.

"So I read in the morning paper. You take off to do a benefit and you end up saving the life of a vice president; and, according to the paper, you're somewhat of a national hero. Fortunately for you, however, the attentions of the media have now switched over to Walter Reed. Hope you enjoyed your fleeting moment of fame."

"Didn't go looking for any fame, Frankie . . . you know me better than that. Hopefully the others were mentioned as well."

"Yes they were—briefly. How were Briana's performances? Did she bring in the crowds?"

"Bring in the crowds is an understatement. She packed both the cafeteria and courtyard to overflowing, for all three performances, I might add."

"So all in all it was a good weekend for the hospital . . . and apparently for you as well," Frankie said, with a little added emphasis.

Michael intentionally refused to acknowledge the last part of Frankie's comment. "The benefit itself was well attended. It will be awhile, however, before the final results are in. With any luck, we'll have brought in enough to meet our goals."

"You've come back with an added glow to your face, so obviously you were pleased with the events of the weekend—the ordeal with the vice president being the exception."

"All in all, yes."

"Any problems with the plane?"

"Flew like a bird. Why the interest in the plane?"

"Oh, nothing," he answered, evasively. "Kind of thought that maybe something was wrong . . . took you almost a full hour to come up to the house after pulling into the hangar. Never known you to hang back that long before, that's all. Then to go directly up to your room without stopping off to at least say goodnight first; a little out of character for you."

Michael was at a loss for an explanation without having to reveal what actually took place out on the plane. He wasn't the quick thinker that Briana appeared to be in these situations. God, but how she could fire off the quips, even if they were mostly filled with little white lies.

"Briana and I were sitting on the plane discussing the events of the weekend, that's all."

"And I was born yesterday," he fired back, not wanting to let Michael off the hook—but deciding to do so after noticing the increased redness in Michael's cheeks. "Your breakfast is ready—here or in the dining room?"

"In the dining room, please," Michael replied, as he got up from his chair. That was a safe place, he figured, knowing that Frankie would leave him alone in the dining room—which he did. Michael knew that Frankie had reason to doubt that the weekend ended up being only about the benefit or the vice president. He could sometimes hide his feelings from his parents—but never with Frankie; he was too good at reading minds, as he was at solving murder mysteries. This brief encounter with "Frankie the Inquisitor" in the kitchen was making him feel more like a child than an adult. He gave serious consideration to coming right out and telling Frankie about what transpired this weekend between he and Briana—but obviously not revealing everything.

Shortly after breakfast, he decided to go down to one of the local free clinics. All things considered, helping out at the clinic would, he hoped, take his mind off of Briana. He would love to have given her a call, but knew that she was going to be tied up all day in the recording studio.

Midway through the day at the clinic, his cell phone began to vibrate in his pocket. He was wishfully hoping it was Briana calling during one of her recording breaks. Glancing at the phone, however, he immediately recognized the number as coming from DWB. He found the call surprising as their next trip was not due to start until early February—unless they were calling in regard to the benefit in Etenia.

"Michael," he answered.

"Hi Michael, it's Sandy. We heard that you had quite a turnout in Etenia this past weekend . . . congratulations."

"Thanks, Sandy. I have a hunch this call is more than about the benefit, right Sandy."

"You always were the perceptive type, Michael. And yes, you are correct. We know that you signed up for a mission in February, but we're in desperate need of help right now in Bolivia—La Paz, to be exact. As you've probably read or heard, they've been hit by a once in every 25 year flood—twice now. As with the previous flood, they reported breakouts of both dengue fever and malaria. Hospitals and clinics servicing the poor have, in many cases, been severely damaged or destroyed. You've been in these situations before, so you know well what major flooding can do."

"Yes I have, a couple dozen times. Maybe more."

"We've got three doctors and four nurses already lined up. We've already gained clearance by the Bolivian government to come in and help. I won't lie to you, you know me better than that; we need both you and your plane. If you have other commitments, I understand and respect that too. We can always fly them and their equipment in commercially."

Michael immediately thought to himself that this request was unfortunate timing. There was the issue of Briana—that was his one and only "commitment" right now. This request was not a situation that he'd had to face before; the needs of a flooded city and countryside as opposed to his own needs—and those of Briana's. Why now of all times?

"Michael, are you still there?" Sandy inquired.

"Sorry Sandy, just trying mentally to pull up my commitments from this tired brain of mine. It's been a long weekend. When do we leave?"

"Thank you, Michael. We're tentatively shooting for Wednesday. That will give us time to make the arrangements here for others to fly to Nashville, along with flying in the standard medical supplies you'll need. And I know that you'll need time to make your flight-plan arrangements. I'll send you an e-mail later this afternoon with all of the particulars—names of those going with you, when they'll be arriving in Nashville, etc."

"I'll look forward to their arrival. We apparently have an arrival date in La Paz; do we have a departure date?"

"We have a two-week commitment from the others . . . back on the fourteenth. Is that a problem, Michael?"

"No, not at all—simply need to reschedule some minor commitments I had previously made. They can be easily rearranged," he lied.

"Good. And Michael . . . thanks for taking this assignment on such short notice. You know we try not to do that, but disasters only happen when we least expect them."

"I'll look forward to your e-mail, Sandy . . . and let the others know that I look forward to working with them."

"Will do, Michael, thanks."

"Be sure to give my love to the girls."

"Will do. Bye!"

"Bye!"

This was obviously the last phone call Michael had expected to receive. He had looked forward to spending one-on-one time with Briana this week—and hopefully making love to her. If she didn't call him after the recording session ended, whenever that was, then he would call her. He was looking forward to hearing her voice, but not the sharing of this most recent news. He could only imagine that she would not take it well. In fact, she just might tell him to kiss off—much like previous women had done due to his various commitments that took him outside of Nashville.

How he made it safely home from the clinic, he wasn't sure. His mind was so wrapped up in Briana that he didn't remember the actual drive home. He did remember calling Frankie, however, to let him know that he was on his way—the reward being that he was able to sit down to a much-needed hot meal shortly after arriving home.

"Frankie," Michael said, halfway through dinner, "I'll be flying out of here on Wednesday for La Paz, and seven others will be joining me. We'll be back on the fourteenth."

"I don't recall any La Paz trip on your calendar," Frankie commented at the unexpected news.

"Got a call from DWB while at the clinic—another case of severe flooding. Can't say I'm overjoyed at going, but I've never quite learned how to say no yet. Anyway, medical equipment and supplies should be arriving sometime tomorrow. If you can run them out to the hangar, I would appreciate it. For the larger items, as usual, have the drivers take them directly out to the hangar via the back road. You know what to do for those packages labeled for refrigeration. I'll call the maintenance folks first thing tomorrow and have them service and refuel the plane. Not sure where the others are coming from, but they should stagger in Wednesday morning at the latest. Sandy will be sending me their arrival times via e-mail this afternoon. I'll work up and file the flight plans tomorrow . . . that should about do it."

"Aren't you forgetting something?" asked Frankie, with that certain tone of voice that let Michael know that he was being coy.

"I'll bite. What's that?"

"Briana; you'll need to break the news to her."

"Frankie!" Michael said, wanting to leave the issue off the table. "I'll be sure to give her a call . . . maybe tonight if I get around to it." He immediately regretted his response to Frankie's question, knowing full well that Frankie was smarter than to accept his statement as an honest answer—but the damage was already done.

"Maybe you should call her as you're taxiing down the runway;

wouldn't want to disappoint her any earlier than you have to, now would you?"

"Okay, Frankie, I give up . . . you win. Yes, Briana and I have become what they say in today's vernacular, 'an item.' Are you satisfied now that you pried it out of me?"

"Thanks for confirming something I already knew. Even this morning I could see that certain look on your face and in your eyes."

"Do I get your nod of approval, Father Frankie?"

"You most certainly do. I liked her from the first time I laid eyes on her; call it a 'father's intuition.' Now make sure that you call her right after you finish with your dinner—as if I even need to remind you. Other than that, you know that I won't interfere in your relationship; I never have in the past. You're an adult, after all."

"Thanks for the vote of confidence . . . that I'm an adult, that is. Now, if you'll excuse me, I'll head upstairs and place a call." Michael then rose from the table, leaving part of his dinner behind, and took the stairs two at a time to his study.

His call to Briana's private phone rang four times before going to voice mail. He thought of leaving a detailed message concerning his mission Wednesday, but then thought the better of it as he wanted to hear her voice again.

"Briana! This is Michael . . . before you retire for the evening, please give me a call. Until then, bye. P.S.— I hope your recording time in the studio went well today . . . missed you . . . bye again."

Setting the phone down, he wondered if she missed him as much as he missed her—of course she did, he quickly concluded. A moment later he picked his cell phone back up and spent the next half-hour figuring out how to download a distinctive ring tone for Briana's number.

After a number of false starts, he eventually succeeded before picking up a journal to read—falling fast asleep in the process. At nine-thirty, he was startled awake by her unique ring tone—which happened to be one of her songs.

"Hi there, beautiful," he said into the phone.

"Hi yourself, handsome," she fired back with a note of excitement in her voice. "I noticed your missed call on the way out of the studio, but decided to wait until I got home before calling you. Wanted to climb into my cozy, warm bed when I called you. How'd your day go?"

"Uneventful; spent the better part of the day down at one of the free clinics. How about your long day in the studio?"

"I would have to say that it was extremely productive, actually. It took the entire day to record four songs—one of which I wrote last night about you and me."

"Say what? And here I was under the false impression that I would not become fodder for one of your songs."

"Not to worry; I kept it generic. Nothing in the song will tie you back to it. Your reputation is safe—for now anyway," she added, teasingly.

"And does this song have a title, by any chance, just so that I'll recognize it when I hear it?"

"Well of course it does, silly. It's called, Take My Hand."

"Care to sing a few lines?"

"Sorry . . . no sneak previews. You'll just have to wait. I plan on releasing it as a single shortly, but not until I judge how it's received during the first few weeks of my tour. After a few weeks of trying it out on my poor fans, I should have a good feel for whether to release it or not. In the meantime, because you may not be at any of my concerts, I'll have a prereleased copy dropped off for your listening pleasure, if I don't deliver it myself. If all is good then, and only then, will I include it on my next album—once we finish fully recording it, that is."

"Don't you know better than to keep your man waiting and wondering?"

"Now don't you go trying to make me feel guilty, Dr. Michael Thomas. I don't want to spoil the surprise."

"Well, then . . . you sure must have stayed up late last night writing it."

"Not really. I had most of it worked out in my head on the drive home from your place. The rest of it came together in the studio. After it's released, the media and my fans will obviously be looking for the object of my affections—which is you, of course. I'm not ready to go public yet about you and me as I enjoy my privacy. And I'm guessing that you do to."

"I've never had the media trying to break down my door to talk to me . . . until this vice presidential thing, that is. But Frankie knows how to keep them at bay."

"Frankie definitely has your back."

"And speaking of Frankie," stated Michael. "I need to prewarn you. He quickly figured out, without my having to say anything, that you are secretly trying to take advantage of my virgin body."

His comment about "virgin body" was briefly followed by silence from Briana. "Are you really a virgin, Michael?" she finally asked, inquiringly.

"No," came his one-word response.

"Oh, I'm not surprised, given that you are soooo much older than me," she replied, in a kidding tone. "And here I thought all along that you would have waited for me."

"I tried, but you kept falling asleep on me in my dreams," he responded, with notable humor in his tone that even she couldn't help taking notice of. Briana found herself laughing at his response.

"Good comeback, Michael, good comeback."

"Not usually as quick or as good as yours, I'm finding out. You've been around far more than your physical age would lead one to believe."

"One has to grow up fast in this business to have any chance at survival. Speaking of survival," Briana continued, "I'm not sure how I'm going to survive on tour without seeing you. I don't know, and neither do you probably at this point, but if ever you make it to one of the cities I'm performing in, come in through the stage door. I'll leave a note with the security guys to let you in. That way you can have a side-view seat to watch the show from . . . and maybe I'll even allow you to try and steal a kiss from me before I go on stage. How does that tempting offer sound to you?"

"I may take you up on the offer, you little temptress."

"Temptress! I like the sound of that. I may even tempt you more after the show in my bus, if you aren't careful," she teased.

"Not to change the subject on you, though I do like the subject, but I have news, and not necessarily good news." There was a moment of silence on Michael's part before continuing. "I received a call from DWB today while at the free clinic." He paused once again while looking for the courage to continue with the unsettling news. "They asked that I ferry seven others to La Paz, Bolivia—the day after tomorrow—and I reluctantly accepted the request." He then waited for her response, but was met with stony silence. "Are you still there, Briana?"

Following another moment of silence, she eventually answered. "Yes, Michael. Not exactly the kind of news a girl wants to hear."

"Trust me, Briana, there was no way that I wanted to have to tell you this, either. The floods down there have been catastrophic . . . the folks at DWB were in a real pinch for a pilot and another doctor. And I, unfortunately, happen to be one and the same."

"How long will you be gone?" came her slightly subdued question.

"They have a commitment from the others for two weeks. Back on the fourteenth."

"Bad timing all the way around," she said, dejectedly.

"What do you mean by bad timing?"

"The day you return is the same day I leave for my month-long Christmas tour. That means another six weeks apart. I'm beginning to think that the gods are conspiring against us," she said, sullenly.

This time, Michael was the quiet one before finally responding. "Maybe the gods are testing us. I firmly believe that we will survive the test and come out stronger because of it," he said, trying to sound convincing.

"I guess that's what I should have expected when falling for a flight surgeon . . . and you for a travelling performer. But you're probably right—we will come out stronger for the absence."

"I know we will," he responded, continuing his attempts to sound more reassuring. "I'll call you from La Paz, though I'll warn you in advance, cell phone coverage may be nonexistent. But I'll try."

"Okay," she stated, sounding even sadder as it was all sinking in.

"I know you probably had a tiring day in the studio, so I'll let you get some much-deserved sleep . . . and I promise to fantasize about being under your bed covers tonight."

"I like that thought—only make sure that I don't fall asleep in your dreams," Briana said, with a half laugh.

"Trust me, my dreams will find ways of keeping you totally awake. Goodnight, Briana . . . I'm missing you already."

"Probably not as much as I'm already missing you. Goodnight, Michael."

At that, the two of them hung up. Both were obviously disappointed by the turn of events that put on hold the eventual consummation of their relationship—something they were both eagerly looking forward to. Given that it was ten o'clock by the time he hung up with Briana, he headed off to his bedroom to shave and shower before calling it a night. As expected, sleep did not come easily for him. His wide-awake fantasies of keeping Briana "awake" fought valiantly against his body's need for sleep—but sleep finally won out—as it always does in the end.

The next morning for Michael had come too soon, as deep sleep had eluded him. Following an early breakfast, he set about tackling the various tasks confronting him with only one day to prepare for his departure. His first call went out to the flightline maintenance crew to fuel and check out the plane. His next task was to map out which airports he would land at for refueling prior to his final destination. Once that was determined, he would then be able to electronically file his flight plan for La Paz.

Aside from the medical supplies that would be arriving today, he had his own personal medical and clothing bags to pack. The more tasks he had to attend to, the better it helped to keep his mind away from Briana. His constantly thinking of her only raised his level of frustration, which he knew was not healthy—but knowing that did little toward relieving the frustrations he was experiencing.

His day ended late with a phone call from Briana who, it turned out, had managed to keep busy herself with another full day in the recording studio. They kept their conversation light rather than dwell on their inevitable separation—with Michael throwing a multitude of questions at her about the art of recording music in a studio. Once she returned from her tour, she made a promise to invite him to one of her recording sessions. Their conversation lasted close to an hour, with neither one of them wanting to be the first to say goodnight and goodbye—but Michael finally took the initiative on his own—painful as it was.

Chapter Twenty

THE NEXT MORNING, AT MICHAEL'S INVITATION TO THE OTHERS, FRANKIE was kept busy feeding breakfast to four of the volunteers who had flown in the day before. Immediately following breakfast, they all pitched in helping to store their personal gear into the belly of the aircraft—along with the received medical supplies that were awaiting them in the hangar. Shortly before noon, the three remaining team members arrived at the house. Frankie transported the three of them out to the hangar along with enough food, as was customary of Frankie, to feed an army; not one of them would likely die of starvation or dehydration on the long flight to La Paz.

By one-thirty in the afternoon, they achieved liftoff for the 3,800-plus nautical mile flight to La Paz. According to Michael's projections, based on brief refueling stops in both Miami and Bogotá, Colombia, the entire flight would take upward of nine hours—assuming he encountered average high altitude wind speeds along the way. With favorable conditions, he calculated an estimated arrival in La Paz of ten-thirty in the evening—at the earliest. A later arrival time than he would have liked, but little he could do about it given their late start.

While in flight, Michael received notification from ATC to be cautious and alert when entering the air space around El Alto International Airport. The airport, located eight miles southwest of La Paz, is one of the world's highest airports at 13,325 feet; turbulent winds running along and through the mountain ranges can, at times, play havoc with even the largest of aircraft—advice Michael was more than willing to heed. The flights into and out of Nashville, Miami, Bogotá and eventually into La Paz would be handled under "LIFEGUARD" designation—meaning that he would receive priority status for both take-offs and landings and also enroute sequencing; a designation he had become familiar with on his various mercy flights.

The team of doctors and nurses knew before leaving their home states that this was not going to be an easy assignment—and they would not be disappointed. The temperatures were higher than the normal average of 58 degrees for December, and the humidity was even higher; little surprise, then, to any of them regarding the large outbreak of both dengue fever and malaria. The well-organized Deployment Team at DWB had the foresight to send along three mosquito-proofed tents—two for sleeping and a larger one which would operate as a clinic—mostly serving those living on the hillsides outside of the city of La Paz itself.

Part of the flight was, in fact, met with turbulence, but not in the air space immediately prior to landing at El Alto Airport; for that, Michael was thankful, given the essentially moonless night. Forced to fly around some of the turbulent areas, however, they did not touch down in La Paz until shortly after eleven; the real work now lay ahead of them.

Arrangements had previously been made to have the eight of them, along with their gear, transported by charter bus to where their field hospital would be set up; the exact area had been prescouted and secured by the Bolivian Red Cross. It would be almost one-thirty in the morning before they arrived at their clinic site. Unfortunately, the bus driver had to make a number of detours around impassable roads before finally reaching their final destination. Sleep would not be possible, of course, until after they had pitched the three tents. All of them were fortunate enough to have been able to catch some sleep on the flight into La Paz—not so the case with Michael, however, who by this time was operating on sheer adrenaline; flights of this nature and duration can take their toll on even the most seasoned pilots.

By three in the morning the tents were fully erected, with Michael hitting the sack as soon as the first sleeping tent had gone up. Given the long flight behind him, the team knew he deserved the first shot at sleep. The patient cots, tables and medical supplies had been offloaded from the bus, but not set up as yet; the rest would have to wait until first light—which today would come a little before six.

By seven o'clock, the team had all of the equipment and supplies ready to go for the first in a long line of patients. It came as no surprise to the seasoned volunteers that the lines would begin to form long before the team was ready to see them. Even without the availability of telephones or computers, word of their arrival generally began to spread long before the bus left to pick them up at the airport. Free medical care, especially under these conditions, was considered a hot commodity; many, unfortunately, would go untreated.

The days were long as they put in upward of eighteen hours each day in order to meet the needs of those waiting in the long lines; many were carried in on makeshift stretchers and left behind by those who carried them to the clinic. These were, invariably, the ones who required the most intensive medical care the team could provide—when they could provide it; not all were made whole. For twelve consecutive days and nights, more silent tears were shed than laughter shared. This was not the kind of volunteerism for the faint of heart—Marine boot camps were considered kinder than these conditions.

On their ninth day in La Paz, they were presented with a patient whom they could not help. She was both young and extremely beautiful. She had been an aspiring model who was medically double-jin-xed—having previously been diagnosed with atrial septal defect—commonly referred to as a hole between the two upper chambers of the heart. The DWB doctors were not equipped to perform some-thing as delicate as heart surgery, and the tents would hardly classi-fy as a sterile environment. Her attending team physician also noted an advanced case of cataracts in both eyes—unusual for someone so young—deemed to be hereditary, he surmised. The cataracts were another diagnosis for which they were not capable of providing care, due largely by the fact that none of them were trained as ophthalmol-ogists—let alone by the lack of proper surgical equipment.

Her attending physician made his case to the others for bringing her to the United States for surgery. This option was not something generally encouraged by the folks at DWB headquarters due to limit-ed budget constraints. Aside from DWB considerations, however, the greatest obstacle was finding a way to get her into the U.S. This would require both passport and a visa—not something likely to happen giv-en the five working days remaining before they packed up their gear and flew home.

As the patients filtered in and out of the oversized tent for care, dis-cussions between the eight of them continued as they worked. There was eventual consensus amongst them to make every effort to fly her out. How to fly her out of Bolivia and into the U.S. legally was one of many considerations to be taken into account. Was there an American Consulate in La Paz? Dr. Tan believed there was and suggested that one of them ask that question of the Bolivian Red Cross representa-tive who routinely stopped by in the afternoons. Would the Bolivian government grant her permission to leave? Status unknown—though they all thought there was no reason to believe they would not—given her medical situation.

Will the high altitude of jet travel place undue pressure on her heart? Michael assured them that this would not be a problem given that the cabin was pressurized. Where would the patient receive care and who would serve as her sponsor, her advocate, to see to it that medical and financial matters related to her care were handled during her stay in the U.S.? This issue alone turned out to be the second biggest sticking point of all. The seven team members talked about their work and family responsibilities—with the exception of Michael. Seven pairs of eyes were homed in on him—and he knew it. They knew that he had the necessary medical connections and financial resources to help her out.

He could easily do it, he thought, as he had the free time that the rest of them apparently did not. He had many friends and acquaintances—due in large part to his parents—in the medical profession who could perform the needed surgeries—possibly at a reduced cost. She could stay at his home with little inconvenience to him; there was always Frankie to keep an eye on her when he wasn't around. Frankie, he reasoned, would love the idea of having someone else around to dote over like a father.

Michael's personal concern, however, was the question of how all of these commitments would affect his much desired time alone with Briana. As soon as the question entered his mind, he realized that Briana would be starting her month-long Christmas tour the same day he was to return home. Every question he threw at himself led to the conclusion that he could, in fact, handle her care with little or no impact to his life; he eventually relayed as much to the team.

His decision brought a new sense of relief and motivation to the team of volunteers. They now had a goal before them other than simply providing medical care to the long lines of patients continuing to gather outside the clinic tent. When the Red Cross representative stopped by that afternoon to unload fresh food and medical supplies, the young woman's attending physician approached him with their request.

His first reaction was that it was highly unlikely to occur before their departure on Tuesday. Unlike goal-driven workers back in the U.S., most Latin Americans process things at a much slower pace. Something of this nature, he advised them, could take upward of two weeks on an expedited basis, though most likely longer.

The representative's response put an immediate damper on the enthusiasm of the team. Michael, however, was not put off by the initial response. He had been involved in far too many of these DWB missions to know that with the right incentives, things can be moved along with haste. With all of the team members watching, he reached back, pulled his wallet out and extracted a sizable amount of currency.

While handing the money over to the representative, he said, in a polite manner, "Please see to it that she is ready to go with us no later than early Tuesday morning. Here is her name and address."

The representative, looking up at Michael, replied, "Yes, doctor, I see to it she here, with papers, first thing Tuesday morning." And with that he turned around and hurried out of the tent and back into his vehicle. Michael knew that some of the money would quickly make it into the driver's own pocket.

Michael then called for the next patient while the others looked at him in awe of what they had witnessed—some of the team members had tears in their eyes. The attending physician who handled her initial visit walked over to Michael, shook his hand, and said, "Thanks," before returning back to his patient.

In terms of receiving any form of consent from the DWB staff, Michael assured himself that none was needed. This was his plane to bring her back to the states—and he would personally assume any and all medical and financial responsibilities associated with her care. He would also bear the future expenses of returning her back home on a commercial flight to La Paz—but not before she was deemed medically fit to return home, however.

On Tuesday morning, they were all involved in the process of loading the medical equipment and supplies onto the bus. Just before finishing up, they caught sight of the all too familiar Red Cross vehicle approaching along the dirt road with his horn honking. After pulling to a stop in front of the bus, the representative climbed out of the vehicle and went around to the passenger side. Immediately after opening the passenger door of the vehicle, a young female climbed out holding a single bag—a bag that most likely carried her worldly possessions. The sight of her brought tears to two of the nurses along with her attending physician. "Miracles do happen," one of them was overheard to say. Michael knew, however, that in reality, it wasn't exactly a miracle—for the poorer the country, the more money talks.

As the driver handed over the passport and visa papers to Michael, he immediately climbed back into his vehicle and headed back down to the affluent parts of the city—a city built largely on the backs of the poor. Though he knew little Spanish, her attending physician went over to the young lady, took her by the hand, and led her up and onto the bus.

When the last of the gear was loaded, they made the slow journey back to the airport for their flight back home. Once planeside, the team wasted little time in stowing the supplies into the cargo hold while Michael attended to his preflight responsibilities. When all were onboard and the door secured and latched, Michael requested the required clearance from ground control to taxi to the main runway. Upon reaching the end of the runway, he was given final clearance for takeoff. With a clear morning sky before him, Michael raced down the runaway and lifted off at precisely ten o'clock, La Paz time, for the long journey home.

After glancing at the two documents handed to him earlier, Michael learned that she was 21 years of age, stood five feet eight, weighed 125 pounds and had brown eyes. He already knew that her name was Bonita Lucia de Borbón. If his recollection of four years of Spanish still held up, he took a guess that Bonita meant something like "pretty one"—and pretty she most certainly was. She should have an exciting future as a model, or perhaps even an actress, when she returned to her homeland, he mused.

Michael knew that the flight home would test the limits of his concentration—like the others, he too was tired. Glancing back into the cabin, he could see that the others wasted little time in reclining back and falling sleep—all except for Bonita, who was sitting in the co-pilot seat. With mercy flights in mind, Michael had the eighth seat removed in the cabin to allow room for a stretcher.

Michael was glad that he had this time alone to talk with Bonita. He came away knowing more about her than he did some of his lifelong friends—she held nothing back from him. Unlike many girls in her immediate community, she graduated from a Catholic high school, managed to complete a few courses in English—though she and Michael primarily conversed in Spanish. She had a hearty laugh which would burst forth whenever Michael grossly mispronounced a particular Spanish word—which he did often.

She turned to modeling when she was sixteen, she confided, as a means to pay for her education, for her parents were poor as they struggled to raise a family of seven children—she being the oldest. Her father was a carpenter, when he could find work that is, and they lived in a rented small house with three bedrooms and one bathroom. Following graduation, she pursued modeling on a full-time basis until her eyesight forced her to leave; falling off the edge of the runway could be hazardous to one's health, she laughed. Someday, she relayed to Michael, she hoped to save enough money to be able to attend college. After graduating from college, her primary focus was to help her younger brothers and sisters attend college, as well. She truly believed that education was the only way toward breaking the cycle of poverty that her own family had known for generations.

Though they are poor, her parents had claimed for years that her father is a direct descendant of Spanish royalty; a duke, she believed, who escaped to Bolivia when Napoleon overran Spain. Whether this was factual or not, she had no way of knowing. Her parents also claimed that their lineage was purely Spanish, through and through; unlike the majority of Bolivians today who are primarily of mixed heritage.

It became readily apparent to Michael that in spite of her medical problems, she retained an optimistic outlook on life and her chances for a happy future. If the American doctors could fix her heart and restore her severely limited vision, Bonita promised Michael that in whatever accomplishments she achieved, she would do so as a dedication to him. Michael was both touched by her words and convinced that she would, in fact, achieve her every dream. But first, it was up to him to make her whole again.

Glancing back through the cabin once more, he noticed that everyone was fast asleep again after leaving Bogota for refueling—and would most likely remain so until touching down in Miami for the last of the refueling stops. He didn't fault them for catching whatever sleep they could—he only wished he could do so as well.

Upon landing in Miami, he taxied directly to the end of the corporate terminal building for the purpose of clearing both the aircraft and passengers through customs. Given that their flight was medical in nature, the entire process took less than one hour; even Bonita's quickly procured visa held up to detailed scrutiny.

Once customs were cleared, two members of the team departed into the main terminal with their luggage; one taking a shuttle flight up to Orlando, another up the coast to D.C. As soon as the plane had been refueled and they were taxiing along the apron, Michael, with instructions received from ground control, lined up behind six other planes readying for takeoff. While waiting, he gave Frankie a quick call to alert him of their new house guest.

One hour and forty-five minutes later, he gently guided the plane down outside of Nashville. Thanks to strong tailwinds on a good portion of the flight, Michael was able to shave close to an hour from his projected afternoon arrival time of five o'clock. After taxiing up to the terminal, he assisted with the removal of luggage for the remaining team members. They would stay in a Nashville hotel for the night before catching morning flights to their home destinations.

After buttoning up the aircraft once again, he taxied around the perimeter of the airport to the access gate to his property and hangar. As soon as the engines were shut off inside the hangar, he noticed Frankie standing over by the side door. Michael was tired and chose to call and ask for Frankie's help in unloading some of his personal bags and belongings. Unloading the medical equipment and what was left of the supplies could wait until tomorrow—if he didn't sleep through tomorrow, that is.

Following Michael's introduction of Bonita to Frankie, Frankie made quick work of helping load the necessary items into the back of the cart; once everything was loaded they headed up the path to the garage. After placing everything in the elevator, the three of them then proceeded up to the main level.

Bonita, glancing up at Michael, asked, "Are we in hotel?"

As tired as Michael was, he had to laugh, and laugh hard he did. He had forgotten all about the cultural and physical differences that separated their two worlds; especially given her roots, though she had experienced more than most given her modeling exposure. Even Frankie had to chuckle at her question, though more subdued about it than Michael's open laughter. Or, Michael thought, was she possibly seeing things differently than they were because of her blurred vision? He would have to keep that in mind, when and if she questioned something in the days to come.

"No, Bonita," he finally said, "we are in my home. This home is a lot different than most American homes, so don't think that all Americans live like this; they don't."

"I see," she replied.

"Michael! Bonita!" Frankie interjected. "Would the two of you like dinner?"

"Bonita, are you hungry?" Michael asked.

"Yes," came her quick reply.

"Then yes, Frankie, the lady is hungry, so we'll eat just as soon as you can pull a meal together—you included."

"Good. I'd hate to throw out the chicken and dumplings I have warming in the oven. Give me fifteen minutes to set the table and bring the food out. Oh, and her room has been prepared. End of hallway."

"Thank you, Frankie, and the timing is perfect . . . I want to run Bonita and her bag up to her room first thing anyway." Michael and Bonita then reentered the elevator and proceeded to the top floor. Passing along the hallway, he first pointed out his bedroom, study and two other bedrooms before reaching what was to be her room.

"This will be your room for however long it takes to get you all fixed up. Why don't you go ahead and freshen up a bit before dinner.

When you're ready, you can come down to the main level by taking either the stairs or the elevator; close the gate, pull the lever and push the number one."

"Gracias, Dr. Thomas, I be down shortly," she replied.

"Bonita, in this house I go by the name of Michael, not Dr. Thomas. Or you can call me Miguel—same thing, different language."

"Gracias, I will."

"Can you see well enough to navigate around the room and the bathroom, or would like me to show you where everything is?"

"No, Miguel. I think I find everything on my own." And with that she turned and began exploring what was to be her very own bedroom.

Michael remained in place and watched as she, with her limited vision, moved around the room. Without knowing for sure, he believed that she was in awe of her surroundings. He finally left her and headed off to his own room to freshen up, as well.

"So tell me, Bonita," Frankie asked as they were finishing up with dessert, "was the chicken and dumpling dinner as good as your mother makes?"

"Better, much, much better. My mother good cook, but this creamy, rich. I take recipe home with me, no?"

"Bonita," Michael interjected, "you can take home any recipe for which you survive the meal . . . right, Frankie?"

"Cute, Michael, very cute. Ignore any mention of my cooking that Michael makes, Bonita. He actually worships my cooking."

"Worship might be too strong a word," Michael countered.

"As I've told Michael many times over the years, Bonita, he can hire a new cook and household manager anytime he feels the need. And years later he's obviously still in love with my cooking and doesn't want to take a gamble on another cook."

Bonita eventually found herself laughing at the verbal exchange that was taking place between the two of them—which was ongoing during the most of the dinner. Her first day in America and she was already feeling right at home with both Frankie and Miguel.

"Frankie and Bonita," Michael said, as he rose from the table. "If you two will excuse me, I have this urgent need to crawl under my bedcovers. In fact, I seldom ever take the elevator, but this is one night I'm going to make an exception. I simply don't have the energy right now to even think about climbing the stairs . . . and Frankie, would you please entertain Bonita until she is ready to retire?"

"It would be my pleasure, Michael. I believe the first thing I'll do is teach her how to do up the dirty dishes."

"Frankie, I no longer even have the energy to argue with you." Turning to Bonita, he said, "Goodnight, Bonita, I'll see you in the morning for breakfast."

"Buenas noches, Miguel . . . and muchas gracias for bringing me to America."

"You are most welcome, Bonita." Michael then turned and headed straight for the elevator. This has to be one of the toughest trips I've ever been on, he thought. Even should Briana still be in Nashville, he knew that he couldn't muster the energy to call her; tonight he was interested in only one thing—sleep, and lots of it.

Chapter Twenty-One

MICHAEL MANAGED TO SLEEP FOR THIRTEEN HOURS STRAIGHT. EVEN SO, HE was still feeling somewhat groggy. Nothing a long hot shower wouldn't cure, he told himself as he made his way into the shower. Ten minutes later he reluctantly turned off the water. Almost thirteen days of taking sponge baths would drive anyone to commit shower overdose, he reasoned.

While descending the stairs, he heard the sounds of beautiful piano music playing on the radio—not something Frankie normally did this early in the morning, so he could only assume that it was Bonita's doing. He followed the music into the living room where, to his utter amazement, he witnessed Bonita playing away at the baby grand piano, with Frankie sitting on the couch watching and listening. The first thought that came to Michael's mind was, where did she learn to play the piano that well while living in the slum areas of La Paz? And to top it off, there was no sheet music before her—not that she would be able to read the notes anyway, given her blurred vision.

He leaned against the entrance to the room and listened as she continued right into the second stanza of Beethoven's Sonata Pathetique, one of his mother's favorite pieces. It was also one of Beethoven's slower masterpieces which allowed his father to dance around the living room with his mother. Glancing over at Frankie, he noticed an appreciative smile set on his face—not something Michael was used to seeing on Frankie. When the piece ended, Michael was the first to acknowledge her performance.

"Bravo! Bravo!" Michael exclaimed, loudly.

When she turned around on the piano bench, Michael could see that she was surprised by his unknown presence.

"Yes, Bravo!" chimed in Frankie.

"Gracias," she replied, somewhat embarrassed at being noticed by Michael. "I hope I not wake you up, Miguel."

"A train running through my room would not have awakened me, Bonita. The smell of Frankie burning my breakfast would have, however. Speaking of which, is anyone hungry besides me?"

"I hate to disappoint you, Michael, but we had our breakfast hours ago . . . you know . . . when normal people usually eat breakfast." Frankie never was one to be shy about throwing digs at Michael—even in the presence of Bonita. "I'll leave you alone with Bonita while I prepare your breakfast," Frankie stated, as he rose and headed off to the kitchen.

"Thanks, Frankie."

"You sleep good, no?" Bonita asked.

"I obviously slept very well, indeed. Let me ask you, Bonita, where did you learn to play the piano so well?" Michael inquired, as Bonita joined him on the couch.

"At school—favorite nun teach me."

"She apparently taught you very well. That was a beautiful piece you played; one of my mother's favorite pieces, I might add."

"Gracias. You play piano, Miguel?"

"Let's just say that I play at it. I've had years of lessons but never quite achieved the level of perfection that you apparently have. Not to change the subject, Bonita, but I want you to know that I will be making a number of calls after breakfast to arrange the necessary surgeries for your heart and eyes. Okay?"

"Gracias. I be debted to you," she replied, with the utmost sincerity.

Michael had to admit to himself that he loved her broken English—he found it delightful in its own way. To save her any embarrassment, however, he chose not to correct her—as she had made few attempts at correcting his own feeble alterations of the Spanish language—outside of those instances where she could not contain her laughter.

Noticing Frankie entering the dining room with his breakfast and coffee in hand, Michael excused himself and headed off to eat. Following his breakfast, he went upstairs to his study to make arrangements for her potential surgeries. After consulting with a few colleagues, Michael concluded that the cataract surgery could precede the heart surgery—more out of schedule availability than for any medical concerns.

He was able to book an appointment with an ophthalmologist for tomorrow morning for a preliminary screening. If the physician found her eyes to be as Michael described them, the actual surgery—thanks to a cancellation—would take place on Monday afternoon; the cataract surgery being the least complicated of the two pending surgeries.

With that behind him, Michael then set about the task of setting up the appointments to repair the hole in her heart; this, he knew, would require more upfront work prior to the actual surgery itself. This would entail a blood workup, a physical examination, along with an echocardiogram to determine the exact location of the hole. The results of this workup would determine the type of surgery required—open heart or via catherization.

Following a number of calls, he was able to set in motion two schedules, a presurgical examination and an echocardiogram—both on the following Wednesday. Following her work-up exams, the physi-

cian would then be able to determine the appropriate surgical procedure required; a preliminary date for surgery was set for Friday. Elec-
tive surgeries were not normally scheduled the day before Christmas,
but the cardiologist made an exception for Michael as a professional
courtesy. Michael was quite surprised that it took a full two hours of
coordination to set everything up. He could now better empathize
with what the general populace would have to go through to set up
similar appointments.

With the necessary appointments out of the way, he picked the
phone back up to place one more important call. When that call was
completed, he then headed downstairs to share the schedules and surgeries he had set up with Bonita. Not finding her in the living room, he
eventually located both she and Frankie in the kitchen, sharing lunch.

"Hungry?" Frankie asked as Michael entered the kitchen.

"Thanks, but no," he replied, as he sat down at the table with the
two of them. Michael then proceeded to share her various appointments for both tomorrow and next week. Even after Michael's explanation of the possible surgical procedures with Bonita, she appeared
unfazed by it all. He had to attribute this to her desire to be whole
again—especially where her eyes were concerned.

"Bonita, can you be ready to go somewhere in an hour?" Michael
asked.

"Sí, Miguel," she replied immediately. "Where we going, Miguel?"

"We are going nowhere . . . but you are. I've called an acquaintance
of mine, married to a fellow doctor, and she will be arriving shortly to
take you shopping—clothes shopping to be exact. We need to fill up
that empty closet of yours. Are you up for a little shopping in America?"

"Sí," she replied, eagerly. "But you no have to do that, Miguel; you
doing enough already."

"You were a model once. You know firsthand how nice clothes made you feel. We can't have you going out in the same clothes day after day. It's my treat."

"Gracias, Miguel, gracias," she said, like a young child about to go shopping for new toys.

"Now why don't you go upstairs and make yourself all pretty for shopping. Oh, by the way, her name is Roberta. She's only a few years older than you, so trust her judgment when she helps you pick out clothes, okay?"

"Sí, Miguel, Sí," she answered, as she rose and quickly headed out of the kitchen.

Once she was out of earshot, Michael leaned in and said to Frankie, "Roberta will be keeping a running tally of the purchases, so please pay her in cash from the safe when she turns over the receipts."

"Not a problem," responded Frankie. "This is generous of you, Michael," he added with unusual sincerity.

"I haven't violated her privacy by checking out her closet, but I have to believe that she only brought with her two, three at the most, changes of clothes. Some nice clothes will help Bonita in dealing with the challenges she's going to face, what with the multiple appointments and surgeries. Meanwhile, with her out shopping, I'm going to head down to the clinic for a few hours; should be back around six. I don't expect Roberta and Bonita back any earlier than that, as I've also asked Roberta to take her to dinner after shopping."

"Okay, see you around six for dinner."

Michael rose from his chair and headed back upstairs to grab his medical bag before riding the elevator down to the garage. In the twenty minutes it took him to reach the clinic, he had only one thought on his mind—Briana. The obvious fact that he missed her was an understatement. Dealing with Bonita's medical issues and working at the clinic helped to take his mind off of her—somewhat. He missed being around her a whole lot, and he knew it. He was also acutely aware that it would be a number of weeks before he had the opportunity to see her again. If only her singing tour would be canceled for some reason, then all would be well in his life.

When he returned home a few minutes after six, Bonita had yet to return from her shopping extravaganza and dinner with Roberta. Knowing that she was probably eating dinner with Roberta about now, he and Frankie sat down to their own dinner. Following his meal, Michael headed up to his study in an attempt at making some headway on the accumulation of medical journals that arrived during his trip to La Paz. An hour later, he sensed the arrival of the wandering shoppers. The dead giveaway was the continuous laughter that wafted up the stairs and into his study. This was a definite sign that the two shoppers had experienced a fabulous time spending his money. Placing the journal down on the side table, he rose from his recliner and headed down to check out the gaiety below.

And sure enough, there were boxes and bags galore near the open front door—with Frankie coming through the doorway with yet another load.

"What is all this commotion I hear down here?" Michael said as he started down the stairs. Surveying the loot, he jokingly added, "It looks as though you ladies purchased one of everything you laid your eyes on."

"I'm sorry, Miguel, Roberta make me buy," Bonita responded.

"Is that true, Roberta?" Michael said, looking directly at Roberta with a smile.

"Yep! Sure did—and proud of it. An opportunity like this comes only once in a girl's lifetime, and we . . . I mean me . . . decided to help Bonita enjoy it with wild abandonment."

Moments later, Frankie reappeared where they were still gathered and handed an envelope to Roberta. Michael could only imagine how much their adventure had cost him—not that he was overly concerned, however. Bonita was a remarkably gifted young lady who deserved every bit of what luxuries he could offer her.

Shortly after Roberta departed, the three of them carried the various boxes and bags to the elevator for transport upstairs. Both Michael and Frankie volunteered to help her unpack her purchases and put them away for her—Bonita, however, would have none of it. She wanted the pleasure of examining every purchase again before putting them away herself. The men made a hasty retreat from her room, leaving everything piled on her bed. Bonita, it appeared, was apparently in seventh heaven.

Chapter Twenty-Two

MICHAEL ARRIVED WITH BONITA FIFTEEN MINUTES EARLY FOR HER APPOINT-
ment with the ophthalmologist. If she were at all apprehensive about
the eye exam, she didn't show it.

Michael surmised that she was still on a "high" from her shopping experience with Roberta yesterday and, he had to admit, she
looked quite stylish in the outfit she wore this morning. Looking as
beautiful as she did, he had no doubts that she could easily reenter
the modeling business back home. He wasn't about to ask her, but he
did wonder why she had not married yet—most women her age in
third-world countries were long married before reaching the age of
twenty-one.

After Michael filled out the required paperwork, they were both
escorted back to one of the examining rooms where Dr. Mandrel was
already waiting for them.

"Hello Bill, thanks for seeing us on such short notice," Michael
said, greeting him on a first-name basis.

"Cancellations have a way of doing that, Michael," he responded,
"though I still would have squeezed you in. Still living out at your
parent's mansion?"

"Same place . . . they'll probably end up burying me there."

Glancing quickly down at his chart before turning his attentions to Bonita, Dr. Mandrel asked, "And this beautiful young lady must be Bonita, I presume."

"I am. Glad to meet you, Dr. Bill," Bonita replied. By her innocent informality with addressing him by his first name, both Michael and Dr. Mandrel found it difficult to stifle a laugh; both looking at each other with amused grins.

After recovering from the innocence of her introduction, Dr Mandrel proceeded on with the examination of Bonita. Without even the benefit of using his ophthalmology equipment, he could clearly see that she had an advanced case of cataracts; how severe and how damaging would have to await the use of his sophisticated equipment.

"Shall we get started, Bonita?" he asked.

"I ready, Dr. Bill."

"Okay then. Climb right up into this chair, young lady, and relax. None of this will hurt you at all. This piece of equipment you see before you will enable me to look deep into your eyes. It's called a slit lamp. It is nothing more than a microscope that magnifies your eyes for me. With it, I can determine both the presence and severity of a cataract, amongst other things. Now lean forward please and place your chin right here."

Dr. Mandrel then spent the next ten minutes looking into her eyes. When he had finished that part of the exam, he then dilated her eyes before taking another look a short time later. At the conclusion of the exam, he gave both of them his diagnosis.

"The eyes are severely clouded—much as you explained on the phone Michael, but not so severe that they can't be saved. There is no question but that we need to perform a little surgery. And the sooner the better," he added. "While the normal process is to do surgery on only one eye per visit, I would like to perform surgery on both eyes on the same visit. Otherwise, we're looking at another surgery a couple of weeks from now at the earliest. I'd like to get the eyes taken care of prior to any potential heart surgery. There are a number of options in terms of lenses. Based on her youth and her personal goals that you previously explained to me on the phone, Michael—piano, college, etc.—I'd like to implant multifocal intraocular lenses in each eye. That way she can possibly avoid having to wear glasses. Would you agree, Michael?"

"You know better than I, Bill. Ophthalmology is not exactly my field of expertise, as you well know."

"Okay then. Multifocal lenses it is." Looking down at his chart, and then back at the two of them, he continued. "I see where we already have Monday set up for surgery. Any questions, Bonita? Michael?"

"No, Dr. Bill," Bonita replied.

"None from me either, Dr. Bill," Michael said, with a grin on his face. It was evident that Dr. Mandrel caught the subtle humor from Michael and quickly replied, "Great, Dr. Michael, then I will see the two of you on Monday. Here's a packet of reading materials that will help in explaining both the surgery itself along with what to expect during the recovery phase. Have Dr. Michael go over them with you, Bonita, line by line by line," he added, with a wink meant only for Michael. "Also in the packet," he continued, "are three prescriptions and over-the-counter eyedrops for dryness, burning or scratchiness; one is a steroid, the second one an antibiotic and the third is for pain and swelling control. I would highly recommend that you have the prescriptions filled before the actual surgery."

"We can handle that, doctor, thank you," Michael replied.

After leaving the office, they entered the elevator and made their way down to the garage level. By the time they arrived home, Frankie had lunch waiting for them in the dining room.

"It pays to call ahead," Michael remarked to Bonita as they both sat down with Frankie.

"So, how did the appointment go?" Frankie asked, having waited patiently for one of them to bring the subject up.

"It went well. Dr. Mandrel will go ahead with the surgery on Monday. From what he saw, he doesn't foresee anything preventing the surgery from being successful. And, with a new set of eyes, Bonita will be able to see just how beautiful she really is."

Glancing over at Bonita sitting beside him, Michael could detect a slight flush rise upon her cheeks. Not only was she beautiful, he thought, but somewhat humble, as well.

"Frankie, can you please get these prescriptions filled before Bonita's surgery?"

"Not a problem, I need to run into town for a little grocery shopping tomorrow anyway."

"Thank you."

The weekend was a time of relaxation for the three of them, aside from Michael and Bonita attending Sunday mass at the cathedral. Though her eyes could not take everything in, she was amazed at how large the church was. Following mass and brunch at a local restaurant, Bonita spent the better part of the afternoon entertaining the two of them on the piano; even Michael was cajoled into joining Bonita for a duet piece. Frankie and Michael were both amazed at how much music she was able to retain in her memory bank. She was probably one of those gifted individuals one reads about, Michael surmised, who can listen to a particular song and immediately play it back. Michael, for the most part, could not survive without having the sheet music before him—he had a decent memory, only not so much where music was concerned.

Monday's afternoon appointment appeared to arrive more slowly for Michael than it did for Bonita. It was not that he was worried about the surgery itself, as much as he was anxious for Bonita to be able to see clearly for the first time in years. At the appointed time, Bonita was escorted into the room where the procedure was to take place. As for Michael, he chose to remain in the waiting room; there's a time and a place for his being by her side, he thought, but this was not one of them. He felt comfortable with her being in the skilled hands of Dr. Mandrel.

An hour and a half later, she was walking out to the waiting room, arm in arm with Dr. Mandrel. Covering both eyes were a pair of patches and her Hollywood-style glasses that Michael had asked Roberta to pick out for this occasion.

"Well, doctor!" Michael remarked, with a tone of anxiousness in his voice. "What's the verdict?"

"After the customary recovery period, she'll be as good as new. Everything went as well as expected. You're now free to take your 'Hollywood Princess' home. Please leave the bandages over her eyes until after you get her home; then you can remove them. Also, it would be a good idea to have her lie down and take a nap. This little box here," he continued, as he handed it to Michael, "contains a protective shield that she needs to wear when going to bed, or anytime she lays down to rest. I'll need to see her for a few minutes tomorrow afternoon, just to make sure that her eyes are properly healing. No need for an appointment; I can catch her between patients as tomorrow is not a scheduled surgery day for me. Any questions of either one of you?" he concluded.

"Bonita, any questions of Dr. Bill?" Michael asked while taking her arm from that of Dr. Mandrel's.

"No . . . muchas gracias for fixing eyes . . . I pay you someday for what you do for me," she said, glancing in what she thought was the general direction of Dr. Mandrel.

"No payment is necessary," Dr. Mandrel replied. "Everything was done as a professional courtesy for Dr. Michael," he added, with another one of those winks. "I've never gone to another country like Dr. Michael has to help others, so anytime he brings someone back, like you Bonita, it's free."

"Thank you, doctor," Michael said with genuine sincerity. "I'll remember that offer . . . and thank you for what you've done for Bonita."

"You are most welcome—now beat it so I can get to my next surgery," he said with a smile. After Michael shook hands with Dr. Mandrel, he guided Bonita out the door and back to the elevator for the ride down to the parking garage. The two of them were both silent on the ride home—more from relief that it was behind them than for any other reason.

Frankie, of course, was overjoyed at hearing the positive news. After some discussion of the surgery, Bonita let Michael know that she felt tired and wanted to lie down. Michael then escorted Bonita up to her room where she immediately laid down on her bed. He then carefully removed the bandages from her eyes that Dr. Mandrel had previously placed over them. After retrieving the protective shield from the box, he placed it over her eyes, securing it around her head with the attached elastic band.

As Michael was finishing up with Bonita, Frankie came into the room proudly holding a bell in his hand.

"Listen to what I have for you, Bonita," he said, as he rang the bell before placing it into her hand. "All you have to do is ring the bell and one of us will come to you the minute we hear the ringing."

Bonita, apparently amused that someone would actually come running at the sound of a bell, shook it. Michael and Frankie both observed the enormous smile that lit up her whole face. She was obviously pleased with her new toy.

Taking the bell away from Bonita's hand, Michael said, "I'm placing it right here on the nightstand where you can easily reach it. Okay, Bonita," Michael continued, "you're now ready for your nap. When you awake, all you have to do is ring the bell and either Frankie or I will come back for you."

"Gracias, Miguel," she responded, in a sleepy voice.

The two of them left her room, closing the door partway behind them. Frankie returned to the kitchen to start dinner preparations while Michael chose to remain close by in his study.

An hour and a half later, Michael was awakened from his own nap, one he had never intended on taking, by the sound of a ringing bell. As he entered her room, he found Bonita sitting up in bed.

"So, have a good nap, did you?" he inquired.

"Sí, gracias," she replied. "I ready to get up now."

"Okay. But first I need you to lie back down while I put these various drops in your eyes—we need to keep them protected and moist at all times—very important."

She slid back down on the bed and rested her head on the two pillows. Michael then removed the eye shield and applied the drops while sitting beside her on the bed. First one set of drops, then a wait of five minutes before applying another set of drops. After the last of the drops was applied, he set about dabbing around her closed eyes with a tissue.

After a few minutes had passed, Bonita asked, "You wait for me—I use bathroom, please?"

"Of course I will, but first I have to ask, can you see any improvement in your vision?" he inquired, with added curiosity.

"Sí—little better."

"It's early yet. Don't be discouraged if you don't see everything perfectly right away. As the pamphlet said that I read to you over the weekend, it could take up to a week before your vision returns to where it should be . . . sometimes longer."

"I remember," she said, as she slid off the bed and carefully made her way to the bathroom.

When she reappeared five minutes later, the two of them took the elevator down to the main floor. Frankie apparently had heard the bell as he was spotted carrying some of the dinner items into the dining room just as they appeared. Following dinner, and after Frankie had cleared everything away, she serenaded the two of them on the piano again—with eyes comfortably closed.

A little after nine o'clock, she informed Michael that she was ready for bed. He allowed Bonita her privacy while she changed out of her street clothes and into one of her recently acquired nightgowns. Once she was in bed, he reapplied the various eyedrops before placing the shield over her eyes.

"I'll be right down the hallway," he informed her, "so ring the bell if you need anything."

"Okay . . . I will," she replied, quietly.

Michael closed her door halfway again before heading off to his own bedroom. Even he felt tired after the day's events. Following a brief shower, not even thoughts of Briana kept him from falling fast asleep.

The next morning, Bonita informed Michael that she thought she could see about the same as yesterday. This gave Michael an indication that recovery for her might take a little longer than normal. Given the severity of her cataracts, he wasn't the least bit surprised by this revelation. Following another one of her early afternoon naps, Michael once again applied her drops. In short order, they would be leaving to see Dr. Mandrel for the follow-up exam.

While Michael was waiting for Bonita to finish freshening up, Frankie came up the stairway.

"What's up, Frankie? It's not like you to be climbing the stairs," Michael remarked, upon seeing him at the top of the landing.

"Briana's father will be here in a few minutes, Michael."

"And the purpose of this visit?" Michael inquired, with a fair amount of curiosity.

"Something about dropping off a CD for you, from Briana."

"Oh! It must be that single she talked about releasing. Let him know that I'll be right down. I'm waiting for Bonita to finish getting ready."

Frankie then headed downstairs and waited by the phone for Alan's call saying that he was at the gate. After receiving the call, Frankie headed to the front door to await his arrival, and opened the door just prior to Alan reaching for the doorbell.

"Good afternoon, Frankie," said Alan, upon seeing him at the door. "Is Michael available?"

"He'll be down momentarily, Alan; he is tending to Bonita at the moment."

The name Bonita had never surfaced during their conversations at dinner, so it caught Alan a little off guard; nor did he recall Briana having mentioned the name before. Right in the middle of his thoughts, he glanced up and watched as Michael and this unknown "Bonita" person began to descend the stairs. Bonita had on her Hollywood glasses and was hanging tightly onto Michael's arm. The first thing Alan noticed, of course, was that she was strikingly beautiful— as in Hollywood beautiful. Given the stylized glasses, along with the fashionable clothes she was decked out in, he wondered if she wasn't either an actress or a model.

"Hi, Alan," Michael called out, while still halfway down the stairs.

"Hi, Michael," Alan replied, still with a note of curiosity and rising suspicion in his voice.

After stepping off the last stair, Michael made the proper introductions.

"Bonita, this is Alan Price. Alan, Bonita."

"Please to meet you," Bonita said, with her unmistakable Spanish accent.

"Pleased to meet you as well, Bonita," replied Alan, still feeling in the dark as to how this beautiful young lady, and noticeably Spanish, fit into the household picture.

"Frankie mentioned something about a CD from Briana," Michael said, in a way that came across as a given fact.

"Yes indeed. She asked that I personally deliver her prereleased single. She said you knew of it," he added, as he handed over the CD to Michael.

"Yes, I do know of it. Briana and I talked about it prior to my leaving for two weeks. Speaking of Briana, how is the tour going so far?"

"So far, no hitches. Every concert sold out within hours of going on the market."

"Having heard her sing, I'm not surprised. Would you mind telling her hi for me the next time you talk to her?"

"Absolutely—I usually talk to either her or her mother every day, so I'll be sure that she receives your message." Alan was still finding it difficult to keep his eyes off this mysteriously, unknown Spanish beauty while talking to Michael.

By this point in the conversation, Michael was starting to get a little antsy to get Bonita on her way to see Dr. Mandrel. He couldn't quite understand why Alan was hanging onto the conversation; or was it his need to get moving that made it appear as though he were hanging on?

"Bonita and I have a date with a doctor shortly, so I'll apologize upfront to you, but we need to get moving."

"I totally understand, Michael. It happens all the time in the music business, as well." They have a date? With another doctor? A double date, perhaps? "Enjoy the CD," Alan added, bringing his thoughts back from their wanderings.

"Given that Briana recorded it, I'm sure I will. And now we have to get moving . . . so, if you'll excuse us."

"Sure thing," Alan replied, as Michael and Bonita headed down the hallway and around the corner to the elevator. Frankie, who had remained to the side, opened the door and Alan quickly exited. Frankie could not help but notice a perplexed look on Alan's face as he left, but quickly dismissed it.

When Michael and Bonita returned from the quick follow-up examination, the first thing Michael did was to let Frankie know that she received a clean bill of health—her eyes were healing as expected. Dr. Mandrel confirmed Michael's suspicions that Bonita's vision appeared to be taking a little longer than average—but there was no cause to be alarmed. On the drive home, Michael was encouraged by Bonita's upbeat demeanor, in spite of the "longer than usual" healing diagnosis issued earlier by Dr. Mandrel.

The next challenge before Michael and Bonita was that of the potential heart surgery. Her first appointment tomorrow was to be at ten for the echocardiogram, followed by a physical workup at one—the break between appointments would allow the two of them time for a nice lunch between appointments.

Wednesday morning came quickly enough, with the transthoracic echocardiogram only taking forty-five minutes. After leaving the Cardiology Clinic, they opted to walk the three blocks to the restaurant where Michael had made reservations for lunch. Immediately upon entering the restaurant, it was obvious to Bonita that it was a cut above any she had seen before—even in magazines. Candles were burning on those tables that were occupied, the patrons were all well-dressed, and place settings with fancy cloth napkins sat upon neatly ironed, white tablecloths.

As the maître d' was in the process of guiding them to their table, Michael's eye caught sight of a familiar face at a table with two other men—it was Briana's father, Alan. Realizing that Alan had taken notice of him, Michael acknowledged his presence with a slight wave as he continued, arm-in-arm with Bonita as they followed the maître d' to their table. Once seated, Michael considered going over to Alan's table, before quickly deciding against it; they only had so much time left before her appointment with Dr. Olson.

Bonita was deeply impressed with the atmosphere, service and food—and said as much more than once. Michael, not frequenting these restaurants often, had to agree with her assessment. This, he thought, would be an excellent place to romantically entertain Briana some evening. He wouldn't be surprised at all, however, if she had already been here before, given that her father was currently dining here; a father, he noted, who spent a considerable amount of time glancing their way. Before Bonita and he had finished with their own lunch, Alan got up and left the restaurant with the two men.

Upon the completion of their meal, and with a little extra time remaining, the two of them took a leisurely stroll back to the clinic for their meeting with Dr. Olson. Michael had chosen the doctor as her cardiologist based on comments he had overheard his parents make some years back—another one of their many university connections. Michael recalled meeting Dr. Olson at a number of social events his parents had thrown at their house. Given her strong sense of humor and good looks, along with her easygoing personality, it early on became apparent to Michael why the doctor was always invited to their parties.

After one of the nurses had conducted some preliminary work, Dr. Olson walked into the examination room with a broad smile on her face. "Hello, Michael," she said, "long time no see. In fact, I believe the last time we crossed paths, you were still a young pup about to finish medical school . . . am I not correct?"

"Partially correct," Michael answered. "The last time we were together actually was at my parent's funeral."

"Ah, I try to put those thoughts out of my mind. I like to remember the happier times." Glancing at Bonita still sitting on the examination table, she turned her attentions to her. "And this absolutely beautiful lady must be Bonita. Is Michael taking good care of you, dear?"

"Sí, good care," she replied, somewhat meekly.

Glancing back at Michael, the doctor asked, "And how are the eyes coming along?"

"Surgery was successful and her vision is slowly clearing up, though it might be next week before she is able to see perfectly. Dr. Mandrel sees no complications or problems that would impede any potential heart surgery."

"Excellent then! I had the opportunity to go over the echo results during lunch and there appears, in fact, to be a hole between the two chambers—a classic case of ASD—though a little larger than I would like to see. It's a good thing you brought her in when you did."

Turning back toward Bonita, while at the same time placing the stethoscope in her ears, the doctor said, "I'm going to listen to your heart and lungs now, dear." After a few minutes of listening, the doctor removed the stethoscope from her ears and jotted down some notes to go along with those previously made by the work-up nurse.

"Well," she said turning back to Michael. "She definitely has a heart murmur, no question about that. Her blood pressure is high, her heart skips beats, and she has a notable shortness of breath—all of which comes as no surprise, either. All of her symptoms, as you know yourself, have manifested themselves as a direct result of the hole. We definitely need to get her into surgery this Friday. Like most doctors, primarily for family reasons, I would not normally schedule any surgeries the day before Christmas. However, based on our conversation of last week, I felt it was prudent to get her in as soon as possible if, in fact, she required surgery."

"And we both thank you very much for that," Michael said, with a tone of sincerity.

"According to the echo," Dr. Olson continued, "the hole is located midway in the upper chambers. Based on that, I see no need for open heart surgery; cardiac catheterization should do the trick. And, given her youth, she should be as good as new in no time. Any questions of you two?" she said, in conclusion of her overview.

"Not here," Michael responded. "Bonita?"

"No, Miguel."

"Then I will see the two of you early Friday. I see you have the pre- and post-operative information in your hand, Michael. Be sure and go over it with Bonita so that she knows what to expect Friday. Most patients, I find, like to know what to expect, as do you and I."

The doctor then shook hands with both Michael and Bonita before turning and exiting the room. Michael extended his arms and helped Bonita down from the table, and together they exited out the other door. Bonita remained silent until long after they had entered the car and were halfway home.

"I be okay?" she asked, in a quiet, concerned voice.

"Yes, you'll be fine," he replied, reassuringly. "This will be an easy surgery on you. The doctor will make a tiny cut right here," Michael added, while touching a spot on his own leg to show her. "Then she is going to slip a tiny tube up your artery with a patch inside of it. That patch will cover the hole in your heart. It won't take her any time at all. Given that you have an early surgery on Friday, she may not have to keep you overnight. It all depends on how things look to her when she visits you later in the afternoon which, I assume, she will. And the best part is, you won't feel a thing—you'll be sound asleep during the entire procedure."

"Okay, that make me feel better," she responded, with a little more lightness to her voice.

"I'll go over everything with you when you tell me that you're ready to sit down and discuss it, either tonight or sometime tomorrow; your choice."

"Okay, maybe later . . . maybe tomorrow . . . take nap first when get home."

Once up in her room, Michael reapplied the individual drops before slipping the eye shield over her eyes. She did look beautiful, he thought, as he stared down at her lying under the bedcovers. As beautiful as she was, it was Briana, however, that he wanted to be looking at under this cover—or any cover for that matter. Their coming together again was not that far off, he thought. Bonita, it turned out, had been an enormous diversion for both his mind and time since first they met; though he wished the circumstances surrounding her health had not been present in the first place. With those thoughts racing through his head, he returned to his study to await the "ringing of the bell" from the "Spanish Princess."

Thursday would be a free day for the two of them before the scheduled heart surgery early Friday morning. Given her ongoing need for the application of eyedrops, Michael opted out of going into the clinic on Thursday. He knew that Frankie was capable of applying the eyedrops, but Michael felt the need to keep a personal eye on her for any signs of healing complications.

At six-thirty Friday morning, Michael and Bonita were on their way to the hospital for her surgery. After explaining the whole procedure to Bonita in detail yesterday, along with what to expect during the recovery period, she seemed more at ease with herself—engaging Michael in nonstop conversation as he drove. With her vision gradually improving, she explained the letter she was able to write to her family yesterday—and how much she missed them all. In spite of the comforts she had been experiencing while living here, she was eager to go back home. Michael found that quite touching, given that most people coming to America end up wanting to stay here; especially when coming from poorer conditions as Bonita has—but in her case, it was a clear testament to the power of love for family.

A half-hour after leaving home, Bonita was taken away for the standard presurgical preparations, giving Michael a loving hug before disappearing through the doorway with the nurse. Michael was given the option by Dr. Olson to observe the surgery, but chose to remain in the waiting room. He wasn't quite sure why he opted out—but he did. Maybe, he thought, it was because he felt that he had grown too close to her—like a parent or sibling. And, like an expectant parent, he paced the waiting room and read magazines without remembering what he'd read. Eventually, when what seemed like hours had passed but hadn't, Dr. Olson came through the door into the waiting room. She walked over to the only person in the waiting room—Michael.

"Congratulations, Michael, you are now the proud guardian of what will soon become a healthy young woman."

"It went smoothly? No complications?" Michael inquired.

"Nary a problem, went right up to the hole, patched it up clean as a whistle, and backed out without a hitch. Just the way your parents taught me to do it. By this time tomorrow, you'll notice a greatly improved young lady."

"I don't know how to thank you enough, doctor. She's a great young woman with many dreams to fulfill. This will get her on her way. Thank you."

"I'll be honest with you, Michael. I accepted the patient, and resulting surgery, on behalf of your parents. They both did a lot for me at the university besides being close personal friends. In the past, I could never find a way to repay them for their many forms of generosity—and now I have through both you and Bonita. My surgical fees have been waived as a 'professional courtesy' on behalf of your parents. And with that having been done I can sleep better at night knowing that a debt has been repaid."

"I . . . I . . . don't know what to say," Michael finally stammered out, at an apparent loss for words.

"You don't have to saying anything. I was as much talking to your parents as I was to you. They were great role models for a lot of doctors—myself included—extremely compassionate people. And I firmly see that in you as well, Bonita being the prime example. I'm sure your parents look down at you with more pride than a hundred parents combined could ever muster up in their souls."

"I . . . I . . . " Michael still couldn't get anything more out. So he did the next best thing—or perhaps the best thing. He took three steps in the direction of Dr. Olson and gave her a hug like she probably had never experienced before, at least from a thankful "guardian."

When the two finally separated, Dr. Olson said one more thing to Michael. "I would ask you to pay it forward, but I know that you already do through DWB, much like your parents before you. Now go put on a mask and gown and get yourself down to the recovery room. I think someone might be waking up and wanting to see a familiar face. I'll see you two later this afternoon. If I don't get some last minute family Christmas shopping done between now and then . . . you may be doing surgery on me tomorrow." With those final words, she turned and walked out the door.

After the doctor retreated from the room, Michael shed more than a few tears. After regaining his composure, he did exactly as the doctor had ordered. He procured both a mask and gown from the nurse's station and went in to check on the "Spanish Princess." She must have heard the creaking of the door as her eyelids made an effort to open—and open they did to Michael looking down at her. When Bonita appeared to recognize the face, Michael could see a slight smile emanating from her lips.

"Don't try to say anything, Bonita," Michael said, softly. "The surgery went perfectly; you're going to be better than new. Rest is important . . . so close your sleepy eyes and go back to sleep. I'll be back shortly—most likely after they move you to your own private room."

Like a good patient, she let her eyelids drop down to a closed position. Michael waited a few minutes to confirm that she had actually drifted off to sleep—and she had. With Bonita resting comfortably, Michael decided to wander down to the cafeteria to grab a quick bite to eat. Out of consideration for Bonita, who was not allowed to eat prior to the surgery, he had chosen not to eat, as well. If for no other reason, outside of actually being hungry, eating right now was a way to fill up the time while she slept.

From the short time he was gone until he returned, they had moved Bonita to her own room—a room with a view of a beautiful landscape that appeared to run forever. Upon entering her room, he fully expected to find her still somewhat groggy but, to his surprise, she wasn't. To listen to her talk, one would never have gotten the impression that she had come out of heart surgery barely two hours ago.

While together, they laughed and smiled as they watched the same nurse come in a number of times to check up on her. The real smile, however, didn't appear on her face until the meal tray was placed before her. With Michael's help, she sat up in bed and promptly proceeded to eat every morsel on her tray—even the crumbs didn't stand a chance of escaping her hungry mouth. Michael, to say the least, was amused by it all—the scene reminded him of Briana's appetite.

Michael found the similarities between Bonita and Briana striking. They were both the same age, both were strikingly beautiful, tall, loved to eat, considerate of others and musically inclined. The only difference he could bring to mind that set them apart was Briana's mischievous nature. Thinking of this difference, the first thing that came instantly to mind was the comedy, The Taming of the Shrew. He wasn't convinced, however, that she was tamable—nor would he want her to be.

At four o'clock, they were eventually paid the much awaited visit by Dr. Olson.

"And how has our beautiful patient been doing while I was out being crushed in the mall by last-minute male shoppers?" she stated, looking directly at Bonita.

"I fine, doctor," she quickly answered.

"I'll say she's fine," chimed in Michael. "She devoured every morsel of lunch and still wanted more."

"That's a good sign indeed, especially knowing that it was hospital food she ate. Don't tell anyone, but I eat most of my meals outside of the hospital cafeteria. Something tells me that I'll live longer that way. Now let's have a look at you, young lady."

After taking her time to check her over, she took out a pen from her white lab coat, picked up her chart and wrote the words, "Patient released to the care of Dr. Michael Thomas."

Michael was pleased at this early release, but apparently not as happy as Bonita, however. The doctor heard the words "muchas gracias" from her more often in one minute than she had heard from any patient before.

"I know it's like singing to the choir, Michael, but I have to caution you to be vigilant in the monitoring of her vitals—any abnormal changes, slight as they may seem, bring her back in immediately. We don't want to take any chances."

In spite of the fact that they were both doctors, Michael listened intently to what she had to say with the utmost respect. Michael had a deep appreciation for another person's knowledge—and Dr. Olson was the leader of the pack when it involved matters of the heart.

"Thank you, doctor. You have my assurance that she'll be monitored closely. I'll restrict her activities until I know she's on the mend."

"Good enough," replied Dr. Olson. "And Merry Christmas to the two of you."

"Merry Christmas, doctor," Bonita stated.

"Enjoy your new life, Bonita," Dr. Olson remarked before turning and walking out the door.

"Are you excited about coming home now?" Michael asked.

"Happy . . . very happy," she responded, with obvious joy in her voice.

A few minutes later, one of the nursing assistants came in to help Bonita change back into her street clothes. Michael, not needing to be told, discreetly went out into the adjoining hallway and placed two short calls; he remained there until the assistant had given him the okay signal to reenter the room. The two of them then helped guide Bonita down into the wheelchair for the ride to the parking garage below. Once in the garage, Michael retrieved his car and returned to where they were both waiting. After gently helping her into the passenger seat, he securely fastened her seatbelt. Next stop—home.

Chapter Twenty-Three

PULLING INTO THE GARAGE AFTER LEAVING THE HOSPITAL, THEY BOTH noticed Frankie waiting by the elevator with a wheelchair by his side. Standing on the other side of the wheelchair was an attractive young lady that Bonita had never seen before.

One of the two calls Michael had placed was to a close nurse acquaintance of his whom he had hired to look after Bonita when he couldn't be available—or, for those moments when she would prefer the assistance of a female.

Following formal introductions, Michael lifted Bonita out of the front seat and gently placed her into the waiting wheelchair. After the four of them were in the elevator, Rebecca and Michael then took her straight up to her room while Frankie got off on the main floor. Michael quickly retreated to his study to allow her time to change into more comfortable clothing; which, he remembered, she had plenty to choose from given her recent shopping adventure.

Fifteen minutes later, he returned to find Bonita comfortably resting in bed. Knowing full well that she would likely fall asleep shortly, he placed the eye shield over her eyes after applying the necessary drops.

"Would you like something to eat before you sleep?" Michael asked.

"After I wake," came her sleepy response.

"Okay; you sleep, then eat," Michael said.

"And how about you, Rebecca, can I have Frankie bring you up some dinner?"

"I would love some dinner, with milk and coffee please, if you have either."

"Milk and coffee we have. I'll go down and see where Frankie is on dinner." Before Michael turned to leave, he glanced down at Bonita—the "Spanish Princess" looked to have already fallen asleep.

"Frankie!" Michael called out, as he entered the kitchen. "Would you consider rustling up some dinner with a glass of milk and coffee for Rebecca?"

"Two steps ahead of you, Michael. I have a folding tray stand over there and dinner will be out of the oven in five minutes. When I return, I'll get everything dished up for us. Is Bonita hungry?"

"Sound asleep. I have a feeling she'll be out for awhile."

"No problem—I'll reheat hers when she's ready."

Michael headed back upstairs to check on Bonita. While she was still sleeping, he checked both her blood pressure and pulse. Even with the cuff wrapped around her arm she never stirred. "All systems look good," he whispered to Rebecca. Michael then began to give Rebecca a briefing on the two surgeries and the various medications to be given to Bonita.

Frankie came in a few minutes later and presented Rebecca with her dinner on the folding tray. Michael and Frankie then left Rebecca to eat and headed back down to have their own dinner.

Following dinner, Michael went back upstairs to check on his patient once more, finding her vitals to be stronger than before.

"Sleep has always been one of the greatest medications for healing—and it doesn't cost a dime, either," Michael stated to Rebecca. "But then you already know that."

"I've always been a great fan of sleeping; even before I knew of its medicinal benefits," Rebecca replied.

"I'll be down the hallway in my study if you need anything," Michael whispered to Rebecca.

With her mouth busy eating a cookie, Rebecca simply nodded her concurrence. He felt comfortable having Rebecca over as she was one of the most accomplished surgical nurses he ever had the opportunity to work with—and he'd worked with many.

As he walked into his study, the first thing he noticed was the CD from Briana's father still lying on the corner of his desk. He immediately felt a slight twinge of guilt run through him at not having taken the time to listen to it yet—but he would now. He lifted the CD out of its case, noting first that the title of the song was Take My Hand. He then inserted the CD into the player, pushed play and quickly retreated to his recliner to listen—and listen he did. It was a beautiful love song, sung with an emotion by Briana that he hadn't even heard, or felt, at the benefit. After it ended, he immediately jumped up and hit play again—he needed to take in the lyrics one more time—and hopefully store them to memory. He was utterly astounded by what they lyrics said—but in a good way.

Take my hand my darling
And I'll lead you down
The road that leads to me—leads to me

Take my hand my love
And we'll walk forever
On the cotton—cotton clouds of love

May you never see a lonely day
Or spend a single night alone
May our love be as the song of time
That continues on and on—on and on

I was an ordinary person
A simple soul—a grain of sand
And then you looked my way
And then you held my hand
And then—I was everything

So take my love my darling
And you'll have my love
For a life—lifetime too

So take my heart my love
And I'll surely know
That it is safe—it is safe

May our love for each other be a guide
For all the world to see
May the love we feel grow stronger
As we live together day by day—day by day

I was an ordinary person
A simple soul—a grain of sand
And then you looked my way
And then you held my hand
And then—I was everything

So come—my beautiful love
And you'll never, never, never know
The end of time or love—the end of time or love

He was even more taken by her lyrics the second time around, so he rose to hear it once again—that was, until he thought he heard the sounds of talking down the hallway. Instead of hitting the play button, he quickly left the study and made his way down the hallway to Bonita's room.

"How are you feeling, Miss Sleepy Head?" Michael inquired as he entered her room.

"Sleep long time, no?" she replied.

"Yes, you did manage to sleep a long time. Are you hungry, by any chance?"

"Frankie is only moments away from bringing up her dinner," Rebecca interjected. "Bonita asked me to go down and find Frankie—she is one hungry girl. If I didn't know you better, Michael, I would think that you've been intentionally starving this poor girl."

"Nope! Simply one healthy appetite. We need to keep the little lady well nourished; known to be the best ingredient for whatever ails you, along with lots of sleep. While we're waiting for your dinner, let's check your vital signs, Bonita."

"They're great, Michael. I checked them a few minutes ago: 118 over 76 with a resting pulse of 60," Rebecca interjected. "Wish I could have those numbers on my best day."

"Well then, let me at least get some fresh drops in your eyes, young lady."

"Done," Rebecca responded, just as quickly as before. "Right after I took the protective shield off. Both of her eyes look pretty good to me; but then again, I'm not a doctor."

"Doctor or not, I'm starting to get the feeling that I'm no longer needed here. Wait!" he exclaimed, "I need to see how the incision is healing on her thigh and apply a fresh gauze."

"Done—it appears to be healing perfectly—no signs of infection.

Speaking of which, she finished taking her antibiotics. And yes, you are needed here, just not at the moment. We girls have a lot to talk about—mostly about men," she added, with a wink directed at Bonita.

"On that note then, I think I'll turn around and go downstairs to be harassed by Frankie—less painful," he replied, giving her a wink of his own. He then turned around and headed back down the hallway. Instead of harassing Frankie, however, he turned back into his study and began to play the recording, over and over again.

Each time he listened to the song, he came away with more un-answered questions. Is she asking for my hand as a romantic gesture of two lovers? Or is she asking for my hand in marriage? Can any of these words be a true reflection of her feelings when we haven't even uttered the words "I love you" to each other? Or did one of us? Have we allowed our physical needs to cloud the bigger picture of love and commitment? If there is love between the two of us, can it realistically survive the absences that will surely come to be because of our respec-tive traveling professions?

Needing to get away from his thoughts of Briana, he returned to Bonita's room to check up on her one last time before retiring for the night. It came as no surprise to find her already asleep. Rebecca, meanwhile, was fully engaged in a magazine in the dimmed light.

"I gather she is doing well?" Michael inquired of Rebecca quietly.

"All systems are functioning well. The dinner, no surprise, made her sleepy again. Given the hour, she may sleep through the night. I've brought my own night bag, along with a change of clothes, so I'll climb into bed beside her. I'm a light sleeper, so I'll know if and when she moves or wakes."

"It's Christmas Eve, Rebecca; why don't you go home to your hus-band tonight and for all of Christmas day. Husbands and wives should not be separated on Christmas."

"I'd consider the offer if he were home, but he isn't. His father suffered a heart attack three days ago . . . so he flew off to Seattle to help his mother cope with the situation."

"Sorry to hear that . . . then you will celebrate Christmas with the three of us."

"Thanks. Now back to sleeping beauty. I've kept a running chart of her vitals, medications, drops, etc., if you wish to review them, Michael."

"No need to," Michael replied. "You seem to have everything under control. It's getting late—a long day—so I think I'll retire myself."

"Goodnight then, Michael—we'll see you in the morning."

"Goodnight, Rebecca," Michael said, as he turned and headed to his own bedroom. Leaving his door slightly ajar in case he was needed, he headed off for a quick shower before drifting off to sleep shortly after his head hit the pillow.

Chapter Twenty-Four

AT SIX-THIRTY THE NEXT MORNING, MICHAEL WAS AWAKENED BY THE sound of laughter emanating from the direction of Bonita's room. This was a telling sign, he thought, as it gave the impression that all was apparently well with her. He arose from his bed and got dressed before heading down the hallway to check out his patient.

"Good morning and Merry Christmas, ladies," he said, as he entered the room. "The two of you sleep well last night?"

"Sleep like log," came Bonita's quick response. "And Merry Christmas to you, Miguel."

"And you, Rebecca—did you sleep well too?" Michael inquired.

"Same log as Bonita's."

"I would check her vitals and all that, but I have a sneaking hunch that they've already been taken," he said, while looking directly at Rebecca.

"They have been taken, and she is well on the road to recovery. She now has one healthy sounding heart," she added with a smile while looking at Bonita. "I can see her entering a triathlon by this time next week."

"Let's make it two weeks. I'll be right back—need to grab something out of my medical bag." He turned and headed back down the hallway and into his study. When he returned, he sat down next to Bonita who was still propped up in bed.

"Now lean forward a little bit while I look into your eyes," he said, as he raised a handheld ophthalmoscope up to her eyes. He carefully scanned each one for what seemed like an eternity to Bonita. After replacing the device in his shirt pocket, he said directly to Bonita, "I've never seen such perfectly beautiful eyes as yours. The real question right now is . . . how is your vision?"

"I see much, much better . . . even read magazine, till Rebecca say no more."

"Rebecca is right, Bonita. It's okay to see if you can read, but we don't want you putting any undue strain on your eyes just yet. They need to heal a little bit longer. And now, with your heart as good as new, you should be getting plenty of oxygen and nourishment to your eyes."

"Okay, Miguel," she responded.

"Are either one of you ready for breakfast?" Michael asked as he rose from the bed. "I know I am."

"Hungry," came Bonita's response.

"Make that two," chimed in Rebecca.

"Make that three," Michael added. "Would you like breakfast in bed or in the dining room?" Michael asked of Bonita.

"Dining room, please."

"Dining room it is, then. While you two get yourselves ready, I'll go down and throw Frankie out of bed," he said, with a devilish grin on his face.

"No wake Frankie up . . . he need sleep maybe," Bonita said, with a concerned look on her face.

"Not to worry, Bonita, I'm sure that Frankie was up hours ago. He always beats me up in the morning. I'll see you two ladies downstairs whenever you're ready."

"Give us ladies a good thirty or so minutes," Rebecca stated. "We both could stand a good shower before getting dressed."

And, true to his word, he found Frankie in the kitchen frying up bacon. "It looks as though we have some hungry mouths to feed," Michael remarked in passing, as he headed straight for the coffee pot. "The two of them will be down in approximately thirty minutes . . . something about showers and getting all dolled up," Michael added, before sitting down at the table.

"Merry Christmas, Michael," Frankie said.

"And Merry Christmas to you as well, Frankie." At that very moment, Michael became aware of an unfamiliar scent in the air. "There's a sweet fragrance coming from somewhere . . . it smells as though the outdoors moved indoors," he said, as he continued to sniff the air. "Any idea what it is, Frankie?"

"Sure do—it's a little something I brought in from the back forty," he responded. "Thought the ladies might enjoy it."

"Are you looking for me to start begging for the answer?"

"Nope. For a doctor you apparently have a lousy sense of smell identification."

"Frankie, it's Christmas after all—quit being your usual self for one day."

"It's a surprise for the ladies. Don't spoil it by asking too many questions."

Intentionally choosing to ignore Frankie at this point, he picked up the morning paper that he knew Frankie had already devoured while everyone else slept. He managed to get through most of the paper when he thought he heard a familiar sound.

"Speaking of the ladies," Frankie stated while scrambling eggs. "I do believe that I hear the humming of the elevator. They sure didn't waste too much time coming down. Must have been hungry for my cooking."

Ignoring Frankie's comment, Michael turned his chair around so as to better catch sight of the two of them when they entered the kitchen; and he waited, and he waited some more, until finally hearing Bonita's voice from the living room.

"That is beautiful."

"It certainly is," acknowledged Rebecca. "And to think that it wasn't even there last night."

By now, Michael's curiosity had gotten the best of him, so he pulled himself up from the chair and headed off in the direction of the voices. He spotted the two of them staring off into the living room at the object of their admiration—a Christmas tree; a fully decorated tree with multicolored lights and silver tinsel everywhere. Underneath the tree were four wrapped gifts. Michael could only assume that they were the four he had previously asked Frankie to wrap for the two ladies.

"Beautiful, isn't it?" Michael said, as he approached the two of them.

"You put it up, Miguel?" Bonita asked, still in awe.

"I wish I could take credit for it, ladies—but all the credit belongs to Frankie. We haven't had a tree up in the house since my parents passed away."

"Breakfast is ready!" Frankie announced as he made his way to the dining room table with a rolling cart full of food and drinks.

"Frankie, that is one beautiful tree," remarked Rebecca.

"Sí . . . beautiful," seconded Bonita.

"Thank you, ladies . . . I did it for you two. No Christmas is complete without a tree under which to lay one's gifts, or so they say. Now sit down everyone, please, before the food gets cold."

"I'd have to agree with the ladies, Frankie," Michael remarked, as he joined the others in being seated. "When did you find the time to do all of that?"

"Cut the tree and brought out all of the decorations while you two were at the hospital. Brought the tree in first thing this morning and put up the decorations. Didn't take long at all."

"You have to be kidding," remarked Rebecca, while cutting up her sausage. "That would have taken me all day."

"Did it this morning, I tell you. After breakfast and dishes, we'll see about opening some gifts."

"I no get anyone gift," remarked a slightly embarrassed Bonita.

"Neither did I," responded Rebecca in kind.

"None needed," replied Frankie, in an attempt to minimize their obvious sense of embarrassment. "There's a time to give and time to receive. This year it is both of your turns to receive."

"Frankie's right," Michael interjected. "Bonita, you have been a gift to this otherwise bachelor-run household. You've given Frankie and me something to look forward to when we awake—a purpose, a reason to look beyond our normal, sometimes boring routines—and we're going to miss you deeply when you return home. As for you, Rebecca, you've given us the skill of your profession, and I couldn't be happier for your being here to help us—it means a lot to me, not only medically, but personally. Thank you."

From the expression on both of their faces, Michael's words appeared to have hit home; a renewed sense of joy and gaiety took hold during the rest of their meal. When the last of the meal had been eaten, the three of them retired to the living room to take in the tree and engage in idle conversation. Meanwhile, Frankie cleared the table and placed the dishes and silverware into the dishwasher.

When he returned from the kitchen, he knelt down at the base of the tree and pulled out the gifts, two each for Bonita and Rebecca. Presenting the nicely wrapped gifts to the ladies, he wished each one of them the merriest of Merry Christmases before taking a seat alongside Michael.

"You first," Rebecca said, glancing at Bonita sitting next to her on the couch.

"You sure?" Bonita asked, feeling slightly uncomfortable with all three sets of eyes upon her.

"Of course I'm sure! Go ahead and open one of them," Rebecca encouraged her again.

Bonita slowly and carefully began unwrapping the first of her two gifts as though the decorative wrapping were more valuable than the gift itself.

"Oh my!" Bonita exclaimed, as she lifted the lid on the small jewelry box containing earrings loaded with small diamonds. "They beautiful," she added, with an obvious expression of gratefulness in her eyes. "Muchas gracias—both of you."

"You are most welcome," Michael stated, pleased at the look in her eyes. "Every pretty girl should have at least one pair of nice earrings for those special moments in her life."

"Now it's your turn," Frankie said, looking over at Rebecca who was still admiring Bonita's earrings.

Rebecca looked down at her lap and picked up one of the two similar-sized gift boxes. And, like Bonita, she slowly and carefully began unwrapping the gift.

"Oh my goodness!" she exclaimed, at seeing the multi-diamond encrusted, twin-heart pendant. "It's absolutely gorgeous, you two—thank you, very much. It's way, way more expensive than I deserve," she added.

"Nonsense," replied Frankie. "You deserve every diamond encrusted upon it, and more. Now it's your turn again, Bonita."

"Okay," she responded shyly in acknowledgement, as she began to unwrap a larger package.

"Oh no!" she blurted out with obvious wonderment in her eyes.

"Way too much money . . . I tell Roberta in store . . . way too much money," she remarked, while holding up the blouse, pants suit and matching jacket for all to see.

"Roberta told us that you liked the outfit very much but wouldn't let her buy it," Michael commented. "So, if you want to blame anyone, blame Roberta."

"Muchas gracias, everyone . . . nice Christmas," Bonita said, in an appreciative voice. "Rebecca, open gift," she added, looking sideways at Rebecca.

Rebecca, looking down at the remaining package on her lap, picked it up and began carefully unwrapping it.

"Michael! Frankie! You shouldn't have," she exclaimed, after opening the jewelry box containing earrings to match her pendant.

Both Michael and Frankie said nothing in return. The look on the women's faces made for their own Christmas gifts. Following the passing of his parents, neither one of them felt much like setting up a tree or exchanging gifts—except for this tree, future Christmases would more than likely be no different.

"Why don't you ladies go upstairs and try on your jewelry," Michael suggested. "I'll be up shortly to have another look at your eyes, Bonita."

"Okay," the two of them said in unison. Gathering up their gifts, they quickly left the living room and headed straight for the elevator.

Once they were heard going up the elevator, Frankie remarked to Michael, "That was generous of you, Michael. You brought a lot of joy to the ladies, both of them with their loved ones being far away this Christmas. From the looks on their faces, it apparently meant a lot to the two of them."

"You and I both know, Frankie, that money isn't an issue with either one of us. The monies spent on the gifts were worth every smile they produced."

"May I ask how you came upon the gifts for Rebecca on such short notice, Michael?" Frankie inquired.

"Actually, they were meant for Briana. But I can get her something else later, before she returns from her tour. Now, if you will excuse me, Frankie, I need to go upstairs and attend to some important eyes."

Christmas day at the Thomas house was an enjoyable occasion for the four of them—with the ladies proudly displaying their jewelry like peacocks. Bonita entertained them with Christmas music on the piano and Frankie served up a roasted turkey for dinner with all the fixings—much as one would expect on a day such as this. The memorable day ended with lights out for all four of them at the early hour of nine o'clock.

Michael strolled into the kitchen early the next morning, catching Frankie at the table reading the Sunday paper. Michael headed directly over to the coffee pot and poured himself a cup before turning around and asking, "Care for a warm-up, Frankie?"

"No thanks, Michael. I've already drunk the good stuff—the rest is yours."

Michael had to chuckle to himself. One day after Christmas and Frankie was back to his usual self—throwing those little jabs to let him know that he's loved. With cup in hand, Michael sat down at the table across from Frankie. Frankie slid the paper across the table toward Michael—all except the obituary section.

"Why do you even bother with the obituaries? You don't have friends or family living here."

"Making sure that my name isn't in it, that's all. One never wants to wake up in the morning and be caught by surprise, you know."

Michael knew better than to pursue the subject. Frankie was just being Frankie, he mused, as he pulled the paper closer to him.

"Not much to read in the paper this morning," Frankie volunteered. "Except for the entertainment section, perhaps," he added, with an unusual tone in his voice.

"Something tells me, Frankie, that you intentionally want me to read that section, right?"

"Thought you might be interested in an article written about Briana's Christmas tour—read it or not, your choice—but reader beware."

As Michael thumbed through the paper, he found the entertainment section buried at the bottom and pulled it out. On the upper front page of the section was a picture of Briana—and directly alongside her picture was an article titled, "Where is the Song?" Michael read the article from beginning to end—all without saying a word—though his mind was going into overdrive with questions. Frankie, meanwhile, had long risen from the table and was in the process of preparing their breakfast. Michael hadn't even noticed.

After reading the article twice—to make sure he didn't miss anything—he took a deep breath and leaned back in his chair. Our song—where is it? Michael wondered. The author of the article reported that the song was enthusiastically received by her fans during the first part of her tour—even clapping and cheering for her to sing it again. Then, not even halfway through her tour, it ceased to be a part of her performance. Why? Why would a singer take a new song that had become so popular and cease to sing it again? That was the question the author asked—and now Michael found himself asking the same question, as well. Why? Not that he considered himself a good judge of music, but Michael thought that Take My Hand was one of the most beautiful love songs he had ever heard.

Something was missing in this puzzle—something was seriously missing, he thought to himself. Was she no longer feeling the emotions that went into the creation of the song? If so, why? They hadn't spoken to each other since he left for La Paz. When last they talked, he recalled, it was about their tomorrows—not any potential goodbyes. Or was pulling the song even a goodbye? Maybe, he thought to himself, that he was reading too much into it. It was possible that she had other reasons for ceasing to sing the song.

"Michael, breakfast is ready," Frankie said, as he passed by him on his way into the dining room with some of the food.

He wasn't able to call her from La Paz because there was no cell phone reception—but he remembered forewarning her that it may be the case. And Briana had let him know that her cell phone was usually off during most of her touring days. He clearly remembers her saying that they would have to fantasize about each other.

"Michael!" Frankie called out again, as he came back into the kitchen for the last of the food. "The ladies are waiting for you in the dining room."

"Huh!" Michael said, suddenly becoming aware that someone was talking to him.

"Breakfast!" Frankie exclaimed even louder as he passed him by once again. "The ladies are waiting."

"Oh! Sorry," he said, as he rose from his chair, leaving behind his cold cup of untouched coffee and the article.

Eating breakfast with the three of them did little to free his mind of "Their Song." Or, he thought to himself, "The Missing Song." When he had finished with his breakfast, he excused himself and headed up to his study, closed the door behind him and fell back into the recliner. As he laid back in the recliner, he began thinking so hard and long about the article that he actually wore himself out—and drifted off to sleep.

Once again, it was laughter that pulled him from his slumbers. The laughter, not surprisingly, came from Rebecca and Bonita as they walked past his closed door in the direction of Bonita's room. Michael thought about going back to sleep, but ultimately decided against it. Besides, he thought, I need to make that obligatory appearance to check on the status of my patient—even though she's currently under the ever-vigilant care of one of the best nurses. If for no other reason, he thought, he would make an appearance anyway, just so Bonita didn't get the feeling that he was ignoring her.

Pulling the recliner back upright, he pulled himself up and out, opened his door and made the walk down the hallway to where the ladies were still in the process of laughing.

"You ladies sure find enough things to laugh about," Michael said, as he entered the room.

"We still haven't left the subject of men—they give us so many reasons to laugh," teased Rebecca, with a smile.

"That's okay, and understandable," he responded, "as long as I don't hear my name being mentioned in between the laughter, that is."

"You have nothing to worry about, Michael," replied Rebecca. "We haven't gotten to you yet . . . but close," she added, while glancing at Bonita, who was propped up on two pillows resting against the headboard.

"My apologies to the two of you for my behavior at breakfast," Michael stated. "I wasn't intentionally ignoring either one of you; my mind had simply gone off on a brief vacation, as Frankie would oftentimes say."

"Not a problem," replied Rebecca, to Michael's apology. "We were able to gossip about you right in front of you, and you appeared to not even care—or possibly even hear us."

It's a good thing Rebecca doesn't live here, Michael thought. Between her and Frankie, he wouldn't stand a chance against their not so subtle humor directed at him.

"So, Bonita," Michael said, "you haven't said a word since I came in. Cat got your tongue?"

"What cat?" she replied, questioningly.

"Oh, sorry . . . one of those sayings we Americans use from time to time. How are you feeling?"

"Feel good. I see good—not tired like before."

"Best news I've heard all day—and it's still early. As long as I'm here, let me take a peek at your eyes again. He then eased himself down onto the bed next to her and, while leaning in, checked out both of her eyes through the ophthalmoscope.

"Perfect—both eyes," he said reassuringly to Bonita. "But you still need to keep taking the eyedrops, at least one of them, for a long time—very important. You will also be taking the antibiotic for your heart for a long time also, maybe six months at the most. You can't risk getting your brand new eyes and heart infected—understand?"

"Sí, Miguel—I understand." This was followed by a moment of hesitation before she spoke his name again. "Miguel!" She said, more in the form of a question than a statement.

"Yes, Bonita," Michael replied, in a quiet tone.

"When I go home? I miss family."

Michael was taken aback by her question, as he hadn't quite expected her to inquire this early on; especially given the two surgeries she'd endured within the last four or five days.

"We will get you home as soon as you're healthy and ready to go. But first we have to see Drs. Mandrel and Olson one more time. They are the ones who will give the clearance for you to go home. Speaking of which," he continued, "we have an appointment to see both of them the day after tomorrow. Can you hang in there that long for an answer?"

"Okay . . . that be good."

"I promise you, the doctors and I will get you home as soon as your health allows. So tell me," he asked, "do you have a heart doctor and an eye doctor back home?"

"No," she reluctantly admitted. "Too much money."

"That's my point, Bonita, we don't want to send you back home until you're fully healthy. Do you understand what I'm trying to say?"

"Sí, Miguel," she replied. "I stay here till healthy."

"Good—get healthy and we'll have you back home with your family in no time—maybe in time for the New Year. And now," he said, as he pulled himself up and off the bed, "if you feel up to it right now, I'd like to suggest that you either go downstairs and play the piano or go outside for a short walk with Rebecca—but whatever you choose, don't overdo it."

"Walk sound good . . . then piano maybe," came her soft, feminine reply.

"Rebecca, she's all yours," Michael said, as he turned and headed back down the hallway and into his study. If the follow-up appointments with the two doctors come back with positive results, then it might be possible that she could be going home by the weekend. With that in mind, Michael decided it was time to map out a long-range medical plan for Bonita's eventual return to La Paz—along with other plans to ease her transition back home—and her future.

Chapter Twenty-Five

"Good morning, Frankie," Michael said as he entered the kitchen and headed, as usual, straight for the coffee pot.

"Sleep well?" Frankie replied.

"All things considered, not bad," Michael said, as he sat down at the table.

"Sleep doesn't always come well when you have a lot on your plate," Frankie said, more an inquiry than idle chatter.

"Can't find any argument with that, Frankie. And speaking of a full plate, I'll be flying off to D.C. around nine this morning. I have a one o'clock appointment with the Bolivian Ambassador to work out some last-minute details concerning Bonita. It's only an hour and a quarter flight, so with any luck, I should be back around six or so. Once in the air on the flight back, I'll give you a call, but don't hold up dinner for the ladies on my account."

"Will do. I can't imagine what you have planned that couldn't be handled over the phone, however," Frankie inquired.

"A lot of technical details to work out—I don't want to leave anything to chance concerning Bonita. On a related note, I have follow-up appointments scheduled with both doctors tomorrow. There's a good chance that Bonita will be returning home soon, providing she gets the clearance from the two of them."

"That is good news . . . but I'm going to miss her. She's brought a lot of joy, music and a sense of purpose to this house."

"You're not alone in those feelings. Rebecca will be leaving us also—tomorrow night I believe. The medical clinic she works for will be returning from their yearly Christmas break—going to miss her too."

"Make that two of us. Given your flight is at nine, would you like breakfast now or when the two of them come down?" Frankie asked.

"Now would be fine. Should the ladies inquire, and they most likely will, tell them that I had to go into D.C. on DWB business this morning; no need to explain anything just yet."

"I think I can handle another one of your little white lies, Michael. I'm used to it."

"Frankie, step out of character for once and be nice for a change."

"If I did that you'd think you had a stranger living in the house. We wouldn't want that now, would we? What we could use in this house is the touch of a woman . . . on a more permanent basis."

This was not the kind of comment that Michael wanted to hear right now. Thoughts of Briana had taken up enough of his time since she entered his life; but something was not right between them and he knew it—or at least sensed it. So, for the time being, he had been focusing his attentions, as best he could anyway, on Bonita. After she was no longer here, he knew he would have to find other ways to occupy his time and thoughts.

"Would you like to eat here, or in the dining room?" Frankie inquired of Michael, interrupting his troubled thoughts.

"Here's fine," Michael said, as he set the morning paper aside.

Michael finished off his breakfast quickly before excusing himself to tend to matters of this morning's flight and subsequent visit with the ambassador. After freshening up, he grabbed both his medical bag and notebook concerning Bonita before returning downstairs to the kitchen. With a quick goodbye to Frankie, he descended down the elevator to the garage, climbed aboard the cart and headed out to the hangar. It was still a little early, so he took his time conducting the standard preflight checkup. At nine fifteen, his wheels left the runway on a clear and sunny morning bound for Washington, D.C.

His meeting with the ambassador and a member of his staff went smoothly—they were appreciative of his more than generous requests and promised, on an expedited basis, to do what it took to bring them to fruition. A cash contribution by Michael to their favorite Bolivian charity helped to seal the deal. The commitment on their part to expedite his requests, though costly, took an enormous burden off Michael's mind. By five that evening, the plane's wheels touched down back home—in plenty of time for dinner with Frankie and the ladies.

With his mind relatively free of both Bonita's short- and long-range needs, the dinner conversation with the ladies was much more energetic than it had been in the past few days. He was pleased to hear from Rebecca that Bonita had more bounce in her step throughout the day without even feeling the need for an afternoon nap—that alone was a clear indication that her heart was returning to normal. She was able to read without difficulty, though Rebecca still placed some limits on her reading time. She even managed to send off another letter to her parents telling them all about her recovery and Christmas experience in America.

Following breakfast the next morning, Michael and Bonita headed out for their two doctor appointments. The first stop was with Dr. Mandrel, who gave her eyes a clean bill of health. Continue with one of the eyedrops, he advised, giving her extra samples to take back with her to La Paz. He informed the two of them that he saw no further need for follow-ups, but cautioned Bonita that she should continue to be seen by an ophthalmologist once she returned to La Paz. Michael assured the doctor that those arrangements were already being looked into.

The second appointment, with Dr. Olson, followed an hour later. As with the first appointment, Bonita was given full clearance to return home; antibiotics would need to be continued daily, and the need to be seen regularly by a cardiac specialist was a must. As with Dr. Mandrel, Michael assured the doctor that those arrangements were also being coordinated.

On the ride home following the two appointments, Bonita appeared to Michael to be somewhat subdued—only answering questions or responding to Michael's idle chatter. Halfway home, Michael, being a little concerned about her silence, finally inquired.

"Bonita, you received some good news, but you seem a little quiet. Is something bothering you?"

"I be leaving soon. No more Frankie. No more Rebecca. No more Miguel. I be missing everybody already."

"Well," Michael responded, "you'll be happy being back with your family, which is where you belong. And you know how to write, so we'll be looking forward to whatever letters you may want to send our way. You'll be going back with a lot of envelopes with our address on them. Postage has also been included. That tells you that we want to hear from you—we want to know what you're doing with your new lease on life. Okay?"

"Okay. That nice of you: stamps and envelopes," she stated, in appreciation of his thoughtfulness.

"Whatever letters you send this way we will share with Rebecca, as you two have become close friends this past week. None of us will ever forget you, Bonita. And hopefully you won't forget us . . . even when you become famous some day."

"I not forget any of you—promise."

"I believe you, Bonita."

Michael pulled the car into the garage and parked. Coming off the elevator on the main floor, they immediately caught a whiff of Frankie's cooking. Turning into the kitchen, they spotted Rebecca reading the paper while Frankie appeared to be entertaining her with his "how to cook" instructions, while at the same time vigorously stirring something on the stove; whatever it was, it smelled positively heavenly to the two of them.

"Not for lunch if that's what you were thinking," Frankie stated, sensing the two of them behind him without turning around. "You'll have to wait for dinner—lunch will be served in five minutes," he added.

"Hi you two," Rebecca said, "how were the appointments?"

"I go home," Bonita joyfully responded.

"That is good news," Rebecca stated, with obvious excitement in her voice as she rose to give Bonita a big hug. "So tell me, when are you going home?"

Bonita, unable to answer that question, looked over at Michael who was leaning against the wall.

"Not sure yet," he responded. "Possibly Saturday . . . or Sunday. After lunch, I'll give the travel agency a call and see what we can work out. And yes, Bonita received a clean bill of health from both doctors, thanks in large measure to your care, Rebecca."

"I had a good patient, unlike many I've had to deal with in my career. I only wish they were all like Bonita."

"The dining room table is already set up," Frankie interjected, "so why don't the three of you take this conversation out there. I'll have lunch out to you shortly."

With that dismissal by Frankie, they headed directly into the dining room. During their lunch of meat sandwiches and fruit salads, the ensuing conversation centered on the topic of how they were going to miss Bonita—and how she, of course, was going to miss the three of them. It was mostly an attempt at lighthearted conversation, though all could easily distinguish the underlying sense of sadness in one another's voices; those feelings would only become more intense between now and her actual leaving.

As Frankie began clearing the table, the three of them rode the elevator upstairs together. Rebecca and Bonita headed straight to their room for another round of drops in Bonita's eyes. Michael, meanwhile, headed off to his study to place a call to his travel agency. Thirty minutes later, the agency called back with available options for Saturday. Given the distance, there were no direct flights to La Paz, and all would require layovers of varying times. To minimize putting any undue physical or emotional stress on Bonita, Michael chose to fly her out of Dulles International on a direct flight to Lima, Peru. He also opted to personally fly her into Dulles; given his DWB credentials, he could stay with her right up until it was time to board her flight. Being informed that connecting flights would not get her into La Paz until shortly after midnight, he requested that she be put up in a hotel adjacent to the airport—personalized ground transportation to be provided at all stops. From there, the following morning, it would be a short two-hour flight into La Paz. Michael informed the agent that a specific La Paz address would be provided no later than Friday at which Bonita was to be dropped off. As a means toward further minimizing any potential travel worries, Michael instructed the agent that all flights, hotel and ground transportation expenses were to be paid in advance. Someone as young and naive in the ways of travel as Bonita, and given the opportunistic mentality of others, could easily be taken advantage of, he reasoned. By three o'clock, Michael received confirmation on all flights, ground transportation and hotel accommodations for her overnight stay.

With the logistics of getting her back home behind him, and with only three full days left, Michael decided to set Thursday and Friday aside for whatever Bonita wanted to do; one option being to take in some sightseeing of the Nashville area. Michael had to remind himself, however, not to tax her energy level this early after heart surgery; he chose to discuss all of this with her over dinner. There was always the possibility that Rebecca would have some ideas as to what they could see and do. Need to pick her brain before she leaves this evening for home and back to work tomorrow, he thought. The generous amount of money he was paying Rebecca for tending to Bonita on a 24-hour basis was worth every penny spent—and he knew it.

The evening meal was a feast to end all feasts. If ever Frankie had gone out of his way in the cooking department, this meal was it. Tonight was "Spanish Night" at the Thomas house. Prior to the meal itself, for which no one was allowed near the kitchen, he presented them with a vintage 2003 red wine, Contador—compliments of Michael's wine cellar, of course. For an aperitivos (appetizer), he served up "Ceviche de atun"—a Peruvian style yellow fin tuna ceviche, with sweet onions, cilantro, cucumber, fresh corn; coconut milk, aji Amarillo, and sweet potato. For the platos (main course), he presented them with a choice: Pollo—an organic young chicken breast, parmesan cheese potato cake, baby bok choy, with natural jus-garlic sauce. The second choice was "Costilla"—braised short ribs, potatoes, piquillo peppers, green peas; and natural jus–white wine sauce. And if that didn't fill them up, for dessert he served up "Croquestas de chocolate"—almond-crusted chocolate croquettes, lemon gelatin, and coconut foam.

When they had finished with the meal and dessert, even Michael felt the need to announce to all gathered that it was a meal to die for—but hopefully no one would tonight. Frankie, a modest man by nature, was reveling in the praise that was being heaped on him throughout the meal. It hadn't been since the death of Michael's parents that Frankie came upon the opportunity to display his culinary skills in high fashion. Though it required a lot of preplanning and work, he felt it was worth all the smiles and praise he received in return; especially from Bonita.

"Tell me, Frankie," Michael inquired. "You are not Spanish, and you have never served anything like this before—even for my parent's social dinners. So, be honest, where did you come up with the menu selection?"

"You're absolutely correct, Michael, I am not Spanish." A long silence followed as if that were the answer to Michael's question.

"Frankie!" Michael exclaimed, in a raised voice. "We are waiting."

"Okay, the truth it shall be. The menu is actually the work of Executive Chef Manuel Romero, of a Spanish restaurant located in New Haven, Connecticut. I believe the restaurant is called Ibiza. And no, I have neither met the gentleman nor partaken of his culinary skills. I have no idea if he is even still there. A dear friend of mine had eaten there, however, and couldn't find enough kind words to describe his experience. Knowing that I'd probably never travel to New Haven, he sent me a copy of the menu, and from that menu came this meal in honor of Bonita. It was the only means available to me to give her a taste of home away from home. End of story."

"Frankie . . . very, very good," Bonita said, for probably the tenth time tonight. "You make me feel home."

"Thank you again, Bonita. At least someone around here appreciates my cooking."

Michael intentionally chose to ignore Frankie's teasing.

"Bonita," Michael called out, "I believe Frankie left out one important detail about the meal, which is that you have to pay for the meal by playing the piano for us—that is, if you're up to it. And Frankie, we will all help get the dishes out to the kitchen so you can enjoy the fruits of your labors with us."

"Thanks, but no thanks. The leftovers need to be gathered up and stored in the refrigerator as soon as possible. I can hear the piano in the kitchen, so you three go ahead. And Bonita," he continued, looking directly at her, "if you know Silent Night, I would appreciate your playing it for me in honor of my parents. It was their favorite Christmas song."

"I know song, Frankie," Bonita replied. "I play for you."

And play she did. For an hour and a half she entertained them—with Frankie joining them in the living room after putting the leftover food in the refrigerator. The actual cleaning of the dishes, he figured, could wait until later—if not tomorrow. About nine o'clock, the wine and food, coupled with the day in general, had worn them all down. Rebecca was the first to rise.

"This girl is going home to get a good night's sleep and prepare to head out to work once again," she stated as a matter of notice to the other three.

Realizing that her new friend was departing for good, Bonita slid out from the piano and gave Rebecca a hug that lasted a long time. When they finally pulled apart from each other, it was easy to see the tears flowing from the two of them.

"Muchas gracias, Rebecca, for taking care of me . . . for making me well," Bonita said, in a crying voice.

"You are most welcome," replied Rebecca. "My husband and I love to travel, so if we ever make it to South America, we'll visit you for sure, okay?"

"I like that you visit me—friends never say goodbye, no?"

"No they don't. They simply say, see you later . . . or until we meet again. And someday we will," Rebecca added. "And Michael! Frankie! Thank you for your hospitality. I considered this stay a vacation with a loving family—not a job assignment."

"You were the one, not me," Michael stated emphatically, "who helped in restoring Bonita's health so quickly. If ever I become a patient, you are the one nurse I would select, above all others, to take care of me. And Rebecca," he continued, "when the dust settles, we'll be asking you and Ed to join us for a social dinner—right, Frankie?"

"Absolutely!" Frankie exclaimed. "Just let me know in advance what your favorite foods are."

"Ed and I will gladly accept the offer." She then went over to Bonita who was standing alongside of Michael, and gave her one last hug before turning and heading straight for the elevator that would take her down to her car; tears were still streaming from Rebecca's eyes as she departed. When Michael glanced down at Bonita, he noticed that tears were still flowing from her eyes, as well. Well, he thought, at least her eyes were remaining moist.

It would be a full minute before any of them made a move from where they were standing. Frankie eventually turned without a word and headed back toward the kitchen. Michael and Bonita soon followed suit and headed upstairs to make ready for bed. When Bonita was settled into bed, Michael went in and applied eyedrops, dabbed around her eyes, and then turned the lights off before partially closing the door and making his way to his own bedroom. It was a good day with an emotional ending—an ending all knew was coming but were ill-prepared to deal with when the actual moment arrived.

The following day was a relaxing one for the three of them. Michael spent part of the day on the phone with the Bolivian Ambassador's office tying up financial matters. Bonita played the piano in be-tween taking walks outside and sitting next to the koi pond feeding the fish; she was enamored by the fact that the fish would actually come to her. Michael and Frankie eventually joined her for lunch alongside the pond. Come dinner time, they all sat out by the pool feasting on grilled hamburgers and hot dogs. Michael was pleased in his obser-vations of Bonita as she appeared to have a lot of energy; afternoon naps having become a thing of the past.

Thursday morning found Michael in Bonita's bathroom teaching her how to apply her own eyedrops in front of the mirror. Michael chastised himself for having not taught her this earlier—she was, after all, a big girl. He reminded her, as the doctor had previously, that even though she could see clearly now, the drops were still a necessity for some time to come.

Following the "teaching moment," they headed down to say good morning to Frankie and to have breakfast. Today was going to be a busy day for the two of them, so Frankie made sure that they had a filling breakfast before they departed for their guided tour of Nashville and surrounding areas. The tour, however, would be conducted from the back seat of a limousine; if Michael was going to enjoy the sights along with Bonita, he decided that a limo would be the ideal way to do it.

By nine o'clock, the two of them were descending the outside stairway to the awaiting limousine—a sight which left Bonita's mouth agape. When the seasoned-appearing driver came around and opened the door for them, she was even more impressed—she felt as though she were a member of royalty. The look of wonderment on her face told Michael that he had made the right decision in going all out for her second to last day in Nashville and for that matter, in America.

Their first stop was the Belmont Mansion, built in the 1850s by one of the wealthiest women in the country at that time. Before leaving the mansion, Michael picked out a cross pendant for Bonita's mother. They followed that with a tour of the Grand Old Opry, the Belle Meade Plantation, and the Country Music Hall of Fame. From there it was on to the Nashville Zoo at Grassmere before stopping to dine at the well-known Stockyard restaurant for a late lunch.

Michael knew better than to wear her out, so many of the sites they visited were viewed courtesy of the limo windows. Following lunch, they went on to visit the famous Jack Daniel's Distillery where Michael purchased a bottle of their finest whiskey for Bonita to take back to her father. The limo then took them to Stones River National Battlefield and Carter House—both scenes of Civil War actions.

Once the touring part of the day had concluded, they stopped off at Morton's Steakhouse for dinner—an experience unlike any Bonita had participated in before. White-shirted, bow-tied waitstaff seemed to outnumber the patrons. They were seated at a white table-clothed table with a burning oil lamp for added ambiance. The first item set before them was an egg and onion loaf of bread—exclusively made by a local bakery to Morton's exacting specifications.

Following the delivery of the bread, they were greeted by a wine steward who presented them with a vast array of some of the finest wines available to choose from—including some of their finest that ran upward of $5,000 a bottle. Once their wine of choice was selected, they were next greeted by a server who rolled out a cart containing wrapped displays of many of their available dinner choices. The server proceeded to describe each cut of the prime USDA meats available on the menu. Also on his display cart were live lobsters shipped in daily from Maine; Bonita, however, felt a little uncomfortable at watching the live lobsters crawl around on the display cart. The two of them eventually ordered oysters on the half shell and filet mignon—both washed down with the red wine Michael had ordered.

For dessert, Bonita chose the New York cheesecake while Michael went with the cinnamon apple pie with Haagen-dazs ice cream. The most enjoyable part of the dinner, however, was the free-flowing conversation that passed between them. From the gaiety in her voice and the look on her face, it was obvious to Michael that she had thoroughly enjoyed the experience—but then again, so had he.

The events of the day brought him to the realization that there was, in fact, another life beyond that of doctoring—a realization that even his parents knew all too well before him. He made a silent commitment during dinner that he would include such events in the future with friends and acquaintances—but only if they included Briana. He deeply cared for Bonita, and regretted not a moment of her having entered his life; it was Briana that he both wanted and needed to fulfill him, however.

It was well after eight before the limousine dropped them at the house. The ride back was filled with more silence than conversation. Michael could tell that both the meal and long day had taken their toll on Bonita. After sharing the events of the day with Frankie, Bonita excused herself and made her way up to her room to prepare for bed. Michael followed behind her ten minutes later to apply the eyedrops and place the protective shield over her eyes. After watching her slip under the covers, he flipped off the light switch and made his way back downstairs.

Michael and Frankie spent the next half-hour discussing last minute preparations that needed to be attended to before Bonita's eventual flight home on Saturday—and then Michael too headed up to bed.

It would be almost eight-thirty the following morning before Bonita came downstairs—finding both Michael and Frankie conversing at the kitchen table over coffee.

"Good morning, Bonita," Frankie greeted, upon seeing her.

"Well, look who finally woke up," Michael quickly added. "Frankie was about ready to serve you breakfast in bed."

"Me tired," she said as she seated herself at the table.

"After yesterday, I'm still a little tired myself," Michael remarked.

"Have good time yesterday," she offered. "Take home good memories."

"Good—same here," Michael stated. "I was born and raised here but have never taken the time out of my life to see most of the places we went to, so it was good for me to get out and see the sights. All thanks to your being here," he added.

"Maybe see our sights someday?"

"I would love that—but hopefully not during any of your major floods."

"I know you two probably ate too much last night," Frankie interjected, "but either of you interested in breakfast?"

"I eat something light, no?" Bonita responded.

"How about some oatmeal and toast?" Frankie offered.

"That be good."

"And you, Michael?"

"I could actually go for some scrambled eggs, bacon and toast, if you don't mind."

"Oink, oink," Frankie said, as he rose from the table.

Michael ignored Frankie's insinuations, while at the same time, Bonita was trying to figure out exactly what is was that Frankie had just said. At Michael's insistence, Bonita and he left for the living room, leaving Frankie alone to prepare their breakfast. Bonita, knowing that today would probably be her last opportunity to play the piano for some time to come, went directly to the piano. Michael wasn't sure of the piece she was playing but, as usual, it was beautifully played. He knew, with a feeling of great sadness, that he was going to miss these precious moments with Bonita.

Following breakfast and after the table had been cleared away,

Frankie spent the better part of the morning assisting Bonita in the fine art of packing. Knowing that she was returning home with far more than she came with, Frankie had the foresight to pick up a three-piece luggage set with a matching carry-on bag. While they were engaged in packing, Michael busied himself out in the hangar to prepare the plane for tomorrow's early flight to Dulles International; a flight he was not exactly looking forward to—for obvious reasons.

All of this activity was notable for the lack of humor, jokes and ribbing that had become a part of their daily routine over their time spent together. Bonita was overjoyed at the notion of finally going home—but at the same time deeply saddened at the thought of leaving. Michael and Frankie were happy for her soon-to-be reunion with her family—but her gain was their loss.

Michael, seeking a way to ease the tensions created by her leaving, and feeling the need to get out of the house, made reservations at a downtown restaurant for the three of them. Frankie, of course, was delighted at the invitation, not because it meant that he wouldn't have to prepare dinner—but because he was able to be a part of Bonita's last evening in Nashville. It was to be his final opportunity to say good-bye, without having to contend with the harried activities that would surely ensue come tomorrow.

The dinner turned out to be a complete success, not because of the dinner itself, but for the intimate conversation shared between them. Absent were the usual jabs that Michael and Frankie would normally be throwing at each other during meal times. Instead, the conversation centered on Bonita—more specifically—her dreams and aspirations. She once again shared her desire someday to attend college as a means to help her siblings attain a better future—not to mention her desire to help her parents out financially. She also had aspirations of learning the piano well enough to be able to perform at weddings, funerals and various social events—all for the sole purpose of bringing in added money for the family. And, last but not least, she shared her desire to fall in love, get married, and to raise a family of her own—but hopefully outside of the types of neighborhoods she had become all too familiar with in her own upbringing.

She had first shared some of those aspirations with Michael on the flight from La Paz to Nashville. He believed back then that she would one day achieve her dreams and now, more than ever, he knew she would one day make it all come to fruition. Unbeknownst to her, he had already set in motion the things necessary to assist her in those aspirations. The real work, however, would be up to her—but he knew deep down that she would be up to the many challenges that lay ahead of her.

The ride home from dinner was a quiet one. The dinner, coupled with wine and the inevitability of tomorrow coming too soon, had gradually taken its toll on the three of them. Michael and Frankie stepped off the elevator on the main floor while Bonita continued on up to the top floor. Knowing that she had a full day ahead of her in terms of flying, Michael had suggested that she retire early—so she immediately set off to do just that.

Both of them drifted off to the living room where Michael placed a classical CD in the player and hit play before seating himself into one of the cushioned chairs. Frankie made himself comfortable in his favorite love seat and picked up his book. As Michael listened to the piano music, he closed his eyes and allowed his mind to travel back to the three days with Briana in Etenia; they were, without question, the best three days of his adult life. He had no idea, however, if those days would ever play themselves out again. Shortly after ten, he was awakened by a gentle hand coming to rest on his shoulder—he rose and went upstairs to bed.

By six the next morning, all three of them were up and quietly preparing for what they knew was to follow. A half-hour later, they were seated at the dining room table for their final meal together. Light conversation filled the air, but any mention of her leaving was avoided—a classic case of avoidance out of fear that the tears would fall hard.

When breakfast was finished, Frankie made no attempt to clear the table. Instead, he went up to Bonita's room, retrieved the suitcases and moved them into the elevator. From there he went down to the garage, loaded them onto one of the golf carts and headed out to the hangar. Pulling alongside of the plane, he got out and promptly proceeded to place the luggage into the cargo hold. Once the luggage was adequately secured, he headed back to the house for the moment of reckoning.

Coming off the elevator, he headed back into the dining room where he spotted Michael in a tight embrace with Bonita. Though she had her back to him, he knew that she was crying, while Michael had his face buried deep within her hair. Frankie was convinced that Michael was weeping, as well. When it came time for Frankie to give her a hug, could he hold back his own tears? He wasn't convinced that he could hold back—nor, given the circumstances, did he really care.

When the quiet sobbing finally subsided, Michael slowly released his hold on Bonita. He then pulled a neatly folded handkerchief from his shirt pocket and gently erased the signs of tears—but he could do nothing about her reddened eyes. Frankie knew that the moment of truth was upon him, so he slowly approached Bonita until he was mere inches away from her. He then took hold of her for a brief moment before releasing her.

"Please, write us when you get the chance," Frankie said, with a touch of sadness in his voice that Michael hadn't heard since his parents' funeral.

All Bonita could do was nod her head yes. If she said anything at all, she was afraid she would burst into tears again. Frankie quickly kissed her on the forehead, turned and exited the room. Michael then picked up her carry-on bag with one hand and took her hand with the other. From there, the two walked in silence to the elevator for the ride down to the garage. After climbing into the cart, they made the short trip out to the hangar without saying anything. Bonita stepped out of the cart and proceeded up the stairs into the plane. Once inside she made her way to a seat halfway back on the right side. From this vantage point she could easily view Michael as he piloted the plane. Once onboard himself, Michael secured and latched the door and made his way to the cockpit, but not before helping to adjust her seat belt. Twenty minutes later the wheels lifted off the runway into a sun-filled, cloudless sky.

Michael's mind was so preoccupied with thoughts of Bonita sitting quietly behind him that he barely remembered the flight itself; it was as if the entire flight were flown on autopilot—and Michael wasn't pleased with himself for letting his mind wander like that.

Upon arrival at the airport's corporate jet center, her luggage was loaded onto a service vehicle and they were driven to the departure terminal. Upon reaching the upper floor of the main terminal, Michael assisted Bonita through the check-in process. After passing through security, they then made their way along the terminal to her assigned gate, finding two seats by the window in which to await her call for boarding. Throughout the morning, few words were spoken between them—until now.

Pulling a small envelope from inside his jacket pocket, he handed it to Bonita, saying, "This is for you—please put it in your purse. You never know when you might need some extra spending money between here and your arrival home. When you arrive at the airport in Peru," he continued, "someone will be there to take you to your hotel. That someone will be holding up a sign with your name on it down at baggage claim. They will see to it that both you and your luggage make it to the hotel. They have already been paid. Any meals or whatever else you may decide to buy at the hotel, charge to your room, which is also paid for. The hotel will see to it that you get back to the airport in time for your flight to La Paz. The driver will also see to it that you get assistance in getting your bags to the proper check-in counter.

Once you land in La Paz, someone will be there to take you home. Look for your name again in the baggage area—the driver has been paid in advance, as well. Don't let any of the drivers ask you for money, and no tipping. And here," he continued, as he pulled another envelope from inside his jacket and handed it to her, "is a letter from Frankie and me to you. Once you're all settled in and the plane is in the air, you may open it. I know I threw a lot at you right now, but I have to ask: any questions?"

"I never able to repay you," Bonita finally said, after some hesitation.

"I hope you never repay me." Michael responded. "It's Frankie's and my gift to you."

"You already do too much for me."

"Bonita!" Michael said with emphasis to get her attention. "Do either Frankie or I appear to be hurting financially? No! We are two bachelors with more money then we could ever spend on ourselves. You just promise us that you'll work hard at whatever career path you choose to follow. When we see your name up in lights, or read about your successes in magazines, then we'll know that you have repaid us, okay?"

"Okay. I work hard . . . make you and Frankie proud."

"That is all we ask—nothing more. And one other thing. You be sure to write us like Frankie asked this morning. If you want, you can write your letters in Spanish and I'll read them to Frankie."

"I write often. Maybe in Spanish, maybe in English."

Bonita had barely gotten those words out of her mouth when the announcement came over the speaker system for first-class passengers to begin the loading process.

"It sounds as though they're calling you to go aboard already," Michael said, with a sense of reluctance in his voice.

"First class?" Bonita exclaimed, looking at Michael in disbelief.

"Yes—first class. The "Spanish Princess" needs to go home in style. Besides, that's the only section of the airplane that gets good food and personalized service. I've sat in cramped economy sections more than once, and I have to admit, I didn't like it—nor would you."

Michael then rose up from his seat and extended his hands to Bonita. Taking hold of her outstretched hands, he gently pulled her to an upright position. While facing her, he pulled her body into his. A few seconds later he released her, placed his hands on both sides of her face, and gave her a quick kiss on the lips.

"Hasta que encontremos otra vez, Bonita . . . until we meet again," Michael repeated in English, as a tear began to form in his eye.

"Sí, Miguel, Hasta que encontremos otra vez. And we shall."

She then lifted herself up on the toes of her feet and quickly gave Michael a kiss right back. With that, she turned and headed straight for the ramp leading onto the airplane, turning around only briefly for one last look at "Miguel" before disappearing out of sight. Michael, at that moment, could care less if those around him noticed the tears streaming unashamedly down his face. At that very moment, he said goodbye to something far more important than his pride.

Michael could have left at that point, but something kept him there a bit longer. He felt nothing less than a deep sense of loss. By the time he was driven back to his own plane and was about to climb the stairs, he turned and watched as her plane raced down the runway and lifted into the air. He waved, not knowing if she actually saw him or not, as another tear quickly formed. Twenty minutes later, he too was racing down the same runway for home.

A half-hour later, Bonita reached into her purse for the letter Michael had given her to read. Carefully unsealing the envelope, she began to read:

Dearest Bonita,

I'm not sure where to begin other than to say that both Frankie and I are missing you already. During your short stay here you have managed, by your presence, to bring a lot of joy into our household— into our lives. We looked forward to your risings each morning, as one would a bright and beautiful sunrise on a clear autumn day. We both looked forward to those many times when you would sit at the piano and entertain us with your flawless pieces that are someday destined for a stage. You are a better piano player than you give yourself credit for. Frankie and I both agree, which is a miracle in itself, that you should be playing the piano more often so as to become more fully proficient at it. So, with that in mind, you will find a new piano in your parent's house. Think of the two of us every time you sit down to play. Someday, when you record your first CD, you can send us two bachelors a copy.

Oh, did I forget to mention that your parents are now living in a new home in the suburbs of La Paz? The airport driver will take you directly there. Unlike your parent's rented, three-bedroom house, this one comes fully furnished and has four bedrooms—one of which is just for you. Why should you have your own bedroom, you ask? For the simple reason that a girl needs her own quiet space to do her college work in.

Oh, did I also forget to mention college? Well I guess I did. Beginning with the upcoming quarter, you will be attending the University of Mayor de San Andres, a university close to your parents' new home. What field you choose to major in is clearly up to you—music, of course, is only one of the many choices available to you. If you choose not to attend college—that is fine too. Both tuition and books for four years have already been paid for. A stipend for any miscellaneous expenses has also been deposited with the university in your name. Your assigned counselor, so I have been informed, is Senorita Catalina Garcia-Ramirez. She will be your first point of contact.

As was mentioned by me on a few occasions, and by the two doctors that operated on you, medications must be continued and follow-up appointments with local specialists are a must. A medical insurance card will soon follow in a separate mailing. Recommended doctor's names will also be included in the mailing. Frankie, Rebecca and I have a lot invested in your health, so please, do not skip seeing the doctors just because you appear, in your own mind, to be feeling healthy. Okay?

Oh, a friendly reminder. Take the money out of the envelope that I gave you at the airport, and slip it into your purse—if you haven't already done so. Inside the envelope, you will also find a prepaid credit card, in your name, with a credit balance of 8,250 Brazilian real. Every college girl needs to keep up with the latest in everyday fashion trends. Good clothes, as you know from your stint as a model, are a vital asset to a beautiful college girl—and that would be you.

Frankie and I would have mentioned these things while you were still at the house, but for some unknown reason, it slipped our minds.

We bachelors seem to have such terrible memories. I only hope you won't be mad at the two of us.

Well, Bonita, as you can see by reading this, I am not much of a letter writer, so I'll quit while I'm ahead. Have a pleasant flight home, take care of your health, and write when you get a chance— though Frankie and I both know you'll be busy with your college studies. We miss you—and we love you.

~Love, Miguel & Frankie

"Ma'am, is there something wrong?" the flight attendant asked of Bonita.

All Bonita could do was shake her head no as her tears continued to pour onto the letter resting in her lap.

"If you need anything, ma'am, simply push that button right above you and I'll be right here; even if you just need someone to talk to for a bit, okay?"

Chapter Twenty-Six

WITH BOTH REBECCA AND BONITA NOW GONE, THE FORMER ROUTINES around the house returned to normal—though a sense of emptiness permeated the bachelor household. Even the bantering that normally took place between Michael and Frankie was more subdued; a reflection of their missing Bonita deeply.

To keep himself busy, Michael returned to assisting at the free clinics. If nothing else, it helped to clear his mind of the emptiness that filled his heart—not so much for Bonita now—but for Briana. "Their Song" had yet to return to the airwaves and the media, from time to time, continued to print articles questioning why; but no one questioned why more than Michael. Nor in the media were there any responses from Briana as to why she no longer sang the song. He went to bed at night wondering why and arose wondering why—but no answers were forthcoming—so much for sleep being the panacea of what ails you, he thought.

Briana's Christmas tour was scheduled to run until its final performance on the twelfth—seven days from now. Michael, in spite of his own dreams and desires, knew deep down that Briana would not call when she returned home from the tour. Something had happened between them for which Michael had not a clue. Could their relationship and longing for each other have been replaced by someone else? No, came his quick answer. As short as their relationship was, he truly believed he knew enough about her inner character that she was above dumping him for someone else. It had to be something far more serious than that—but what?

Sitting down at his desk, Michael decided to Google her Christmas tour. For reasons even he couldn't explain, he wanted to know where she was this afternoon. When her home site came up, he clicked on "tour schedule." This, in turn, brought up every one of her performance dates from mid-December through the final performance on the evening of January twelfth. A quick glance at the schedule indicated the tour beginning on the west coast and finishing up on the east coast—New York City to be exact; no performances, he noticed, were scheduled for Briana's hometown of Nashville.

Today's performance was to be at eight o'clock in Chicago so, he wondered at length, what would she be doing at three in the afternoon, her time? Even though she most likely would not get to bed before midnight on performance nights, he seriously doubted that she would still be in bed this late in the afternoon.

This tour information led nowhere—nor did he fully believe that it would. Sliding the chair away from the desk, he returned to his recliner and plopped down. No sooner had he made himself comfortable than he instinctively reached for his cell phone. Scrolling through his address book, he pushed "talk" when he came to Briana's name—and he waited—for what he wasn't sure. He wasn't even sure what he was going to say if and when she answered the phone.

Without even hearing a ring tone, he immediately received a message he wasn't expecting to hear—The party whom you are calling is not accepting calls from this number. He suddenly felt the heat rising in his head as he leaned further back in his recliner. His phone number had been intentionally blocked. At that moment, he felt worse than if he'd been slapped in the face; for if that were to happen, at least he'd have had some answers. She would have been standing before him—in the flesh. There would be pain, but at least there would be answers, as well. He could live with answers, even if the answers were not to his liking. Right now, however, there were none—other than the painful realization that she had written him out of her life forever—by a robotic message, no less.

Could he accept the rejection and move on with his life? He wasn't quite sure yet. He knew he'd have to move on eventually—as he had in previous relationships—but this one hurt far deeper than the others combined. Without the actual words spoken between them, he knew that he was in love with her—even if she wasn't in love with him. But he felt that she was at one time until—until he didn't know when. It was the not knowing when and why that ate at him the most. And with those thoughts and unanswered questions racing through his mind, he fell fast asleep in the recliner from mental exhaustion.

An hour later, he slowly began to stir from his sleep. He was awake now, but lacked the energy or the willpower to rise from the recliner. Fifteen more minutes consumed by thoughts of Briana passed before he finally made the effort, though reluctantly, to leave the comfort of the recliner. When he finally did, he went straight into his bedroom, changed into his swim trunks, and headed down to the pool. He hadn't been in the pool once since Bonita came to stay with them—it felt relaxing, even though he felt the soreness in his muscles from the long period of disuse. Following a long shower to take the tightness out of his muscles, he joined Frankie in the kitchen.

"You're a little early for dinner, Michael," Frankie stated, upon seeing him enter the kitchen.

"I know . . . a little bored at the moment. A lot of activity around here with Bonita and all . . . then nothing. Maybe I should run up to Etenia for a few days—keep myself busy."

"You could," Frankie remarked, "but it won't fix what ails you at the moment."

"Frankie, are you trying to tell me something without actually telling me something?"

"You could say that."

"Let me guess. It has something to do with Briana, doesn't it?"

"You could say that," Frankie answered, for the second time.

"Spit it out, Frankie. What are you trying to say?"

After a moment of hesitation, Frankie finally spoke his piece. "What I'm trying to say, Michael, in a roundabout way, is that you're in love with her, but you no longer feel that she's in love with you. And you've been sitting around stewing about it for days on end, and haven't done one thing about finding out what happened between you two. And don't even try to deny any of this because I know better—and you know that I know better."

"Touché! Frankie hits the bull's eye again," Michael exclaimed, giving in to total defeat at the hands of Frankie. "So, Oh Wise Master, where did I make a wrong turn that would make her not want to have anything to do with me?"

"In one word," Frankie clearly stated, "Bonita."

"Bonita!" Michael loudly exclaimed. "Bonita?"

"Yes, Bonita," Frankie repeated, for the second time.

"It can't be. Bonita arrived the same day that Briana left for her tour. They haven't even met. In fact, I haven't even talked to Briana once since Bonita came onto the scene."

"Doesn't matter; she still knows of her. Briana knows that Bonita is tall, slender, young and beautiful . . . a 'Spanish Princess,' as you have so named her. Briana is more than jealous—she feels betrayed. That's why you have become *persona non grata* in her life."

"Frankie, I hate to admit that you're usually right in most matters; but not this time. No one knows of Bonita with the exception of the two doctors, Rebecca, Roberta and you. None of whom have ever talked to Briana since the tour began."

"Michael, I hate to burst your bubble, but someone else has seen you with Bonita—twice I believe."

Michael thought of what Frankie had just said for a half minute before it finally dawned on him. "Oh my God!" Michael yelled out, with the light finally coming on in his head. "Alan Price . . . her dad . . . here . . . at the restaurant. Oh my God!" He exclaimed one more time.

"Now does it all make sense?" Frankie kindly asked.

"Absolutely. Briana has cast me aside for a relationship that never was . . . at least romantically."

"You know the old saying, Michael, 'perception is reality.' Based on what little her father could honestly tell her, she has perceived that you are/were involved in an affair with this unknown Spanish beauty. Can't say that I would have thought any differently myself if I were in her shoes."

"Now what do I do, Dr. Frankie?" Michael asked, in an obvious plea for advice.

"As you well know, I typically steer clear of matters of the heart— it's like stepping in quicksand to do so. But, if you're sincerely asking me for my advice, I'll give it this one time."

"I'm asking," Michael stated, looking for Frankie's wisdom to bring Briana back.

"Write a letter," Frankie calmly stated.

"Write a letter?" Michael asked, wondering why a letter.

"Have you tried calling her lately?"

"Yes."

"And?"

"She's blocked my calls from getting through."

"Okay. And if you staked out her place in an attempt to talk to her in person . . . there's a good chance that she'll have a restraining order placed against you, and your reputation doesn't need to take a hit like that. Remember, Michael, you're dealing with a woman scorned—or at least she thinks she has been. That's why I suggest a letter. It doesn't have to be wordy—simply state the facts. If that doesn't work, then just possibly you weren't meant for each other, in spite of your heart telling you otherwise."

"A letter it is then. Thank you, Frankie."

"You're most welcome, as always. Her condo address, by the way, is in the address book by the living room phone."

"Is there anything you don't think of, Frankie?" Michael inquired.

"Not too much. Remember this, Michael, it's a lot easier to see the total picture when you're standing outside as opposed to being in the middle of something. Just a little something my father passed onto me."

"Wise man," Michael said. "Like father, like son."

"Michael, you're wasting time. Get yourself upstairs and get the letter written."

"Okay! I get the message, Dr. Frankie." Before heading upstairs, he quickly grabbed an oversized mug and filled it to the brim with coffee. This letter writing might take awhile, he mused.

"Michael!" Frankie exclaimed loud enough to get his attention. "Nothing long; one or two pages max."

"Okay, I get the message—again," Michael responded, as he quickly made his way out of the kitchen and up the stairs to his study. Pulling the stationery forward with his initials embossed on it, he began to write:

My Dearest Briana,

Before you decide to tear this letter into a million and one pieces, let me explain something of importance to both you and me. First off, allow me to tell you that I love you. And it is because of this love that I feel for you that your apparent rejection of me has caused me so much pain—more than you could ever comprehend.

And thanks to Frankie, I now believe that I understand what has possessed you to remove me from your life. Please let me explain the circumstances that led to your unfortunate misapprehensions concerning me. Prior to leaving La Paz, I was asked (begged actually), by my fellow team members, to bring a young lady home with us on the return trip.

Her name is Bonita, she is 21, tall and, yes, she is beautiful. But all of that was meaningless for her future. She had two serious medical strikes against her for even having a future. She had a hole between two chambers of her heart. She also had a severe case of cataracts that prevented her from seeing anything more than ten or so feet in front of her. Both symptoms were treatable—but not in La Paz—as she could ill-afford the necessary surgeries to give her a chance at having a meaningful life. And because of the severe flooding there, the hospitals were too busy dealing with emergency cases only.

At the insistence of the medical team that I was with, I flew her home with us to stay with Frankie and me. I saw her through two surgeries—one to correct her vision and the other to patch the hole in her heart. I did exactly what you would have done under similar circumstances. Oh yes, I also provided her with a nurse to stay with her—24 hours a day. She even slept in the same bed with Bonita at night.

Shortly after receiving the blessings of the two doctors who treated her, I sent her back to La Paz on a commercial flight—she desperately wanted to be with her family. She is a beautiful young lady—but she isn't you—and it is you that I want and need.

If Frankie is right (and when isn't he?), he believes that your father, who saw Bonita with me on two occasions, once at the house on the way to her doctor appointment, and a second time at lunch between two doctor appointments, came away with the wrong impression. When he saw us both times, I can only assume that he saw Bonita hanging onto my arm tightly. Why? Because she could not see well enough after having just undergone surgery on both eyes, hence the dark glasses she was wearing.

I don't know what to say beyond what I have shared with you in this letter. If the reasons for your rejection of me are not related to Bonita, then please, set my mind at ease by sharing your reasons. Please.

Love You, Want You, Need You —

Michael

P.S.—Please call me—if you haven't already burned my phone number, that is.

After rereading the letter to ensure that it said what he felt needed to be said, he folded it and placed it inside an envelope. With the envelope in hand, he left his study to go downstairs to find the address book. Before reaching the top stair, however, he noticed the address book lying on the hallway floor. Frankie doesn't miss a beat, does he? Michael thought to himself with a half smile on his face. Picking up the book, he quickly retreated back to his study where he addressed the envelope to Briana—placing the words "Personal" in the left hand, bottom corner. After placing more postage than required on it, along with his personalized return label, he headed downstairs.

"It's all taken care of, Frankie," Michael stated, as he marched into the living room. "And you'll be proud of me . . . I kept it to two pages—short and sweet."

"That's good, Michael." Frankie replied while looking up from his book. "It'll go out first thing in the morning," he added.

"Fair enough; she won't get the opportunity to read it until after she returns from her tour, anyway. May not even have time to go through all her mail then . . . may take a few days."

"That would be my guess as well, Michael. Maybe her mother or an assistant screens her mail. Can't say that I know how those Hollywood types and singers handle such things. I know how things work around here."

"Very efficiently, Frankie, very efficiently. Thank you."

"I don't know about you, Michael, but I'm starting to get a little hungry."

"Make that two," Michael replied, in concurrence. "Need any help in the kitchen?" Michael asked, even though he already knew what Frankie's response would be.

"Michael, I didn't stay out of your love life, so feel free to rustle up some grub for the two of us. I'll be right here in the living room reading, so please let me know when dinner is ready and on the dining room table."

Michael was flabbergasted at what Frankie had just said. What happened to "stay out of my kitchen?" Michael wanted to know but was afraid to ask. Once he regained his composure, he got up from his chair and headed off for the kitchen.

"Michael! Stay out of my kitchen!" Frankie stated, in a commanding voice as he arose from his chair and headed straight for the kitchen. "You managed to mess up your love life—don't need you messing up the kitchen and dinner too."

Michael had to smile at what Frankie had said—or was that commanded? Either way, he was relieved. The thought of even attempting to prepare a meal was overwhelming. Better to perform open heart surgery than attempt cooking; especially with Frankie as his sole tasting judge.

Over dinner, Michael discussed the idea of going on an extended vacation somewhere; he just wasn't exactly sure where that somewhere was. He only knew that he could no longer sit around to await a call from Briana—if a call was even to be received.

"Where would you like to go, Michael?"

"That's the problem; I'm not totally sure. I've been to many places around the world, but those have always been on DWB missions. I'm thinking that I need some sunshine and warm beaches. Hawaii is one option . . . never been there . . . but then you know that."

"Great place. I'll pack your bags first thing in the morning."

"Not so fast, Frankie. Are you intentionally trying to get rid of me?"

"Now whatever gave you that notion, Michael?" Frankie asked, with a grin on his face.

"Oh, something about breaking a speed record to get my bags packed might have something to do with it."

"Only trying to help, Michael, only trying to help," he repeated for effect.

"I think I'll mull it over for a few days first. Never was one to make rash decisions—you know that."

"I know it all too well; but every now and then you need to let your instincts kick in and go for it."

"Like I said, I'll mull it over," Michael stated, before rising from the table and heading upstairs to his study to read before retiring for the night.

Following breakfast the next morning, Michael headed over to the free clinic, which was beginning to see an influx of influenza patients. Most of the patients he saw could ill-afford the cost of a flu shot—hence the increase in the number of patients.

Returning home a few minutes before six, Frankie informed Michael that they had received a letter from Bonita.

"And what did she have to say, Frankie?"

"Don't know. I've learned a lot of things over the years but never did learn how to read Spanish."

"Oh . . . well then, let's get comfortable in the living room and see what's new in her life."

After sitting down, Michael pulled the letter out of the opened envelope and began to read aloud:

Dear Miguel & Frankie,

Sorry I haven't written earlier. I have been busy since returning to our new, fully furnished home. Thank you both for everything that you have done for my family and me. I know that I could never repay you for your generosity. The house is beautiful and my bedroom is the envy of my new and old girlfriends. I'll send pictures later. The baby grand piano is located in the den—it is so beautiful. I've been practicing every single day since I returned home—thank you both, so very much.

I have already seen both doctors that you recommended, Miguel. They are both very nice to me. My vision is now 20/20, and the heart doctor says that my heart is doing well also—thanks to the two of you and Rebecca.

I have also met with my counselor, who is also very nice, and will be pursuing a degree in music. I am eagerly looking forward to starting classes next week. I am learning how to use the laptop computer that was sitting on my new desk when I arrived home— it is so neat and will help me in my studies. Thank you again for the opportunity you two have provided me.

My father has now found full-time employment with a large construction company in the city—so that has been wonderful news for our family. Not sure if you two had anything to do with it, but they actually came looking for him.

Shortly after arriving home, I took my whole family out to a lovely restaurant—but not fancy like the ones you treated me to, Miguel. It was the first time that my brothers and sisters have ever been to a nice restaurant. Hope you are not upset with me for spending some of your money on them. I think that it gave them something to dream about and hopefully to work hard for as they grow up. I know that my brief stay in America has helped me to envision a future beyond what I have known in the past. Thank you.

In closing, let me say one more time—thank you both, and Rebecca, for making me well, taking care of me, buying me nice clothes, feeding me delicious meals (Frankie) and all of the other things that you have done. Thank You—Thank You—Thank You.

Love Always,

Bonita & Family

P.S.—Please give my love to Rebecca

"Nice letter," Frankie remarked. "She writes well in her native language. I think she'll do well in college."

"Yes—smart young lady, indeed."

"Why didn't you tell me of the things you did for her and her family? A new home, money, piano, computer, college, doctors. Did your visit with the Bolivian Ambassador have anything to do with this?"

"Yes, that's exactly why I went. I had to move fast, and they were the only ones I could think of to help pull it all together quickly. I would have mentioned it to you before, but I guess I plumb forgot—my mind has been on other matters of late."

"Well, forget or not, that was extremely generous of you, which doesn't surprise me. Your parents had done similar things in the past, but not quite to that extent."

"Not necessarily trying to emulate my parents . . . simply felt that she had a bright future ahead of her, given a little help. Now, how about a little dinner? Never did have lunch today."

"Coming right up. I've got a roast, potatoes and carrots, along with biscuits, warming up in the oven. Wash up and I'll see you in ten minutes."

Six more days and counting, he thought to himself as he laid back in his recliner following dinner. Five more days until her final performance—then home the following day—but not to him. What played on his mind the most was how long it might be after her return before she read the letter. It was the unknowns like this that were tearing at his mind. What happened to the uncomplicated life I used to enjoy? he wondered. Whatever happened to the . . . Right in the middle of his thoughts of Briana, his cell phone began to ring.

"Hello," he answered, not immediately recognizing the phone number.

"Hi, Michael, Brendan Murphy here. Did I catch you at a bad moment?"

"Nope—sitting here contemplating the meaning of life," Michael replied. "What's up, Brendan? A little late for you to be calling, isn't it?"

"Sorry for the late call, Michael. We need your help, but only if you're available. Flu bug—patient load has overwhelmed us. To make matters worse, two of our doctors, along with four nurses, are out of commission. I know what you're thinking, not as exciting as patching up a vice president."

"Must be the cafeteria food, huh?" Michael quipped, in an attempt at some light-hearted humor. "You and I don't need any more vice presidential surgeries, thank you very much."

"I agree on the vice president thing. One is enough to last a lifetime. As for the cafeteria food causing the flu, wouldn't doubt it. Anyway, what are the chances you can help out until the flu crisis clears up?"

"Nothing on my schedule at the moment, Brendan. Outside of planning for a potential vacation, which can now wait. How about I fly up first thing in the morning. Will that work?"

"That would be perfect; see you then. And Michael . . . thanks."

"Wouldn't miss the opportunity to catch the flu for anything," Michael quipped again. "I'll see you in the morning."

"Until then, bye." Brendan said, before hanging up.

Michael closed the cover on his phone, got up from the recliner and headed downstairs to find Frankie.

"Frankie," Michael said, as he entered the living room. "Need to run up to Etenia first thing in the morning. Any chance of a six o'clock breakfast?"

"I think I can handle that. What's up?"

"Flu bug—it decided to wipe out some doctors and nurses along with bringing in a large influx of patients. Consider it my vacation."

"Okay—see you at six."

"Six it is then." With that, Michael turned and headed upstairs—this time to make ready for bed given the early rising time. He wanted to be in the air no later than seven-thirty. Following a shower, he went straight to bed—though thoughts of Briana prevented him from falling fast asleep. Six days until she's home kept running through his head.

Chapter Twenty-Seven

MICHAEL GUIDED THE JET ONTO THE RUNWAY IN ETENIA AT EIGHT-THIRTY. After going through the normal shut-down routines inside the aircraft storage hangar, he was greeted by one of the staff members from the hospital. A short ride later and he met up with Dr. Murphy at the main desk of the Emergency Room.

"Thanks for coming, Michael, and in the nick of time. We're down one additional doctor, two nurses and one orderly, along with other staff members."

"Dropping like flies, huh, Brendan? Maybe I should turn around and fly back home. Only teasing," Michael quickly added. "It looks as though you have a full waiting room," he continued, while glancing back at the room. "Give me a moment to change and I'll take the next priority patient."

"Thanks, Michael," Brendan stated with gratitude. "I'll see you between crises."

"My pleasure," Michael replied, as he headed toward his locker in the doctor's lounge.

One day led to the next as Michael, along with the other doctors, struggled to keep up with the patients flowing into the Emergency Room waiting area. While the conditions and equipment were better than on DWB missions, the hours were no different. Upon completion of fourteen- to sixteen-hour shifts, he would ride home with Dr. Murphy and literally collapse into bed. This routine, in itself, was inconsequential as far as he was concerned, as there appeared to be no significant other to occupy his time. He hadn't given up on Briana coming back into his life, but as the days progressed, his belief in their future together was looking dimmer.

By the fourth day, the various medical personnel who were previously out sick began slowly trickling back to work. They were still short one doctor and two nurses, however, but Dr. Murphy gave his assurances to Michael that it would be okay for him to go home. As the flu crisis began to wane, so too did the numbers waiting to be seen.

Even though he was free to go home, Michael had already made up his mind to stay for one more day. If Briana were still in his life, he knew that he would have left immediately for home. But given that she appeared not to be, and with more free time available to him, he decided to sit down with the administrative staff for an overview of the benefit of six weeks ago. Up to this point in time, he had only received bits and pieces of information.

The following day, at the appointed hour of three o'clock, Michael entered the conference room set aside for his requested meeting. Already gathered were the CEO and CFO for the hospital, along with a communications specialist. Michael had worked with all three before when he first initiated the idea of a benefit. At first, they were skeptical that a small town such as Etenia could ever expect to raise any sizable donations—at least any that would make a dent in their much-needed capital improvement goals for the hospital.

When the funds began to pour in shortly after the benefit, however, they became believers. Per the computerized presentation, the hospital to date had received over one point five million dollars in cash donations and pledges. As the donations and pledges continued to come in, the CFO anticipated totals nearing the two million dollar mark—approximately five hundred thousand above their goal. When the presentation was finished, Michael walked out of the meeting happier than when he walked in. The efforts of all involved had paid off for the benefit of the citizens of Etenia—for this he was pleased.

At the conclusion of the meeting, Michael went back to the Emergency Room to meet up with Dr. Murphy. The two of them wandered over to the "Flu Bug Cafeteria" for a bite to eat; a term coined by Michael in jest, but which seemed to have been adopted by staff members, as well. Michael felt more than a little guilty for having coined the phrase in the first place.

Following a light meal, Dr. Murphy dropped Michael off at the airport for what was not, as previously planned, to be a flight back home. Michael had decided at the last minute to fly on to New York City rather than flying directly back to Nashville. He knew this was to be Briana's last performance of the tour, so he made up his mind to check out her earlier promise of an open backstage pass at all of her performances. It was a gamble on his part, and he knew it, but one he felt that he had to take. Try as he might, there was no way that he could get Briana off his mind. And there was no way that he could fly back home without trying, without knowing. Before leaving Etenia, he gave Frankie a courtesy call to let him know of his change of plans.

After filing his flight plan and performing the standard preflight checks, he was racing down the asphalt runway at six o'clock for the one-and-a-quarter-hour flight to New York City. The skies above were relatively clear but windy, with only a few clouds passing between him and the sliver of a moon. In a matter of minutes, he would be flying comfortably above even the few clouds that were there.

The flight to John F. Kennedy International Airport was smooth with a strong tail wind to push him along on his way to Briana. This was one time he was extremely grateful for a tail wind as it appeared that his arrival at Madison Square Garden would be close to her eight o'clock start time. He looked forward to seeing her on a professionally crafted stage—unlike the makeshift stage in the hospital cafeteria.

He brought the plane down onto the runway at seven-fifteen and guided it into a rental stall for visiting pilots. Moving quickly through the terminal, he reached the place where a stand of taxicabs waited to pick up fares. As he would soon find out, it was easier to fly into New York than it was to make his way to Madison Square Garden; another good reason, he thought, for living in Nashville.

With his nerves on edge following the harrowing ride through the city's various highways and boulevards, the driver eventually made it to the Garden at fifteen minutes past eight; fifteen minutes later than it would have taken under normal traffic conditions. He had to chuckle to himself at the thought that the "show must go on" in spite of his late arrival. The driver drove to the area where the performers and staff made their way into the building. The first thing he spotted was a traveling bus with the name "Briana Price" painted on the outside in elegant script lettering. It was apparent that well-known performers like Briana love to travel in luxury, but then again, when you spent as much time on the road as she did, he couldn't fault her.

After paying the driver, he then made his way over to a booth where an elderly gentleman was sitting inside reading a magazine, and what appeared to be two security personnel standing about ten yards to the left of the booth. He had heard of "gate crashers" before, but there was little chance that anyone would make their way safely past these two men without the correct pass in hand.

"Good evening," Michael said, to the elderly booth attendant. "My name is Michael Thomas, I believe my name is listed on your roster for a backstage pass."

"One moment," the attendant said, while setting his magazine aside and scanning up and down his clipboard. After a half minute of checking for his name, the attendant stated, "Sorry, sir, but I don't see your name on the sheet."

"You're sure now?" Michael questioned, on the off chance that he simply passed over his name.

"Positive, sir," he responded, politely but professionally.

"Miss Price assured me, prior to the start of her tour, that my name would be listed for all of her performances, not knowing which one I would be able to make."

"Sorry, sir, if your name isn't listed, we can't let you in. While you appear reputable enough, we still can't let you in," he stated apologetically, as having said the same words a thousand times over before.

"Her mother, Debra Price, travels with her. Is there any way you can get a message to her that I'm here?" Michael asked.

"Possibly, but no guarantees," he responded, while apparently jotting Michael's name down on a scrap of paper. "Bob . . . Frank," he called out while looking in the direction of the two security guards now watching Michael. "Would one of you see if you can locate Debra Price for her okay to let Mr. Thomas in for the show?" When one of the two guards approached the booth, the attendant handed over the scrap of paper with Michael's name on it. The guard, without saying a word, headed through the gate and into the stadium.

"This may take a while, sir," the attendant said flatly.

"Thank you," Michael responded, "I have little choice but to wait."

Michael knew that he was taking a huge gamble on his name being listed for a back door pass, but it was a gamble he knew he had to undertake. Briana herself had made the offer, and he found it difficult to believe that she would renege on that offer unless there was a valid reason; that reason, of course, being an outright rejection of him. If not allowed access to her performance, by verbal request to Debra herself, then it would imply, without question, Briana's outright rejection of him in her life. The best he could hope for is her reading his letter—a letter waiting for Briana upon her return to Nashville tomorrow.

Fifteen minutes would pass ever so slowly before the guard made his return to the booth attendant. After the guard whispered something to the attendant and walked away, Michael approached the booth.

"Sorry, sir," the attendant said to Michael, "but no backstage pass is being granted."

There was no appearance of disappointment on Michael's face. In the fifteen minutes of pacing back and forth, he had already expected the worst. While he was not happy with the response from Briana's mother, his gut told him that this and any subsequent performance would go on without him. He then entertained the idea of going around to one of the main entrance gates to check out the possibility of buying a ticket from one of the scalpers, but quickly changed his mind. He couldn't bear the thought of watching her perform with the knowledge that he was not wanted here.

"Thank you," he politely stated to the attendant before turning and walking away.

"Sorry," the attendant said one more time.

Michael then slowly walked around the stadium to the front where a few taxis were lined up. Instead of going back to the airport, he instructed the driver to take him to a hotel—any hotel in the heart of the city. He knew that he was in no mood to fly home. With his level of concentration elsewhere, now was not the time to be in control of an aircraft. After being dropped off at the Ritz-Carlton Hotel, Michael proceeded through the check-in process where he was assigned the last available room.

"Any luggage, sir?" the clerk asked.

"Yes," Michael replied. "It's at the airport. Once up in my room, I'll have the flight service company retrieve it from my plane and send it over. Please have it delivered to my room as soon as it arrives."

"Not a problem, sir. I'll have it sent up immediately."

"Thank you," Michael responded as he slipped a twenty dollar bill across the counter. With that, Michael then headed straight for the bank of elevators. The first thing he did after entering his room was to give Frankie a call.

"Hello," Frankie answered.

"Frankie, Michael. I had every intention of flying back tonight but decided against it at the last minute. I'm at the Ritz-Carlton; will probably stay here a day or two. Maybe see some sights, visit the DWB offices, who knows. At this point I'm just going to wing it."

"Good for you, Michael. A few days away without distractions or obligations will be good for you."

"That's what I'm counting on, Frankie. I'll give you a call when I know for sure when I'm flying home."

"Okay, enjoy yourself. See you when you get home."

"Thanks, Frankie. See you then. Bye."

"Bye, Michael."

Chapter Twenty-Eight

WITH THE LAST OF THE PERFORMANCES BEHIND HER, BRIANA AND HER mother flew directly home to Nashville early the next morning. It was considered another successful tour, if sold-out performances were any measure of success—and they were in her line of business. From a personal standpoint, however, it was a major disappointment. She was not happy. Michael's apparent "affair" with some Spanish beauty devastated her; it tore at the very essence of her heart and soul.

She admitted to herself that her past relationships with men could be easily counted on one hand—maybe even half a hand. But Michael was different—or so she had thought at one time. He was the "prize" she had long hoped for. He was kind, generous, treated her like a lady, forgiving and understanding; the attributes that ran through her mind were many. He was everything any woman could ever hope for—except faithful. Unfaithfulness was the last thing she would have ever expected of him—the one negative aspect that she could never tolerate in a man. She could forgive him for a lot of things—but not this. He was finished, history, a thing of the past.

When she heard the news from her father, she'd cried longer than she had ever cried before. Even with her mother's arms wrapped tightly around her, they could not diminish the tears and the searing pain she felt deep inside of her. She had been more than willing to give up her virginity for him. In fact, she wanted desperately to give up her virginity for him. Her very being yearned to take him in her arms and give him everything a man could desire—and then some. Nothing would have been deemed too good for "her Michael."

But all of that was in the past now—though the pains had remained deep inside of her. Her attempts at casting out the "demon" had been futile up to this point—try as she might. She privately wished that he would die in a car wreck just as his parents did or, better yet, a plane crash would be more fitting. But then again, she quickly thought, either one would have been too quick and painless. No, a slow burning at the stake would be better. And she would be the one adding small pieces of wood to the fire as he helplessly watched. Burn, Michael, burn—feel the pain that you have inflicted upon my trust, she cried out silently. Yes, a quick death, she thought, would be a grave injustice—burning at the stake it shall be. And when you have breathed your last, I shall burn you eternally in a song. Your dishonorable reputation shall live until the end of time.

"Briana!" her mother said, pulling her thoughts away from the destruction of Michael. "You need to eat. You've lost seven pounds already—seven pounds you could ill afford to lose in the first place."

"I'm not hungry, mother." Briana replied, without much emotion in her voice.

"No man is worth dying for, especially Michael. Count your blessings that you found out about him early on."

"I know," she replied, while picking at her dinner simply to appease her mother.

"If I hadn't stopped by to feed you the past two days, you'd be all skin and bones, which you sort of are already."

"Gee, thanks for the compliment, Mother."

"You're a big girl now. Take it from someone who's been there before your father came into my life. I know what you're going through—been down that road myself—more than once I might add. Each time I thought the world was going to end . . . then I met your father. To this day I don't even remember their names. Michael will eventually be forgotten as well; trust me on that."

"I know you're right, Mother . . . it's just hard right now. You start having big dreams of forever after . . . and then they're crushed by the person you so believed in."

"Life has a way of doing that. But life can also bring happiness if you let it in. Trust me, dear, there will be happier tomorrows, but you have to let go of the past first."

"That thought might make for a good song, don't you think?"

"Yep! I think it has potential; and so does your future."

"Okay, Mom—I'm beginning to feel better already. You have a way of bringing light where only darkness sometimes exists."

"That, my dear, is what mothers do best. We may not always be right, but we're not always wrong, either."

"Okay. Thanks for the pep talk. Why don't you go home now and I'll sort through the mail—it will keep my mind occupied until bedtime."

"Fair enough. I need to get back anyway and see how Ryan's coming along on his science fair project. Give me a call if you need anything."

"Will do. Talk to you tomorrow."

"Bye," her mother said, as she rose from the couch and let herself out the door.

Briana then pulled the box, mostly containing fan letters, over to the couch and took a seat. As she opened them, one by one, she found nothing different than from the past—fans wanting her autograph, request for signed pictures of her, letters from male fans expressing their undying love for her, and even proposals of marriage. Other letter writers expressed their thankfulness to her for being their hero, their role model, for being an inspiration in their own lives as they struggled to find themselves.

And then she came across one that she had never imagined would ever be there—one with Michael's return address on it. She suddenly felt the heat rise in her face, far hotter than when she "lost it" with Michael on the plane. Even her eyes began to burn as the tears slowly began to fall, eventually turning into a torrent of tears which no dam was strong enough to hold back.

Without hesitation, she immediately flew off the couch in a rage and headed for the shredder in her study. She turned on the shredder and was about to insert the letter when she had a change of heart. Shredding is too good for the likes of his letter, she thought to herself. Besides, it may end up in a hundred pieces—but it will still be there. No, I have a better idea for the likes of Michael Thomas, she proudly convinced herself.

With a new plan in her head, she walked back out to the living room and headed straight for the fireplace. "Yes! This is what I will do to Dr. Swine," she cried aloud. "He shall die a thousand deaths by fire. He shall come to know the fires of hell that await his soulless soul—and all at the hands of the very woman he so callously scorned. You shall not be allowed to escape the hands of the Grim Reaper this time," she shouted at the letter. "Your attempts at an apology shall go unread, for your words are meaningless to me." She then flipped a switch and the gas burner immediately came to life. No matter that the fireplace was not intended for the actual burning of combustible materials; for this, she knew, called for desperate measures. She needed to watch it burn as if it were actually Michael burning at the stake; the end result being a total cleansing of her heart, mind and soul. "Burn, Michael, burn," she screamed and cried as she threw the unopened letter on top of the flaming gas.

Over and over again she called out for him to burn while she envisioned him crying out for mercy—but she would not hear a word of it as she laughed at his demise. And laugh she did until the last scrap of paper turned to a grayish ash. It was over, she assured herself; he's gone forever from both my life and this world. No longer will he be able to control my thoughts and destroy my dreams, my future—from ashes to ashes, as the saying goes. Tomorrow, she thought, when the ashes were cooled, she would gather them up and send his final remains swirling and screaming down the toilet. "Yes, Michael," she sobbed, "even your ashes shall join the stench of filth from which you were born."

When she deemed the ritualistic burning finished, she went calmly over to the couch, picked up a writing tablet and pen from the coffee table, sat down and began to write:

Fly Boy

So fly away —fly boy
To the skies you know so well
Fly away—fly boy
Fly fast and far away—fly boy
From the hearts you left to die

Your words are full of air
Like the sky upon which you fly
Unseen beauty before you
Unlike the hearts you left to die

After writing only a few stanzas, she threw the tablet back onto the coffee table, fell back on the couch and was fast asleep from the labors of her self-exorcism. She was —finally—free of Michael at last

Chapter Twenty-Nine

EVEN THOUGH HE WAS STILL DISAPPOINTED FROM EARLIER EVENTS, MICHAEL managed to get in a full nine hours of uninterrupted sleep. Glancing out the window from his 32nd floor room, he was able to take in a full view of Central Park from his southern-exposed window. He knew that the park was large but had no idea just how massive it really was until now. If one wanted to get lost, he thought, this park was the ideal place to do it.

With no obligations before him, he took his time shaving and showering before heading down for a leisurely breakfast in one of the hotel's many restaurants. After breakfast, he left the hotel and began wandering the streets in search of nothing in particular. He was content just to stroll by himself with no preplanned destinations in mind. Time alone to think, to ponder, to forget, to observe the pedestrians rushing by him—all appearing to be in such a hurry to get somewhere. As for Michael, he was in no hurry to get anywhere.

By five o'clock, he found himself to be both tired and hungry, having not taken the time out for lunch. He wasn't exactly sure where he was at the moment, he only knew that he didn't have the energy left in him to walk back to the hotel—he had done enough walking for one day. After attempting to wave down a number of cabs passing by him, one eventually pulled up to the curb. Climbing in the back seat he instructed the driver to take him back to his hotel. On the ride back, he took notice of the fact that cabs seemed to outnumber the cars in the Big Apple; a reflection of the lack of parking, he assumed.

After being dropped off at the hotel, he wasted no time in heading directly to one of its restaurants. Without hesitation, he ordered a steak and lobster combination. By the time he finished with his dinner, there was little reason for anyone to wash his plate as there was not a scrap of food left on it. Feeling better now with a solid meal under his belt, he headed in the direction of the main lobby. Finding a comfortable chair to sit in, he took a seat and proceeded to read the morning paper while observing people coming and going through the lobby. From his observations, he concluded that residents and visitors alike were of the monied class. But then again, he'd sort of surmised that given the cost of his own room. After finishing off the paper, he went up to his room, showered and fell into bed totally exhausted.

Following a second night of restful sleep, he once again went down for breakfast and coffee. He had no plans for today but decided that his sore legs were not up for a lot of walking. With the assistance of the doorman, he was able to grab a cab immediately. Michael was quick to note that they apparently like hanging out around the more expensive hotels, not that he could blame them for following the wealthy; in New York City, it appeared to be all about money.

In just under ten minutes, the cab driver dropped him off at his destination: DWB Headquarters. Having worked with them for a number of years, he felt that it was high time he met them in person. Sandy was the only one still working there that he, along with his parents, had met personally for a social function at her and her family's house some six years before. Four hours later, Michael was blown away by all that he had learned from talking with the various staff members, Sandy included. He had to remind himself from time to time that their reach around the world was far wider and more involved than just the missions he volunteered for. If for no other reason than visiting DWB Headquarters, he was grateful for having come to New York City.

Given that it was still early afternoon, and at Sandy's suggestion, he grabbed another cab and headed for the Statute of Liberty; a landmark he had seen from the air but never close up. Knowing that he was heading for home today, but being in no hurry to do so, he next opted for a three-hour cruise on the Hudson River. It was an unusually warm day for the time of year so he relished the breeze in his face as the cruise ship motored along its way past many historic sites. By the end of the cruise, he felt more refreshed and relaxed than he had for some time. So, to both top off and end the day, he hailed yet another cab—this time for dinner at Morton Steakhouse of New York, located in the heart of midtown Manhattan.

The service and food here, he discovered, was as excellent as the one where he and Bonita had eaten in Nashville. The only difference being that he had no one to share the meal with. That, he admitted to himself, would have been the perfect ending to a great two-day adventure. He nevertheless accepted it for what it was and was thankful. Another day—maybe.

At the conclusion of dinner, he hailed another cab for the short ride back to the hotel. Instructing the driver to wait, Michael proceeded directly to the front desk to retrieve both his suitcase and medical bag. Once the two pieces of luggage were placed in the trunk, he settled in for the twenty-minute ride back to JFK International Airport, calling Frankie en route. After refueling, he sped down the runway at ten o'clock for the flight back to Nashville—the loneliest two-hour flight he had ever had to endure.

Chapter Thirty

WHILE THE WEATHER OUT OF NEW YORK CITY WAS CALM, NASHVILLE'S weather report was an altogether different story. Michael was alerted by the ATC to expect strong winds and torrential downpours; not the kind of weather any pilot cares to fly straight into. He and his jet, however, had experienced these weather conditions before. Michael instinctively knew that if the conditions became too severe close to his arrival, he could simply fly around the storm and land somewhere else to wait it out.

The cruising speed for a Citation CJ4 is rated at 451 knots, though Michael typically never pushed it beyond 350 on any given flight—with rare exception. This evening, however, he chose to reduce even that to 300 knots. This further reduction in speed was done in the hopes that the storm would have pushed through by the time he arrived in Nashville; if not the full storm itself, then at least the worst of it.

Twenty-five minutes out, he received word from Nashville ATC that the storm had subsided somewhat, but to expect possible wind gusts of 60 miles per hour. Given the size and weight of his plane, Michael was not unduly alarmed at the projected wind gusts; the torrential rains, though they had lessened in intensity, were significantly reducing sight visibility for most pilots. Again, his plane was equipped with an instrument landing system, so the lack of visibility, he figured, should not be a significant factor as he approached the airport. In the middle of his thoughts his radio came to life.

"Flight Surgeon November three-one-four, maintain 200 knots or less for spacing into Tune Field, you'll be following a single-engine Cessna 172 Skyhawk."

"Roger, 200 knots or less spacing into Tune Field, Flight Surgeon November three-one-four," Michael replied back in acknowledgment. Given the winds and the uncertainty of the Cessna ahead of him, Michael chose to reduce his speed even further to 180 knots.

At five minutes out, he was given final clearance from the Nashville approach controller for the instrument approach to runway two-zero. Given the poor weather conditions, he could not visually see the Skyhawk except for the blips from the Traffic Collision Avoidance System (T-CAS) located on his instrument panel.

Michael was somewhat surprised that a light aircraft, especially one as light as that particular aircraft, would be flying in this kind of weather. Even with his own heavier plane, he could feel the wind gusts buffeting the plane. At four miles out, he could see by the T-CAS that the Skyhawk was mere seconds away from touching down, so he chose to slow his plane down to 140 knots and configured for landing.

Michael's distance would allow more than ample time for the Cessna to exit off the runway prior to his own landing. He had been a long time away from home, and he was looking forward to seeing Frankie again; right now, he would even settle for a cantankerous Frankie.

Michael's touchdown onto the asphalt pavement was picture perfect in spite of the winds as he sped down the runway at approximately 120 knots at touchdown. He instinctively reduced power to both engines to idle, applied the brakes and deployed the thrust reversers to assist in slowing the aircraft.

With the monsoon-like rains beating against his windshield, coupled with a darkened sky, Michael never saw what was coming until it was too late. The Skyhawk had cleared itself off the main runway when a blast of wind, later recorded to be 73 miles per hour, hit the lightweight plane head on and carried it back onto the runway. Michael was still doing 90 knots at the moment he caught glimpse of the Skyhawk sliding into his path. Given the speed and the situation before him, there was virtually no time to react. His plane had, as they say, reached the point of no return. Both engines were in idle mode and the distance between the two aircraft was less than a hundred yards; there was simply not enough speed left in his jet to safely climb back up and over the Skyhawk.

Michael was powerless to do anything at this point except ride out the impending collision and hope for the best—but fortune was not aboard his aircraft on this given night. The Skyhawk itself was totally destroyed upon impact. The occupants probably never knew what hit them. As the media would later report, the pilot and his passenger were both killed instantly. What was not immediately known, however, was why the Skyhawk pilot failed to proceed, per procedure, onto the safety of the adjoining apron? Or had it, in fact, made it to the apron but was carried all the way back onto the landing strip by the high wind gust? This would be left up to investigators from the National Transportation Safety Board to solve later.

Michael's nose-landing gear was instantly taken out by the Skyhawk's lone engine. This, in turn, caused the nose section of his plane to immediately set down hard onto the asphalt runway; the impact being so quick and violent that the nose section separated totally from that of the cabin section. The nose section, with Michael still strapped to his seat, began tumbling down the asphalt runway until finally coming to rest in the grassy median. Meanwhile, the cabin section came to rest approximately fifty yards behind him. Given the location of the fuel tanks in the wings, the cabin section immediately burst into a fireball of flames; even the torrential downpour failed to put a damper on the estimated 200 gallons of unspent fuel fanned by the winds.

It would be seven minutes before the first wave of firefighters and other rescue personnel were to arrive at the scene of the accident; personnel from two other stations arrived three minutes later. John C. Tune Airport, though publicly owned, was too small an airport to support its own onsite fire department. All fire, rescue and medical-aid support required for the airport was contracted out through the neighboring Nashville Fire Department. In the case of an aircraft fire, foam spraying trucks would be immediately dispatched from Nashville International Airport.

Based on Michael's preflight filings, the ATC notified the first responders that only he was on board his aircraft; therefore, their initial attentions were directed at the nose section of the aircraft, not the cabin section that was currently being consumed by the fire. Memphis ATC could provide no information on the number of people aboard the Skyhawk as no flight plans were on file. A quick check by the rescue team assigned to the Skyhawk revealed that no rescue of life would be needed this night.

The ensuing rescue efforts on Michael's behalf were made all the more difficult by the high winds and the continuing downpour. With lights from the fire engines focused on the nose section, rescue personnel climbed in and found Michael still strapped in his seat. The five-point restraint harnesses he faithfully used was a reassuring sign to the rescue personnel; had he not been securely strapped in place with this highly recommended system of safety belts, his body would have instantly become a human projectile. In this scenario, the chances of him surviving a crash of this magnitude would have been close to zero.

A quick check of his vitals revealed that he was still alive, though unconscious. The most obvious sign of injury was to the side of the head which was bleeding profusely. A large, sterile gauze was quickly placed over the wound, followed by an ace bandage wrapped around his head to keep the gauze in place; all in the hopes of stopping or, at the least, reducing the amount of blood loss from the head wound. Not knowing the full extent of any additional injuries just yet, the paramedics knew they had to be careful when lifting him out of his seat amid what remained of the cockpit; this was not to be an easy task given the scattered debris of broken glass and twisted metal pieces strewn everywhere. Following some quick problem solving, a ladder truck was deemed the best option available to minimize injuries; not only to Michael but to themselves, as well.

A ladder truck was quickly turned around and backed up to within ten feet of the rear opening of the nose section. With the ladder in a level position, a stretcher was placed on it and secured in place. The ladder itself was then slowly and carefully extended into the nose cone of the plane until it reached just short of Michael's seat. After applying a neck brace, the paramedics then released the seat belts from across his chest and lap. When the belts were released, they began the arduous task of easing his body carefully up from the seat and onto the stretcher. With little room to maneuver, this turned out to be no easy undertaking. Once they were able to lie him down on the stretcher, a rain shield and blanket were placed over him for protection from the driving rains—as well as for warmth to minimize any effects of shock should he awake.

After securing his body to the stretcher, they then gave the signal to begin slowly easing the ladder back out of the cockpit. As soon as the stretcher was fully outside of the plane, the straps connected to the ladder were removed. Four rescue personnel then proceeded to lift the stretcher up a few inches while the ladder was retracted from beneath it.

Michael was then quickly moved onto the runway to an awaiting Medevac chopper at exactly 12:45 a.m. With the stretcher securely in place, the chopper immediately ascended with a certified flight nurse and a flight paramedic on board for the quick trip to Vanderbilt University Medical Hospital—where, ironically, not only had his parents taught, but where Michael received his own medical training.

After landing on the roof located above the Emergency Room, hospital personnel were there to unload Michael and escort him down the oversized elevator which, by design, exited directly into the emergency room hallway. He was quickly transported to an assigned operating room where a team of doctors and surgical nurses were awaiting his arrival.

His life was now in the hands of some of the same medical staff that he knew personally from his own medical training days, or through association with his parents—some of whom were taught by his parents. The initial screening placed him in the category of "critical condition." Michael was still unconscious when he arrived in surgery, which the surgical team attributed to an apparent blow to the right side of his head; an easy assumption to make in this case given the deep laceration and significant swelling. The swelling, thought to be due to internal bleeding, was of critical concern to those working on him. His head would be their first priority—much as it was for Michael with the vice president just a month and a half ago.

Both his right forearm and lower leg were also severely damaged, as broken bones could easily be seen protruding from both areas. Any internal injuries, other than those readily observed, would have to await MRI scans and x-rays. The team of doctors and surgical nurses, though shaken by who their patient was, went quickly to work.

An hour after Michael was transported to the hospital, Frankie entered the surgical waiting room—to describe his mood as being distraught would be an understatement. Frankie's whole life, since the first day Michael was bought into the family, had been devoted to him; he was the son he one day hoped to have of his own—but didn't. Thanks to Michael's foresight, Frankie's name was always listed on his flight plans to be notified in case of incidents such as this—a trait he had learned and followed religiously from his parents, but obviously hoped would never have to be implemented. Frankie was also listed on Michael's Medical Directive, giving him the ultimate authority in making medical decisions on Michael's behalf should he become medically incapacitated—as he was now.

The wait was long and hard on Frankie. There were no other visitors currently in the room to keep him distracted; most people were fast asleep in the comfort of their homes. Come late afternoon, however, he knew that the room would be filled to overflowing with medical associates and acquaintances once the word got out; but for now, time passed into eternity with the clock on the wall appearing to tick backward instead of forward.

The hour on the wall clock eventually indicated three o'clock in the morning—and still no word had come out of the operating room. He was tired, but resisted the urge to close his eyes and rest—all out of fear of missing something. Two other families had eventually entered the waiting room since his arrival, talking quietly amongst themselves in the opposite corner. They were apparently going through the same grieving process as Frankie. Even with his own grief to deal with, his heart went out to them.

An hour later, what appeared to be a doctor came into the waiting room and headed directly for Frankie. Reaching Frankie, he immediately took a seat alongside of him.

"Hello, Frankie, I don't know if you remember me. I'm Dr. Mitchell, the lead surgeon for Michael's care."

"Right now, doctor, I don't even remember who I am."

"Under the circumstances, that's understandable."

If his memory served him correctly—and right now that was questionable—he recalled the doctor as having been over to the house for social parties that Michael's parents had thrown—but right now, he wasn't positive on that in spite of his otherwise excellent memory.

"I'll give it to you straight, Frankie," the doctor quietly started out with a demeanor of obvious compassion in his voice. "Michael is in serious condition. He's currently in a coma, the result of a severe blow he took to his head. We had to go in and remove foreign debris that had embedded itself in his skull. He has four broken ribs, one collapsed lung, multiple fractures to his right side—arm and leg to be exact. He had lost a considerable amount of blood when they brought him in, but we now have that stabilized. In addition, we currently have him on a respirator to assist his breathing until his collapsed lung is able to work on its own.

"Our main concern, however," the doctor continued, "is the damage done to the head. As I mentioned, the small pieces of debris have been removed; blood vessels have been repaired. We are now in a wait-and-see mode. We do know that his comatose state came about as a result of a blow and/or the deep laceration. What we don't know is how long it will take for him to come out of the coma—it could be today, it could be tomorrow—or perhaps well after that. We don't know ... and I apologize for that. Every case similar to his is actually unique. He has now been moved to Intensive Care. There will be a nurse stationed in his room around the clock. We don't like surprises, so one of us will remain at the ready should he require additional surgery; both because there is always that possibility and out of professional courtesy to Michael. I assure you, each one of us who worked on Michael feels your pain. We know him, and some of us have either spent years working alongside his parents, or were taught by them. So, needless to say, we and this hospital have a personal interest in his recovery." With those final words came a moment of silence by the doctor.

Frankie had been silent up to this point. What could he say other than to fire off a bunch of questions—none of which came to mind at the moment. He, the doctor, was the source of information that Frankie desperately needed to hear, even if it wasn't good news.

"Thank you, doctor," Frankie was finally able to say. "I appreciate your telling it to me exactly as it is concerning Michael's present condition and prognosis. At least my mind can relax a little now, knowing that Michael is resting comfortably. As you said, now it's a waiting game . . . for all of us."

"Yes, a waiting game. One other issue before I leave you, Frankie—that being the media. I was informed before coming in here that they're bunched up outside of the emergency room entrance, obviously in search of a story given his recent involvement with the vice president. As his legal guardian, you have a choice. Either instruct us to say nothing, or allow us to give out basic information concerning our prognosis; whichever you decide, we will respect your decision."

"Feed the beast," Frankie quickly replied without hesitation.

Dr. Mitchell was more than a little surprised at Frankie's quick response. He knew from experience that Michael, along with his parents before him, enjoyed their sense of privacy. But he chose not to question Frankie's decision, nor, as it turned out, did he have to ask.

"I know what you're thinking, doctor," Frankie said, interrupting the doctor's thoughts. "But I give you my utmost assurances that Michael, in this one instance anyway, would fully approve of what I'm authorizing you to do. I'm betting on something eventually happening that will help to speed Michael's recovery along, if he doesn't recover shortly on his own."

"Okay," the doctor responded, with a sense of curiosity in his voice. "You know Michael better than all of us combined, so I'll take your word on it. Now, if you have no further questions, I'll go off and take on the 'Beast' as you refer to them; which, by the way, is a fairly accurate description of what they are sometimes."

"Thank you," Frankie responded.

"One last piece of advice: I don't foresee Michael coming out of his coma real soon—at least not today—so I would suggest that you go home and get some sleep. You, along with the rest of us, may be in this for the long haul, so we all need to take our rest when and where we can get it. By the way, do you have a phone number so I can get in contact with you should there be any major changes?"

"Yes, but I have neither pen nor paper on me."

The doctor then reached into his shirt pocket, extracting both a pen and two of his business cards. "And your number is?" he asked of Frankie.

The doctor then wrote the number down on the back of one of the two cards, handing the other to Frankie. "This is my number. Don't hesitate to call me any time. I sincerely mean that."

"Thank you," Frankie said, as he placed the card in his shirt pocket. "I'll obviously be spending a lot of time in the waiting room—for however long it takes—so be sure to stop by when you're in the neighborhood."

"I will, Frankie, you can count on it. Now, if you'll excuse me, I have the media to attend to before returning to an important patient. Take care, Frankie." The doctor then rose from his seat and made a quick retreat out the back door.

Frankie, taking the doctor's advice, got up and quickly made his way down the hallway to the stand of elevators that would take him to the parking level. Time to take the doctor's advice and catch a few winks before returning later, he thought to himself.

After awakening three hours later from a restless sleep, Frankie sat down at the kitchen table with black coffee in hand and unfolded the morning paper. Not to his surprise, there was nothing about the plane crash in the paper. Given the hour of the accident and when Dr. Mitchell had taken on the media, the presses had already been rolling for the morning paper. Frankie surmised that he would see comprehensive newspaper coverage of the accident, along with Michael's current medical status, in the Sunday edition.

After finishing off a light meal of oatmeal and toast, Frankie headed back over to the hospital. Having not received a call from Dr. Mitchell, Frankie could only assume that there were no changes concerning Michael's condition. Arriving at the nursing station and inquiring, his premonitions proved correct.

Leaving the Intensive Care nursing station, he wandered down the hallway to the waiting area. As soon as he walked in, he was greeted by someone attempting a smile, but failing—it was none other than Rebecca.

"Hi, Frankie," she said, as she got up from her chair and came over to give him a hug. "Thank you for leaving a message on my answering machine this morning. The question right now is, how are you doing?"

"I'm glad you could come—a familiar, friendly face when I needed one. How am I doing, you ask? Not so hot at the moment."

"I know exactly how you feel; I've been here under similar circumstances before. And I don't mean my patients . . . I lost my younger sister to a skiing accident at Cloudmont while waiting in this same room."

"Sorry," Frankie solemnly said. "I didn't know. In that case, I guess you do know how I feel right now."

"I do," Rebecca replied. "It hurts deeply . . . it tears at your gut because you feel so helpless. There are times when you start to wish that it were you in Intensive Care . . . not Michael . . . not my little sis."

There was a moment of silence between them before Rebecca asked of Frankie, "So what have the doctors told you so far about Michael?"

"He's currently in a coma—they removed debris from the side of his head. Collapsed lung, broken bones in his right arm and leg, four broken ribs, I think. Listed in serious condition."

"Oh my!"

"As Dr. Mitchell put it, it's a waiting game right now. Speaking of which, have you by any chance seen Dr. Mitchell stick his head in here?"

"No I haven't, but then I've only been here fifteen minutes."

"Shouldn't you be at work?"

"It's Saturday, Frankie."

"My God! Not even eight hours have passed, and already I've lost track of which day of the week it is."

"The actual day of the week will mean nothing to you, Frankie. Not until Michael is finally released from the hospital will you go back to even caring about what day it is."

"I'm guessing you're right. Who cares what day of the week it is? Saturday, huh? Maybe I should wander back down to the nursing station and see if Dr. Mitchell is even going to be in today."

"No need to ask, Frankie—I already did. Julie at the main desk informed me that Dr. Mitchell will be here for Michael seven days a week—for whatever length of time it takes. Dr. Mitchell was another one of those students who were guided through medical school early on by Michael's parents, and he apparently hasn't forgotten what they did for him."

"That's comforting to know," Frankie responded.

"As the word spreads, Frankie, you'll see more and more of his real friends paying their respects right here in the waiting room."

"It will most likely be front page news tomorrow," Frankie stated.

"I'm sure it will. It was all over the early news channels this morning. Something about "doctor who saved vice president's life in critical condition." Or something to that effect. The whole city will soon know who Dr. Michael Thomas is."

"That's what I'm counting on." As soon as Frankie had said that, he immediately regretted it.

"What do you mean by that?" Rebecca inquired.

"I put my foot in my mouth—totally uncharacteristic of me—I apologize. Someday, when the time is right, I'll explain it to you."

"Okay. In the meantime, I'll pretend that I never heard you."

"Thanks . . . I appreciate that."

"What about Bonita? Are you going to tell her about Michael?" Rebecca inquired.

"No. We got a letter from her recently; by now she has started college. Knowing her, she would pull out of school and fly up here. Michael wouldn't want that."

"College, huh? That girl didn't waste any time after getting back," Rebecca commented. "Good for her. Any other surprises I'm not aware of concerning Bonita?"

"Can you read Spanish?"

"A bit rusty, but yes. South American Spanish is a little different than what we learned in college, though it should be close enough for me to figure out."

"Good, because I can't. I'll bring her letter in tomorrow. Then you can read firsthand what Michael has done for her; in typical Michael fashion."

"I can't wait." Rebecca replied, with a hint of curiosity.

Frankie and Rebecca then spent their time going on to other topics, reading outdated magazines and making much-needed coffee runs. It would be high noon before Dr. Mitchell found his way to the waiting room, just as the two of them were returning from one of their coffee runs.

"Hi Frankie," he said as he entered the room via one door and they another. "Well, Rebecca, what brings you here on a Saturday?"

"I'm one in a long list of Michael's friends," she proudly stated to Dr. Mitchell.

"Yes, he does have many."

Turning back to Frankie, he said, "No change up to this point. We'll take him off the ventilator tomorrow . . . see how well he can breathe on his own. Everything we patched up appears to be healing as expected. We're pumping plenty of nourishments into him to help the healing process; the added oxygen helps, as well. Other than that, I don't know what else to share with you. As we talked about earlier this morning, it's a waiting game."

"When can I see him?" Frankie inquired.

"Unfortunately, not until we move him out of intensive care. It's a sterile environment—can't risk any infections at this point. Just possibly, in a day or two, we'll make a decision about moving him into a private room. Once that happens, then you'll be able to see him. There's a strong possibility that just hearing your voice will help to bring him out of his coma. If there are no other questions, then I'll go back and check on the latest status of our mutual patient."

"None, doctor," Frankie answered.

"In that case, I'll probably see you later this afternoon or early tomorrow morning." With that said, Dr. Mitchell turned and disappeared back through the door.

Both Rebecca and Frankie remained in place until shortly after six o'clock. With no words of encouragement coming forth from any doctor, they both decided to call it a night. Their sitting in the waiting room for hours made no difference to Michael—though they both wished it had.

Bright and early Sunday morning, Frankie jumped into the golf cart and headed down to the main gate to pick up the morning paper. Once back, and with fresh-brewed coffee in hand, he sat down at the kitchen table and opened up the front section of the paper. Sure enough, taking up the entire lower half of the front page was not only an article on the plane crash, with pictures of the plane wreckage, but a picture of Michael, as well. Where or how the media obtained the picture of Michael, Frankie had no idea—but at least it was a good one. Some reporter, or group of reporters, he thought, obviously did an excellent job of researching Michael's life up to this point. The article, in fact, spent more ink on Michael's life than it did on the plane crash itself. They referred to his work with the free clinics in Nashville, his time spent helping out at the hospital in Etenia, including being the mastermind behind the benefit there; they rattled off missions he went on at the behest of DWB; they referred to his parents being the guiding force in his life. They even mentioned the fact that he was able to talk Briana Price into performing at the benefit in Etenia. Of course, the article referred to him as a "hero" for saving the vice president's life. When Frankie finished reading the article on the continuing page, he was brought to tears. The references to Michael's life simply reinforced what he already knew, and the reasons for which he had always been proud of Michael. He could have written the article himself, with the exception of the "hero" reference, and it would have remained the same.

Being that it was all he could handle of the paper for one morning, he pushed it aside and prepared himself another light breakfast of oatmeal and toast. The thought of cooking for only himself caused him to lose interest in cooking altogether. Anything quick and easy was his new motto—at least until he brought Michael back from the hospital.

By eight o'clock, he was back in the waiting room alone before eventually being joined by Rebecca an hour later. Michael's condition had not changed from the day before. They learned, from Dr. Mitchell personally, that the ventilator had been turned off and that Michael was now breathing comfortably on his own. That alone was a good sign.

Reaching into his shirt pocket, Frankie pulled out the letter from Bonita and handed it to Rebecca. "The letter from Bonita that I promised you. This will be a real test of your Spanish."

"Thank you," Rebecca replied, as she unfolded the letter and began to read.

"Wow!" Rebecca stated, after reading the letter. "You and Michael were quite generous."

"You know Michael very well; he doesn't take sole credit for anything. I wasn't even aware of any of it until after Michael read her letter to me."

"Yep! That's our Michael," Rebecca exclaimed in acknowledgement of Frankie's statement.

The waiting room turned out to be a beehive of activity. Friends, fellow doctors and nurses, along with other acquaintances, passed in and out of the waiting room throughout the day; at least those who had turned on their TV or read about Michael in the Sunday paper. So many flowers had arrived, along with get-well cards, that Frankie and Rebecca could no longer find table space to set them on. Both

Frankie and Rebecca were deeply touched by this outpouring of concern for Michael.

At Frankie's insistence, he and Rebecca sought out a number of nursing stations in the hospital—donating flowers to those patients who had received none—or would most likely not receive any. By the end of the day, they had managed to give away the majority of the flowers sent on Michael's behalf. Michael, they both agreed, would have wholeheartedly approved of their actions.

By five o'clock, the last of the visitors had left, resulting in a quietness that was almost eerie in its silence. If nothing else, the many visitors went a long way toward breaking the tedious silence and solitude of waiting and thinking of Michael. After grabbing a bite to eat together, Rebecca headed for home with an armful of flowers as a reminder of Michael—not that she actually needed any reminders. Frankie headed for home a short time later after receiving the latest updates from an associate of Dr. Mitchell's.

On Michael's third day at the hospital, his team of doctors agreed that he was ready to be moved to a private room; access to be strictly limited to those closest to Michael. At Dr. Mitchell's request, Frankie provided a short list of potential visitors; exceptions, the doctor assured him, could be made, but only with Frankie's prior approval.

With the exception of a few visitors, Frankie spent the day alone with Michael, since Rebecca had gone back to work. With his attention focused solely on Michael, he found it difficult to concentrate on the novel he brought with him to the hospital. On the fifth day, he stopped off at a newsstand and purchased nine magazines to supplement the outdated ones in the visitor waiting room, not so much for himself as for the other visitors—shades of what Michael would have done, he thought to himself.

Shortly after returning from lunch in the cafeteria, he was met by Archbishop Lowney at the nursing station.

"Thank you for coming, Father," Frankie greeted him.

"I wish it were under different circumstances, Frankie," he replied in response. "It seems like only yesterday that I buried his parents—an event I'll never forget given the outpouring of love I witnessed. Their legacy and impact on this community, and beyond, was displayed by the large gathering of friends and colleagues at the cathedral," the Archbishop concluded.

"Nor have Michael or I forgotten that day," Frankie responded, as he led the Archbishop to Michael's room.

Standing alongside Michael's bed, the Archbishop immediately opened his prayer book and began the sacramental prayers for the Anointing of the Sick, as requested yesterday by Frankie. Frankie sincerely believed that Michael would have approved of the Archbishop's appearance at his bedside; much as Michael would have done for him under similar circumstances. Following the reading of prayers, the Archbishop quietly said his goodbyes to Frankie and departed.

Chapter Thirty-One

SUNDAY MORNING FOUND BRIANA HUMMING ONE OF HER SONGS AS SHE pushed around the scrambled eggs in one fry pan and flipped the bacon over in the other. Ever since her recent exorcism ordeal she was back to eating as before, sleep came easier and she no longer allowed herself to think of Michael—at least in polite, ladylike terms, that is. She was pleased with her new self—or was it just her old self reborn?

After spreading a thick layer of jam on her toast, she carried the two plates over to the kitchen table and sat down. Taking a sip of orange juice, she pulled the morning paper closer to her. The cover story was another in an unending series on the various conflicts around the world—topics she no longer cared to read because they depressed her. Flipping the front section over, she knocked over her orange juice at what she saw. There, staring directly into her face, was a picture of Michael—the same Michael who she had already burned at the stake—Michael, the "betrayer of women."

She didn't bother to clean up the spilled orange juice as it began to trickle over the side of the table and onto the floor. Two killed instantly, she read—"it should have been him," she quickly said out loud. The cabin section burned—"he should have been in it," she again loudly proclaimed. A coma?—"may he remain in a vegetative state for as long as he lives." A hero? she continued to read. "No, they have it all wrong—he is a 'betrayer of women,' remember?" And to think that this was the first man to bring her to an . . . no, she couldn't even get the word out; the thought of that experience with Michael on the plane immediately caused her blood pressure to rise.

By the time she finished reading the article, her breakfast had long gone cold. She didn't care, never even gave it a thought—her appetite had quickly disappeared the moment she first glanced at the picture of Michael—"Michael, the Betrayer of Women," she said out loud again. "The very Fly Boy who will hopefully never again bring shame to another woman. Justice has been served—the gods have unleashed their wrath upon him and handed him his just reward." After getting all of this out of her system, a sense of relief washed over her body as she cast the paper aside.

Briana eventually pushed herself away from the table, picked up her plate and dumped the contents down the disposal. With a hot washcloth in hand, she returned to the table to wipe up the spilled orange juice. After rinsing out the washcloth in the sink, she returned to clean up the floor. Tossing the wash-cloth into the sink, she then gathered up the morning paper and promptly threw it into the garbage can; she wanted no reminders of him lying around. He had haunted her life for weeks—but no more. Some may see him as a hero, but she knew better. Thanks to the plane crash, she was finally able to move outside of his grasp—both mentally and physically. It's a new beginning, a time to move on, she told herself.

Then her cell phone rang. She knew from the ring tone that it was her mother calling.

"Hi Mom," Briana said, as soon as she flipped open the phone.

"Good morning, dear . . . happy Sunday," she stated.

"What's up? You can't be back from church already?" Briana inquired.

"Didn't make it. Your father is a little under the weather. Don't know if he caught the flu bug or what."

"Well, I hope you and Ryan are staying away from him, or at least wearing a mask."

"I've locked him in the bedroom and told him not to come out until he feels better. He's propped up reading the paper as we speak."

"Good. Slide his food under the door and sleep in my old room," Briana suggested.

"I plan on it." After a moment of silence, Briana's mother continued. "Did you happen to read the paper this morning?"

"By that do you mean the article on the Betrayer?" Briana replied, in a strongly, sarcastic tone. "He got what he deserved," she added.

"Briana!" Her mother exclaimed, in a raised voice. "That isn't Christian of you—not the way your father and I raised you."

"Sorry," Briana responded, without meaning it.

"Two people were killed, and Michael is in a coma, not something you should ever wish for, even on your worst enemy. We didn't have the TV on yesterday, and apparently neither did you, otherwise we both would have known about the plane crash earlier."

"Mother, I have finally been able to put him out of my thoughts—and then I find his picture staring right at me this morning. Not exactly what I wanted to see first thing in the morning. And yes, my sympathies go out to the families of the two who were killed."

"You know the Christian motto, Briana: forgive and forget."

"Easier said than done, Mother."

"I'd ask that you come over here to chill out if it wasn't for your father being sick."

"Thanks for the offer, but I think I'll just curl up on the couch and read . . . maybe write some music. I've got to come up with two more songs in order to finish the next album . . . haven't been in the mood lately."

"The album is important, dear, but you also have to start preparing for Seattle and San Francisco in two weeks. It's unlike you to wait until the last minute."

"I know, Mother, I'll start first thing tomorrow morning."

"I think I hear your father crying out for me, so I'd better run. If you need anything, anything at all, honey, call."

"Okay," Briana responded, knowing she wouldn't be needing anything from her mother.

"Talk to you later, dear."

"Bye, Mom."

Briana pulled the afghan over her and slipped down on the couch, her head resting on one of the many decorative throw pillows. She was tired and emotionally drained after reading the article about Michael, but refused to admit that Michael was the cause. She closed her eyes and soon drifted off to sleep.

Chapter Thirty-Two

THE MAGAZINES FRANKIE HAD PURCHASED WERE OBVIOUSLY WELL READ, he mused, as he passed by the waiting room on his way to see Michael; though he did notice that a few of them appeared to have gotten up and walked away. Oh well, Frankie thought, not the end of the world.

Dr. Mitchell had stopped in shortly after Frankie arrived for his visit with Michael. The report from the doctor was the same as yesterday, which was the same as the day before—no change; words he has come to expect as the days rolled on, one after the other. Out of desperation for Michael's recovery, he started bringing an abridged version of the Bible with him to the hospital—openly praying aloud to Michael as he lay there with various tubes running in and out of his body.

Rebecca continued to visit each night on her way home from work—for which Frankie was grateful. Aside from nurses and doctors coming and going, the hours passed slowly in silence. He could have chosen to stay home, or simply reduced the hours spent in Michael's room. But he knew, without even having to think it, that Michael was his life, his sole reason for getting up every morning, both before the accident and, more importantly, now.

Day nine came and went without change. In spite of the intravenous nourishment, Frankie could see that Michael was slowly losing weight. His upper body, kept strong and muscular by his daily swim routine, was slowly beginning to fade away. Day after day of watching Michael's physical deterioration caused increasing moments of apprehension to creep into Frankie's thoughts. When negative thoughts did come his way, he prayed even harder to chase them away. Did Michael not want to come back? Frankie wondered. Were thoughts of Briana's apparent rejection of him so ingrained in his subconscious mind that his desire to live was no longer there? While Frankie always had the uncanny knack of reading Michael's mind whenever the need arose, this time it failed him.

Passing by the nursing station on day ten, following a late dinner downstairs, he was handed another stack of get-well cards sent in care of the hospital. Sitting down alongside of Michael, he opened them one by one and read them aloud to him; something he had done every day since the cards first began to arrive. He found it rather amusing that hundreds of cards would be sent to Michael, or any patient for that matter, while they were hospitalized—but few, if any, while they were well. He made a mental note to send his sister a card thanking her for being a good sister and to let her know that he was thinking of her.

The next to last card he came to was one bearing the seal of the vice president's office. Fully expecting to see a preprinted card inside, he was surprised to find a handwritten letter signed by the vice president's wife herself. Though the outside of the envelope was clearly addressed to both Michael and Briana, the letter itself was addressed to Briana. It read:

Dear Briana,

My husband and I have been following the progress of Michael on a daily basis. You can't imagine how deeply saddened we both are at not only the accident itself but his apparent slow recovery. The two of us have been praying daily for not only Michael but for you, as well. I know from firsthand experience what you are going through.

Michael is very fortunate by having you in his life when he needs you the most. Though you are going through your own grieving process, never underestimate the power of your love in Michael's eventual recovery and healing; he needs you by his side now more than ever— as I know you are right now as you read this letter. As the saying goes, "Love heals all wounds."

When I first saw the two of you together at the hospital in Etenia, I knew instinctively that you two were meant for each other—call it a wise old woman's intuition. I've personally seen a lot of doctors over these many years, but never have I been so impressed with what I saw, or felt, in Michael. His whole mind and demeanor exuded compassion; and for that reason alone, I hope you consider yourself one lucky young lady to be such an important part of his life. Whenever he glanced your way, I saw nothing but love in his eyes. It was apparent that he worships the very ground you walk on.

I'm speaking to you as a woman who has been down the road of love, both in the past and currently. We women sometimes have to go the "extra mile" to keep our relationships young, fresh and exciting— but the rewards in the end are worth those efforts. When we hit those rough patches in life, as they are for you now, that is when we women need to be strong and supportive. Right now, as Michael fights for his own survival, is when you need to muster up all the love within you that you obviously have for Michael—much as I did a few months ago for my husband. Remember—Both Love and Trust will carry you through even the roughest of times.

Love & Prayers,

Dottie

*P.S.—I'll still be looking for those invitations. And Briana, thank
Michael for making my husband whole again.*

Briana should have been reading this letter to Michael, not I,
Frankie said to himself. What exactly took place in Etenia between
Michael and Briana, he wondered, that would cause Dottie to spend
so much of the letter devoted to issues of love? And what was this "invitation" that she was waiting to be sent to her? Could it be a wedding
invitation? Knowing Michael, he would find that hard to believe so
early in their "unacknowledged" relationship. It was at this point of
questioning that he decided to place the letter back in the envelope
and put his curiosity aside for another day.

Instead of going straight home that evening, even though it was
later than usual, Frankie decided that it was time to pay someone a
visit—someone who should have been at Michael's side from the beginning—but sadly wasn't.

Frankie pulled up to the new, high-rise condo complex just past
ten o'clock. He was thankful for finding an open parking place only
fifty feet from the entrance to the building as he felt exhausted from
the longer than usual day at the hospital. As he was walking in the
direction of the main entrance, a man and woman were exiting a cab.
He paid little attention to the couple as his mind was on other, more
weighty matters before him.

"Frankie, is that you?" exclaimed a male voice.

Frankie, having quickly been brought out of his pensive thoughts
by the call of his name, shifted his glance in the direction of the unknown voice.

"Well, if it isn't Drs. Jerry and Darlene. What a pleasure running into you two. I haven't seen the likes of you two for close to five years. Or has it been longer than that?"

"Five years it has been," Darlene answered. "At the funeral, I believe. But given the number of people who were there, I'd hardly expect you to remember specific people."

"Yes, it was the funeral," Frankie responded, thinking back to Michael's parents.

"And what, pray tell, brings you way across town to our humble neighborhood, Frankie?"

"I'm here to drop off some jewelry that Ms. Price had left at our place a few months back. She apparently had left them on Michael's plane when he flew her back from a hospital benefit in Etenia. I've been waiting until she returned from her recent tour to give them back." What Frankie intentionally didn't share with them was that Briana had actually mailed the jewelry back a few days after returning from her tour. He could only assume that they must have been a gift from Michael to Briana while they were together in Etenia.

"I'm almost afraid to ask, Frankie, how is Michael doing?" inquired Darlene.

"He's holding his own, though still in a coma. The doctors are cautiously optimistic that he'll pull out of the coma eventually. For now, it's just a waiting game on all of our parts."

"If there's anything we can do, don't hesitate to ask, Frankie," Jerry added.

"Thank you, I'll keep you two in mind, but thankfully, he has a very dedicated team of doctors and nurses looking after him."

"Okay then," responded Darlene. "It's getting cold out here; why don't we all go inside. If you like, Frankie, you can join us for the elevator ride up. We live on the same floor as Ms. Price; just down the other end of the hallway from her unit. Besides, by coming in with us, you can avoid having to deal with our building's security. Any and all visitors have to be willing to give up their first born when visiting anyone here," she added with a chuckle.

"I'd appreciate that, thank you," Frankie said, grateful for her assistance in getting past a security guard that he hadn't known about. And sure enough, off to one side of the lobby was what appeared to be a guard sitting at an expensive, ornate-appearing desk.

"Good evening, Drs. Manning. How was the opera?" he inquired.

"Very good, as usual, Patrick," Darlene replied, as they continued walking towards the elevator.

"You all have a good evening, you hear," he threw out as the elevator doors closed behind the three of them.

Once inside, Jerry retrieved a key card from his wallet and inserted it into a slot on the elevator wall. At the appearance of a green light, he pushed the number 18. Frankie was amazed at how quickly they reached the top floor, unlike the elevator at home. When the door opened, the three of them stepped out into a small foyer but remained in place.

"Frankie, I only wish we had bumped into you under better circumstances," Darlene remarked. "But know that Jerry and I have been saying many an extra prayer for Michael's recovery."

"Thank you both. Given the circumstances, Michael can use all the extra prayers offered up on his behalf. And thank you for bringing me in and up to Ms. Price's floor. You apparently saved me from a lot of potential grief."

"Our pleasure," Jerry replied. "If we hadn't come by when we did, we most likely would have seen you in the lobby dealing with security come morning. And just so you know, it doesn't take an elevator key card to return to the lobby. Once inside, just push the L. You can always get out of this building, but not always in."

"Thank you, I'll remember that."

"And by the way," Darlene interjected, "Briana's is the last unit on your left. And with that, we hope to be hearing good news concerning Michael real soon."

"As do I," responded Frankie. "Good night, and thank you both again."

"Good night, Frankie," stated Darlene, as she and Jerry headed off down the hallway.

Upon reaching Briana's door, he lightly knocked three times rather than using the doorbell. When no answer came, he knocked a little harder and waited. When the door eventually opened, he knew immediately that his presence had caught Briana totally off guard—as well he imagined it would.

"Frankie!" She exclaimed, with a surprised look on her face after regaining her composure. In spite of her feelings about Michael, she had nothing but love and respect for Frankie. And because it was Frankie himself standing before her, she had no intentions of slamming the door in his face.

Then there was an unmistakable silence between them; a silence that would have gone on forever had not Frankie spoken up.

"Briana, I'm probably the second least person you either wanted to see tonight or, for that matter, ever expected to see again. I didn't come here tonight to trouble you or place any undue stress on you. I only have one question that I would like to ask you—and then, I promise you, I will leave immediately."

Briana stood there saying nothing, for words escaped her.

Frankie hesitated for a moment before continuing. "Briana, did you by any chance receive and read Michael's letter that he mailed to you?"

Briana hesitated for a long moment before answering. "Yes and no . . . I burned it . . . unopened," she replied haltingly with a sudden feeling of guilt rushing through her body. This sense of guilt was caused by the possible knowledge that her answer would most likely be hurtful to Frankie—and she wasn't wrong.

Frankie then gave her a look that burned right through her eyes before speaking again. "That's too bad; that's really, really too bad. And like I said, I had only one question of you . . . and you answered it. Thank you." With that having been said, he turned and begin walking down the long hallway without saying another word—not even a goodbye.

By the time he had reached the halfway point to the elevator, she yelled out his name in a tone of panic. "Frankie!"

But he kept on walking.

"Frankie!" Briana shouted even louder the second time. "Don't leave, please. I'm begging you—please don't leave." What made her call out his name and want him back? She wasn't quite sure. She only knew, or at least she felt something deep inside of her, that whatever brought him here, this late at night, must have been of paramount importance; and she needed to know what that was. All of a sudden, she had a terrifying sense within her that she had done something horribly wrong.

At last, just before reaching the foyer of the elevator, he turned around and looked down the long hallway in her direction. He said nothing as silence continued to engulf them once again.

"Please, Frankie . . . come back and talk to me . . . please," she quietly pleaded with him.

Frankie stood still for what seemed like an eternity to her before slowly making his way back along the hallway and through her still open doorway. Briana followed him in and closed the door.

"Please, have a seat, Frankie," Briana said quietly, motioning to one end of the couch. After he had taken his seat, she took a seat at the opposite end of the couch.

"Your being here, Frankie, tells me that I should have read Michael's letter," she stated, calmly.

"Yes, Briana, you should have," Frankie responded just as calmly. "Not just for Michael's sake, but yours as well. Had you read the letter when you returned home, there is reason to believe that Michael would not be currently fighting for his own life, much as he has for others as a doctor. Or maybe, just maybe, he's not actually fighting for his own life; maybe he's given up . . . I don't know. Am I laying the blame on you for Michael's present condition? Most certainly not. He was simply in the right place at the wrong time. He was coming home. A day earlier . . . a day later . . . who knows."

Frankie then spent the next hour on the couch with Briana, going over every detail of Michael's purely professional relationship with Bonita. In a matter of minutes from his beginning to tell the story, she was crying. By the end of the story, she was bawling. When he had said all that he felt needed to be said, he set the jewelry box and Dottie's letter on the coffee table, rose from the couch and, without saying another word, let himself out the door, leaving it slightly ajar; even from the elevator foyer, he could still hear her sobbing.

Chapter Thirty-Three

AFTER AN UNUSUALLY RESTFUL NIGHT OF SLEEP, FRANKIE ROSE EARLY AND left directly for the hospital. He had lost interest in preparing even the simplest of meals at home, so he started relying on the cafeteria for his meals. Quickly finishing breakfast, he headed up to see Michael. Upon entering Michael's room, he knew at first glance that nothing had changed from the day before—even without one of the doctors having to tell him.

A half-hour later, while Frankie was staring out the window seeing nothing but emptiness, he turned at the sound of the door opening— it was Briana, as he knew that it would be. It took only a quick glance on his part to notice that she apparently had not slept well last night— if at all. In uncharacteristic manner for a professional performer like herself, it also appeared as though she had not even bothered to apply makeup before arriving at the hospital. The one important and telling thing that Frankie did notice, however, was that Briana was wearing the jewelry Michael had apparently bought for her—the same jewelry he had left on the coffee table the night before.

"Morning, Frankie," she said, almost too softly for him to hear. She glanced towards Michael's bed, but the curtain was drawn halfway around it. "Thank you for putting my name on the list to see Michael."

"Your name was number one on the list from the first day. As a matter of fact, it was one name ahead of my own," he responded truthfully. He then motioned for her to come around to the other side of the bed where Michael could be seen.

The tears immediately started to emerge within seconds of seeing him, tubes in his arm and a large bandage of some sort covering one side of his head. The longer she stared, the more the tears flowed. After last night's ordeal with Frankie, she was surprised that she even had tears left to cry.

After Frankie's visit last night, she regretted doubting Michael's love for her. She regretted burning his letter without first giving him the opportunity to explain—especially if that explanation was in written form. She regretted having burned him at the stake. She regretted everything since the day her father had told her about Michael and Bonita. Michael had placed his undying faith and trust in her, he believed in her, even when she pulled less than admirable stunts—like telling people that she was his fiancée; and yet he had forgiven her— without hesitation. Oh, he made her squirm a little alright, but then again, she deserved it, and she knew it. After the discussion ended, she remembered Michael taking her hand during the walk back to the hotel. He forgave her, while she, hearing about Bonita, slammed the door in his face, burned him at the stake, and yes, even flushed him down the toilet.

Was she not a Christian? Did not her own mother advise her on Sunday to forgive and forget? She not only ignored Michael, but her mother, as well. Maybe she wasn't as grown up as she thought she was; all she knew for sure was that she wasn't sure of anything anymore. Well, that's not exactly true, she told herself. I know that I am deeply, madly in love with Michael. "My Michael," to be exact.

She readily admitted to herself that she had blown it. Trust, at least according to Dottie, being the cornerstone of any meaningful relationship—whether the relationship is business, social or romantic. And she blew it—big time. If it hadn't been for her, the plane crash would not have happened—in spite of Frankie's assurances to the contrary. Frankie had alluded to her last night that Michael had stayed longer in Etenia and New York because there was nothing worth rushing home for—meaning her. The only reason he flew to New York was because of her. She had never experienced so much guilt and remorse in her entire life until she heard those words from Frankie last night.

Yes, it was she who should have been burned alive, not Michael. She was the one who should have been bound to the stake and allowed to cast the match upon the wood. The Grim Reaper should have taken me away, she told herself; and the gods should have struck me down hard, but not without making me suffer first. Yes, she reminded herself again, she'd screwed up—big time. And if Michael wasn't to pull through, or never regain consciousness, she knew she would have to live with that knowledge for the rest of her life. A life she couldn't even imagine now without Michael being in it.

She wasn't quite sure why, but she approached the side of Michael's bed cautiously, as if he were about to rise up and strike her down—but approach she finally did, until she was only inches from the side of the bed where his chest was. There was no turning back, however, as a part of her forced herself to face the consequences of her actions. With tears gently cascading down her cheeks, she sat down on the bed beside him, being careful not to touch those areas that she knew were injured. She remembered Frankie telling her that he took a deep gash to the head, obviously the area that was bandaged. She could see the cast on his right arm that was resting on top of the bedcovers. She also remembered Frankie telling her that his right leg was casted, as well. And then there was something about cracked or broken ribs and a collapsed lung. Oh my God!

she exclaimed, to herself—it's a miracle he's even still alive. And all because of me.

Frankie pushed a chair over for Briana to sit down on—but she remained seated on Michael's bed. A few moments later, she turned sideways on his bed and gently lifted his uninjured arm up before carefully setting it down along his left breast and thigh. To Frankie's utter surprise, she then slipped off her shoes and carefully climbed into bed alongside of Michael—being careful not to touch any broken or injured parts of him. She scooted up to the point where the top of her head brushed up just below his shoulder. With both hands resting in her own lap, she began to sing, ever so softly, "Their Song."

She wanted Michael whole again; she wanted so desperately to pull him into her naked body and make passionate love to him—not he to her—but her to him. She wanted to make it up to him for all that she had done against him—her actions, her thoughts, her omissions. She stood ready to give him every pleasure she possibly could—willingly. Never in her short life had she been so willing to give her all to a man.

Frankie, meanwhile, was in awe at the sight of her crawling into bed with Michael—but in a good way. He had never heard the song before, but he sensed that it was their song, or the missing song, as the various media had referred to it. As she sang the song, tears began slowly flowing from Frankie's eyes. He loved Briana. He'd loved her from the moment she first appeared in Michael's life. Not so much be-cause she was who she was, but because of the immediate change—for the good—that he witnessed in Michael following their first breakfast together. His whole world appeared to take on new meaning when she entered his life. Though Michael never openly admitted any affection for Briana at the start, Frankie could clearly see it in both his eyes and in his overall demeanor.

As Briana was just beginning a second rendition of the song, Dr.

Mitchell came into the room; he was momentarily stopped in his tracks by the sounds of singing coming from the other side of the curtain. When he eventually walked forward and came in sight of Briana lying next to Michael, still singing, he was stunned. Who was this woman, anyway? he wondered. He was about to say something until he noticed Frankie raising his index finger to his lips, as a signal for silence.

Moments later, glancing back down at the two of them in bed together, both Frankie and Dr. Mitchell witnessed movement—not from Briana—but from Michael. The length of his left arm slowly slipped off his chest and came to rest between Briana's breasts and her stomach. Briana immediately ceased her singing but remained frozen in place.

Had it fallen of its own accord, they all wondered privately? The answer to their question came a half minute later. Michael's arm slowly rose from between their two bodies, sliding across her breast in the process, eventually coming to rest on her side. His fingers then began to move slowly around on the outer side of her thigh as though he were giving her a massage; the same manner of massage he had previously applied to her temple, resulting, on two previous occasions, in putting her to sleep. But no longer, she vowed, would she fall asleep on him again—at least not until he had taken her—and she him.

Moments later, with the touch of his hand and fingers on her thigh, Briana began to cry. At first quietly in a futile attempt not to cry, but then the torrential tears came forth as though it were the evening of the plane crash itself. Dr. Mitchell was not surprised by Michael's apparent actions—it was a scene he had witnessed more than once in his twenty years of practice. In spite of the fact that he was a doctor—and had observed this scene before—tears rolled from his eyes, as well. He was a witness to something for which even the best medical care in the world could not always make happen.

The scene taking place before Frankie's eyes was what he had hoped and prayed for when he visited Briana last night. While he never did find true love himself, he was acutely aware of its healing power. His visit to Briana was not an arbitrary decision—he felt deep in his heart that if Michael had any chance of pulling out of his coma, it would take a strong dose of love to do it. He was praying that Briana's love, at this moment in time, would be enough to bring Michael back to the here and now. He too shed tears, unashamedly.

As Briana continued to lie beside Michael and her tears turned to quiet sobbing, both Dr. Mitchell and Frankie saw something else move besides Michael's arm upon Briana. His eyelids rose, revealing two sleepy-looking, cloudy blue eyes. At first, they appeared to take in both Frankie and Dr. Mitchell standing in front of the window—before eventually lowering down to the figure lying beside him. Upon seeing the top of her head, he forced his arm a little more to her back and gave a gentle pull to bring her body closer to his. She felt his tug and snuggled in closer to him, even though there was little room left between their two bodies. The pull by Michael caused Briana to cry even more—she knew that her Michael was back—back where both she and he belonged.

Dr. Mitchell then pulled the curtain all the way back as he moved to the opposite side of the bed. Leaning over, he looked directly into Michael's eyes. Michael, while now massaging Briana's lower spine, looked up at Dr. Mitchell and gave him a wink. That one, simple sign told him that Michael had successfully pulled out of his coma; the power of prayer, love and a woman's touch was all it took, he thought. He could oftentimes heal the body, but it took something far more powerful, as in Michael's particular case, to heal the mind and heart—Briana's love.

By this time, Frankie had ceased his own tears—he was now at peace knowing he would soon have his son back in the house and, hopefully, Briana with him. She was a good woman, a good match for Michael. He was convinced that she was simply misguided in the past by circumstances both unseen and unknown to her at the time. It was unlikely, he thought, that she would ever again doubt the cornerstone of every significant relationship—especially in love—trust; without trust, no meaningful relationship can exist. He was convinced that Briana now knew this.

Briana reluctantly pulled herself carefully out from under Michael's arm and slid off the bed. She then moved up closer to Michael's head, sitting gently back down on the bed, and began rubbing his left temple softly with her fingers—all while staring down at the two eyes staring back at her. Neither Frankie nor Dr. Mitchell could see Briana's eyes, but they both noticed the gentle rolling of tears from those of Michael. There was no need for words between them right now, for they both knew where they had been and where they were going.

Briana then pointed her finger at herself before cupping her hands in the shape of a heart, then eventually pointing down at Michael. It was her first open admission of her love for Michael. The wink of his left eye told her that he had gotten her message. And the tears came once again.

"Okay," Dr. Mitchell said, interrupting the silence that had consumed the room. "I need to run some mental acuity tests on Michael while I still have him awake. If you two will retire to the waiting room, I'll let you know when I'm finished . . . most likely in a half-hour's time."

Briana slid back off the edge of the bed, looked down at Michael, and said, "I'll be waiting for you Michael . . . forever, if that's what it takes." And with that, she and Frankie left the room.

"Frankie," Briana said, as they walked down the hallway together, arm in arm, "how could I have been so stupid?"

"Briana," Frankie calmly replied, "given the information your father shared with you—and he did so with your best welfare at heart—anyone would have reacted the way you did. It's not your fault; I would've reacted the same way. In fact, I probably did a few times back when I was your age. That may go a long way to explaining why I never married. See, even I apparently have made some mistakes along the road of love."

"But I never gave Michael a chance to explain. I never called him, never wrote him . . . I even blocked his calls from my phone. And yes, I even burned his letter without reading it. I simply cut him out of my life altogether."

"And therein lies a lesson for you, Briana," Frankie commented. "Michael never once questioned his love for you. He tried calling you, he wrote you that letter, he flew all the way up to New York to be with you, even though he knew from the onset that the trip wasn't likely to turn out with a happy ending. For the first time in his life, he believed in love, he believed in you. Against everything that implied that you wanted nothing to do with him, he held on to hope. The relationship, or lack thereof at the time, was eating at him—but still he held on to hope; it was the only thing he had left to hang on to. That's how powerful his love for you was—and is. As you well know, he is an intelligent, handsome young man, aside from being wealthy. Any number of women would have loved to have been a part of his life, but he held out for that one special woman who would capture his heart and never let go—and that one special woman he waited for, as it turned out, was you. I knew it from the moment he first laid his eyes upon you that you had captured his heart. I'm not exactly sure what took place between you two in Etenia, but when he came back I could see love written across his face and in his eyes. That's when I knew for sure that he was madly, deeply in love with you."

"And I with him, Frankie," Briana interjected.

"I believe now, Briana, that you've come full circle in your own heart—that you now realize there isn't anything Michael wouldn't do for you. And knowing you, better than I think you know yourself at times, I'm convinced you'll find ways to make it up to him. He's an uncommonly forgiving person, much as his parents were. And you'll find out soon enough that he won't be bringing up in conversation your misguided lack of trust in him. That simply isn't Michael."

"Believe me, Frankie, I've already experienced Michael's forgiveness, more than once, I might add. And yes, I will make it all up to Michael . . . and then some."

"I have no doubts about that, Briana, none at all. And Briana—welcome to our family."

At that, Briana immediately became misty-eyed. She stopped, looked Frankie straight in the eyes before throwing her arms around his neck—and cried. Frankie wrapped his arms around her, as well; thinking at that very moment—now I have both a son and a daughter.

Epilogue

THREE DAYS LATER, WITH BRIANA, REBECCA AND FRANKIE BY HIS SIDE, Michael was discharged from the hospital. Rebecca had taken a long-term leave of absence from work in order to assist Michael at home during his convalescent period. Frankie was in charge of providing nourishment for his body and Rebecca was responsible for changing out bandages, keeping the wounds clean and monitoring his vitals, including his mental acuity.

Briana was solely responsible for providing, as Dottie had previous-ly suggested, TLC—the most important contribution to the overall healing process. This time around, however, she was not going to let him out of her sight—or touch. She stayed by his side twenty-four hours a day, sleeping with him at night, bringing gentle comfort where she could—her naked body pressed closely against his. Over the ob-jections of her promoters and fans alike, she canceled her upcoming performances; she knew now, thanks to the wisdom of Frankie, where her priorities were. Make no mistake of it, she loved entertaining her supportive fans—but she loved her Michael more.

During the ensuing days, she would sing to him in the living room while playing the piano or her guitar. She would always begin these moments with "Their Song" and finish her concert for one with the same song. On warm days, they would sit together out on the balcony or down by the pond and talk quietly and lovingly about life, love, marriage, children and, most of all, trust; though it was she who broached the topic of trust, not Michael.

Later in the evenings, she would take him back upstairs and undress him before wheeling him into the shower and bathing him—with her naked, as well. Tender acts of love quickly replaced any self-conscious thoughts of being naked before one another. Given his inability to pursue her physically, due in large part to his two casts, healing rib cage and head wound, she wasted no time in taking the initiative to make sure that his needs were met—either in the shower or later in bed. Because of her, Michael had almost died in the process of proving his love for her. Briana knew that she had a lot of making up to do for "Her Michael," and she wasted no time in doing so.

About the Author

MICHAEL JENNINGS WAS RAISED AND EDUCATED IN SEATTLE, WASHINGTON. He was the fourth born of a large Catholic family of eleven children. He remained in Seattle until joining the Navy shortly after graduating from high school. After completing his naval service, he went to work for The Boeing Company while attending college.

In 1971, he relocated to Denver, Colorado where he pursued his college degrees on a full-time basis—graduating from Loretto Heights College (now Regis University) in 1973 with two B.A. degrees (Behavioral Sciences & Sociology) before moving on to the University of Colorado where he obtained an M.A. degree in Sociology (1974). In 1978, he returned to Seattle and The Boeing Company before taking early retirement in 2003. Aside from writing his first novel, *Flight Surgeon*, he has written a full-length musical play, *Blind Love*, which awaits musical composition of the lyrics. He has also written, in conjunction with his youngest son Ryan, a play for his eighth-grade class, *The Man Who Lost His Way*. In addition to plays, lyrics and short stories, he has crafted over two-hundred poems, along with an animated story for young readers (*Fluffy*); all of which remain to be published.

He has two adult children, Brendan and Ryan, and has recently taken up residence in Scottsdale, Arizona, where he spends his days and evenings working on his next novel between swim breaks. He is a voracious reader of novels and attends mass weekly at his local parish.

www.ingramcontent.com/pod-product-compliance
Lightning Source LLC
Chambersburg PA
CBHW020322180626
46812CB00001B/7